promises we meant to keep

ADRIAN J. SMITH

EREKA PRESS

promises we meant to keep

Cover Design by Perrin of The Author Buddy

one

"My stomach's in knots!" Kamryn winced as she held the phone tightly between her ear and shoulder. There was only so much gossiping she could manage without bringing the conversation with her best friend back around to the fact that she was starting her first day at Windermere Prep.

"Take deep breaths, Kam." Greer's voice was calm, nearly on the edge of patronizing, but not quite there. Yet, at least.

Kamryn knew she was being annoying, because she'd voiced her anxiety and her nerves more times in the last hour than she could count. And here she was, saying it again. "I know. I know. I *am* taking deep breaths. I promise!"

She finished shoving a few notebooks into her satchel, and damn if she would admit her hands trembled. She hadn't been back on this campus since she'd graduated. But she'd wanted to come back, desperately for years, and now she was finally here. The move had been quick—so unexpected—and she'd only just arrived the day before, so finding a clean pair of slacks and her bag for work was harder than she'd expected it to be when she'd woken up early that morning.

"You've got this. I'm not sure why you'd want to go back to your high school, but you've been adamant for years that you wanted to." Greer was again speaking her own language to calm Kamryn down.

"I have! I loved this place growing up." Kamryn pocketed her keys as she shut the door behind her. Students would be arriving in the next few days, ready to move into the dormitories where she'd be the new house parent. Everything was so new as much as it was the same. "It's just weird, you know? Everything looks like I remember it, almost, but it's different at the exact same time."

"Hmmm." Greer always made that particular sound when she was deep in thought. Kamryn missed her dearly. She wished they lived closer, but her move out to Windermere added another hour to the trip. And with the time constraints on Kamryn with the new job, it was going to be impossible to get together any time soon.

"I've got to go." Kamryn wished she could stay on the phone longer. Talking to Greer eased the tension in her chest. It always did. But she had to start her day. Hell, she had to start her first day at her new job, and not toss her cookies in the meantime—which she somehow managed to do every first day at school.

Today would be different though, right?

The long walk to the administration building seemed fast. The nerves running through Kamryn's body were nearly too much and overloaded any good sense she had. Not that she had much of that to begin with. She wasn't just coming back to Windermere as a teacher, she was coming back as the Head of School, an emergency and definitely temporary placement until the actual Head of School was out of the hospital and recovered.

It was temporary. At least she kept telling herself that. Because if she got her hopes up, then she'd be devastated at the end of the semester when things didn't work out right. When the board told her she didn't have enough experience or she wasn't mature enough or she wasn't ready for the responsibility. Certainly they would tell her that.

Because what else would they say?

Not "job well done."

Not "keep going into the next semester."

Not "keep this job for the foreseeable future and then we'll talk about tenure."

Or better yet, "here's tenure! You don't even have to try to get it!"

Pushing the dreams aside, Kamryn followed the sidewalk to the administration building. She wasn't bringing in all of her books and personal effects yet. Not since this was supposed to be only one or two semesters while Dr. Waddy recuperated from his stroke. She would just use what she had and make do like she always did.

She'd been a scrappy kid when she needed to be, so what difference would being an adult make now? Except those damn nerves were still running rampant in her stomach. She really needed to get those under control.

Kamryn dropped her satchel on the desk after she let herself in with the key that groundskeeping had given her yesterday. She pulled out her laptop and her notebook and then stared at the desk before putting anything down. Everything was basically how it had been left weeks before when Dr. Waddy had collapsed on it. Pencils and pens strewn about, papers with random things she probably should read and figure out so she knew what was happening and when, and a computer that she still didn't have access to.

What the hell had she been thinking? She wasn't ready for this job. She'd applied on a whim since it had been the only open position that she somewhat qualified for, and when the board chair had called her for an immediate interview, she'd been scared shitless and beyond surprised.

But it had happened.

And here she was.

Moved into the dormitories since it was the only available housing, and she wasn't going to make Dr. Waddy and his wife move out in the middle of a medical crisis—a place she'd never truly anticipated living again, even though it was her dream.

She just had to not screw this up and then maybe they would offer her a permanent position—even if it wasn't Head of School.

The knock on her door startled her, but it was a welcome distraction from what she was facing on the desk in front of her.

"Dr. Ogden, the staff is ready for you in the conference room."

"Right." Was her voice shaking? Shit, she really did have to get that under control. Slow, deep breaths. That's what Greer had told her. She could do this. "I'll be there in a minute."

"If you don't mind, I can clean up in here while you're debriefing everyone."

"Yeah, uh... okay." That sounded like a really good idea. Mrs. Caldera, the long-serving secretary, was going to be a godsend for certain. Kamryn remembered her from when she was a student, and the woman had to be close to retirement, but thank all things holy that this wasn't the year she was gone and Kamryn wasn't stuck with a first-year administrative assistant while also dealing with the consequences of the former Head of School having a stroke.

"Dr. Ogden?"

"Yeah. I'm going, sorry." Snagging the mechanical pencil that she saw first thing, Kamryn propped the notebook and computer under her arm and headed out of the office. The conference room was...where exactly? She hadn't really been there when she was a student, and the memories were so far back in her brain that she wasn't sure she could even call them forth.

"Second door on the right!" Mrs. Caldera called.

"Thanks!" Kamryn said back loudly. That was the best thing ever. She really needed to keep Mrs. Caldera around. Just so that she had someone who was going to show her the ropes, because at this point, Kamryn wasn't convinced that the staff were going to give her the benefit of the doubt in anything.

At least five of them had taught her, though most of the teachers had retired by now and everyone else was new. She was going to have to prove herself at least three times over just to win their hearts as temporary Head of School. It was sheer dumb luck that she was in this position, and Kamryn was no idiot about it.

The door to the conference room was solid glass and heavy. When had they replaced that? Kamryn managed to hold back her grimace as she pushed it open. Inside were all of the teachers. Not just around the table, but around the edges of the room, seated and staring at her.

Fishbowl effect to the max.

Kamryn hadn't prepared herself for that.

She cleared her throat and set her things down on the one open place at the table. She wasn't even sure she could look up and into the eyes of the staff she was now in charge of. She had experience teaching, yes, and she had some experience in administration. But being in charge of everything and everyone? Having to answer to the board and run the school? Yeah, that was more than she'd bargained for. Well, not really. She had bargained for it. She just had to make sure that the risk paid off in the long run.

Kamryn dragged in cool air and blew it out slowly. *Stop this insane worrying, Kam. You're better than this.* And she was better than her anxiety. She knew that. She just had to get her feet under her to keep moving forward, and another two days would have been totally welcome for her to accomplish that.

"Good morning, everyone," Kamryn said, glad her voice wasn't wobbling or full of anxiety. If she could manage to fake it until she made it, then she would. "I know I haven't met all of you yet, but I'm looking forward to it."

It was like someone had stuck blinders over her eyes. She couldn't actually see the faces of the people in the room with her. She was in some sort of alternate-reality state. Oh well, this was going to have to do for now.

"I'm Dr. Ogden. I'm temporary Head of School while Dr. Waddy is recovering."

"Do you know how he is?" Someone in the back spoke up.

Kamryn's stomach dropped. In the rush of everything, she had failed to get the one update that people were going to want.

And that was probably her first major failure as a leader in this school. What was she fooling herself into? She had to do better.

"I don't have a recent update yet," Kamryn said, leaning back on her skills of avoidance to tackle this one. "I'll make sure to find out by the end of the day and let you all know. I'm sure the students will be just as anxious to know when they return in a few days."

"Yes, they will be."

Kamryn froze. That voice was one she hadn't expected to hear, at least not yet. Which was ridiculous. She should have. She knew that Dr. Elia Sharpe was still a teacher at the school, that she was the head of the English department, and that she hadn't moved up in the ranks to become admin like she'd said she wanted to all those years ago.

Raising her gaze to meet the cool blue eyes of the teacher sitting precisely to her left, Kamryn balked. She hadn't expected to feel this way in front of her former teacher. She hadn't thought that it would make a difference to her—and yet, it did. Something about Dr. Elia Sharpe always seemed so impersonal and distanced, like she was a greater-than-thou character in a book that Kamryn swore she never read but actually lived for. She'd looked up to Dr. Sharpe throughout her entire career at Windermere, and now, Kamryn was Elia's boss.

Elia?

Could she even call Dr. Sharpe by her first name now?

That seemed impossible.

"Yes, they will be, and I'd like to let them know as much as I possibly can." Kamryn straightened her shoulders. She remained standing, wanting the added height difference between her and the staff to give her some kind of element of authority that she still wasn't sure she was worthy of. "I'll make sure that they have all the resources they need to process this trauma and this *temporary* transition."

She made sure to emphasize *temporary* because she certainly didn't want it getting back to the board that she was trying to take over and make a million changes. Not while she was still on their short list for permanent positions should Dr. Waddy never make a full recovery.

"That's good to hear, Kamryn."

That tone, that name, falling from Dr. Sharpe's lips should have been the warning that Kamryn needed. No one had called her by her given name except her grandparents in a very long time. And no one should be addressing her by that name in this room —not right now. They should be calling her Dr. Ogden and nothing else.

She had worked hard for that degree, and she had worked hard for her education. And it was a simple sign of respect. The fact that Dr. Sharpe was doing the opposite was a very personal and intentional point that she was making.

"Absolutely, *Dr. Sharpe.*" Kamryn made sure to use her proper salutation, emphasizing it even. If Dr. Sharpe did it again, then Kamryn would probably correct her, but not this first time. Kamryn wasn't such a brute that she would ruin a good thing while it lasted—if it could be a good thing at this point.

Turning to the rest of the group, Kamryn prepared the speech that she wrote late last night over the glass of whiskey that she had desperately needed in order to calm some nerves.

"I haven't had much time to sit down and sort things out, so this meeting is going to be short today, and I'm going to assume that most of you know what needs done. I was only hired for this position last week, and the notes that were sent to me were scant at best. I know we need a secondary co-leader for the Speech team, and that we need someone to help with Model United Nations. Any takers?"

Two teachers in the back of the room shot their hands up and asked for MUN. Kamryn took down their names in her notebook. She'd sort out the rest later. "And for Speech?"

No one volunteered.

Her stomach plummeted. From her recollection, Dr. Sharpe was the main leader for Speech. She'd taken Speech when she was in school, and she'd learned a great deal from Dr. Sharpe. But the fact that no one was willing to work with her was going to be a stretch.

"Anyone?"

Still silence rained through the room.

"Right. I'll work on that issue later."

"If I may," Dr. Sharpe started quietly, "I've been leading Speech for the last four years alone. I don't need a co-leader."

Kamryn pressed her lips into a thin line. She wasn't going to take that for an answer. There was some reason that position wasn't fillable, and that no one wanted to volunteer. And it wasn't just that fact that bothered her. It was a flat-out safety issue for Elia and the kids.

Oh, look, damn. That hadn't taken long for her to mentally make the switch to calling her Elia.

"We can talk about that in my office after the meeting."

"And by your office, you mean Dr. Waddy's?" Elia's gaze was sharp and perceptive. She'd always been that, and Kamryn should never have expected anything less.

"Yes." She moved on from that moment, pushing past Elia's discomfort along with her own and straight on to everything else that they needed to discuss. She set up meetings with each individual department to go over even more details and then she dismissed the group.

But Elia remained seated, stoically staring at her as the room emptied.

Fuck.

Kamryn didn't have to prove herself to the board.

She had to prove herself to her former English teacher who clearly had a chip on her shoulder and didn't want to accept the fact that Kamryn had been hired for this position.

"You said we needed to talk," Elia finally spoke once the last person was out of the room and the door was shut.

"Yes," Kamryn said. "In my office."

"I'd prefer to talk here, if this works just as well. Then we don't have to move."

Kamryn paused for a moment, weighing her options. This was a power move from Elia. But was it one that she wanted to fight right now?

Absolutely not.

Plopping her butt down into the chair next to Elia's, Kamryn stared at her. "Fine."

two

"When's the last time you worked with a co-leader on Speech?" Kamryn settled her notepad down in front of her as she seemed to melt into her seat.

The muscles strained at the corners of Elia's jaw as she clenched her molars hard. She'd never gotten out of that habit no matter how many times she'd attempted to drop it, and in the last month, it'd been far worse.

As soon as Miller Waddy had his stroke, Elia had put her name in for the position to help fill the gaps until he could return. The board had allowed her to live in the silence of no response for three weeks until they hired a temporary but longer-term replacement.

That had stung.

She'd given and devoted her life to this school. And to add salt to the wound, they'd hired her former student, who certainly didn't have as much experience as she did. Kamryn Ogden was a sight for sore eyes, however. She'd certainly grown up in the last twenty years since she'd graduated.

Was Kamryn just as nervous as Elia about this conversation? She hadn't seemed to be when she'd started it.

"It's been five years."

"Five..." Kamryn blew out a breath and ran her fingers through her shoulder-length dirty blonde hair.

It used to be lighter in color, probably from spending so much time outside in the summers. Elia had found Kamryn reading books under the sugar maples more times than she could count. But now Kamryn's hair was dark, and she'd gained weight, not just in her body but in her cheeks, which were much fuller now than they had been.

"Do you realize how dangerous that is?" Kamryn straightened her back a little, pressing her palm into the table. "Not just for the kids, but for you."

"It's how it's always been." Elia clenched her fist under the table. She didn't want to be dealing with this, not now. If she couldn't be the replacement for Miller while he was out and couldn't be trusted with even that small amount of power, then why would she ever consider allowing Kamryn to walk all over her? She wouldn't.

"You and I both know that's a lie."

Elia shuddered, but she managed to contain it to where she didn't think that Kamryn saw. Because Kamryn was right. It hadn't always been that way, she'd just used that excuse for years because it was how she'd managed to get out of having a co-leader. And she hated that Kamryn was so easily calling her out on that.

"Dr. Howard co-led with you when I was on the team."

Elia's lips thinned and the muscles in her jaw tightened even more. "Yes, she did."

"And wasn't there a parent volunteer, too? At least for when we were traveling." Kamryn scratched the side of her head before shaking it. "I can't remember her name."

Elia sure as hell wasn't going to fill in that blank for her. The last thing she wanted on the face of the planet was to remember *that* woman. Well, in all honesty, Yara hadn't been the problem at all, but that situation had nearly ended Elia's career.

And it was why Elia never wanted to work with a co-leader again, even though it was also the perfect example of why she needed one. But Kamryn didn't know anything about that, and Elia was determined to keep it that way. The last thing she needed was for her history to come up and bite her in the ass again, especially while she was still hoping the board had a short enough memory to potentially give her the Head of School position should Miller not return.

"Mrs. Cole!" Kamryn smacked her hand lightly on the edge of the table. "What was her first name?"

"Yara," Elia mumbled, closing in on herself even more.

"Right. Anyway, you need a co-leader, or the Speech team won't be happening this year."

"What?" Elia stilled, her heart thudding hard. Kamryn was pulling out the big guns for this one, wasn't she? Pushing her weight around when she hadn't even been here long enough to take a breath.

"I'm serious, Dr. Sharpe. It needs to happen. Like I said earlier, it's for your protection as much as the students. We don't need anything untoward happening."

Did she know? Panic rose in Elia's chest, trying to claw its way out, but she managed to keep it locked away, at least for now. "I understand what you're saying."

"Good. And since no one volunteered this morning, I'll do it."

"No." Elia was going to put her foot down on this one. She didn't need administrative supervision to run the Speech team, something she had been doing for over two decades now. She wouldn't put herself through that.

"Then the Speech team won't exist this year."

"The meets are already booked." Elia looked straight into Kamryn's dark brown eyes. "I'm not going to cancel an entire season for our students, especially the seniors who are looking for scholarships to college."

"Then we're agreed." Kamryn leaned back in the chair, a smug smile gracing her full lips.

"No, we're not in agreement."

"Then no Speech team."

"Kamryn!" Elia's voice rose along with her anger, and she couldn't hide it this time. She wasn't going to play this back-and-forth game. "You don't have the authority to do this."

"Actually, I do, and it's by the board's direction. This is a safety issue, nothing else. And if no one else on staff will join you, then I will. I think it'll be nice to dip my toes back into the competition world. Giving my own lectures every week gets a bit tedious. A challenge would be nice."

Elia's mind spun. How could this possibly be happening? She didn't need her former student to watch over her like she was a new teacher who was going to screw everything up. If this came down from the board, it might just be further punishment for what had happened eighteen years ago. But it shouldn't be. That was done and over with. She'd been proven innocent so many times over.

But stigmas were real. And she'd never be able to escape this one, would she?

"In your last evaluation with Dr. Waddy, he suggested that you spend the summer finding a co-leader. It seems you didn't do that." Kamryn stared directly at her.

Elia had been filleted open and laid bare. She couldn't do this. It was worse than eighteen years ago almost, and only because this was Kamryn—her former student who had taken the job that she deserved. And hell yes, she deserved it.

But the fact that Kamryn was throwing out her annual evaluation? She definitely had more information than she'd let on in that all-staff meeting just ten minutes ago. She'd been prepared for this conversation, and she'd allowed the suddenness of this move to work to her advantage and to take Elia off guard, as if she'd known that Elia would be resistant to the idea.

"Dr. Sharpe." Kamryn's voice was firm but steady. The words weren't angry—more a call to come back to the conversation at hand.

How long would it take for Kamryn to start calling her Elia?

"I don't suppose there is another choice, is there?"

"There's not," Kamryn responded. "Except you stepping down from Speech entirely, but I can't imagine you doing that."

"Why not?" Elia asked before she could stop herself. What was it that Kamryn was seeing that she wasn't? What was keeping her here and entertaining the ridiculous idea that she wasn't capable of doing this on her own?

"Because when I was a student here, I was fairly convinced—along with many other students—that you loved the Speech team more than teaching English." Kamryn folded her hands in her lap. "And the fact that you're still leading the Speech team all these years later confirms that."

"I'm also head of the English department."

"You are." Kamryn nodded. "And why aren't you the assistant Head of School? Or better yet, Head of School all together? Surely, Dr. Waddy wasn't chosen over you."

Elia paused. She raised her chin up, eyeing Kamryn over carefully—perhaps even looking down her nose a little. What game was this woman playing? And she was a woman. She wasn't a kid anymore. She'd changed in these twenty years, and Elia wasn't sure she could see anything of the former student who had been mostly smiles, laughs, and burying her nose between the pages of more books than Elia managed to read in a year.

"You're assuming that I applied when Miller was hired." Elia barely resisted the urge to cross her arms. "And if you remember correctly, assumptions are deadly in debate."

Kamryn paused at that, the reminder of where they had once been in terms of power and authority clearly uncomfortable for her. But Elia reveled in it. It put them back on the same footing, which was uneven at best. Two could play this game, and Elia was going to be just as prepared for it next time.

Because this war between them was only just beginning.

"I do remember," Kamryn said slowly, keeping her voice steady as she locked her gaze on Elia's. "I also remember that assumptions are necessary in debate. We have to anticipate where our opponent is going next with the argument. But, Dr. Sharpe, we're not opponents. Are we?"

"I don't know." Elia hollowed her cheeks, ready to stand up and leave as soon as she got a chance. She needed to escape back to her office soon. "Are we?"

"I would hope not." Kamryn's brow knit together in concern. "Why would we be?"

Pushing back and standing, Elia grabbed her notebook off the table and pressed it against her chest. From here, she could stare down at Kamryn and have all the power in the conversation—at least that was what she was telling herself. "I'll see you at the first Speech practice."

"Sure," Kamryn answered, staying put.

Now *that* was a power move. And damn Kamryn for being the one to pull it. Elia pressed her molars into each other even harder than before, and she walked out of the room without looking back. She closed her eyes as soon as she reached the garden at the front of the administration building.

The jealousy that had gotten into her was beyond anything she'd experienced before, but Kamryn had been right. She'd wanted that position, for far longer than when Miller had suddenly left it open for the taking. She'd wanted to be Head of School from the moment she'd stepped foot on this campus, and it hadn't been until last month that she'd had the temerity to even attempt to apply for it.

And Kamryn had no idea why.

That much was clear.

But damn her for bringing all of that up and more. Elia had been so open with her students in the beginning, allowing them to see her hopes and dreams just like they allowed her to see theirs. It had been codependent and wrong of her, and she'd since stopped that behavior, but where had that left her? She was still a damn good teacher, but she hadn't worked toward those dreams she'd once held, and the one time she had, Kamryn had stolen it out from under her.

The cool air, a sure sign that fall was coming rapidly, refreshed her. Elia closed her eyes briefly to center herself before walking back to her office in the Social Sciences building. It was the smallest building on campus, but it had been her home for so long that she wasn't sure she could live without it in her life in some manner.

Elia sat down at her desk and turned her computer back on. She stared at the sign-ups for Speech and at the schedule she'd already planned out. Adding in another adult would help, as much as she didn't want to admit it, but it would also increase costs and she'd need to rework some of the rooming arrangements she'd already made.

She rubbed her hand against the back of her neck and immediately closed out of everything. Sadness swept through her. *Yara.* That had been the best and worst mistake of her life, hadn't it? And she wasn't ever going to be able to escape her past nor the promises she had made to herself so very long ago.

To become Head of School.

To be a damn good teacher.

To fall in love and have a family.

But she was getting closer to fifty every single year and none of that had really happened. She'd allowed her teaching to become stagnant. She couldn't remember the last time that her name had been up on the favorite teachers lists that the students put together every semester. She wasn't young or hip, and she didn't have new ideas or energy for her lesson plans anymore.

Working with a former student?

Not only that, but having her former student be her new boss?

Maybe it was time for her to give up and retire.

It definitely called out her age, even if Kamryn had been one of the first students she'd taught. Elia had started at Windermere the year before Kamryn had, and she'd taken over Speech that second year. Not that Kamryn would remember or know that.

This wasn't a sign that she was old and decrepit, was it?

Elia wrinkled her nose at that thought. She'd never admit to that. Ever. But she would admit to the jealousy that was still raging through her chest and down into her fingers. The fact that the one time she had taken the chance to apply for a position she was most certainly qualified for, and she hadn't even been given a chance?

Yeah, that stung.

But it was far worse knowing that Kamryn was in that position now.

Cursing herself under her breath, Elia pulled up her lesson plans for the first week of school. It was routine and habit to go through them even though they hadn't changed in at least twelve years now. At least not in any major ways. Without holding back, Elia poured her entire focus into the task at hand—teaching her students.

That was what she'd been hired for, wasn't it?

She just had to make it through this semester until Miller was back. Then everything would be back to normal, and she wouldn't have to deal with Kamryn any longer.

three

Kamryn had spent the last hour going through the calendar with Mrs. Caldera, and by the end of it, she was ready to tear her eyes and her ears out. Miller Waddy hadn't been keeping up to date with anything it seemed, which meant that she had quite the mess to clean up. His being out for the last few weeks didn't help either, especially when the assistant Head of School was out on parental leave.

Pursing her lips, Kamryn rifled through the desk to find the few things she knew she would need, but it felt odd and like a violation. She would ask Mrs. Caldera to pack up Dr. Waddy's things by the end of the week—at least the things in the desk that were personal items. That way she could focus better.

Now that she had a moment to breathe and think—what the hell had been up with Elia Sharpe? That was more of an attack than Kamryn had anticipated from her favorite teacher. She hadn't ever expected to be put on the spot like that, to have the power play so early on—well, she had, but not with Elia Sharpe.

She stared at her phone and debated whether or not to call Greer back, ask for more advice. But that wouldn't really help very much because Greer hadn't gone to school there. She didn't know

Dr. Sharpe before, and if Kamryn explained who she was now, that would certainly taint Greer's opinion of her.

The phone on her desk rang, and Kamryn startled at it. She wasn't exactly sure how things worked here, if Mrs. Caldera would screen all her calls to the office or not. Kamryn reached for the black standard office phone and held it to her ear.

"Dr. Ogden speaking."

"Kamryn, it's Heather."

Kamryn smiled at the name. Heather was the only reason she'd known the position was open in the first place, and she'd jumped at the chance to apply as soon as Heather's text had come through. "Hey."

"How's the first day going?" Heather asked.

Kamryn was about to tell her all the drama with Elia, but she stopped herself. Heather was on the school board now, and they weren't close friends. There was a new twist to their relationship, and Kamryn had to be vigilant in how she treated it. "Not bad. Do you have an update on Dr. Waddy?"

"He's still in ICU from my understanding." Heather sounded stressed.

Kamryn could only guess why, but she was sure having such a major medical event happen so close to the beginning of the school year when there were already a number of other positions in flux wasn't helping anything. "Any idea how his recovery is going? Some of the staff were wondering, and I'd like to be able to give them an update."

"No, I don't, sorry. You might try getting hold of his wife. She'd have more information than we would."

"Right, I'll try that." Though Kamryn didn't love the idea of bugging the woman whose husband had collapsed in this very room from a stroke only a few weeks ago. "Were you just calling to check in?"

"Mostly. The board was curious if you'd found volunteers for those extracurricular teams." Heather paused, and the silence was pregnant with some sort of tension that Kamryn wasn't able to name.

"Uh, yeah. I did, actually." Kamryn picked up a pen and started to flip it back and forth between her fingers. She focused on it while she debated what else to add to this part of the conversation. Heather had been the one to bring it up to her, so she'd taken care of it as her first order of business at the meeting.

"Even for the Speech team?"

"Yes," Kamryn responded.

"And Elia Sharpe didn't give you any trouble with that?"

That's what this was about. Kamryn glanced toward her open doorway and decided to lower her volume. She didn't need anyone to overhear what she was going to say and only get half the conversation. "No, she didn't. In fact, she said it would be good to get back to how it was when we were in school."

"Really?" Heather seemed surprised by that.

Kamryn could understand why, especially if this was something Heather had been pushing for a while. She likely would have come up against Elia's backbone at least a time or two. "Sometimes it just takes the right person to ask."

"Right," Heather said, dropping her tone. "Well, I'm glad. It'll help keep the students safe."

"It absolutely will." Kamryn started to draw spirals on a yellow pad. "Let me know if you hear anything about Dr. Waddy. I'd really like to give the staff an update before the students get here."

"I will." Heather's voice had that tone to it, the one that was half-fake and half-real.

Which was rather unexpected. Kamryn hung up, squared her shoulders, and rolled her neck. She really needed to sit down and figure out what she was doing for the rest of the day. She needed to prioritize everything.

Bending over her desk, Kamryn lost herself in organizing. This was at least one thing that she could accomplish today—even if it was the only thing. When Mrs. Caldera knocked on her door lightly, Kamryn stretched her back, an ache settling into the center of it.

"Lunch is only being served for the next thirty minutes today."

"Oh." Kamryn glanced down at the work that was spread over the desk. "Go on ahead, then."

"You're not coming?"

Kamryn's back went up. She had so much work to get done. It wouldn't be the end of the world for her to skip one meal. "Tomorrow."

"Make sure you eat dinner." Mrs. Caldera pointed a finger at her. "I'll bring you back a snack."

"Thanks." Kamryn smiled a little, and as soon as her office was empty, she went back to work.

"I brought the schedule for you."

Kamryn jerked with a start. She blinked her dry eyes toward the door and tried to relax the muscles in her neck and shoulders. Elia Sharpe stood in her doorway, the light from the window in the office outside of it shining against her back and giving her an ethereal glow.

"Schedule?" Kamryn shook her head in confusion. "Schedule for what?"

"Speech." Elia stepped forward and dropped the papers onto the desk with a soft thump. "Since you'll need it."

"Ah. Thank you." Kamryn stared down at the papers that were now covering what she had been working on. Her head ached, no doubt from the stress, and from staring at a computer screen and Dr. Waddy's scribbled handwriting all day. "They're only serving lunch for thirty minutes today."

Elia frowned slightly before catching it and smoothing her features out again. "Lunch was an hour ago, Kamryn."

"Oh." Kamryn glanced at the clock on the far wall, realizing way too late that it had been a whole lot longer than she'd thought. Covering her embarrassment, Kamryn picked up the papers Elia had dropped on the desk and started to skim over them. "How many kids are on the Speech team this season?"

"Twenty-six. Not including any incoming students or new students that would like to join." Elia crossed her arms.

"How many do you anticipate?"

"No more than ten new."

"Shouldn't be too bad a crew then." Kamryn settled the papers back down. She wasn't entirely sure why Elia was bringing her these instead of just emailing them over, or why she would dare to come into the office after the disaster they'd had earlier that day. "Was there something else you needed?"

"I thought you might appreciate a bit of an orientation." Elia spoke slowly, as if choosing her words carefully and trying not to make a mess of this conversation.

Maybe she wasn't as changed as Kamryn had thought this morning. Relaxing slightly, Kamryn canted her head to the side and waited a beat before responding. "Orientation?"

"Usually any new staff gets an orientation. I realized belatedly that Miller is usually the one who does this, and the board for the Head of School position. I wouldn't be surprised if that was missed in the...chaos of the situation."

"You're right, it was missed." Kamryn's lips pulled up into a gentle smile. "But I don't think I need an orientation to the school. Thank you."

"Your choice." Elia started toward the door, her long legs carrying her swiftly away from Kamryn's desk.

"I could use an orientation to the board."

Elia halted, her shoulders so rigid that Kamryn wondered if they would break. Slowly, she turned and faced Kamryn, her cheeks pale and her eyes wide. "I don't deal with the board often."

"Doesn't mean you don't know who the players are. There seem to be a lot of missing communications between Dr. Waddy and the board and the board and Dr. Waddy. I'd like to rectify that before I leave if I can—maybe help get everyone on the same page." Kamryn didn't tear her gaze from Elia. There was something here that was off. Elia looked scared almost.

"That's something you'd have to talk to them and Miller about, not me."

"I understand, but I'd like an outsider's point of view, if possible. And since you offered an orientation—"

"To the school," Elia corrected, "not to the board."

"The board is what leads this school, and there's a lot amiss there. They don't even have an ethics review committee."

"I know," Elia said, and then shook her head.

Had she not wanted to say that? Had the great Elia Sharpe who prided herself on her speech and debate skills let something slip? Now Kamryn was fascinated.

"Would you consider being on it? Not only as someone who has high ethical standards, but as a connection point back to the school?" Kamryn stretched her legs out under the desk.

"Absolutely not." Elia shook her head sharply. "And don't for one second think that I'm someone with high ethical standards. I might surprise you."

"That would surprise me." Kamryn frowned.

"Good." Turning on her heel, Elia walked out.

Kamryn was left in the wake of anger that followed. At least it felt mostly like anger, but something was under the edge of it that she couldn't really put her finger on. Sighing heavily, Kamryn picked up the papers Elia had given her again.

Elia Sharpe was clearly going to be her problem child.

Yet, she had offered a helping hand, so perhaps Kamryn was overthinking the issue. In fact, she'd been the only one to outwardly offer help on anything. Mrs. Caldera was just doing her job, but the board had basically left Kamryn to fend for herself.

But she'd never seen Elia so shut down before. What exactly had happened to the woman she remembered? The one who was her teacher, who was passionate and energetic, and open? Because this woman was closed off and icy. Not just icy. She was liquid nitrogen in a bottle, sucking the air and freezing everything around her that she touched.

Kamryn shook her head.

She had to stop thinking like that. It wasn't going to do her any favors in the long run. She had to keep an open mind about everyone who was here. It was the only way that she was going to survive her temporary position.

Her cell phone buzzed on the top of the desk. Kamryn smiled when she saw Greer's name light up on the screen. Sliding her thumb across the screen to answer the video call, Kamryn set the phone up against the computer screen and grinned broadly.

"Lunch time?" Kamryn asked.

"Yeah." Greer leaned down and wrinkled her nose. "Has the first day been as bad as you thought it would?"

Kamryn flicked her gaze toward the open door and stood up immediately to shut it. She needed privacy for this one. Plopping back into the chair, Kamryn sighed heavily. "It could be better. I'll tell you more about it when I'm not in the office."

"That bad, huh?"

"Not bad." Kamryn pursed her lips. "Interesting for sure."

"Oh, I sniff a good story."

Kamryn chuckled. "Why are you calling on your lunch? I thought you had a long day today."

"Yeah, I did too." Greer's face fell. "I'm being laid off."

"What?" Kamryn's eyes widened. "Are you serious?"

"I knew it was coming." Greer lifted her shoulders up to her ears and dropped them. "They want the boys to start preschool, which means that my position is kind of pointless. No use for a nanny when the kids are in school."

"Greer..." Kamryn frowned. "You'll find another position."

"I know I will. It's hard though, leaving the boys. I've been with them for five years straight. They're my babies." Greer gave an over-accentuated pout. "At least I have until the New Year with them."

"What about Andra's wedding?"

Greer smiled. "They said that I could still have that time off for the wedding, not for anything else. So no bridal shower, no bachelorette party. They want to use as much of my time as they possibly can."

"Greer." Kamryn wanted to drive over there and hug her best friend, but it was damn near impossible to do that right now. And they both knew that.

"I'll be fine. It isn't the first time this has happened."

"I know, but it's hard."

"It is. But worth it." Greer forced a smile and winked. "Is everything as much of a mess as you thought it was?"

"More. Which I probably should have suspected. I've been digging into the board a bit. I still find it really odd that they wouldn't just hire from within for this." Kamryn ran her fingers through her hair and stretched again. She really should get up and take a short walk somewhere. It'd be good for her.

"What'd you find?"

"Nothing." Kamryn frowned. "At least not yet. But I have taken care of two issues that the board wanted me to work on. There's a third one that I think is going to be a bit harder."

"What's that?"

"I need to form an ethics committee. Want to be part of that?"

"Hell no!"

They both laughed, the lightheartedness of this conversation exactly what Kamryn had needed. Sometimes it was like Greer was psychic when it came to these kinds of things. When they settled again, Kamryn looked directly at Greer. "Think you can sneak away on Friday and come to town? They're having their fall festival. I remember it always being amazing."

"I'll see what I can do, but no promises."

"Perfect." Kamryn ended the call shortly after and rolled her shoulders.

With her first day done that meant her first week was nearly in the books, and while she'd be bringing a lot of the work home with her that night, it had been well worth it. And she hadn't created chaos yet, so that was a good thing too. Picking up the phone on the desk, Kamryn searched for Dr. Waddy's home number. She really had to make this call, no matter how much she didn't want to. But she needed to update the staff like she'd promised.

four

"I nearly forgot the festival was tonight," Elia said, turning to her best friend, Abagail, and smiling. They'd gone out for dinner, Elia really needing to get away from the school and from the jealousy that was raging within her. It was taking over everything she had attempted to do that first week of school, and every time she'd seen Kamryn, it had gotten worse.

She'd avoided Kamryn as much as she could, but it was impossible in a school so small. The kids arriving had been the sanity she'd needed, and meeting up with Abagail was her chance to unwind and vent. And boy had Abagail heard it over dinner.

"Remember when we were in our twenties and we used to come to this thing every year?" Abagail laughed lightly, holding onto the takeout containers in her left hand.

Elia nodded, shoving her hands into her pockets. It was supposed to get chilly that night, the first night that it'd truly feel like fall, though it wasn't set to last very long. "Yeah." Elia's gaze was drawn to the town square, with the lights that were up year-round casting a glow onto the cobblestones and the people that loitered underneath them.

"Let's go tonight," Elia said in a rush, an impulse that she hadn't known she'd still possessed. Then again, she'd done a whole lot impulsively in the last two weeks, including just about every interaction she'd had with Kamryn.

Why couldn't she get that woman out of her head already?

"I can't," Abagail responded. "I've got that early morning meeting, remember?"

"Right." Elia shoved her hands a little tighter into her jacket, clenching her fists. She wasn't ready to go back to the school, not just yet. She needed a bit more time than she'd had away from that place, somewhere to find her center again and to step away from the insane jealousy that kept her up at night.

"But you should hang out for a while."

"I..." Elia was about to object, since her introverted self wasn't someone who would just stay alone at an event if she could avoid it, but something caught her eye. There was a loud raucous laugh not that far off, but the tone of the voice sounded very familiar. "Can you stay just a few more minutes?"

Abagail looked at the square and then back at Elia. "A few."

They walked together, closer to the square, saying nothing. Elia was comfortable with that silence, wanting it, craving it even. She didn't need to talk to Abagail to know what she was thinking, or that Abagail was just as curious about Elia's change in mood as Elia was.

They stopped by the first booth, and Elia paid for one spiked hot apple cider and one not spiked. She handed the alcohol-free one to Abagail and sipped on her own. The warmth spread down her throat and into the top of her chest, warming her even more. It used to be a lot colder for these events, but the tradition of having all the fall things never quite stopped.

Once again looking around and observing, Elia took everything in. She was sure there were likely a few students out here tonight. The older ones typically came out to enjoy one last weekend of freedom before the school year really took over and consumed their life.

Speaking of... there was Bristol. "Hey, Dr. Sharpe."

"Bristol." Elia smiled at the soon-to-be young woman. She'd

been on the speech team for all the years she'd been at Windermere, and they'd soon be spending a lot of time together. "Enjoying the festival?"

"Oh yeah!" Bristol's eyes lit up. "One last hurrah!"

Elia could understand the sentiment, but she kept her reaction calm. She nodded to Bristol. "Then enjoy away. Don't let me stop you."

"Speech is on Tuesday, right?" Bristol leaned up on her toes. It was her nervous tic. Her gaze slid from Elia to Abagail before she bounced back down onto the flats of her feet.

Did she think they were dating?

It wouldn't be the first time, though she and Abagail had never considered it.

"Tuesday at four."

"I'll be there!" Bristol grinned broadly before she skittered away.

"How do you think coaching Speech is going to go with your former student now your co-leader?" Abagail asked in hushed tones as her shoulder brushed against Elia's. She took a quick sip of her drink.

Elia's jaw clenched again. She'd given herself a migraine twice now because of that bad habit, which she really needed to get over. Rolling her shoulders and purposely loosening her muscles, Elia raised her gaze to meet Abagail's. "I'm not concerned about her abilities."

"Didn't think you were," Abagail mumbled into her drink.

Elia winced. "I don't need a co-leader."

"You do, and you just don't want to admit that she's right." Abagail had that sickening *I'm right* smirk on her lips, and Elia turned away so she wouldn't have to face it.

Logically, she knew that Kamryn was right. That the board was. This did add a layer of protection and safety to the entire Speech team, but that didn't mean she liked it—especially because the solution was Kamryn herself.

That laugh echoed in Elia's ears again. She looked around the square, trying to find the source and pinpoint why it seemed so familiar, but she didn't manage to find it.

"Elia, what harm is there in some extra help?"

"It's not the help I'm worried about."

"Then what is it? Because you've been on edge for three weeks, and something has to give soon."

Elia sighed heavily, wrapping her hands around the cup of spiked cider and taking another sip. She wasn't ready to answer the question. She wasn't ready to face the truth of why this hurt so much. Right now, she wanted to sit in that anger a bit longer, and she wanted it all directed at someone who could very easily distract her from the real reason why she was so upset by it all.

"Fine, keep your silence." Abagail sighed. "Call me when you're ready to talk, okay? I promise I'll answer this time."

Elia chuckled lightly. "You're going out of the country for two weeks. I don't think you'll have time to take my call on your whirlwind vacation with your newest fling."

"Oh, you never know." Abagail smiled. "I need to get going. But seriously, Elia. Call me when you're ready to get over yourself and actually talk about what's going on."

"I will." Elia latched her hand onto Abagail's arm and gave her a gentle squeeze. "Have a good trip."

"I always do." Abagail wrapped her free arm across Elia's shoulders and gave her a side hug, pushing Elia's boundaries for physical comfort. But they both knew that Abagail was the only one that Elia would allow to do this. "See you."

"Email me when you get there."

"I know the drill, boss!" Abagail laughed as she stepped away.

The warmth was suddenly gone. Elia hadn't realized how much of that had come from Abagail's very presence until that moment. Sipping her drink, Elia stared down into the cup. She would finish drinking it and then she would head back to the school for the night. That would force her to stay out just a little longer. It'd be good for her in the long run.

There was that laugh again.

Elia was drawn to it, trying to figure out where it was coming from. She was determined this time to figure out why it sounded so familiar. Carefully walking through the throng of people, Elia followed the noise until she stopped short.

Kamryn.

Her boisterous laugh was what Elia had heard, and it tickled the recesses of her memory because it had been so very long since she'd heard it. Swallowing back the disgust, Elia stared. Kamryn was being obnoxiously loud, something Elia hadn't ever seen before. Her movements were all over the place.

Staying put, Elia sipped her drink again, observing. What was it about Kamryn that irked her so much? Was it actually Kamryn herself or was it something else entirely? Elia listened carefully to the music and the voices around her. She could fade in here, fall into the background, and no one would know that she existed.

But her entire being was centered on Kamryn.

Maybe she was just happy? She seemed to be with friends.

A small group of women surrounded Kamryn, five women to be exact. One of them looked familiar, but Elia couldn't make out her face from this distance. She was the one facing Kamryn so it was hard to see, but Kamryn's facial reactions didn't exactly say that she was excited to be there. There was something hard about them, something stiff.

Elia caught sight of Bristol and two other girls from the Speech team hanging out by the band that was playing. They giggled as they pointed toward a group of boys who were also seniors at the school. That was hopefully not going to make for some interesting drama throughout the school year, but Elia would keep her eye on it if she could.

Kamryn lifted a small cup to her lips and chugged it. Elia frowned. That was definitely alcoholic, and if she remembered correctly, the vendor who had those cups specifically sold shots and nothing else. Elia watched as Kamryn threw the cup into the trash next to where she was standing and then turned back to her group of friends. She wobbled slightly.

This was going to turn into something else entirely, something that Elia wasn't sure she wanted to deal with. But she couldn't let Bristol or any other students who were out tonight see Kamryn make a fool of herself. She would embarrass the school, and the school was having enough issues right now. It didn't need any added ones.

Dropping her half-full cup into the nearest trash, Elia started to weave her way through the throng of people. She couldn't let Windermere go through another scandal on her watch, although at least she wouldn't be the one who caused this one or was at the center of it.

Straightening her shoulders and plastering on the best disappointed face that she could manage right now, Elia walked. She had to move all the way to the back of the crowd in order to get around them. She wasn't a person who would just push through people to get where she was going, especially when she was trying not to make a scene.

She'd text Abagail all about the drama when she got home that night. But this incident only confirmed exactly what Elia had thought from the start. Kamryn wasn't fit to be temporary Head of School, and the board shouldn't have hired someone so young and immature to take on the position. They should have hired Elia, someone who had a reputation with the school—good or bad, it didn't really matter—but someone who knew how to control themselves.

As she approached, her stomach twisted into knots. Kamryn definitely wasn't herself. Elia had never seen her like this—not just drunk, but loud and boisterous. It was so forced, like she was trying to cover something up. But what exactly was it?

Elia rounded the last small group of people. Kamryn's eyes lit up when she reached her, going from surprise and shock to bold and knowing. Kamryn tipped back another one of those small brown paper cups that no doubt had *a shot* in it that was actually equal to three shots and way overpriced.

"Elia!" Kamryn slurred.

She was definitely drunk.

Elia approached cautiously, with the goal to mitigate any drama or scandal that could result from this. She needed to get Kamryn under control and back to the school where she could sleep this off and forget tonight happened. Well, probably not forget. Elia wouldn't let her do that. She would remind Kamryn of the stupidity of this moment every chance she got, especially if it made a difference in keeping the school safe from her stupid mistakes.

Kamryn snagged Elia's hand and jerked her close. She leaned in, up on her toes and pressed her lips to Elia's ear. Elia's entire body shuddered. Only Abagail touched her like this, and even then, it was far more reserved than whatever Kamryn was doing right now. This was... this was nearly intoxicating in and of itself.

The scent of alcohol wafted to Elia's nostrils, and her stomach churned with it. "Kamryn—"

"Please just go with it," Kamryn whispered, managing somehow to keep her voice so quiet that even Elia who was right next to her had to strain to hear what she said.

"I'm not—"

Kamryn's lips covered hers, cutting off anything that Elia was going to say. Kamryn's hand slid behind Elia's neck, her fingers diving into the rough hairs at the back of Elia's neck, the ones that were graying but that she ignored because unless her hair was up no one could see them.

Gasping, Elia parted her lips to say something. But the words were lost again when Kamryn slid her tongue against Elia's. Those shudders from before turned into shivers of pleasure. Elia wrapped an arm around Kamryn's side when she started to sway to the right. She propped Kamryn back up and had to use her other arm to prevent her from falling the other direction. She was surprised to find that she was essentially hugging Kamryn in a tight embrace.

Elia sighed, physical sensations floating through her and sparking alive. It had been a long time since a kiss had managed to do that. Not since she'd kissed anyone, but since it had been such a basic physical reaction. Elia relaxed and pushed into Kamryn, tangling their tongues as her eyes fluttered shut for a brief moment before her mind came back to her.

Pulling away, Elia kept her arms around Kamryn, scared that she was going to topple over herself in her drunken state. And there was no mistaking it now. Kamryn was sloshed.

"So you're her new girlfriend."

five

With the fall festival lights and energy spinning around her, cold washed through Kamryn as she stared at her phone.

> *Greer: I'm so sorry I have to cancel tonight. The boys have the flu and there's a huge event. I have to stay and take care of them.*

Kamryn wanted to write back how angry she was. Instead, she rolled her shoulders and stared out at the town square where the fall festival had already kicked up. She'd managed to pry herself away from her desk after two weeks of working pretty much nonstop just for Greer to cancel on her tonight. And this had been their second attempt to get together.

Instead of writing what she wanted, she sent back a quick message about how she understood and they'd catch each other another time. She wasn't supposed to be here alone. She needed Greer for her own protection, because she'd heard through the grapevine that Lauren was supposed to be here. The grapevine being Andra, who had managed to sneak a text to Kamryn to give her the heads up.

Greer was supposed to be there along with Andra, but they'd each been pulled away, leaving Kamryn alone. So very alone. Which was all she had been feeling the last two weeks. She couldn't for the life of her get the teachers at the school to give her the time of day when it came to breaking down the boundaries of boss and employee. And Elia Sharpe had been making her life a living hell—well, probably not intentionally, but she hadn't been making life easier.

Kamryn bought a drink and stood watching the band on the stage. It was never first-rate bands who performed during the festival nights, but this one wasn't bad. She'd have to check out their website and see if they had more music than just this.

She'd needed an escape. That had been why she'd come and that was why she was going to stay. It had nothing to do with Lauren and her newest fling—the Replacement as Greer had named her. Kamryn finished her drink and slowed her breathing. She could do this. She could stay out here on her own and avoid her ex easily enough. Once Lauren showed up, Kamryn would leave.

"Kam?"

So much for that. The chill that ran through her wasn't because of the cold this time.

"Lauren." Kamryn forced the smile onto her lips. Why hadn't she ever moved far away from home? Greer had, and she didn't have to put up with this drama. It was high school all over again—well, in some ways. "I was just getting another drink."

"We were too." Lauren's gaze was cool and locked on Kamryn's. "Let me buy you one."

Was this a good idea? Absolutely not. But the move had been expensive, Kamryn could use the drink, and Lauren was offering.

"Sure."

The new piece of ass on Lauren's arm, because she hadn't budged from that position yet, scooted even closer as they walked toward the small vendor on the far side of the stage. Kamryn ordered a round of shots for everyone, surprised when they came in small paper cups the size of Styrofoam coffee cups. It meant there was about three times the amount of liquor in there.

They stepped to the side, and while Lauren and the Replacement sipped their shots, Kamryn tilted hers up and chugged it. She immediately went back to buy two more. It wasn't a wise decision by any means, but it was going to get her through the night. The second shot she also chugged, but the third she held tightly in her hand.

"I'm not sure we've been properly introduced," Kamryn said, the heat from the alcohol rushing through her body and warming her limbs. "I'm Kam."

"Rosie. You're not as pretty as I imagined."

Kamryn jerked with a start. She moved her gaze from Rosie to Lauren, who at least had the audacity to look ashamed by that comment. Is this really who Lauren had chosen over her? Right then. Kamryn took a breath and sipped the shot in her hand. "We can't all be divas."

Rosie chuckled. "Lauren's certainly one, don't you think?"

"Sure," Kamryn remarked offhandedly. It wasn't Lauren that she was going to have an issue with tonight. It was the Replacement.

"So are you dating anyone new? Or still pining over this one?" Rosie ran her hand over Lauren's arm possessively.

Had Kamryn just gone to the set of *Mean Girls* without realizing it? This woman was outrageously ridiculous, and the fact that Lauren was just standing there not doing or saying anything was equally insane. This wasn't the Lauren that Kamryn had been in love with. This was someone she absolutely didn't like.

Which, honestly, helped put some things into perspective.

"I have a girlfriend." The words were out of Kamryn's mouth before she could stop them. The worst part was that if it had just been her and Lauren, she probably wouldn't have lied. But there was something about the Replacement that irked her so much she felt compelled into lying. "We just started dating, so it's all very new."

"Is she here tonight?" Rosie's eyes lit up like she'd just been given a new toy.

"Oh, um, she was supposed to meet me, but—" Kamryn stopped talking. What was she doing anyway? She shuddered and took the shot in her hand, crumpling the cup up and throwing it into the nearest trash can, which happened to be right next to her. She laughed loudly and shook her head. "I'm getting another one. You all want one?"

So much for letting Lauren buy the booze. As soon as they nodded, Kamryn went to order one more shot for each of them. When she returned there were two more people standing with Lauren and Rosie. She should have taken the opportunity to leave while she had the chance. They were talking briskly, clearly they knew each other, and Kamryn was left out of the circle, yet again.

That was how it had always been with Lauren. Kamryn had always felt like she was one step outside of being included. Rushing back into that feeling didn't help her situation. Neither did the fact that her head was spinning from the shots she'd already taken.

"Guys, this is Kam, Lauren's ex."

"Thanks, Rosie." Kamryn tried to hide the ire in her tone, but she wasn't sure she managed it. She shook their hands quickly after handing over the shots and then held hers. Did she really want to take it? She was already drunk, and she was going to have to call for a ride back to the school before she tried not to let the students who were in the dormitory in on the fact that she was drunk. She really should have thought this through better.

"Kam was just telling us about her new girlfriend. She's here, right?" Rosie sneered again, her nose wrinkling and her upper lip rising. "Or does she even exist?"

"She exists," Kamryn said, doubling down on her lie. She was going to die when the truth came out, and she'd never live it down in her circle of friends. Luckily Greer and Andra would probably laugh about it later when it wasn't so fresh and stressful.

"Then where is she?"

Kamryn laughed, shaking her head. She was never one who was very good at lying. It had been her downfall throughout her entire life. Lauren, however, was very good at lying and keeping secrets. Kamryn looked up, her gaze meeting none other than Elia Sharpe's cool blue eyes. Elia didn't look very happy. Her cheeks were hollowed, her lips pursed, and she was walking very purposely in their direction.

There had been rumors all those years ago about Elia Sharpe being a lesbian, but they'd never been confirmed. Coming back to the school, Kamryn had known they'd been true. She was wiser now, and more aware of things going on around her. At least, she liked to think that sometimes.

Elia was four steps away.

Surely Elia would save her this time. She'd saved Kamryn many times over the years, and that moment of kindness when she'd offered an orientation kept coming back to Kamryn's mind as *that* being the true Elia Sharpe.

Tipping her head back, Kamryn swallowed the last shot in two gulps before tossing the cup in the trash. She walked directly up to Elia, clasping a hand on her arm to stop her forward motion and leaned into her ear. Her heart hammered so loudly she swore the entire town could hear it.

Elia would save her.

That was the only thought than ran through her crazy, alcohol-riddled mind. Kamryn paused when she sucked in a breath, getting a deep scent of Elia's subtle shampoo, the coconut that wafted off her and straight into Kamryn's belly. This wouldn't mean anything. Elia hated her. And Kamryn was beyond trying to get Elia to like her. She didn't need it. She was only going to be at Windermere for this first semester and then she would have to head on to find a new job somewhere.

"Please just go with it," Kamryn whispered, her lips brushing the soft skin of Elia's earlobe.

It was everything she hoped for in five simple words. Backing away slowly, before she could lose her gumption and face the lie that she'd told—or rather face Rosie and the lie at the same time —Kamryn moved in again.

"I'm not—"

Kamryn kissed her. She moved in, pressing their mouths together and cutting off the objection or the confusion that she knew Elia was about to have. She kept her grip on Elia's wrist strong, but she moved her other hand up and threaded her fingers into Elia's hair, tangling the strands and holding onto her even tighter.

When Kamryn expected Elia to pull away, she didn't. She parted her lips, opening for more. Kamryn closed her eyes, tilting backward and pulling Elia with her and deeper into the kiss. There was no way a straight woman would kiss another woman like this—there was something queer going on here, and Kamryn had confirmed it. Although that hadn't been her intention.

All she'd wanted was for Elia to save her.

To save her from the embarrassment of standing in front of the ex she swore she was still in love with, but also the ex's new girlfriend, who was just a snotty brat with a mean streak ten miles wide. Kamryn shivered, stepping closer to Elia and deeper into her embrace as Elia's hands came up and surrounded her, held her there.

Their tongues touched and tangled. It was tentative at first, but then Elia let out a gentle and sweet moan that Kamryn was never going to forget. No music from the band or chatter from the crowd would ever cover that up.

Elia gasped and pulled away, still holding onto Kamryn.

Save me...

But Kamryn was pretty damn sure that she didn't say that out loud.

"So you're her new girlfriend." Rosie's voice grated on

Kamryn's nerves, and Kamryn tensed. There were people surrounding them. Lauren was here. She'd just witnessed—fuck, what had Kamryn done? She was such an idiot.

Elia turned away from Kamryn, the confusion she'd had on her face masked in an instant. Although her look hardened shortly after. Kamryn followed Elia's gaze to where it landed on Lauren. Shit.

"Dr. Sharpe," Lauren said, pursing her lips and shaking her head. "I didn't expect this."

"I didn't expect to see you here either," Elia answered, those cool tones filling her voice again.

Kamryn wanted to crawl into a hole and never emerge now. She wanted to crawl away, hide, pretend nothing of tonight had happened.

"What's it been? Twenty years?"

"Almost—in the spring. I was planning on going to the reunion." Lauren sounded amused now.

"You two know each other?" Rosie asked.

"Dr. Sharpe taught English at Windermere, where Kam and I met."

And where they'd first fallen in love. Definitely not the last time they'd fallen in love. Though so much had changed over that time, and they weren't the same people they'd been when they were teenagers.

"Oh...intriguing," Rosie said, clapping her hands together. She faced Kamryn purposely, a light in her eyes that scared Kamryn to her very core. "Are you someone who usually has mommy issues?"

"I think we should go...home." Elia seemed to stutter over the last word.

Was she trying to fold herself into the lie? Was she actually trying to protect and save Kamryn from any further degradation? Kamryn tightened her grasp on Elia's hand, needing it not only to keep her feet steady but to know if what she'd hoped for was actually happening.

"So soon?" Rosie interjected. "But I'd love to get to know Kam's new girlfriend."

Elia knew that Kamryn and Lauren had dated all those years ago. Didn't she? Or had she been clueless about it? Kamryn couldn't remember, and with twenty years in between, did it really matter?

"There's really not that much to get to know," Elia said.

Kamryn looked at her, the side profile of her face in the dim light not revealing too much. Elia tightened her grasp around Kamryn's back, which was a warm reminder of the way Lauren used to do that.

"Well, how did you two meet?" Rosie asked.

"High school, obviously." Lauren rolled her eyes and chugged the shot that Kamryn had bought her just before all of this went down.

"Well, yes," Kamryn jumped in. She needed to take the lead on this in order to protect Elia from anything damaging that might face her. "But we didn't meet again until a few weeks ago. All of this is very new. I promise."

"We want the story." Rosie sounded excited now.

Kamryn parted her lips in surprise and then looked up into Elia's eyes, waiting for confirmation that this was something they should do. She needed to know what Elia wanted—if Elia would save her one more time.

Six

"Go ahead and tell them." Elia eyed Kamryn carefully. There was something going on here that she wasn't aware of. But she had to make sure that Kamryn was sober enough to walk to the car without looking drunk. There were students here, a few other staff, and definitely family of Windermere.

She'd ream into Kamryn in the morning about her behavior tonight.

"Oh, it's not that big a story. Not really anyway." Kamryn was still looking at her.

If Elia focused on it, she could still feel Kamryn's lips pressed against hers, the tingle from the kiss, the dampness on her lips that Kamryn had left in her wake.

"We want to hear it. I'm Rosie, by the way. Lauren's girlfriend." Rosie was really pushing for this, wasn't she? Just what was she trying to prove?

"Good to meet you," Elia answered, keeping Kamryn tucked into her side. "And Kamryn isn't wrong. It's not a very elaborate story. We're working together at the school, and well, one thing led to another." It was the best she could come up with so quickly. She wasn't an author, so she certainly didn't have a flair for the dramatic or the entertaining.

"Did Kamryn ever have a crush on you when she was your student?"

"God, no!" Kamryn nearly shouted. She was way too loud for there not to be an extra meaning in her words, wasn't she? Even Rosie saw it. Lauren raised her eyebrow, the one that had a piercing through it, and seemed just as surprised by the reaction too. "Dr. Sharpe was—is—an amazing teacher. But I didn't... we didn't... not then."

"No, she didn't," Lauren added, still looking the two them over as carefully as possible. "Kamryn was interested in someone else."

"Oh?" Elia asked, looking at Kamryn for the confirmation. Did Kamryn have a crush on another teacher when she'd been a student?

"Me," Lauren said simply and quietly. She wasn't looking at Elia but at Kamryn, betrayal written across her face. "At least I thought that's the only crush she had."

"It was," Kamryn responded, leaning forward just enough that Elia had to pull back to keep her from toppling over. "I was only into you back then."

"Apparently not."

Kamryn sighed heavily, and Elia tightened her grip on Kamryn's arm. So that's what this was about. "How long did you two date?"

"On and off for twenty years," Kamryn mumbled, turning away to face the band.

"That's a long time!" One of the other two women who had been standing quietly around them the entire time added. "Why didn't you ever get married?"

Kamryn tensed, her entire body going rigid. Elia was up close and personal with her, so she felt it in her own body. That was a touchy subject still, no doubt, and there was no way that Kamryn was going to be able to talk about it.

Jumping in, she made the decision to change the topic. "Those are usually complicated answers. But what about you?

How did you and Lauren meet?" Elia looked directly at Rosie, hoping that the fact she seemed to be running this conversation would pull her to talk about herself instead of being cruel to someone else.

"I met Lauren through Andra, actually."

Kamryn jerked. She was staring at her shoes, her cheeks were red, and her eyes were barely open. Was she holding back tears?

"I'm sure that's an interesting story, but I'll have to hear all about it another time." Elia stated, using her teacher voice that meant she wasn't going to leave any room for argument. "I forgot that I have an early meeting in the morning, so we should get home so we can get some sleep."

"Yeah, that's probably a good idea." Kamryn leaned into Elia's side and let her lead them away from the small crowd.

Elia guided Kamryn through the throng of people, ignoring the stares at her back. There was far more to Kamryn than she'd wanted to believe there was. She'd spent the last few weeks trying to make her out to be the enemy who had stolen a job right from under her, but it was anything but that. Kamryn was a person, someone who came with her own history and problems and pain.

And Elia had unwittingly walked right into the center of it all.

She kept Kamryn upright as they walked toward her car. When they stepped off the curb, Kamryn's voice finally reached her ears. "Where are we going?"

"Back to the school," Elia said, keeping her tone firm and collected. She was upset still about the scene that Kamryn potentially could have caused, that if she hadn't stepped in to collect her it could have gotten really bad. She was upset that Kamryn would ever remotely think that getting drunk in public would be a good idea.

But she couldn't exactly yell at Kamryn right now either. Not while Kamryn was drunk, not while they were still trying to get back to the school. Opening the passenger door and sliding Kamryn into the seat, Elia stepped back after she closed the door and took a deep, steadying breath. Abagail was going to hear all about this before she left for her trip.

Even as adults, Elia was still cleaning up her students' messes.

How did that responsibility seem to always fall onto her shoulders?

At least it used to when Kamryn had been a student. But ever since then, it was different. Elia had made sure of it. She wouldn't repeat mistakes.

Sliding behind the wheel, she turned the car on and lowered the volume on the radio. "So you and Lauren dated." It wasn't a statement. But Elia was insanely curious how that one had happened and how it had ended. While she'd wanted to stick around for the details from Rosie, she was pretty sure that it wouldn't have worked out well in Kamryn's favor.

"Yes. And lived together." Kamryn ran her fingers over her face. "I'm sorry."

"For dating Lauren?" Elia asked, already knowing where this conversation was probably going. She could only hope that Kamryn would remember it in the morning though.

"Well, yes." Kamryn sighed heavily. "But more for putting you in an unethical position. I shouldn't have... That wasn't a very wise..." Kamryn groaned. "I'm sorry I kissed you without your permission."

Permission? That word rang out in Elia's ears. She'd never had anyone ask for her permission, explicitly, to kiss her before. Not in random kisses she'd had as a teenager and young adult or even within longer-term relationships.

But that bit of knowledge, the admission of guilt and pain that seemed to settle into Kamryn from knowing she'd done something without permission intrigued Elia. What would it have been like to have been asked?

Would it have been that much better? Because that kiss out there had been amazing, even with the alcohol, without the anticipation, without the interest between two parties.

"I should have asked for consent. I was wrong."

"Kamryn..." Elia stopped herself. She was about to tell Kamryn that it was fine she hadn't asked, but they would talk about it some other time or just forget that it happened, but she stopped herself. That would be invalidating the confession. "You should have. And to be very clear, I don't plan on holding *that* point against you."

"That point?" Kamryn looked at Elia then, their eyes locking briefly before Elia pulled out into the street.

"Yes. We'll talk more in the morning."

"Now you sound like you're going to make me talk to the Head of School because you caught me drinking."

Elia snorted lightly, a smile that she hoped Kamryn couldn't see playing at her lips. She'd done that many times with many students over the years, though she hadn't ever had to do that with Kamryn. Kamryn had been one of the good kids. Always ready to please, and a very hard worker.

"I suppose I could walk you up to her office in the morning."

Kamryn groaned and sunk deeper into the seat. "Now everything is spinning."

"Because you're drunk."

"Yeah. I am." Kamryn was back to covering her face.

The movement of the car likely wasn't helping the situation. Elia made sure to drive as steady as she possibly could all the way back to the school. She hesitated when she entered the gates, almost taking a right toward the dormitories.

"Is it safe to assume since you were out tonight that you're not the house parent on duty?"

"Hardly. Charlotte's on duty."

"Good." Elia turned her car away from the student dormitories and drove toward the on-campus housing that was reserved for faculty and staff. She'd lived in one of the houses there for the last decade, and it would be a much better place to recover than someplace where students could come in at any moment and need something.

"Where are we going?"

"My house." Elia parked the car and turned the engine off. "So you can sleep this off in peace."

"El...Dr. Sharpe. I don't think that's a good idea. I'll just go back to my apartment."

Elia paused again, looking Kamryn over. This was a mess that Elia felt compelled to clean up. She was more annoyed with that than any kiss that had happened. The warmth from the car was fading with the engine shut off, and she really didn't want to sit there and debate this for much longer.

"I think after kissing me, you've earned the right to call me Elia."

"Oh God." Kamryn covered her face again, shaking her head side to side. She stopped suddenly. "No sharp movements. That was a bad idea."

"Come along." Dragging herself out of the car, Elia moved to the passenger side to get Kamryn out. They walked side by side, Elia's hand around Kamryn's waist again to keep her steady.

Elia unlocked the door and immediately pocketed the keys while she helped Kamryn inside. There's no way she would have made it up the stairs to her third-floor apartment. She put Kamryn onto the couch and then stripped out of her jacket and tossed it over the arm of the lounge chair.

"Think you can take your own jacket off or do you need help with that?" Elia asked, annoyance seeping through her words.

"I can do it." Kamryn huffed, and she started moving and undoing the buttons. "That last shot was a mistake."

"So were the first two." Elia walked around the couch and into the kitchen, pulling out a glass from the cabinet and filling it with ice and water. The last thing she had expected tonight was to be taking care of her new boss.

Her new boss who clearly didn't deserve the job she'd been hired for.

Handing Kamryn the glass, Elia sat down on the chair. "Why did you and Lauren break up?"

"Which time?" Kamryn mumbled.

"Start with the last one." Why was Elia even asking this? Kamryn's life wasn't hers to pry into. And yet, she wasn't sure she'd ever get an honest answer if she didn't ask now, and her nosy sensibilities were playing up.

"We both cheated." Kamryn lay back heavily into the couch. "Not the first time. We never did a really good job of growing up together. Being in a relationship with Lauren was being stuck at sixteen and the first time we snuck off to..." Kamryn stopped talking. "Never mind."

Have sex.

That had been what Kamryn wasn't willing to say. And she'd avoided it because Elia had been her teacher at that point. It would have been on her watch because Lauren had been assigned to Elia's dormitory their last two years at Windermere.

"It's both of our faults."

"Lauren cheated with Rosie," Elia surmised.

"She did." Kamryn wrinkled her nose in the most adorable way. "It wasn't pretty when I found out. Greer calls Rosie the Replacement, but I don't think she's anything like me."

"No, I don't think anyone would accuse you two of that." Elia couldn't imagine that. With what she had witnessed tonight, Kamryn would never be as cruel as Rosie so easily was. Even drunk, Kamryn was apologizing and groveling. That nearly brought a smile to Elia's lips. "What did you do after you graduated?"

"Went to college. Went to graduate school. Got a few degrees, broke my heart a few times. I grew up." Kamryn stared into her glass like it held all the answers to the questions she wasn't asking.

Elia could connect with that. She'd stared down at a glass like that more than just a time or two, hoping for some kind of answer to questions she didn't dare put out into the universe. "Why teach?"

Kamryn looked up at her then. "Is that what this is about? My being the Head of School?"

Elia gave her a slight shrug. "You never told me why you went into teaching."

"There's a lot of creativity that can happen in a school room, between teacher and student. You showed me that. I didn't major in English though, so don't get any grand ideas that I was trying to become you. I wanted to teach because I want kids to have the freedom to explore their interests, who they are, and to find their place in the world." Kamryn looked more sober now than she had all night. "I went into administration because that seemed like the biggest roadblock to any student having the ability to learn."

Elia couldn't stop the smile at that. Kamryn was absolutely right. "And why did you come back here?" That was the question Elia really wanted answered, wasn't it? Why had Kamryn taken the opportunity from Elia to become Head of School? Why had she been passed over again?

"This is where I started. Why wouldn't I want to come back here?"

Putting her hands out to the side, Elia relaxed slightly. She didn't have an answer to that. She had no desire to go back to her hometown. They never understood her, and she hadn't wanted to make them try. Starting new and fresh had been a much better option in the long term. And she would say it had paid off.

"Question back to you...and actually answer this time, please?" There was a plea in Kamryn's voice.

Elia nodded her head, indicating Kamryn could ask.

"Why aren't you Head of School? You told us that's what you wanted to do."

Elia's stomach twisted hard, that pang of guilt and pain coming right back to haunt her. She planted her feet on the floor and pushed herself to stand. She ignored Kamryn as she walked to the linen closet and grabbed an extra blanket and pillow, setting it next to Kamryn on the couch.

"I would have been a better choice than you." Elia straightened her back and put her hands on her hips. "I wouldn't have gotten drunk in public and started a scene in front of my students for starters."

"There were students there?"

"Yes." Elia pursed her lips and let out a breath. "We'll talk more about it in the morning. When you're hung over and awake."

She didn't wait another beat before she walked out of the living room. If Kamryn walked back to the dormitory now, then it was out of her hands. She needed a break from the intensity. She needed to find her center again—that had been the entire reason she'd gone out with Abagail that night.

Changing and crawling under the blankets in her bed, Elia closed her eyes and tried to fall asleep. But she couldn't stop thinking about the town square, the muted yellow lights adding to the ambiance, the band playing on the stage, and Kamryn's lips against hers. The heat from the embrace, the arousal it awoke in her, the base desire to touch and be touched.

Seven

Kamryn flung the blanket off her legs. She was so overheated. Her cheeks were on fire, her body covered in sweat, and nothing was comfortable. Her pants scratched against her skin—wait, pants. Jeans specifically. Pausing in her scan of her body, Kamryn started again, only this time she took better care and went slower.

She still had socks on, her jeans, and her oxford shirt. The buttons pressed into her chest and hurt, so she shifted her weight to ease up on that. Blearily blinking her eyes open, Kamryn looked up at the ceiling above her, not recognizing it at all. It was white, popcorned, and definitely higher than in the apartment she had on the third floor of the dormitory.

Pushing herself to sit up, she instantly regretted the move. Her head spun right along with her stomach, and it took everything in her not to spill whatever was left inside her onto the beautiful hardwood floors. This was too much. The splitting migraine started immediately, and she had to cover her eyes with her hands to keep the light out.

Kamryn took slow and even breaths, calming her nausea before she did anything else. She couldn't let this get the better of her. She had to keep herself together, she had to get back to her apartment, and she had to remain in bed the rest of the day and pretend like last night had never happened. She'd never made such an embarrassment of herself before. And last night was—oh fuck.

The memories of everything that had happened rushed back to her.

Elia.

Kiss.

Talking.

Kamryn cringed. She groaned. She winced and refused to look around the house that she was damn sure was Elia's because that wasn't just a dream, was it? A dream would make everything better. It would mean she hadn't made a complete ass of herself.

The cup of water on the coffee table had been refilled, and next to it were three bottles of medicine. Three different options. Leave it to Elia to think of everything. Without thinking, Kamryn snagged the migraine bottle and downed two of the pills along with the water. She wasn't prepared for the conversation that was coming.

And there would definitely be a conversation.

Elia had made that perfectly clear.

Standing up, Kamryn turned toward the kitchen to find Elia, with a bowl in front of her and a book of crosswords next to her, staring at Kamryn.

"Bathroom?" Kamryn asked. That would at least give her a few more minutes of respite before she had to come back and face the music.

"Second door on the right."

Kamryn walked down the hallway and slid into the bathroom, locking it behind her. What had she been thinking last night? Because surely that was going to be a question that Elia was going to ask her. And she was going to need a damn good answer—and nothing was better than the actual truth.

She went to the bathroom, washed her hands, splashed cold water on her face, and then hesitated before she walked back out into the main living area. Elia hadn't moved from the kitchen counter. Kamryn slid onto the stool next to her, leaning her arms on the counter and closing her eyes.

"I'm so sorry about last night."

"Which part of last night?" Elia's voice was colder than Kamryn could ever remember. Even that first day in the staff meeting.

"If I say all of it, it won't be the full truth. But I do regret most of it." The guilt ate away at what was left of Kamryn's stomach. She hated this. "I did so many things wrong."

"Yes, you did. I didn't think that the board would hire someone so immature as to get drunk in public and pull the stunt that you did."

Kamryn jerked her head upright, her eyes wide as she looked directly at Elia. Where had this anger been the night before? She'd been sure that Elia wouldn't find it now, especially after how sweet she'd been the night before. But this was something else entirely.

"Immature?"

"Yes," Elia confirmed. "If I hadn't been there, it could have ended in disaster and ruining the reputation of the school. You have to think before you act. You're not just a teacher anymore, Kamryn. You're the Head of School. Start acting like it."

Where was this coming from?

"I know. And I'm sorry. And about..." Kamryn gulped. She was going to grovel with the best of them, and she was going to make this as right as she possibly could from every moment going forward. "...about kissing you. I shouldn't have done that. I definitely shouldn't have done it without asking you first."

Elia's lips parted like she was going to say a retort, but then she stopped. She clenched her jaw, the muscles in her cheeks bulging slightly. Elia pushed the crossword book into the center of the counter and leaned into the stool back.

"I was wrong to kiss you without your explicit consent." She'd said that last night, right? She couldn't quite remember, but she wanted to make it clear that this was one of the things that she regretted the most.

"You were upset."

"That's not a reason to hurt someone else or to violate their bodily autonomy." Kamryn rubbed the back of her neck, wishing the medicine would kick in already. This was so difficult with a migraine splitting its way through her skull. "Aside from my behavior that reflected poorly on the school, that's what I regret the most."

"This school has to be your priority. Not some ex-girlfriend you have a vendetta against." Elia picked up her mug of coffee and took a sip. The scent of it nearly sent Kamryn over the edge again, but she managed to withhold the vomiting reflex.

"I don't have a vendetta against Lauren."

"I meant Rosie."

"Rosie isn't my ex-girlfriend." Kamryn rubbed at the center of her chest. This was so difficult to talk about. "Haven't you ever had a relationship end on crappy terms? It hurts, and there's still a lot of pain there for both of us."

"Hmm." Elia's lips pressed into a thin line. "You need to do better."

"You're right. I do." Kamryn straightened her back. "Starting right now. Which is why I'm apologizing to you, if you'd ever stop attacking me long enough to hear what I'm saying."

Kamryn froze. Had she really just said that? She'd wanted to say those words to Elia for two weeks straight now, but she'd never thought that she'd have the gumption to let them loose from her lips. Well, perhaps there were some good things to come out of last night—depending on how Elia took it.

"We've been struggling with each other since my first day here. And I'd really like to start over again, if you'll allow it. I don't want you to see me as a threat. I'm not a threat. I'm in this position temporarily until Dr. Waddy gets back on his feet and can take back over or until the Assistant Head of School gets back from paternity leave. I am only temporary."

Elia stayed so still. Her gaze was sharp and precise, and it was almost a physical pain for Kamryn to look at her. She held her own ground though, needing to make sure that Elia was going to hear what she was saying.

"Dr. Sharpe?"

"Elia," she said in correction.

Kamryn frowned, something niggling in the back of her brain like she should remember it, but it was next to impossible for the words to come to her mind. She shook her head and tried again, "Dr. Sharpe, I'm not exactly sure why you have it out to hate me, especially when I was your student..." Kamryn trailed off, the jealousy she'd detected in Elia from the moment she'd stepped foot onto the campus finally clicking into place. "You applied, didn't you?"

It wasn't really a question. She had the answer already. Elia didn't have to say anything to confirm it. This was hands down classic jealousy and struggle because Kamryn had gotten the job and Elia hadn't.

"Why did they turn you down?" Kamryn asked instead.

"I wasn't given an interview." Elia paled, and everything about her posture pulled in on itself, making her seem even smaller than she was.

"What?" Shock registered through Kamryn. "Why wouldn't they give you an interview? You're perfect for this position, far more than me. Especially as only a temporary fill-in until Dr. Waddy returns."

Elia dragged in a deep breath and blew it out slowly. "What happened last night can't happen again."

"I know it can't. I'll be more careful next time, and I won't make such stupid mistakes." Kamryn ran with the change of topic. This was clearly something that made Elia uncomfortable. "Dr. Sharpe, I'm so sorry that you had to handle the situation like you did last night, and I'm so sorry that I put you in such a compromising position. I'm in over my head with this job. I feel like I'm not even treading water, and no one is respecting me—faculty or the board."

"You need to prove that you're worthy of their respect."

"Theirs or yours?" That was a pointed question, and one that Kamryn only somewhat regretted asking in the heat of the moment.

"You have my respect." Elia stood up and moved toward the kitchen counter. She pulled out bread and a toaster, sliding two slices into it before pressing down the button.

"With all due respect, Dr. Sharpe, I don't have your respect."

Elia frowned and bowed her head slightly. "Elia."

Kamryn shook her head, not understanding.

"Call me Elia, Kamryn. I'm not your teacher anymore. Certainly not after last night."

Kamryn's cheeks burned with embarrassment. It wasn't until that moment that the memory of the kiss came barreling back into her mind, the way they'd wrapped around each other in the chilly night air, under the lights, the sounds and people all around them. But did she dare bring it up?

"I'm so sorry about that."

Elia waved her hand in the air, brushing off the apology. "And stop doing that."

"Doing what?"

"Apologizing."

Kamryn frowned. "I don't know what else to do."

"Eat this." Elia pushed a plate with two pieces of toast in front of her, along with some butter. "It'll help your stomach."

"How'd you know..."

"You're an odd shade of green." Elia started more toast as Kamryn turned to the plate.

She wasn't quite sure that she wanted to eat, at least not yet. She scraped the butter onto the toast and let it melt a bit before she took a small bite and chewed it slowly.

"I didn't think you would wake up so early," Elia said as she sat down with her own toast.

Kamryn finally glanced at the clock over the stove and sighed. It wasn't even seven in the morning yet. "I'm not a very good drunk when it comes to sleeping off the hangovers."

"Fair." The toast crunched as Elia took a bite. "Do you want to try coffee?"

Kamryn hummed to herself and closed her eyes, testing her stomach and debating whether or not she could handle it. "Not just yet. Maybe in a little bit. Why are you being so nice to me?"

"You're not the only one who has had crappy break ups." Elia said nothing more as she took another bite of her toast and stared Kamryn down.

They sat there in silence a while longer, Elia finishing her breakfast and Kamryn nibbling her way through half a piece of toast. Was this all that it was going to take? Getting drunk, kissing her former teacher in a fit of panic and self-deprecation, and then crashing at her house because she was too drunk to walk home on her own? Kamryn winced at that thought. She really had done a number on her already sketchy reputation.

"I've worked in admin before, you know."

"Have you?" Elia asked. "As Head of School?"

"No." Kamryn's cheeks heated again. "Assistant for a few years at Henry Kline Prep."

"Ah."

Elia should have known that if she'd read the CV that was sent out when Kamryn was hired. Either she'd been too mad to read it or the board hadn't actually sent it like they said they did. Kamryn wouldn't be surprised if either was the case.

"Are you ever going to tell me why they wouldn't interview you?" Kamryn took a bigger bite of the toast, hoping this would be the last time her stomach recoiled in response.

"No."

"Fair." Kamryn held her breath. "I suppose I should head back to my apartment soon."

Elia took her plate and rinsed it in the sink. "If you want, or you can stay here a bit longer and recover."

That almost sounded like an invitation. Was it?

"I don't want to impose," Kamryn said, knowing that she had to be polite. She was just getting ready to stand up when another wave of nausea hit her, so she sat heavily back down. "But maybe I'll give it another thirty minutes."

"Wise decision." Elia seemed almost amused by that.

"Ugh." Kamryn groaned. "I have to say it again. I'm so sorry."

eight

Elia paused as she walked from the main desk in the empty classroom toward the white board. Kamryn stood in the doorway, leaning against it, with a smile playing at her lips and her arms crossed. Elia narrowed her gaze but twisted the top off the marker none the less.

"What?" Elia barked out.

"You haven't really changed all that much. You know that, right?" Kamryn seemed so pleased with herself as she stepped farther into the room and leaned against the desk while Elia wrote a few words on the whiteboard.

"I've changed more than you might think."

"Hmm." Kamryn crossed her arms.

Capping the marker, Elia tossed it onto the top of the desk. "We've had twenty new students sign up for the team this year. I've added them to the roster and will figure out housing arrangements when I get a chance, at least for the first couple of meets."

"All business today?" Kamryn asked, her voice nearly a gentle tease.

"I'm only ever business."

"Memory tells me otherwise. But if you want." Kamryn

picked up the piece of paper that Elia had pointed to earlier. "How are we dividing the coaching up?"

"Let's play it by ear." Elia's stomach bubbled, and she realized belatedly that she'd forgotten to grab her snack from her office.

Kamryn's phone rang. "I'm going to take this, if you don't mind."

"By all means." Elia left the classroom, checking the time on her watch before snagging the small bag of carrots she'd left on her desk and returning to the classroom.

Kamryn was still sitting on the edge of the desk, but her shoulders were rounded, and she looked absolutely dejected. Elia nearly stopped what she was doing, wanting to help her out or ask what was wrong, but she didn't. It wasn't her place to do that.

"All right. Yeah, I understand, but I don't think she'll be able to make it." Kamryn's voice trailed off, and she glanced up at Elia, her cheeks reddening. "I'll ask. I promise. Talk to you later. Love you. Bye."

Kamryn dropped her phone onto the desk with a sigh and picked up the paper now, squinting at it as if she was reading it. But Elia knew that move well. She'd used it so many times in her life that she was sure that distraction and refocusing were exactly what Kamryn was attempting to do.

"Since we both specialize in speech, I suppose one of us should volunteer to teach debate." Kamryn still didn't look up from the paper.

"I can do that." Elia popped a carrot between her lips, snapping off a chunk. She didn't take her eyes from Kamryn. "What was the call about?"

"Nothing." Kamryn bristled.

"It upset you."

"A lot upsets me," Kamryn said into the paper, her voice mumbled and quiet.

"Like what?" Elia wasn't sure why she was prying again. But something about Kamryn and who she was now was so different than when she'd been a student there. Elia wanted to know more.

"Like why you're not Head of School." Kamryn crossed her arms, her clothes straining from the move and the fabric tightening the wrinkles right out of it, at least for now. "You still haven't answered that question."

"I never applied until this summer." Elia took another bite of a carrot. "How would I have become Head of School without applying?"

"By actually applying." Kamryn seemed so sure of herself, something in that brutish personality that came with her generation. Elia envied it sometimes, and other times, she was glad to be on the quieter side that tended to fall between the cracks. It meant fewer people were looking at her and trying to find the cracks in her facade.

"I didn't."

"But why?"

"It doesn't matter." Elia's shoulders stiffened. "What was your call?"

"If I tell you what my call was about, will you tell me why you didn't apply?" Kamryn narrowed her eyes, as if that would get Elia to bend over backward and give Kamryn what she was wanting. "Fine, that was Andra. Apparently, Rosie has texted everyone to tell the entire group about my *new girlfriend*, and she was wondering if I needed to change my RSVP for her wedding."

"Oh." Elia's cheeks burned, the memory of that kiss rushing into her face so quickly that she had to turn away. To mask it, she grabbed the marker and turned toward the white board, trying to pretend that she had forgotten to write something up on the board. Deciding on the date, Elia walked toward the board.

"She asked me to ask you... *my girlfriend*... if you were coming to her wedding so she could adjust the seating arrangement and catering numbers."

"Do you want me to go?" Elia clenched her fingers around the marker, keeping it tight in her hand as her lifeline.

Kamryn jerked her chin up, her entire body tightening as her face lit up with confusion. "Go with me?"

"To the wedding." Elia squared her shoulders as she walked closer.

"Why would you want to go to the wedding?"

"That isn't what I asked," Elia added, dropping the marker and standing directly in front of Kamryn. In this position they were nearly the same height, but Elia had all the power. She was standing, and she was prepared.

"I... don't know. It'd be nice to have someone there to help keep me in line since Lauren and Rosie will be there. Have I mentioned that lesbian relationships suck when we're all in the same friend group?"

"I don't think that's exclusive to lesbian relationships," Elia replied. "You don't have anyone else who can come?"

"Greer will be there for the wedding, but that's it. She can't go to anything else. Her work is... she's getting laid off, and so she needs to work as much as possible in order to save up money for when she's unemployed." Kamryn frowned. "Sometimes being an adult sucks."

Elia did smile at that, her lips twitching upward into a small smile. "More than sometimes. What other things are there?"

"Bridal shower. Bachelorette party. All those things that traditional women do."

"And you're not traditional? I seem to remember someone wanting to get married and have a few kids." Elia wasn't sure where she was pulling that memory from, but she definitely remembered something along those lines.

"Dreams change, Dr. Sharpe."

"Elia," she corrected. "Please."

"Elia," Kamryn repeated the name, and it sounded sweet coming from her.

"Dreams do change. Maybe you got the answer to your question in a roundabout way."

Kamryn hummed, again narrowing her eyes. "I don't think so. You wouldn't have applied this year if that was true. You would have just let the board figure it out on their own."

Elia sighed and glanced toward the door. Students would be arriving any time for their first speech session of the semester. She usually looked forward to this day, but Kamryn had been distracting her since she'd walked into the room and Elia had lost all track of time.

How was she supposed to tell Kamryn that she was more right than she thought? Elia had never given up on that dream, but it had taken this long for her to even hope it was a possibility. "What did the board tell you about the position and others who had applied?"

"Not much," Kamryn answered, stretching her hands above her head and moving up onto her tippy-toes. "It was a super quick turnaround, and they made it abundantly clear that this was only temporary."

"So you're just done at the end of the semester?"

Kamryn nodded. "When Dr. Waddy will come back."

"Kamryn..." Elia dragged out her name. She canted her head to the side and stayed very still. "I visited Miller in the hospital last week. He's not going to be coming back at the end of the semester."

"But the board said he would be."

"Even if he wanted to, the stroke did a lot of damage. I'm not sure if physically he'll be able to return to work at all, and definitely not in the next five months." Elia stayed still, glancing toward the door to make sure that there weren't any students coming in. "Maria hadn't told anyone just how bad it is yet, but it's not easy to hide if you go visit him."

Kamryn frowned. "So they probably need a longer term Head of School then."

"They'll likely open up the search in November when Maria can't hide the fact that he won't be returning." Elia hated to think about it, but she'd already mentally started preparing ways that she could help them move out of the Head of School's house in the middle of the winter. It would be difficult, but she had no doubt that this was coming to that.

"Damn," Kamryn mumbled and plopped herself back down onto the desk. "I can stay on for another semester. It's not like I have anywhere else to go, but that's really going to hurt the students and faculty."

Was Kamryn finally understanding the weight of the position? This was the mature side that Elia had seen from her several times in the last few weeks, but she longed to see more of it. And she was spot on. This was going to hurt everyone involved.

"What will you do for income if you don't stay?"

Kamryn shrugged and leaned back slightly. Elia couldn't tear her gaze away, not now. She'd found herself staring at Kamryn more and more lately, unable to stop just watching her.

"Find a new job somewhere." Kamryn frowned. "I wasn't going to give up the chance to get back here if I could, though. That's been my dream since I left."

"Really?" Elia raised an eyebrow.

"Yeah. I guess I could apply for the full-time position when it opens up. Or you could!" Kamryn turned and gave Elia a brilliant grin, one that was full of mischief.

"I wasn't even offered an interview this time around. What makes you think they'd give me one next time?"

"Then let's make sure they do." Kamryn clapped her hands together, her grin getting even brighter.

"Don't you want the position?"

"Yes and no." Kamryn shrugged.

So they wouldn't be going against each other for it? How odd. That bit of jealousy that had taken root in Elia's chest eased slightly. She felt lighter somehow with just that one statement.

"I'll dig a bit and see what I can find out about the interview process and why you weren't included in it."

"Don't dig hard. I've ruffled enough feathers on the board."

Kamryn pulled a face, her forehead scrunching up and brow pulling together with curiosity and confusion, but she didn't push for another answer. "I'll help you out. What's a former student to do?"

"Move on with her life." Elia sighed when she realized too late how the tone of her voice came off. "You could apply yourself."

"Maybe I will. But it won't be any fun if there isn't any good competition. It'll help elevate the search, don't you think?"

Maybe there was something to that. Maybe Kamryn wasn't as naive as Elia had initially thought. She'd obviously held other positions before, so perhaps she knew more about playing these political games than Elia did.

"If you help me, then I'll help you." Was she really going to do this? The idea had taken root, and she wasn't able to shake it. She'd been working up toward it for a while, but it would be a good way to size up the competition and also get what she needed in return. "I'll pretend to be your girlfriend in front of Lauren and Rosie and the others. You help me get an interview for the job —or at least figure out a way to force their hand in explaining why I was denied."

Shock registered on Kamryn's face. "You want to be my fake girlfriend?"

"Weren't you supposed to ask if I was going to the wedding?" There was teasing in Elia's voice that she hadn't heard herself use in years. This was flirting—not flirting with the intention of anything happening, but flirting sheerly for the enjoyment of seeing someone's reaction. In this case, Kamryn's reaction. "I suppose you should ask."

"W-what? Do you want to go? I mean you can go without being my fake girlfriend if you really want to."

Elia heard student voices in the hallway. She stepped in closer to Kamryn, the fronts of her thighs touching the side of Kamryn's leg. She lowered her voice just to make sure that no one else heard what she was saying.

"I'll be your fake girlfriend, Kam." Using the nickname meant something, but Elia wasn't quite sure what it was just yet. "You help me get an interview. Deal or no deal?"

"Elia, there are other ways around this."

"Times up, the kids are here. Deal or no deal?"

"Deal," Kamryn whispered, looking directly into Elia's eyes.

"Good." The smile bloomed on Elia's lips and face, warming her. She was enjoying this far too much. "We'll get together next week to discuss details. Over dinner?"

"S-sure."

Elia stepped back just as the first student entered the room with a loud, "It's time to rock and roll!"

Kamryn still kept staring at her, but Elia had to move away to put some distance between them. She didn't want the kids to get the wrong idea, especially after everything she had been through before. That would be her number one rule with Kamryn. They would keep everything as separate as possible.

"I hope you had a good summer, Ethan."

"The best!" Ethan said loudly, dropping his bag into one of the chairs. He stared up at the white board and groaned. "Devil's Advocate? Really? Do we have to start warm-ups with that?"

"Yes," Elia responded, shooting Kamryn a look of amusement. "You shouldn't like every single practice lesson that we do. It's good to expand your skills."

"Yeah, but starting with *that* one?"

Elia couldn't stop herself from finding joy in this interaction. She'd waited all summer for Speech and Debate to start back up again. It was her favorite extracurricular to teach. "Yes, we're starting with that one. Maybe you all can stump the new Head of School." Elia waved at Kamryn. "She used to be one of my star Speech students back in her heyday. We'll have to see how many lessons she remembers."

"Remembers?" Kamryn stood up sharply. "Oh, I remember them all, Dr. Sharpe."

"We'll see," Elia answered, ready for the lessons to start.

nine

Kamryn checked her calendar and frowned at it. When had that additional Speech team meet been scheduled? She barely had time to get there with the ethics meeting that was starting in three minutes. Those few minutes of respite that Kamryn had managed to find right before the last Speech meeting were the first ones she'd found in weeks.

Her head was spinning with all the responsibility.

Grabbing her notebook and pen, Kamryn walked directly to the conference room. Heather was already in there with Susy Butkis, the board chair. Heather was bent over the table, talking quietly in hushed tones. The tension in the room skyrocketed as soon as Kamryn walked in.

There was no mistaking that. As soon as Heather eyed her, she immediately stopped talking. Something about this didn't feel right.

"Afternoon," Kamryn said, sitting down next to Susy, hoping to keep some space between her and Heather. What were they doing here? This might be the hardest thing she had done so far since taking on this job. It felt that ominous.

Like an ambush.

"How have you been?" Kamryn asked, trying to make small talk in order to ease the tension that was growing in her chest.

"Good," Heather answered quickly.

Kamryn had forgotten how she'd always seemed to have a permanent sneer on her face, her bleached blonde hair just adding to the look, especially when she pulled it back so tight and slicked it to make it look like a helmet.

Susy put her hand on top of a stack of folders and looked each of them over.

"We need to rebuild the ethics team. We've been remiss in getting it together and keeping it functioning, but one of the goals for this school year was to rebuild it—from scratch up if we had to."

Kamryn kept her mouth shut. She agreed that the board needed an ethics review committee, not only to make sure that everyone working on campus was up to date in their background checks and certifications and continuing education, but also for when there were issues. And as much as she would like to believe that there wouldn't be issues, she wasn't an idiot. There were always problems somewhere.

"I thought we'd start with reviewing past cases to see if they are *up to snuff*."

Kamryn managed to hold back any facial reactions, keeping her surprise from the room. "Wouldn't it be a better idea to review the processes and procedures that we already have in place and see where they need improvement, while also trying to maintain and work toward resolution of open issues?"

"There aren't any open issues," Susy returned.

"At least none that have been formally reported," Heather added. "Not that there aren't some that should be reported." She muttered the last part under her breath, but it was loud enough for Kamryn to hear.

"So you want to go through old violations?" Kamryn frowned now, wanting to understand exactly what was happening.

"Yes." Susy grinned. "It'll be the best way to understand what we should be doing and how."

Not necessarily. Kamryn didn't respond though, because she wasn't sure what to say to that. Susy opened up the first file and slid a binder-clipped stack of papers to each of them. One quick glance told Kamryn that everyone had copies of whatever she'd handed out.

Kamryn finally looked down at the top page.

Echoes of misconduct littered the pages, going back decades. Kamryn briefly glanced through them finding page after page. Susy had sliced open Windermere and let it bleed out on the table right in front of them.

Kamryn wasn't an idiot. She knew there were problems. Having them in black and white in front of her hurt. Some of these cases went back to when she was a student.

"Some of these reports were handled well and some weren't. Let's start with the most recent one."

The buzzing in her head was so loud that she barely heard the question she asked. "Do we need to create procedures or are there any that we can follow?"

"We're doing an audit of the complaints at the school." Heather eyed Kamryn carefully. "We want to be transparent with all of our faculty and staff so that when parents complain—and they will complain—we know what we'll need to protect and what we'll need to drop."

Kamryn knew without a doubt that *drop* meant termination. Were they after someone in particular?

"I think we need to have a teacher on this committee, someone who can help represent the other staff and faculty and help us put these procedures in place." Kamryn was still skimming through the reams of paper that she'd been handed. It was information overwhelm at best. "I'd suggest Elia Sharpe."

"No," Susy answered sharply.

Kamryn froze at that. Her shoulders tensed, the muscles tightening to the point of pain. "No?"

"Elia wouldn't make a good member of this team." Susy's voice couldn't be more patronizing.

There was no way Kamryn was going to win this one. She wasn't even sure what battle she was fighting. Was this a witch hunt? She'd thought they'd just been jerks by not giving Elia an interview, or that perhaps there was a reasonable explanation because they couldn't do without a teacher and losing a head of a department when they were already down so many administrative team members.

But this...

Kamryn was floored. Susy was pushing Elia out, and Kamryn had no idea for what. Did any of them actually know? Her heart hammered. Her throat closed up. And she was at a complete loss for words. She needed more information. And she was desperate for it now.

"Is there a faculty member you would suggest?" Kamryn finally asked.

Heather blanched. "It's your job to fill the position."

She had pointed the comment at Kamryn. But Kamryn didn't know the faculty well enough yet, and she certainly didn't know who was doing what and who might have the time or the ability. The ethics team wasn't where you wanted just anybody.

"I still think that Elia Sharpe would be the perfect person for the role. She teaches Speech and Debate, which involves an incredible amount of ethics and discussion of ethics. And she's very good at reading documents and finding what's missing or where the loopholes are."

"She's not the person for this role," Susy said so matter-of-factly that Kamryn knew the conversation was ended.

She'd been shut down. And she hadn't even had a chance to figure out what pile of shit she'd stepped in. Kamryn was sick to her stomach. This wasn't a place for her to have a voice. That much was clear. But she didn't find that an acceptable answer.

They continued down the litany of mistakes that had been made at Windermere Prep.

Reading through the information was enough to make Kamryn want to leave the room and throw up, to hand in her resignation effective immediately. This *job* was bigger than she'd anticipated. She'd never thought it was this bad, that there were this many complaints to sift through.

That couldn't be real, could it?

Miller Waddy had been slacking on the job for a long time. Most of the complaints filed were in the last five years, although there were some dating back decades. Kamryn could only assume that those were for teachers still at the school because otherwise, why would they matter? Which severely limited the number of people who it could be.

Fuck, she thought.

She just had to figure out a plan of action. And her go-to was to talk to Elia, but she was going to have to leave Elia as far out of this one as possible because there was something beyond hinky going on with Susy, Heather, and Elia.

By the time the meeting was done, Kamryn was livid and overwhelmed. More than she had been in the last few weeks of taking on this job at a last minute's notice. She slipped the file into her satchel and ushered them out of the room as soon as she could with their next meeting set up. Glancing at her watch told her that she was already late for the Speech team meeting—in fact, it was nearly over—and she was pretty sure that Elia would survive the rest of it.

Kamryn needed Greer.

With her cellphone in her hand, she called her best friend.

"Pick up. Please pick up the phone."

"What's up?"

"Thank God." The words rushed from Kamryn's lips, and she flopped down in the chair in her office only to immediately stand up again. Energy burst through her in small waves, and there was nothing she could do to control it. She had to talk this out with someone.

"What's wrong?"

"I can't talk much in details..." Kamryn paused. What could she actually say? "How many times did you watch *Mean Girls* when it was released?"

Greer laughed. "You're asking me about a movie? Fuck, I thought you were having a panic attack."

Kamryn had been pretty darn close to that. And just the sound of Greer's voice calmed her down. She loved that her best friend could have that effect on her. "Yeah. I am asking that."

"O...kay. I do remember the movie. I watched it a few times." Greer sounded suspicious now, and Kamryn didn't blame her. It was an odd turn of a conversation, but this was the only way she could say what she wanted to say without actually revealing confidential information. Greer would understand that, eventually. They had a shorthand most of the time that years of friendship had given them.

"Good. That's the meeting I just came from. Exactly that. Mean girls out to get nice girls." Kamryn winced. "Well, maybe it's mean girls out to get mean girls. I don't know. I don't even know where to begin. I feel like I'm caught in the middle of a war I didn't even know was happening."

"Kam." The pity was nearly too much.

Kamryn's eyes watered, stinging from the tears. "I don't know what to do."

"Take deep breaths. Remember? I tell you that all the time. You're shit at it."

That elicited a laugh. This was exactly why Kamryn had called her. Greer would know what to say. "I'm taking deep breaths."

"Are you?"

"Well, now I am." Kamryn groaned. "I don't like this. It makes me nervous. I'm only here for a semester, and then I'm gone. I have a chance to make really good changes, but this one might be bigger than something I can handle in a few short months."

"What's the problem even?"

"Mean girls, remember?"

"Oh, right."

Kamryn ran her hand through her hair and tugged sharply. She was so ready to pull her hair out over this one. And she was pretty sure that she was going to feel this way more as soon as she dug deeper into it.

"You missed practice."

Kamryn spun around, her heart in her throat.

"Elia."

"Elia?" Greer echoed. "Your *girlfriend*?"

"I'll call you later, Greer." Kamryn hung up without even looking at her phone and settled her phone onto the desk. What the hell was she supposed to say? "I was stuck in a meeting."

Elia's face hardened, and Kamryn couldn't read her. "You insisted on co-leading Speech."

"I insisted that you have a co-leader," Kamryn corrected. "That could have been me or someone else, but I'm still temporary Head of School, and I have other responsibilities."

"So do I." Elia's hands clenched at her sides.

Kamryn watched her carefully. Everything inside her told her to tell Elia what had just happened in the meeting, but she couldn't. She had to bite her tongue and keep it all inside, because she couldn't talk about it. Not until she knew what was going on.

"I promise you I don't mean to shirk my responsibilities," Kamryn said, looking directly into those cool blue eyes. "I promise you that."

Something crossed Elia's gaze, changing and morphing, but Kamryn couldn't place it with an emotion. She couldn't figure out what it was. Elia remained where she was, her hands still clenched at her sides.

"And I promise you that if you don't step up for these kids, if you don't show up for them, then you're going to wish you'd never taken this job." Elia's words had a bite. They stung.

It was a promise that Kamryn knew Elia would keep.

Kamryn wanted to collapse. She was tired of holding herself up, of being this strong and put together person that she didn't feel like she was. She'd never been that person, no matter how many times she told herself she was.

"Elia..." Kamryn was on the verge of breaking.

"Don't miss practice on Friday. We have a mock meet coming up, and I would hate for the team not to be ready because you can't be present for them." Elia's stare was so cold.

Kamryn had never seen her like this. Completely closed off from everything in the room. Who had Elia Sharpe become in the intervening years? "I'll be there."

"Good." Elia turned on her toes and walked out of Kamryn's office.

Sighing heavily, Kamryn walked around to her chair and collapsed into it. She pressed her forearms into the desk and rested her forehead on the cold wood. She needed a break. A good break, one that would reset her brain and her heart, because everything was getting so confused.

Was she good at anything?

ten

Each day that passed for Elia since she had confronted Kamryn only bolstered her anger. For someone who had been so insistent on helping with the Speech team, it was ridiculous that she hadn't shown up to the second called practice of the year.

The kids had been disappointed.

Elia had seen it in their faces when Kamryn wasn't there. They might not have said it, but there was something special about having the Head of School on the extracurricular team. Kamryn probably didn't even recognize that.

Walking through the main living space of her house, Elia cleaned up whatever she could find that was out of place. She needed the mundane to be cathartic, but it wasn't working. She couldn't get Kamryn out of her mind or the anger out of her chest.

Cursing under her breath, Elia snagged her phone off the kitchen counter where she'd left it and called Abagail. She had one more day with Abagail in the country, so it was now or never to complain to her best friend.

"You can't miss me already." Abagail's sweet but confident tones filtered through the line.

Normally, Elia would feel an instant ease from that, but today was different. She was unsettled by Kamryn, in more ways than she wanted to admit. But in the ones she was willing to put out into the universe, she was annoyed that she couldn't fix those yet.

"You'll have to tell me all about your plans for your trip." Elia's words were short, and she had no doubt that Abagail could tell that she was distracted by something. That was why Elia had called her in the first place, wasn't it?

"Oh I smell drama a mile away. What's going on?"

Elia bit back the groan she really wanted to let loose and plopped down onto the couch. The very same place that Kamryn had slept off her drunken night of dishonor only weeks ago. Where was she supposed to even start with all that had happened?

"Kamryn is making a mess of the Speech team, and she's only been to one meeting." Elia's head was pounding from the stress. She really should get up and take a pill for that, but she couldn't bring herself to stand up again. At least not yet.

"How is she making a mess of it?" Abagail at least seemed genuinely curious about it all.

"She didn't show up. The kids were so disappointed." Was it the kids who were? Or was Elia the one who was disappointed? Because she'd felt that pang deep in her chest. She'd just ignored it.

"Did she say why she missed it?"

"She got stuck in a meeting." Elia put her foot up on the edge of the coffee table and reclined back. Her house was spotless. She'd spent the last three hours deep cleaning it in an attempt to avoid this phone call. And in the end, she'd given up anyway. "But that's a poor excuse. She has to prioritize the students."

"You're thinking like a teacher, not admin."

Those words stung. Abagail should know that. She'd been through everything with Elia from the beginning, all the ups and downs, the accusations, the suspension, and this last interview debacle. So she wouldn't be saying those words without actually meaning them and the full weight that they carried.

"This is a school. Students have to be our priority."

"They're yours. And I'm not saying they're not also

Kamryn's, but she has other pressing priorities. How do you know she wasn't dealing with a student issue? Did you even ask what the meeting was about?"

Elia pressed her lips tightly closed. She hadn't asked. She hadn't wanted to know. She'd just wanted to be mad about everything. And she had wanted to put Kamryn at the center of all her blame. She was tired of being passed over for positions that she wanted and that she was deeply qualified for, especially for a woman who was fifteen years younger than her and way less experienced.

"They should have hired me for that job," Elia muttered.

"They should have at least given you an interview. Who's to say that Kamryn still wouldn't have been their top pick? You haven't seen her in how long?"

Elia winced. "Twenty years."

"So maybe she's the right woman for the position." Abagail sounded so sure of herself, and Elia hated it. But Abagail was in corporate America, which meant that sometimes she knew and understood these things better than Elia did. "They should have interviewed you, or at least told you why you didn't get an interview."

Elia was pretty sure she knew why, and it was the same reason that she hadn't applied for an administration position in two decades. She probably would have had better chances if she'd left Windermere Prep, but this was her family. And she didn't exactly want to step out into a school that she didn't know and understand.

"They should have," Elia agreed. But deep down inside, she already knew why they hadn't. They were still holding grudges, even eighteen years later. But she didn't want to say those words out loud. She didn't want to give them room to breathe in her space. "But Kamryn needs to realize the influence that she has on these kids. She can change the course of their lives."

"Kamryn was your student, wasn't she?"

"Yes."

"And have you considered the influence you made in her life?"

Elia tensed. She'd thought about it, briefly, but she promptly avoided that one too. She was doing a lot of that lately. The world and life she'd created for herself had been turned upside down so quickly that she was still clawing at whatever she could to keep up.

"What's really bothering you about Kamryn? Is it her lack of ability to do the job, or is it because you still want it so you're putting all your jealousy and anger onto her?"

It was definitely the latter of the two options there. Elia hated that Abagail was so good at calling her out like this. And she hated that it was how she was feeling. Kamryn deserved the benefit of the doubt, and every time Elia moved toward it, something would pull her right back to where she was.

"What did you tell her last night?"

"I wasn't very kind," Elia answered instead of giving details to how harsh she'd been. She wasn't sure she wanted to admit that, even to her best friend. "I need an ally in this."

"You have one in me, but I'm not there." Abagail's voice was tight, and Elia knew there was something else coming that was about to hit her hard. "Perhaps you should find an ally on campus, something you've avoided for eighteen years now."

Elia had shut down after the investigation. During it, too. The entire situation had taken its toll on her, and in order to survive it, she'd leaned only on the relationships she knew she could trust. "I was calling you because you're my ally."

"In everything, I promise." Abagail smiled, the sound reaching her voice and making it sound happy. "And for the next two weeks, you're going to be on your own. Whatever will you do?"

"I'll survive. You know I always do."

"Hmm. I think you should go talk to her. Tell her you're upset about the other day and ask for an explanation—and actually let her talk this time."

Elia swallowed a lump in her throat. She wasn't sure she

wanted to do that. Even though she knew she should, that it would be important. She just hated that she was going to have to break out of her circle and make amends. It was her own fault, of course, but it still didn't mean that she liked it.

"Fine."

"Fine?" Abagail sounded surprised. "That was quick."

"You're right... for once." It was a running joke between them. Abagail was usually right about these types of things, but they always teased each other when they could about it. "I'll talk with her."

"What hold does this woman have over you? It always takes at minimum a week for you to apologize to *me* when you screw up." Abagail laughed lightly. "Is it because she's your former student? Have to still play the holier than thou card?"

"Hardly." Elia glanced at the clock to see what time it was. The sooner they resolved this conflict, the better it would be for everyone involved.

"Why are you so concerned about her?"

Why was she? It was the first time another faculty member had really irked her so much. Sure there were the ones who annoyed her, who couldn't mind their own business no matter what Elia said or did, and the ones who just had odd quirks that she refused to play into, but Kamryn was different.

She was consuming most of Elia's time and thoughts outside of the classroom lately. Elia kept telling herself it was because they were working together on the Speech team, but it was more than that. It really was.

"Elia?"

"It's just an adjustment period," Elia responded, taking the easiest way out possible. "I'll talk to her and apologize."

"Actually apologize?"

"Yes." Elia's lips quirked up slightly at the reminder. She hadn't always been the best about doing that, but she'd tried to learn over the years to be better than who she used to be. Or perhaps it was getting back to who she used to be, before she'd run face first into the realities the world had. "Since I know my mother will ask, are you coming for Thanksgiving this year?"

"I'll look at my calendar and let you know."

That was Abagail's response for everything. But she hadn't missed a Thanksgiving in twenty years, so Elia knew it was unlikely that she wouldn't find the time. She just wanted space to think about it. "All right."

"Are you going now?"

"Yes. Well, I'll text her and see if she has time now."

"Good. Then text me to fill me in on all the groveling you're going to be doing."

Elia rolled her eyes and shook her head, even though Abagail couldn't see it. "I'll call you when you get back from your trip."

"Better yet, I'll pop down to the school for an actual visit."

Elia sighed into the hope of that moment. It would be amazing to have that time with Abagail, to be able to visit with her in person. "Just tell me when."

"Oh, I will. I need to meet this Kamryn who keeps irking you."

Fear ran through her then. She hadn't anticipated that being the reason why Abagail wanted to visit. And she couldn't let the two of them meet. That would spell disaster. "I'll see you soon."

"See you!" Abagail hung up quickly, recognizing Elia's need to end the conversation.

Staying on her couch, Elia stared at her cellphone and debated. It would be so easy to avoid for longer, and Kamryn probably wouldn't think twice about it. But she'd promised Abagail and herself that she would at least begin to make this right.

Elia hit Kamryn's name on her phone and pressed it to her ear. It was now or never, and she needed to get this done and over with.

"Dr. Ogden."

Elia paused. She'd called Kamryn's cell phone, not the office, right? Moving the phone from her ear briefly, she checked, and sure enough she had called the cell.

"Kamryn," Elia said. "Are you busy?"

"Uh..."

Elia clearly heard rustling of papers and clicks on a keyboard.

"I have a few minutes. What do you need?"

"Do you have a few minutes to talk in person?" Elia clenched her fist and then unclenched it. She really needed to teach her muscles to relax better. "This will be easier in person than over the phone."

"Oh." Kamryn sighed lightly. "Yeah, I can meet. When?"

"Now?" Elia was hopeful. If she put this off much longer, then she'd probably avoid it altogether. The sooner the better for sure.

"I'm on house duty, so you'll have to come here."

Elia tightened. It had been a very long time since she'd been to the dormitories. Most of the time she met up with teachers elsewhere, not that she did a whole lot of that in general. And she'd moved into a house on campus as soon as one had become available because of the accusations that had flown her way. She'd thought everyone would feel more comfortable with that than if she'd remained a house parent.

"Okay. Give me ten minutes." Elia hung up before saying anything else. An unsettled panic rested in her chest. She could do this. She could go up to Kamryn's apartment, and she could have this meeting.

They needed to resolve at least one problem today.

eleven

The knock was polite and quick. Kamryn hadn't expected Elia to actually show up, despite the fact that she said she was coming. Her apartment was barren because she refused to unpack too much if she was only going to be there for a few months. Most of her stuff was in storage.

Elia stood on the other side of the door, her shoulders squared, a light jacket on, her hair down by her shoulders, and her makeup light today. Kamryn's stomach tightened. This wasn't professional Elia, the woman who dressed to impress at school every day. This was laid-back Elia, the woman behind the teacher-mask, the woman who actually might take a day off.

Kamryn should probably learn that lesson sometime soon.

Greer had accused her of working herself to death more than once in the last week.

"Hey," Kamryn said, since Elia didn't seem to be saying anything at all.

Elia nodded slightly. "Thank you for seeing me on such short notice."

They still stood at the door awkwardly, staring at each other. Kamryn should definitely let Elia in. She should get her some water or something, invite her to sit down. This was a business meeting for fuck's sake. She should act like a boss and not be weak in the knees.

Kamryn cleared her throat. "Uh...come on in."

She opened the door wider and stepped to the side. Elia's energy changed the entire room. Something about her presence made the space seem that much smaller and impossible for her to work with or be in the near vicinity of. Kamryn glanced at the coffee table and couch, where she'd been working her tail off all morning. It was littered with papers, her computer, a couple of pens.

She was ridiculous. Elia's house had been spotless, and her apartment was a disaster. Elia was probably disgusted by it all.

"Would you like something to drink?" God, now she sounded like an idiot on top of the visual impression. "Water or..." Kamryn had to think about what else she might have in the fridge. "I think I have some soda."

She walked directly to the fridge and opened it up. "Yeah, or beer."

Elia's lips quirked at that, a smile playing at them. It was so nice to see. "I think we should forgo the alcohol so early in the day. Don't you think?"

"It's not like we have a very good track record with it." Kamryn grabbed two cans of soda and handed one over to Elia, their fingers brushing in the process. "This is probably the wiser choice."

"For now at least." Elia popped the top of hers and turned toward the couch. Kamryn expected a judgmental reaction, but she never saw one. "I know you're working because you're on duty today, but you really should take a day for yourself."

"At some point, I will." Kamryn bit the inside of her cheek and walked toward the couch, hoping that Elia would follow her. She slid onto it and stretched out a little. She hadn't realized how many kinks she had bugging her in her back until she stopped to focus on something other than work.

"Breaks are good. They improve work productivity and quality." Elia sat down, pulling at the buttons on her jacket and then sliding it off her shoulders. The jeans and T-shirt she wore were a stark contrast to her normal outfit choice.

Kamryn couldn't ever remember seeing Elia look so relaxed, never in something other than slacks or flats. But the sneakers that were definitely well-worn and probably needed replacing were such a welcome and humanizing sight.

"Kam," Elia said, a chuckle in her tone.

"What?" Kamryn snapped her gaze back up to Elia's face.

Elia shook her head, that laugh still lingering in the air between them, teasing them with something damn near friendship. But that couldn't be right, could it? Kamryn was reading way too much into this. Elia was here for...something work-related. That much she knew.

"You're staring at my shoes."

"Oh. Sorry." Kamryn lifted the cold drink to her lips and took a long sip from it. The cold was exactly what she needed to cool her cheeks off. The only downside was now it was very obvious just how hot her body had become in the last few minutes. "What did you need to talk about that couldn't wait until Monday?"

Elia's smile slipped from her lips, and Kamryn instantly regretted the conversation change. She needed that smile back in her life. It was so genuine and perfect, something that lit up the entire room and affected everything within it.

"I came to apologize." Elia's voice was firm as she spoke, a sadness entering into the words although Kamryn couldn't quite figure out why.

"Apologize?" Kamryn frowned. "For what?"

"My abruptness in your office last night." Elia's face pinched. "I was rude."

Kamryn's lips parted in surprise before she closed them tightly. Elia had been sharp and could probably be considered rude, but it wasn't anything out of the ordinary from what Kamryn had seen recently or remembered from the past. Elia was always a direct person, and Kamryn appreciated that. She hated the two-sidedness of people...people like Heather and Susy for instance. Her stomach churned at the reminder of that conversation.

"I want you to know how important it is to the kids for you to be present at the Speech practices. They value you and the fact that you're the Head of School currently and putting the time and effort into them."

Kamryn tuned back into what Elia was saying finally, the words lingering in her brain, but it was taking her way longer than it should for them to register and make sense. She hadn't expected an apology at all. "I know that."

"So they were disappointed when you weren't there."

Shaking her head, Kamryn narrowed her eyes in Elia's direction. "*They* were disappointed, or you were?"

Elia paled slightly, and her cheeks tightened. She moved stiffly as she put her drink onto the coffee table and straightened her back again. "The students."

"Ah. Like I told you, the meeting I had prior ran over its allotted time. Well over it, actually." Kamryn wanted to roll her eyes at that, but she resisted the temptation. She wanted to tell Elia all about the meeting, let her in on the drama that she was facing, but she couldn't. Not with the contents of what the ethics team—if it could even be called that—was discussing. *Witch hunt* still sounded like a better term for it.

"I know, but next time, if you can text me or call me to let me know, then I can mitigate some of the disappointment with the students."

"All right, I'll work to improve on that." Kamryn canted her head to the side and observed Elia. She had gone from an apology straight to some sort of solution in the span of two seconds, and they had very nearly missed the apology in there. That was huge for Elia. Kamryn was sure of that. And she wanted to go back to it, to acknowledge what Elia was doing.

"I accept your apology, by the way. Though I wasn't bothered by your attitude the other day."

"You weren't?" Elia seemed surprised by that.

"No." Kamryn smiled, her cheeks rushing with a gentle heat this time. "I know you have a short temper, and while you were sharp with me, you didn't cross any boundaries."

"Temper… right." Elia frowned into her drink and sighed. "My *temper* has lost me more than a friend or two in the past."

"Well, you won't lose me over it." Kamryn grinned broadly, glad to finally feel like they were back on even footing.

"I wasn't being self-deprecating when I said I wasn't the most ethical person around. I'm not the kindest faculty member here, and I certainly have a penchant for stepping in my own shit on more than one occasion." Elia twisted the can between her fingers.

"Is this supposed to scare me?" Kamryn asked, keeping her tone light. "Because it's not. I remember who you are, and while you weren't my favorite teacher at Windermere when I was a student, you certainly should have been. You weren't my favorite because your expectations of us were intense."

Elia smiled at that. "You're here to learn."

"And learn I did." Kamryn wanted to ease the tension that was in Elia's face, make it disappear entirely. "Didn't mean I wasn't forced into learning sometimes."

"You were always a hard worker." Elia sighed slightly and set her can down. "I just came here to apologize."

"Are you leaving then?" Kamryn wasn't ready to let her go, not yet. And she'd much rather have Elia stay and talk, to give herself that actual break from work that she really needed. And it wasn't until Elia had shown up that she realized just how desperately she did need it.

"What else is there to discuss?"

"We can discuss Andra's wedding if you want." *Or other things…* Though Kamryn wasn't sure what other things entailed. Friendly conversations about hobbies and family and friends would be a nice start. She wanted to get to know Elia outside of the school and away from the student-teacher and boss-employee dynamic they seemed to find themselves locked into.

"All right. You said the bridal shower was first." Elia seemed to settle back into the couch, and that settled Kamryn's racing heart.

"It is. Don't worry about a gift, I've got that covered. And since you're my *girlfriend* it can be a joint gift." Kamryn laughed at her own little joke, and she was glad to see that Elia relaxed slightly. "I'm not planning this one, but I think it's supposed to be fairly standard. Food, open gifts, eat cake, maybe a game or two."

Elia nodded slowly. "It's been a long time since I've been to a bridal shower. I think it was for my niece three or four years ago."

"You have a niece?" Kamryn was tickled by that. She could see Elia playing the doting aunt, the one who would halfway spoil her nieces and nephews any chance she got.

"By marriage. My brother married a woman who had two kids from a previous relationship. They were ten and eight when I met them." Elia played with the tab on the top of the soda can. Was she nervous discussing such personal things? "I suppose this information is helpful for our little *ruse.*"

"Ruse?" Kamryn's eyes widened. "Is that what we're calling this?"

"What else would you call it?"

"I don't know." Kamryn chuckled again. "Why would it be helpful?"

"To make the lie seem more true."

"I told you, Elia, I don't need to lie to my friends."

"You're lying to Lauren. And Rosie." Elia stared at her directly. "And I don't blame you for wanting to do it, either. Rosie is..." Elia paused, searching for the right word, "obnoxious."

Kamryn snorted. "That's the understatement of the century."

"That's yet to be proven. I imagine I know more about you than you about me."

"Why would you say that?" Kamryn asked.

"Because I was your teacher. I know who your parents are, and I know about your brother and sister, and I know about some of your hobbies and interests growing up."

"Oh really? Like what?" Kamryn finished off her drink quickly and leaned in, trying to test Elia. She wanted to know. "What are my hobbies?"

"You're a book lover."

Kamryn paused at that. She couldn't remember the last time she picked up a book that didn't have something to do with education or leadership. But Elia wasn't wrong. She used to have her nose buried in a book for hours every night. It was to the point that her roommate would yell at her to turn the lights off, but sometime during college that had all ended. "I used to be, yeah."

"Used to?" Elia seemed surprised by that.

"I haven't read a fiction book for fun in a very long time." Kamryn swallowed the sudden lump in her throat. "Do you read?"

"Classical literature and poetry."

"Poetry?" Kamryn grinned at that. "You'll have to share some with me. Do you write it, too?"

"No." Elia's voice sounded breathy. Had she attempted to write it at some point and then given up?

"Why don't I believe you?" Kamryn teased.

"Not one single idea." Elia gave her a full smile then. She was stunning, her lips curling upward, the crow's-feet at the corners of her eyes, the fullness of her cheeks when she was truly happy. This was the Elia that Kamryn wanted to see every day, the one who was easy and relaxed, kind to herself.

"Well, I'm going to pry that answer out of you one day or another. Oh, I think I forgot to mention that there's a brunch the day after the wedding. It's for close friends and family, so we'll be expected to be there."

"We?" Elia pointed with two fingers and her thumb between them, moving her wrist back and forth. "They expect you, Kam. Not me."

"But you're my *girlfriend.* So now you're included in that."

Elia's cheeks reddened slightly. "Careful now or I might start believing that word. I did want to bring one thing up before we start this."

"Start what?" Kamryn continued the tease, pushing into it.

Elia, rightfully, ignored her comment. "I want to keep our fake-dating and work as separate as possible. So I wanted to ask how connected Lauren is to the school."

"Oh." The mood sobered instantly, and Kamryn missed the gentle flirting they were both joining in on. "I agree about keeping this separate. There's no reason for anyone here to know that we're attending events together as friends. That's not unusual. But as far as Lauren... she's not that connected to the school. I stayed far more connected than she did."

"She mentioned something about the reunion."

"That was odd, because she's never mentioned wanting to come before then." Kamryn scratched the back of her head. "She came to our ten-year one but only because I made her come. And trust me, it wasn't a pleasant night for either of us because of that."

"All right." Elia didn't seem fully satisfied with that response, but she didn't seem to want to push for a deeper answer, either.

"No one else from the school will be there. None of the rest our circle went to Windermere."

"That makes me feel slightly better." Elia seemed to perk up at that, and Kamryn was glad to see it. She wanted Elia to stay in this place, a place where she was happy and joyful, and probably more relaxed than Kamryn had ever seen her.

"Good. I'm looking forward to this...adventure."

"Ruse," Elia corrected. "I thought we were calling it a ruse."

"That's what you're calling it, my friend. I think I'll call it illicit." Kamryn giggled, not sure what was getting into her. She hadn't felt this relaxed in a long time. Nor had she enjoyed herself in even longer.

"Now that might push the envelope too much."

"No, no, I don't think it does." Kamryn leaned forward, making eye contact with Elia. "The definition of *illicit* is something forbidden. And I do think that fake-dating my former teacher while I'm her boss probably falls well within that definition."

Elia mimicked Kamryn's pose, her voice lowering to barely above a whisper, "I told you that I wasn't a good choice for the ethics team for a reason."

Kamryn's heart thumped hard, and her gaze dropped immediately to Elia's lips. She'd done that before and regretted it. But she wasn't sure she would regret it if she kissed Elia again. The air intensified with tension, and Kamryn could barely keep one foot in the verbal game that she'd most definitely started.

Elia hummed, her lips pressing into a thin line. "I'll see you at practice on Tuesday. Don't forget about our mock meet next weekend." Without another word, Elia stood up and brushed her hands down her thighs. "Thank you for allowing me to apologize."

Kamryn put her hand out to the side and nodded. "You allowed me to apologize and grovel. It's only fair that I should return the favor."

Elia laughed lightly, a full-mouthed grin with teeth reflecting her happiness with the moment. "See you soon, Kam."

twelve

Elia's ears buzzed with the echo of voices. The mock meet had gone perfectly. She couldn't have expected her students, even the new ones, to do any better than they had. She sighed as she relaxed onto the hotel room bed and closed her eyes.

She just needed a little bit of quiet.

The adrenaline running through her body was something she craved, and she enjoyed it so much. It had been her ever-present companion all day, and even through dinner when they were all eating and finishing up their meal.

The kids had it too.

Even Kamryn had been smiling more than she usually did, and Elia hadn't seen her pick up her laptop to get office work done all day. Although she had taken a couple of phone calls during some of the breaks.

Elia was enjoying the silence in her room. She'd needed this to come down from the high of the competition.

Four rapid knocks at her door startled her.

She winced and whined to herself as she pulled her weary legs over the edge of the bed and stood up on them, her feet bare on the carpeted floor. Though she wasn't about to put shoes on either. Her feet were more sore than her legs.

Pushing her face close to the door and looking out the peephole, she was surprised to find Kamryn on the other side. She'd expected a student, someone who needed her for something. Then again, she wasn't used to having another faculty member with her on these trips. Just the parent volunteers.

Sliding the lock, Elia opened the door and canted her head to the side. "Is something wrong?"

"Nothing." Kamryn frowned, her gaze dropping from Elia's face, down her body in a slow perusal until she landed on Elia's bare toes and flicked back up. "Nothing's wrong."

"What do you need, then?" Elia kept her hand on the door, not sure if she wanted to permit Kamryn into the room. It wasn't something that she was generally opposed to, but there was something so personal about the space being hers, somewhere she could unwind and not think about anyone or anything else.

"I just thought..." Kamryn trailed off, glancing down the hallway when another door opened and closed, and they heard giggling laughter that they knew was from their students. "I should probably go check on that."

"They're fine." The sudden possibility of Kamryn walking away made Elia's shoulders tighten. She didn't want Kamryn to leave—not yet, not until she had some answers. "What did you need, Kam?"

"I don't need anything." Kamryn took a step back.

Elia shot her hand out and pressed it to Kamryn's wrist, noticing far too late that Kamryn was holding a small brown paper bag in between her fingers. "What's this?"

"What I thought you might enjoy." Kamryn pulled her lip between her teeth and shook her head, her cheeks reddening with embarrassment.

"Come on in." Elia held the door open, letting Kamryn walk right by her. The hotel room door slammed shut a bit louder than she anticipated, causing her to jump slightly from the noise.

Giving Kamryn the chance to sit in the single chair in the room, Elia sat on the edge of the mattress, her hands on either side of her. Elia didn't take her gaze from Kamryn as she plopped down next to her on the bed and handed over the bag.

"So what's inside? Contraband?"

Kamryn laughed with a shake of her head. "I did think about buying those little shots you can take, the ones you pull the lid off and just take. But I didn't think that would be very appropriate for a new, young Head of School. What do you think?"

Elia knew the dig when she heard it, but it was said with such a kindness that she didn't suspect Kamryn was still hurt over her comments. "Probably a wise choice, this time."

"There's plenty of time to make bad choices." Kamryn's voice was back to that flirting tone that Elia had found so intoxicating the last time they were in a situation like this. It wasn't any less intoxicating this time, in fact, probably more since they were in such small and confined places.

And because this was forbidden.

Elia sucked in slowly as her fingers crunched the crisp bag. Whatever could Kamryn have gotten inside? She was curious, but she also didn't want to spoil whatever this delicious tension was between them.

"Am I going to like it?" Elia asked, still refusing to open the bag.

Kamryn laughed, her eyes lighting up with joy. "Yeah, I think you'll like it. You really are holding onto this like a secret admirer gift."

"Is it from a secret admirer?" Elia's heart pattered steadily, and her entire body warmed with the thought that perhaps Kamryn did like her a little more than a boss should like someone she supervised.

"She's not so secret, now is she?"

That phrasing confused Elia. She studied Kamryn carefully, but didn't push for another answer. They were getting dangerously close to something, but she wasn't sure what exactly. And as much as it scared her, it excited her even more.

Elia took the bag and unfolded the top of it slowly. She built up the anticipation with each passing second. She peered into the opening of the bag, finding a silver handle. Confused, Elia reached into the bag and pulled out a brand-new whisk.

The laughter burbled up from her belly and left her lips in a loud guffaw. "You're kidding me."

"I'm not." Kamryn was fully grinning back at her.

Elia couldn't hold it in any longer. The joy filled her, and she held the whisk up in the air and chanted, "Whisk! Whisk! Whisk!"

Kamryn joined in the chant before they both dissolved into a fit of giggles together. Elia's breathing became rapid and short, and she held a hand to her chest with the whisk still in her fingers. Pressing her free hand against Kamryn's thigh, she clasped onto her, not letting go.

"I thought some traditions should be kept," Kamryn finally said.

Elia shook her head and wiped the tears that were budding from under her eyes. "Do you know how long it took me to weed this one out?"

"How long?" Kamryn settled her hand on top of Elia's, giving it one long squeeze before letting go.

Elia moved her hand off Kamryn's thigh, a sudden coldness washing through her. If Kamryn had been so concerned about consent before kissing, then she probably felt the same way before touching, even when it wasn't sexual in nature. "I'm sorry. I shouldn't have touched you."

"It's all right." Kamryn gave her a sweet smile. "You can if you want."

Unsure about how to feel about that, Elia moved on from it to avoid instead. "It took six years after you graduated to get rid of *the whisk*." She was shaking her head again. "You really want to bring it back?"

"Why not? It was an amazing tradition." Kamryn took Elia's hand back in her own, lacing their fingers.

Elia stared down at their hands. Comfortable. That's what this was. Kamryn wasn't Abagail when touching her—this was far from friendly—but she wasn't put off by it either. She was sure that there was no other intention than to connect physically as well as emotionally.

"Then let's do it in the morning," Elia answered, her voice far wispier than she intended it to be. Normally she'd correct that, but tonight, she didn't have the energy for that. And this felt so nice. Actually, better than nice. This was amazing.

"Don't want to be up until three in the morning every competition talking about the highlights?"

Elia smiled and shook her head. "I'm not as young as I used to be. So three in the morning is well beyond my bedtime. But you're free to stay up that late if you want to start a new tradition." Elia didn't say the second part—that it would likely die when Kamryn left, having no one to continue it that late into the night. What would she do when Kamryn left?

That thought struck her hard.

Elia didn't want to think about it. She couldn't imagine the next semester without Kamryn there. She'd been so helpful in so many ways, and she was such a hard worker. "I think the morning would be a better option, don't you?"

"To use our whisk microphone as our talking stick? Absolutely." Kamryn squeezed Elia's hand again, but she still didn't let go. "What's your highlight though? I don't think I can wait until breakfast for that one."

"Hmm." Elia was going to have to think about that one. She had many. But it had been such a long time since she'd participated in the practice of lifting those good things up and sharing them with others. She missed it. It was such a good practice that she should have kept up, just in a form that didn't involve staying awake immediately after a competition. "Our new students did well, even with only having a month to prepare. They exceeded my expectations."

"That's a good one," Kamryn replied. "And I agree with you. What else?"

"Is this because I have the whisk still?" Elia very nearly handed it over to Kamryn, but she still wanted it.

"Of course. Whoever has it does the talking." Kamryn bumped their shoulders together. "What else?"

"Having you here." The words were out before Elia could stop them, but they were the truth. "I've enjoyed having another faculty—or admin—member here and coaching the team, but having you in particular has a been a ray of sunshine."

"Oh." Kamryn's cheeks turned red, and the moment sobered slightly. "I didn't expect that."

"I like to be unexpected." Elia flipped the whisk around and held it for Kamryn. "Your turn."

Kamryn held her breath as she took the whisk in her free hand, holding it up to her lips like a microphone. "Is this thing on?"

Elia smiled. "Sure is."

"Good. Because being part of the Speech team again has been the exact respite I've needed. Whether we win or not, I'm here for it for as long as I can be." Kamryn settled the whisk onto her lap. "And I hope that's longer than a semester, even if I'm not Head of School anymore."

"Would you stay on in a different role?"

"If one opened up that I was qualified for, I'd certainly apply. But I've also been applying at this school for eight years now. This is the first time I managed to snag an interview, and I'm pretty sure the only reason I was considered is because it was an emergency."

"They're quite closed off about who gets in and who stays out. Very cliquey," Elia replied, taking the whisk back. Their fingers brushed, and heat rushed from Kamryn's hand into hers. She adored that feeling, and the sensations that ran through her body. She wasn't ready to give that up just yet. "All of the prep schools are. At least I've found."

"Have you worked at schools other than Windermere?"

Elia shook her head, the sadness over her circumstances

sweeping back into her. "I worked in a public school before starting at Windermere. But I applied to other schools shortly after you graduated. None would have me."

Kamryn frowned, a deep line forming in the center of her brow. "Why?"

"That's a story for another night."

"You keep saying that and avoiding." Kamryn touched the whisk. "You have the whisk."

Elia's lips twitched, the rush of the moment moving through her and passing instantly. "The whisk is for happy things."

"Ah." Kamryn started to move her thumb back and forth alongside Elia's. "I do hope that someday you'll trust me enough to tell me what happened."

Elia nearly grimaced. She stared out the dark window across from them and extricated her hand from Kamryn's. The moment had gone from comfortable and flirtatious to exhausting and traumatic. She didn't want to remember those years. In fact, if she could forget them and move on, she'd love that.

"I don't make promises that I can't keep."

"I didn't ask for one," Kamryn responded.

Elia's hand was cold with Kamryn's pressed into it. She'd been the one to break the happiness of the moment. That was the only rule about the whisk—sadness wasn't allowed. Although they hadn't told anyone those rules in twenty years. Elia flicked the whisk against her palm.

"Thank you for bringing me this."

"Of course," Kamryn smiled again, pulling those rays of sunshine back inside her and collecting them. She'd always been such a happy kid. She'd never faced trials like Elia had, at least not then. Who knew about the intervening twenty years? "I'll see you in the morning, Elia."

Her name was so sweet from those lips. Elia nodded and watched as Kamryn left the room in silence. She was cast back into the silence she'd started in, the silence she had craved before

—but now, she didn't want it. She wanted Kamryn back in the room with her, laughing and teasing and flirting.

What was happening to her?

She couldn't like her former student, could she?

What if the lie they were setting up and the roles they were preparing to play weren't all that phony?

What if there was more under the surface?

Elia stared down at the whisk still in her hand. She was being ridiculous. Kamryn would never be interested in someone like her. She was too cold, too bitchy, and way too shut off from her feelings for that. Kamryn deserved the world and the sun and the moon and the stars when it came to romance.

Elia couldn't give her that.

Even if she might want to.

thirteen

Kamryn pulled up outside of the country club and parked the vehicle. Elia was pressed into the passenger seat, bundled in a jacket since the temperatures had dropped so significantly in the last week. Kamryn hadn't managed to keep her jacket on.

Her nerves were going haywire.

"There's no reason to be nervous," Elia said calmly from the seat next to her.

"You're not about to lie to all of your friends."

Elia chuckled lightly, a smile playing at her lips but not quite getting there fully. "We could *not* lie."

Kamryn shook her head. "Nope. I'm not ready to admit my first lie to Lauren yet. Well, really to Rosie. Lauren would probably just call me an idiot and walk away."

"Then let's give them the show of a lifetime."

"Are you secretly a theater kid and just never told me?" Kamryn laughed, but it helped settle the last bit of those nerves she hadn't managed to calm before they'd left Windermere that morning. The drive had been pleasant and warm, but now that they were here, it was all rushing back to her.

"No." Elia put her hand on the door. "So you're going to have to carry the bulk of the lies."

"Deal." Not that it was really going to be that difficult. Kamryn was finding more and more that she enjoyed the time she spent with Elia, that they'd finally broken down some barrier between them that was holding them hostage. "Let's go before I chicken out."

"I won't let you do that," Elia said as she got out of the car.

Kamryn took one last steadying breath. She hated that this made her so nervous—not the bridal shower, but the fact that she had to watch Lauren and Rosie do whatever they were doing in their relationship. She didn't want that jealousy to push her to do stupid things.

Finally out of the car, Kamryn grabbed her jacket from the back seat and slid it over her shoulders before snagging the small gift bag she'd put together for Andra. This was the *family appropriate* gift, something off her registry. Kamryn definitely saved the gift that was solely between friends for the bachelorette party and would sneak that to Andra when she could.

She shut the door and stepped away from the car, surprised to find Elia standing right next to her. Without hesitation, Elia slid her hand into Kamryn's free one, lacing their fingers together like they had during the mock meet. Kamryn had to swallow the lump in her throat.

This felt so real.

So much realer than it should have.

"Ready?" Elia asked.

"No," Kamryn answered. "But that doesn't mean we're not going in."

She took the first step toward the large building and pulled Elia along with her. Kamryn led the way inside, finding which room they were supposed to go to and immediately setting the gift on the table that was waiting for them. She took Elia's jacket and hung it up first before taking off hers. The nerves running through her body were insane. They were damn near close to taking over everything.

Elia turned on her sharply and snagged both of Kamryn's

hands. She looked into Kamryn's eyes and gave a very sweet smile. "Feel free to touch me today if you want. I know that physical touch can help with nerves, and I don't mind."

"I… really?" Kamryn cocked her head in confusion.

"Yeah." Elia leaned in closer, pressing their cheeks together and whispering, "Besides, it'll make the fake seem more real to those distant observers."

"You're really into this, aren't you?"

"I need a bit of excitement in my life." The laugh rang through Kamryn's ears and was exactly what she needed to hear. Elia wasn't doing this out of some distorted obligation but because she really wanted to be here.

"Then let's get to it." Kamryn skimmed her hand down Elia's arm from her shoulder to her elbow before she laced their fingers again. She'd just been given permission to not let go for as long as they were there, and she was absolutely going to take Elia up on that offer.

Andra immediately came over as soon as she saw them. She wrapped her arms around Kamryn's shoulders in a big hug and then rolled her eyes. "Remind me to never get married again, or better yet, next time remind me to elope. I can't do this with my mother again."

Kamryn laughed. "I'll try to remember to tell you that, but I'm pretty sure there won't be a next time."

"Oh, you never know." Andra grinned as she stepped back. "And this is Elia?"

"Yes." Elia extended her hand forward, taking Andra's and shaking. "It's good to meet you. Kam has talked a lot about you."

"Has she? I hope not all good things. I know as many of her deep dark secrets as anyone else in our friend group."

Kamryn nearly choked. There was one secret that Andra was completely unaware of. The only person in their group who knew was Greer, and fuck was Kamryn missing her right now.

Andra stepped in closer and lowered her voice. "Lauren and

Rosie are over by the drinks, so I'd avoid that area of the party if you want to avoid them."

"Thanks for the heads up," Kamryn said, forcing her lips into a smile. "But with Elia, I'm not worried about them being here or what might result from that."

It was a lie.

She was worried.

But she wanted it to be the truth, and if she said it enough times, then perhaps she could manifest her own calm, cool, and collected attitude that she desperately wanted to find. She could do this, and she wasn't wrong that with Elia there with her, she had far more confidence that she was going to actually be able to do this.

Elia took one step up to Kamryn's side and wrapped an arm around her back. "We'll be fine, but thank you."

"I heard about the festival drama," Andra continued. "I hope Rosie wasn't too bad. I really am not a fan of her, but I don't feel like I can tell Lauren she's not invited to the wedding."

"I get it," Kamryn said, nodding. "It's between a rock and a hard place to find yourself."

"Yeah."

"Andra!" Her mother called from the back of the room.

Andra rolled her eyes and pointed over her shoulder. "Never again," she muttered as she walked away.

"You know the way to make sure that you never have to do this again is to focus on only getting married once." Elia's comment was sharp, but it was the truth. Kamryn had thought the same thing many times before, because Andra and Garrett hadn't always had the best relationship. There were things Kamryn really didn't like about Garrett—how he talked to Andra sometimes, and about her when she wasn't around.

"Yeah, that would be the ideal." Kamryn pursed her lips and squared her shoulders. "But it's not my marriage to meddle with, and I make it a point to try and not meddle with other people's relationships."

"I promise you it's better not to meddle." Elia squeezed Kamryn's hand tightly. "I used to meddle with Abagail's, and it wasn't good for anyone. She's a fling person, never has a serious relationship. I'm not sure she wants that, but when we were younger, I was always trying to get her into longer-term relationships. It's much easier now that I stay out of her love life and she stays out of mine."

"Good to know that you meddle," Kamryn said with a bit of a laugh. "Is that why you're here today?"

"Oh, that and so much more." Elia looked deep into Kamryn's eyes, as if saying something that Kamryn didn't understand.

Maybe they hadn't torn down the entirety of that block between them. What was Kamryn missing?

"Kam!" Rosie's fake tones hit her ears, and Kamryn winced. So much for them being on the opposite side of the room.

Elia tightened her grasp on Kamryn's hand in an instant, and the silent support wasn't forgotten. Kamryn was so very thankful that Elia had agreed to come, especially since Greer couldn't be here for this. Rolling her shoulders and readying herself, Kamryn turned around to face the music she'd really rather avoid.

"Rosie." Kamryn nodded at her, searching immediately for Lauren. But she didn't see her anywhere. "Where's Lauren?"

She'd been pretty convinced that the two were attached at the hip and couldn't be separated. Then again, she definitely planned on being attached to Elia today, if only for her own sanity and so she didn't pull anything stupid like the last time she'd run into these two.

"Are you obsessed with her?"

"What?" Cold washed through Kamryn's body instantly. That had been a bucket of ice water she hadn't needed, that was for certain. "No, I just didn't expect you to come over without her."

Elia stayed right next to her, that silent beacon of support that Kamryn definitely needed right now.

"Why not? We're friends."

They definitely were not friends, nor would Kamryn ever consider being friends with Rosie. She repulsed Kamryn in so many ways but mostly by her attitude and behavior. It was like Rosie hit the mean girl stage as a freshman and never grew out of it. Until they'd met, Kamryn hadn't been convinced people got stuck in stages like that. She was once again proven wrong.

"How are you two doing? I was really worried when we got together the last time. I thought you were going to break up with the way Elia was glaring at you."

Was this woman seriously struggling with something? In all seriousness, did she have some sort of mental health disorder that caused her to act this way? Because Kamryn wasn't sure she had ever met someone who talked or acted like this before.

"We're doing well," Elia stepped in, thankfully. Kamryn had no clue how to respond to that. "It was bit of a mix of PMS and being annoyed with someone you love. I'm sure you can understand what that's like."

"Oh, I do." Rosie grinned, glancing at Kamryn before looking over her shoulder. "Sometimes Lauren makes me so mad. She told me I had to play nice today. What does that even mean? I'm always nice."

Nope. Rosie was just living in her own little world of chaos and lies. That was exactly what was happening, and now Kamryn at least understood somewhat how she needed to handle this.

"Like she hates that I talk to you. I don't understand why," Rosie continued, pointing at Kamryn.

"Probably because she's protective of me." At least Kamryn hoped that was the case, that there was still some love lingering there between them, enough that they wouldn't wish the worst on each other. "It's impossible to shut off all feelings when there's a twenty year relationship behind it."

"Twenty-two," Lauren interrupted, two drinks in her hand. She shoved one in Rosie's direction, but her eyes were all for Kamryn.

The look was direct, and it stole Kamryn's breath away. She remembered this look. Lauren had given it to her many times over the years, most often when they were broken up and Lauren was ready to get back together again.

But Kamryn couldn't keep playing those games between them. Her body and heart might be telling her that Lauren was a safe person, that she could go back to what was familiar and be loved again, but her brain was raging against her.

She shifted her stance slightly, bumping her shoulder into Elia's. Their fingers laced together tighter, and Kamryn turned, looking away from Lauren and directly into Elia's cool blue eyes, her rounded, heart-shaped face, her hair that was perfectly coiffed and pulled back, the small gray hairs peeking out here and there.

Despite everything between them, all the complications and lack of history, Kamryn was safer staying right here than she was with Lauren. Kamryn had no doubt in her mind about that. And she needed to stay where it was safe. She needed to give up all those hopes and dreams she'd had with Lauren and let them go.

"You're right, twenty-two years," Kamryn corrected herself with a smile on her face. She lifted Elia's hand wrapped in her own and pressed her lips to Elia's skin. "Love like that doesn't go away, it just changes over time, and it's important to find someone who can understand that. Don't you think?"

Elia nodded. "Yeah." The response came out in a whisper, Elia's voice barely reaching over the din of voices in the room. "It's important to find people who accept all facets of who we are."

"So very important."

"Aww, look at them, Laur, they're gushy!" Rosie clapped her hands together. "Maybe they won't break up. We took bets, you know, after you left."

"They took bets," Lauren added, pointing at Rosie. "I stayed far away from it."

"I appreciate that." Kamryn faced them again, but she couldn't stop the smile that had taken hold of her, the ease of being in the vicinity of Elia and continuing this ruse together. It almost didn't feel quite like this was as fake as it should be.

But Kamryn shouldn't fool herself.

Elia was way out of her league, and Kamryn was just getting out of a bad long-term relationship. Finding someone else to be with wasn't anywhere on her priority list.

However, with Elia with her today, she knew that the bridal shower was going to be a breeze. She couldn't wait for the bachelorette party or the wedding. It wouldn't be bad at all. Kamryn dropped Elia's hand and wrapped an arm around her shoulders, tugging Elia into her side a bit tighter.

"But we are taking bets on Andra and this wedding, right?" Rosie added.

"No," Lauren and Kamryn said at the same time.

They had talked about Andra and her boyfriend many times over the years, and they'd both decided that this was something they needed to stay out of. They could support Andra through everything, but some choices and mistakes had to be hers.

Rosie looked disappointed by that response, and then suddenly suspicious. Kamryn wasn't going to wade into that pool of insanity again.

"Elia, I'd like to introduce you to Kathryn." Kamryn didn't wait another minute before she dragged Elia away.

"Who's Kathryn?"

"No one I care about." Kamryn laced her fingers with Elia's again. "Thank you."

"Any time."

fourteen

The tables in the restaurant were filled with students, and the noise threatened to be overwhelming, but Elia was still riding the high from the first actual competition they'd had. She couldn't remember the last time she was so elated because of a competition. Not only had the kids outdone themselves in talent, effort, and support for each other despite the losses they'd experienced that day, but Elia had found herself connecting more and more with Kamryn.

She'd found herself in Kamryn's orbit and unable to drag herself away.

"Dr. Sharpe," Ethan said, making sure to have her full attention.

She turned to face him across the table where she was sitting, at the last second moving her gaze from Kamryn who was sitting next to her. "Yes?"

"I think I'd like to only compete in Congress next time."

"Oh, really?" Elia furrowed her brow at him, but she let Ethan talk. If he was bringing it up, then surely he was serious about it.

"Yeah, it's my best skill so far, and you know how much I hate debate."

She did know that. He complained anytime she had them do

any sort of debate practice. He'd done that the year before as well, so ultimately, this move didn't surprise her. She nodded at him. "You think that you can put more effort into just focusing on Congress?"

"Absolutely!" Ethan was nearly grinning from ear to ear. "So can I?"

"I don't see why not." Elia was already mentally making the changes to the roster and shifting things around. It wouldn't make much of an impact because Bristol could pick up his debate partner easily enough and she'd quite enjoy that. Elia wouldn't be surprised if Bristol became a lawyer or a politician someday. She had the skills for it. Whether or not she had the passion for those topics remained to be seen.

Elia paid the bill and pocketed the card and receipt. When everyone was done eating, she gathered the students together so they could walk the short way back to the hotel. It was late, nearing nine in the evening, but they were all still full of energy.

"Are you sure we shouldn't do the whisk tonight?" Kamryn murmured under her breath as they walked together at the back of the group.

"Breakfast," Elia doubled down. She didn't have the energy to sit in a circle and listen to everyone's highs for the day. She could handle that in the morning. It had taken her years to realize that she needed to limit her time with people in order to recuperate. It wasn't that she didn't like people, but she needed the quiet to find herself again.

"I'll hold you to that." Kamryn bumped their shoulders together. "Or do I get my own personal whisk time tonight again?"

Elia couldn't stop the smile from gracing her lips. Two weeks had flown by, but at the same time they had gone so slowly. She'd been looking forward to this time that she'd have with Kamryn again—one-on-one time, in a way, when they could have those quiet moments.

She had very little excuse to go to the dormitories to visit

Kamryn's apartment and Kamryn had no reasons for coming to her house. Outside of the bridal shower, which had actually been rather enjoyable, they hadn't spent enough time together.

Enough?

Since when had Elia decided there was a quota for the time they spent together? She'd have to think about and debate that one later when she was alone in her room and had the space to think. "You'll have to stop by and see if I even brought the whisk. Maybe I forgot it."

"Oh, I have a backup one." Kamryn giggled and shook her head. "I remember when you *lost* it senior year. I wasn't going to take chances again."

"I forgot about that."

"I didn't." Kamryn laughed again as they entered the hotel.

"Everyone, gather over here a minute." Elia raised her voice so the students all heard her. "Just a reminder that we have to be on the bus early tomorrow, so I want you up and out of your rooms no later than seven. We'll do whisk time on the bus."

The kids erupted with chatter. Elia also knew without a doubt that if she said seven, she wouldn't actually be leaving until like seven-thirty.

But telling them they were going to do something on the bus that they'd thoroughly enjoyed last time might just be enough incentive to get them moving in the morning when they were dragging from staying up late.

Elia stayed in the lobby until all of the kids had gone up the elevators. When she looked around, her eyes met Kamryn's. That surprised her. She'd expected Kamryn to be the first one to her room so that she could get started on some work project that she had going on. She was always working on something.

Kamryn tilted her head toward the elevator. "Do I need to get my whisk?"

Elia laughed as she walked closer and pressed the button. "That sounds like a dare almost."

"Oh, we could play truth or dare with it." Kamryn seemed so excited, her eyes completely alight with joy.

She hated to crush that, but Elia wasn't going to play truth or dare. There were much better ways to get information and not feel pressured into doing something she didn't want to do. Wasn't Kamryn all about consent anyway?

"I think just highlights is a better use for the whisk." Elia stepped into the elevator and paused as she hit the floor she needed.

Kamryn didn't hit her floor.

Elia said nothing as the elevator doors closed. She really wanted to see what Kamryn had up her sleeve this time, and she was pretty sure that Kamryn had a plan. That woman didn't go anywhere without a plan, even if it went out the window as soon as she arrived.

They walked down the hallway toward Elia's room. They'd ended up spending two nights this time because the drive was so long. Elia fingered the key in her pocket before she pulled it out. When she got to her room, she stopped and faced Kamryn full on, still curious as to what was happening and why.

Had this been a relationship, she would know what to expect.

But this wasn't that.

And even though they were friendly with each other lately, they weren't best friends. Kamryn wasn't Abagail, and Elia didn't think that Kamryn would just barge into the room like it was her own. They weren't that close yet.

"What is your highlight for the day?" Kamryn asked, her voice lowering, not quite a whisper, but definitely close to it.

Elia didn't blame her. She didn't necessarily want any kids to overhear what they were talking about either. Glancing down the hallway both ways, Elia took a risk that she normally wouldn't. Except it seemed she was breaking her own personal rules a lot for Kamryn.

Unlocking her door, she stepped inside and held it open. "We'll talk inside."

Kamryn smiled, definitely pleased with herself, as she walked past Elia and hit the light switch as she went. Elia checked the hallway one more time. The last thing she needed was rumors spreading that she and the Head of School were an item. And while Kamryn had been in her room before, she'd come late at night when the kids were all settled. Not right after dinner.

With the door shut, Elia already felt a million times more comfortable. She shed her jacket and threw it over the chair in the corner of the room. She was assuming that Kamryn was going to sit on the mattress like she had the last time anyway. And something within Elia that night wanted her close. It was probably the same reason she hadn't been able to stop looking for Kamryn in the middle of the competition space all day.

Kamryn took off her jacket and put it onto the chair. She sat heavily onto the edge of the bed, and Elia sat next to her.

"Did you really want to know what my highlight was?"

"Of course," Kamryn answered with a smile.

Elia was going to have to think about this one. Because while she could easily call up something good that had happened, her highlight could mean so much more to the conversation they were having. The question really remained whether or not she wanted to continue down the path that she was already set on or if she wanted to get off.

And she just wasn't sure.

This could so easily tip into relationship territory. But was she willing to go that far? Or did she need to pull back?

Elia sighed and leaned back slightly, finally deciding where she should start. "The last time I tangled a relationship with Windermere, it didn't end well for me."

Kamryn frowned deeply, her face falling from the lightness she'd had to a much deeper understanding. Elia was taking this conversation in a completely different direction. "I'm not sure I follow."

"I'm enjoying spending time with you, Kam." Elia stated as simply as she possibly could. She didn't want to give Kamryn any false hope or to confess something that neither one of them were ready to hear or understand. "I'd like to continue doing that."

"We are spending time together." Kamryn instinctively reached out but then stopped. Elia took her hand and tangled their fingers tight. Sometimes talking to Kamryn was easier this way. "I'm not understanding."

"Then perhaps it's best that we leave it at that." Elia gave her a tight and somewhat forced smile. She wasn't sure that she could lead Kamryn through this conversation, at least not yet. She needed to save something for herself in all of this because without that, she might never survive another disaster like the last one.

"Elia..." Kamryn paused, her gaze locked on their joined hands. The pause was pregnant, and Elia gave her the time to find the words that she needed, whatever they were. "Elia," Kamryn started again, finally lifting those stunning brown eyes to meet Elia's. "Can I kiss you?"

A shiver ran through Elia, raising goosebumps along her skin, hardening her nipples, moving farther down her body and right back up. She hadn't been wrong before. This was amazing, so much better than any kiss she'd had before and they hadn't even started a kiss, which she was going to say yes to.

Just being asked...how could she even put that into words?

Elia looked deep into Kamryn's eyes, her gaze that held so much intensity and passion. How had Elia not seen that before? Because it was there now, it was there when Kamryn was talking passionately about something else, it had been there the one time Elia had gone over to Kamryn's apartment, and it had been there during the bridal shower.

But then there was the block. The thing that Elia had been trying to tell Kamryn. The past. And it kept coming back up to bite Elia in the ass when she least expected it. She couldn't let Kamryn take the bad rap for her, and she certainly couldn't face Kamryn when she found out exactly what had happened all those years ago. Kamryn would likely feel the same way as everyone else.

Students first.

No matter what.

Elia shook her head, keeping her hand locked with Kamryn's as she closed her eyes. Sadness swept through her now, her fear overriding any thought to hope and pleasure. "No."

"Oh, I thought..." Kamryn trailed off, looking so confused.

Elia felt for her. She knew exactly what Kamryn had thought, and the worst part was that she hadn't been wrong. Elia wanted it. She wanted to be touched and caressed and checked after. She wanted someone who cared about her, and if that care could develop into love? Even better. Just like she'd always wanted Abagail to find that love and stability, Elia had wanted it for herself more times than she could count.

Yet, she was still alone.

"You didn't think wrong," Elia said, lifting Kamryn's chin with a finger so she could say this as directly as possible. "What you were thinking is exactly what I was thinking, but..."

"There's always a but to ruin things."

"Sometimes." Elia dropped her hand from Kamryn's face, immediately regretting it. She missed the warmth and touch, the intimacy that came with the touch. "This comes back to what I was trying to tell you. When I mix relationships with Windermere, it doesn't turn out well for me."

"What happened?"

Elia shook her head. She wasn't ready to explain that. She wasn't sure that she'd ever be ready to tell Kamryn what had happened eighteen years ago and why she'd subsequently been shut out from anything other than what she was already doing. It had been a miracle that they'd allowed her to be the department head.

"All right," Kamryn said, her voice calm and not angry at all.

That was such a nice change from any other time that Elia had shared this with anyone. She'd been met with anger, disbelief, and then accusation. It had hurt every single time.

"Then we won't." Kamryn gave her a smile. "Fake girlfriends we'll remain."

Elia grinned at that. She'd nearly forgotten that this was how everything between them had started. With a kiss that she wasn't ever going to forget. And with the knowledge that a second kiss, on both their terms, would be astronomically better than the first one.

"Fake girlfriends." Elia held her hand out and waited for Kamryn to take it and shake, as if they were making yet another deal between them. Their relationship had certainly become an exchange of favors at some point, hadn't it? "I'm sorry, by the way."

"Sorry for what?" Kamryn folded her hands in her lap, clearly not wanting to touch anymore. It wouldn't surprise Elia if that made her uncomfortable.

"For giving you mixed signals."

Kamryn ran her fingers through her hair and sighed heavily. "It's clear to me that you're not ready to share. That can be for a number of reasons, but my guess is that it's because you don't fully trust me yet."

Elia nodded slightly. Damn, Kamryn was good.

"Doing anything like I asked, and perhaps like you were thinking, requires trust. If we don't have that, then it won't be good."

"Agreed," Elia murmured. She was so glad that Kamryn understood. "I don't want to repeat past mistakes."

"Me either." Kamryn gave a weak smile then. "So let's make a promise to each other, all right?"

"What kind of promise?"

"A good one."

Elia waited patiently for whatever Kamryn had up her sleeve this time. And she was glad to know that she wouldn't have to wait long.

"Let's promise to keep open minds, and to keep open communication about what we're experiencing, feeling, and all of that. But let's not put the pressure of anything other than budding friendship and fake dating onto it."

"I can promise that," Elia answered, already feeling lighter than she had before. Why was it so easy to talk to Kamryn sometimes? She needed more of that in her life.

"Good. I promise that too." Kamryn's lips pulled upward slightly. "I think I'm going to head back to my room for the night."

"I'll see you in the morning."

"For whisk time!" Kamryn laughed, but it sounded slightly forced compared to before.

Elia nodded, staying put on the edge of the bed. They'd figure this out eventually. They just needed some space for it. As Kamryn grabbed her jacket, Elia answered, "For whisk time."

fifteen

Kamryn was at a loss.

They were making no progress whatsoever, and the fact that she had to sit through yet another one of these meetings was killing her slowly. How was she supposed to form an ethics committee with these two in charge of it? Or even involved in it?

Heather and Susy were chattering away so fast about plans they'd already made outside of this meeting. They expected Kamryn to either follow along with the conversation or just shut up and agree to whatever the hell they suggested.

Well, that wasn't going to happen.

Kamryn wasn't that kind of person and she needed more than that from the people she was working with. Even if she was forced to work with them.

"We need to do intense interviews with all faculty and staff immediately. We'll start those with the English department."

Kamryn froze. Which one had said that? She'd gotten lost in her own annoyances and missed part of the conversation, although she didn't seem to miss the point of what they were trying to do. Kamryn bit her cheek and held her tongue, needing more information before they completely cut her out of the conversation and just did whatever they were going to do without her.

"Yes, let's start there. I think it's best to start with the head of each department, then they can tell everyone it's painless." That was Susy.

Kamryn clenched her fist under the table. She had to stop this. This wasn't what the ethics committee was supposed to be.

Heather turned on her. "You can start with Elia Sharpe."

"W-what?" Kamryn shook her head. "You want me to interview each staff and faculty member, and make sure they're what? Not pedophiles?"

"Exactly." Heather smiled at her gleefully, as if Kamryn had finally figured out the entire point of what they were discussing and was finally on board with it.

"No."

"No?" Susy leaned in, her voice rising not in questioning but in anger.

Most likely because Kamryn even dared to tell her no to anything. How many times had Susy heard that word? Especially from the Head of School? Or did she just assume that the Head of School was her bitch and would do anything that they were told to do by the board.

"No," Kamryn repeated. "I won't start a witch hunt. It's one thing to update background checks, or even make them more in-depth than the previous ones, but I'm not going to interrogate the staff and faculty looking for people who are doing things wrong."

"But it's for the protection of the children."

"It's really not." Kamryn was going to put her foot down on this one, and if she had to, then she'd get even more people involved. And that might be the solution, honestly. And again, they were trying to oust Elia. What the hell was up with that? Neither one of them had given a good reason as to why they were so focused on her. "This is because you're afraid of something, and until you tell me what is so terrifying or file a formal complaint, I won't participate in this."

Susy's jaw dropped. "This is your job."

"No. It's not. My job is to run this school, to educate its students, and to make sure that staff and faculty have a safe and healthy environment to work, and for some of them, live in. Nothing in my job description is to find out every single thing that would put each person on the naughty list. And I won't participate in a witch hunt. Let me repeat that to make myself *very* clear. I *will not* participate in a witch hunt."

Kamryn stacked up her papers and slammed her notepad on top of them. She stood up, pushing the chair out from under her as she gave Susy and Heather a hard look.

"This meeting is done."

"There are going to be repercussions for this," Heather said. "You'll get in trouble."

"Then so be it." Kamryn shook her head and shrugged her shoulders. "But I won't stand by and be speechless while this happens. It's not right. It *is* unethical. And it's ironic that you chose the ethics team of all the teams to host your little witch hunt." Kamryn put her fists on her hips and stared at them again. They really needed to leave before she lost even more of her temper.

She was tired.

It was late.

And this was beyond ridiculous.

It was outrageous.

"This meeting is adjourned," Kamryn said, again trying to push them out of the conference room door.

They finally picked up their things and walked out. Kamryn made sure to escort them out of the administration building. She was pretty damn sure that they would sit in the parking lot for a while and complain about how rude Kamryn was, but she didn't care. She just needed them out.

She shivered as the cold hit her, but she locked the door

behind her and went immediately back to her office. She meant to plop down in her chair, but she couldn't even bring herself to do that. She was way too pissed off. She needed to throw and break something.

Not even a phone call to Greer was going to help her this time.

What the hell did they have against Elia?

Because nothing Kamryn had seen so far warranted this kind of behavior toward her. Elia was insanely professional with the kids, even when they were out on overnight trips. She supported them, and she was never alone with them if she could avoid it. The other times, she left the door wide open so anyone who walked by could see. There were cameras everywhere, and Elia lived on campus.

What was going on? Seriously?

It irked Kamryn to no end, and the fact that Elia refused to tell her. She'd been close to it a few times, but she'd never actually told Kamryn what was holding her back on so many fronts.

"Fuck," Kamryn muttered under her breath. She needed to get out of her head and out of her office. Pocketing her keys and leaving her office the mess that it was, Kamryn left. She didn't even have her jacket, which of course she didn't realize until after she was outside in the near-freezing air.

She'd be fine.

One night without it wouldn't kill her.

Kamryn started with walking around the gardens by the administration building, but then she just let her feet take her wherever she needed to go. When she finally looked up, her brain pounding less but her anger still very present, she realized she was at the small row of faculty and staff houses.

Elia's was the second one from the end of the row on the right.

Could she?

They hadn't exactly left off in the best of places after the last competition, but in the intervening days Kamryn hadn't sensed any grudges or anger between them. In fact, conversing with Elia had been much easier than before.

Clenching her jaw and squaring her shoulders, Kamryn knew what she had to do. She had to go directly to the source. She needed to know what she didn't know, otherwise she couldn't protect anyone. She couldn't do her damn job without information.

Her feet took her swiftly to Elia's small home. The lights on either side of the sidewalk illuminated the path, and the front porch light was on. Kamryn marched directly up to the front door and curled her hand into a fist, knocking hard. Her heart hammered, her arms were so cold that she worried briefly they might fall off, and her toes curled in her shoes in response.

"Kamryn?" Elia said as she opened the door, obvious confusion and then concern in her gaze. "What's wrong?"

"So much is wrong," Kamryn muttered.

"God, you must be freezing." Elia opened the door wider and ushered Kamryn inside, shutting it instantly. She didn't wait as she reached out and pressed her gloriously warm palms to Kamryn's bare arms. "Where's your jacket?"

"I forgot it in my office."

"And instead of going back to get it, you just walked here without it?"

"I took a gander around the garden first. Look, I came here for a reason." Kamryn's tone was sharp, bursting with anger. She knew that. But she couldn't pull it back in or stop it no matter how hard she tried. Not that she was actually trying. That would be giving in to the insanity that had been that meeting. "The board..." Kamryn stopped talking.

What could she actually say?

She should be looking out for her future here at Windermere, along with Elia's future. Elia was a faculty member, not her girlfriend or spouse. Which meant that there were vastly different lines around what they could share with each other. Fuck, Kamryn hated this.

"What happened?" Kamryn finally asked.

Elia wrinkled her brow and shook her head slowly. "I asked you that." She walked away, heading straight for the kitchen and hitting the button on the electric tea kettle. "I'll make us some tea, so you can warm up."

Damn her for being so kind and thinking about something like that. Kamryn didn't move from the doorway though. She really needed answers. She had to know what was going on in order to know what action she needed to take next.

"What happened all those years ago? What are you hiding?"

Elia froze, her entire body going tense. "What are you talking about?"

"I don't know! That's the entire problem. And no one will just come out and say it!"

"Say what?" Elia nearly shouted this time.

The pain in her voice took Kamryn off guard. She breathed deeply, no sound in the air except her ragged breaths in and out as they stared at each other from across the living room and kitchen. "What happened to you at this school that put everyone on edge?"

Elia put her hand up. "I can't..."

"Because I can't protect you without knowing. And they want to fire you or something. They want to put you under the microscope and make you sweat and probably force you out if they can't fire you. And I can't in good conscience let them do that if I don't know what the hell it's for." Kamryn was ready to explode. She needed to release this energy somewhere, and she knew she shouldn't be doing it here. But Elia was the only other person in this equation that had any information.

"Kam."

"No! Don't *Kam* me. Tell me what I don't know. I'm tired of feeling like I'm the only one in this entire school that doesn't know what happened." Kamryn took a step forward, her fists shaking from being held so tightly. She practically vibrated with her anger. "And if you keep this a secret any longer, you're just as bad as them."

"I won't! I won't be forced to tell you what happened. It's my story to tell!" Elia's voice rang through the living room, piercing Kamryn's ears. She'd never seen Elia this upset before. "I won't let them take that one thing that I have left. Not now, not ever."

"But how can I help you if I don't know what the fuck is going on?" Kamryn threw her hands out to her sides, still riding the anger wave as long as she possibly could. "This is why you should have been on the ethics team. Then you could have controlled some of this."

"Don't!" Elia pointed her finger at Kamryn. "Don't even think that. Even if I had agreed, I never would have been allowed to be on that team."

"But why?" It was an angry whine now. The frustration built in her chest, and nothing was working to get rid of it. Kamryn needed to let it explode out of her, and right now Elia was the only target in sight. "I don't understand why."

"You don't have to understand!" Elia shouted back.

"I want to. I want to know." Kamryn took another step. She was finally in the middle of the living room, but she wasn't close enough to Elia. She could see the pain in her face, the hurt and heartache that she was no doubt feeling, but she couldn't see if she was at her breaking point yet. If finally, she was going to tell Kamryn exactly what she needed to hear.

"You don't."

"I do!" Kamryn fired back. "I do want to know. I want to be able to understand what all this underhanded nastiness is about. I can only protect you so much from it without knowing."

"Don't protect me." Elia's voice was a deadly calm. "I don't *need* or *want* your protection."

Kamryn paused at that. Everyone needed that at some point. And Elia had given her that at the fall festival, so Kamryn would return the favor if it was warranted, but at this point, Kamryn didn't even know if it was warranted. "If I don't protect you, then this school will fall apart."

"Let it." The words were so cold. They were said with no fear. Elia stood in the kitchen, her tone resolute and her entire being determined.

"I won't let them turn this into a witch hunt. I won't let them take the entire school down just to get you." Kamryn reached the edge of the kitchen counter, her fingers curling around the counter, her knuckles turning white. She still couldn't feel half of her body from the cold, but she needed Elia to understand how much danger this was putting the school in. If they could do this with one teacher, they would do it with everyone.

And everyone made mistakes.

The point was that not every mistake deserved termination and not every mistake deserved a hanging. But Susy and Heather were making it out to be that Elia deserved all of that and more.

"It's been a witch hunt for eighteen years." The way Elia said that, the dead calm and the painful acceptance, hurt Kamryn deeply. This was what Elia was hiding, this pain and betrayal. It wasn't from a past lover or a family member. It was from the school, and everyone Elia had trusted at some point in her life to be her family away from home.

"I won't allow witch hunts on *my* campus. I won't let them burn you."

"They already have." Elia raised her chin up in defiance, her gaze filled with it.

"They haven't. I know they haven't." Kamryn lowered her voice. That anger was sliding away from her now, finally having had its outlet. But she was left in the pitiful pain that she'd brought up and forced Elia to feel right in front of her, and she hated herself for that. She needed to be better, to do better.

"Kam."

Kamryn ignored her. She didn't want the confession like that. She didn't want to be the reason that Elia couldn't sleep tonight or to force Elia to have to share when she wasn't ready for it, when there wasn't enough trust—

"Kamryn!"

"What?" Kamryn snapped her head up, locking her eyes on Elia's.

"Yes." Elia's entire body went lax, as if that acceptance had morphed into something else, something that she was finally comfortable with, something that they could both tangibly touch and see now.

"Yes?" Confusion clouded Kamryn's thoughts. What had they even been talking about? She'd gotten so lost in her self-flagellation that she hadn't managed to keep track of what they were talking about. Kamryn walked around the counter and stepped in closer to Elia, making sure that Elia had her full attention now. She wouldn't do that again. She wouldn't be the bully that she abhorred, that she was fighting against. "I'm so sorry."

"Shut up and kiss me."

sixteen

Elia's entire body was a live wire. Kamryn stared at her in confusion, and she couldn't help herself. She stayed exactly where she was and held her breath. She had to wait for what she'd said to click into Kamryn's brain—whatever thread she'd decided to follow and couldn't manage to come back from just yet.

"Kiss me," Elia repeated. "I want you to kiss me."

"Elia..." Kamryn trailed off, dragging out her name until shivers ran up and down Elia's spine.

But Elia had exactly what she needed. Kamryn was mad—pissed off and so, so angry—and it was all because she thought what was happening to Elia was an injustice. No one had ever done that for her, at least no one on campus. They'd assumed she'd been guilty the whole time, and Elia had worked her ass off to prove her innocence and clear her name.

But Kamryn... Elia was very nearly in tears. Kamryn had believed her without even knowing what had happened all those years ago. Without being let in on the secret. Elia slowed her breathing and her heart rate. She slid in closer to Kamryn, locking their gazes together.

"If you still want to... that is," Elia said, afraid to touch Kamryn without some sign that this was also what she wanted.

Without warning, Kamryn surged forward. She cupped Elia's cheeks and brought their lips together, mouths pressed in a fiery kiss that hit on every nerve in Elia's body and told her this was exactly what she'd wanted and needed. Every single place that Kamryn touched felt instant sparks of pleasure and ripples of joy. They cascaded through her, hitting every sensitive spot in her body.

Elia moaned, her body rocking into Kamryn's. She'd needed this. Not sex. Not kissing. She'd needed someone to just believe her and tell her she wasn't wrong. That nothing had been wrong all those years ago, that she was innocent, and Kamryn had managed to do that without even saying the words.

"Touch me," Elia murmured through kisses. "Fuck me."

Kamryn growled and turned their bodies, pushing Elia back into the peninsula and pinning Elia between it and Kamryn's body. Elia ran her hands over Kamryn's sides, shoulders, breasts. Her clothes were freezing cold to the touch, and her skin wasn't much better. Elia didn't care. She just needed to feel everything that Kamryn was feeling and more.

"Take it off," Kamryn said as she moved her hands from Elia's cheeks to the hem of her shirt. She didn't wait as she pulled Elia's shirt off. As soon as her skin hit the air, Elia lost track of everything.

She tried to focus on Kamryn's touches, on their skin against each other—hers on fire and Kamryn's ice—and she couldn't. It was a mix of touches and kisses, tongues and fingers. Her head spun, and breathing was getting harder. Kamryn had a hand down her pants and fingers against her, and Elia grunted when Kamryn found her clit and pinched lightly.

"Oh fuck," Elia said. That felt so good. She got wetter in an instant, and she knew without a doubt that this was going to be good sex. This was going to be exactly what they both needed and wanted. "Mouth."

Kamryn pushed Elia's pants down her legs and pulled them off one leg at a time. Then she pulled her underwear down. Elia stared at Kamryn as she stood back up with a wickedly satisfied grin on her lips. Elia breathed heavily, the pause in the action rearing up her libido even more. If Kamryn continued to stare at her like that, like she was going to be eaten up and completely consumed, would she come just from the look?

Reaching behind her, Elia unhooked her bra and let it drop. She didn't move her gaze from Kamryn's face, but Kamryn looked down. Her gaze roved all over Elia's body, lingering in certain places, her cheeks reddening, her eyes widening. Was she fascinated?

Kamryn stepped forward, putting both hands on Elia's hips. She leaned in, her lips brushing against Elia's ear as she breathed. The hot air touched Elia's skin, rushing over her body. Her nipples hardened tightly, and the muscles in her body tensed with anticipation—this time with anticipation of so much pleasure that she was going to completely lose herself in the moment.

"Just go with it," Kamryn said.

Elia was about to object, but Kamryn's grip on her tightened. She lifted Elia up and backward, sliding her easily onto the counter behind her. Elia cried out in surprise, but when Kamryn bent down and pressed kisses to her hips, Elia closed her eyes and lay backward on the counter.

Parting her legs, Elia waited for Kamryn's mouth to be against her. She planted one hand under her head and the other against her breast, teasing her nipple. She was ready to let everything go, to let the world know who she was, for Kamryn to finally find out who they might be together. And she was ready for the leap for herself too, to let go of everything that had been holding her back for all these years.

"Mouth," Elia demanded again when Kamryn still hadn't started sucking and licking her. "Hard."

Kamryn chuckled as she moved in. The vibrations from her voice adding to the sensation. Elia raised her hips and pushed her body deeper into Kamryn's mouth. She'd dreamed of this. After the last speech meet, when she'd all but kicked Kamryn out of her room, she'd dreamed of exactly this.

Kamryn's mouth, hot against her pussy. The cries of pleasure that would fill the air. The freedom that she might just taste. Freedom from her past, from the cloud that had haunted every step she'd taken for the last eighteen years, from all the hopes that she didn't dare entertain, and from all the failures she knew she was going to face.

Elia bit her lip and pulled her nipple hard, the pain rebounding down her body to exactly where Kamryn's tongue was hitting against her. Kamryn moved into sucking before she went back to using her tongue in quick little flicks.

"Ughhhh..." Elia cried out, her back arching on the hard counter. She didn't want this to ever end. She wanted to stay right where she was, splayed out for Kamryn's consumption, and go nowhere else.

Kamryn's fingers against her thigh were the request for more. Elia wasn't going to tell her stop. She wanted everything that Kamryn was willing to give her, everything and more. Elia was getting more and more frustrated by the second when Kamryn didn't put fingers inside of her. Elia had to work to find her voice.

"Fingers. Now."

Elia sighed as Kamryn moved two fingers inside her, gently inserting them and then curling them upward. She tapped once and Elia nearly jumped off the counter. Her entire body tensed and tightened. She hadn't been prepared for just how damn good that was going to feel.

"Amazing," she murmured. When Kamryn did it again, she groaned and knocked her head back into the counter. She brought her arm up to her mouth and bit down on her wrist to hold back her screams. Because that was exactly what she wanted to do. She wanted to let loose everything that she'd been holding back and never look at it again.

Kamryn's breathing intensified as she moved. Deep intakes and slow exhales as she teased. Elia was so close already. She was ready to cascade into her orgasm and let Kamryn hold her while she did it. She tightened her thighs around Kamryn's head, needing to be rooted as best as she could when she did finally orgasm.

Elia closed her eyes, focusing on the sensations and the feelings. Feelings that she had long kept hidden away. Was there love in there? Hope? Was she even capable of those things anymore? With Kamryn, she thought that perhaps just maybe she could be. But it would be so dangerous to let those things out again.

Writhing and struggling to keep still, Elia stayed planted until she couldn't hold back any longer. She flung her arm out to the side and pushed up on her elbows. Their eyes locked. Kamryn's brown to Elia's blue. Elia's heart thudded hard, her breath caught, and she was gone. Crying out, Elia let her orgasm, her pleasure, her life as it was now with Kamryn consume her.

But Kamryn didn't stop right away.

Elia's body twitched sharply as Kamryn slowed her teasing, and just when she thought that Kamryn would back away, she didn't. She picked her pace back up again. Elia briefly thought about telling her to stop, telling her that it was too much, that she'd be too sore in the morning. But fuck she only lived once, and that first orgasm was delicious.

She needed another one.

Staying as upright as possible, Elia watched this time. Kamryn's face was deep against her, buried. The little curls must be tickling her face, but Kamryn didn't seem to even notice them. She was so damn focused, so determined to do whatever it was she was doing.

"That feels so good," Elia said, smiling when Kamryn tried to grin back at her. "Pull my nipples."

Kamryn reached up with her one free hand and cupped Elia's breast. She used her hand to test the weight, the softness, and flicked the edge of her thumb over Elia's hardened nipple.

"Pull them," Elia demanded. "Hard."

Kamryn pinched Elia's nipple between her thumb and forefinger and did exactly as she had been told.

"Ohhhhh." Elia let all the air out of her lungs before sucking in sharply. "Again." That had been exactly what she'd needed. Kamryn did it again and again, elongating how long she held the nipple tight before releasing. Elia was so close already. Her entire body was ripe for pleasure and Kamryn was going to give and give no matter what they did.

"So close," Elia said, holding onto that feeling. This was what she'd needed—the closeness, the connection. She shivered as she came again, holding still against Kamryn's mouth until she could finally find her brain again somewhere—though she was pretty sure it was mush now.

Kamryn moved her finger and thumb across her lips, and then she licked them, sucked them into her mouth and smiled as she stared directly at Elia. "You taste just as good as I dreamed."

Elia's heart stuttered. *Dreamed?* Had Kamryn dreamed of this too?

Dropping her legs to the counter, Elia surged forward and pulled Kamryn up by the chin. She pressed their mouths together, tangling their tongues. She could taste herself on Kamryn's lips, the cold dampness against her cheeks now. It was sloppy. It was pure. It was a promise.

They stayed there for who knew how long. Elia completely lost track of time. When she pulled back, she was grinning. "Bedroom."

"I thought you'd never get to that point."

Elia chuckled lowly. "Oh, we'll definitely be in there for a while."

Kamryn helped her slide off the counter. Elia took Kamryn's hand and led the way up the creaky old wooden stairs to her bedroom. She flicked on the light, wanting to see everything of Kamryn, as much as Kamryn had seen her. She walked backward toward the bed with her hands out to her sides.

"You better get undressed if you're staying."

Kamryn's lips pulled upward. "Hell yes I'm staying."

"Good." Elia reached the bed and stopped when she didn't see Kamryn moving any more. "What?"

"Thank God your bedroom is messy. I was about to think you were some sort of weird perfectionist."

Elia laughed, her voice ringing through the air. "Only in the public-facing spheres."

"That's sexy as hell." Kamryn immediately undressed, dropping her clothes on the floor next to Elia's dirty clothes. Elia didn't care one bit as she watched. Kamryn climbed onto the bed and lay back, her head on the pillow and her look insistent. "Well?"

"Well what? If I had to tell you want to do, it's only fair that you tell me."

"Hmm." Kamryn used her bare foot behind Elia's knee to jerk her forward slightly. "Get on top."

"This is for you, not me."

"Oh, I know." Satisfaction dripped from Kamryn's voice. "This is for me."

Elia climbed onto the bed like Kamryn had asked her to. She got on all fours and straddled her. Bending down, she kissed Kamryn again, keeping their mouths pressed together, while she slid her hands across Kamryn's still chilled skin. They'd have to fix that next. Maybe with a shower, or maybe with that tea she hadn't made yet. But either way, they'd warm Kamryn up.

"Fingers," Kamryn said. "And don't take it easy on me. I'm not exactly easy to break."

Elia took her time exploring Kamryn's body, her delicious curves, her hips, her thick thighs, her amazing ass. Elia was just about to touch her large breasts again when Kamryn grunted. "Enough teasing."

She supposed it was only fair. They hadn't exactly taken it slow in the kitchen either. "How many?"

"As many as you want." Kamryn intentionally parted her legs.

Elia glanced down between them, overcome with joy. She just

wanted to touch, and she was finally given permission to do exactly that. She tenderly touched at first, seeking to know exactly where Kamryn liked it best, where she was most affected.

"Elia..." Kamryn said on a warning. "Fingers. Now."

Payback was a bitch, but Elia was willing to let it slide this time. Inserting one finger at first and then a second, Elia waited. Kamryn was so tight around her. She wasn't sure that she'd be able to fit a third finger in right away, not without some stretching and teasing first. Elia took a steadying breath, she centered herself so she could focus on what was coming next, and then she did exactly what Kamryn had done.

She tapped—a repeated and regular rhythm.

Kamryn curled upward, her face twisting in pleasure. She gripped Elia's wrist tightly until her breathing evened out, and then she relaxed a bit more. Leaning forward, Elia trailed kisses up Kamryn's stomach to her breasts. She pressed the heel of her palm against Kamryn's clit, adding to the pleasure that she was already feeling.

She pulled Kamryn's nipple between her lips and sucked gently before flicking it with her tongue. She stayed there, listening to every change in Kamryn's body, the way she moved, the telltale signs that what Elia was doing was good and wanted. She tuned her entire body into Kamryn's.

There was nothing else but the two of them there in that moment.

"Elia," Kamryn cried out. "Don't stop. I need this. I need you."

Elia shuddered as those words washed over her. She listened to them, let them echo in her mind until Kamryn shouted her name again, squeezing Elia's fingers deliciously as she came and came and came.

Collapsing next to Kamryn, Elia let out a light laugh as she stared up at her ceiling. She was so relaxed. Sore already, but far more relaxed than she had been in ages. Kamryn turned on her side, trailing a hand down her side and stopping at her hip.

"Can we try that again? But slower this time," Kamryn asked.

Elia smiled, surging up to meet Kamryn's lips in a kiss. "Yes. After a break."

"Yes, after a break," Kamryn agreed. "A much needed and much deserved break."

seventeen

Kamryn loved that warm feeling of a good sleep and waking up surrounded by it was exactly what she'd needed. But whatever pesky alarm was going off seriously needed to stop. Groaning, she shifted and buried her face deeper into the back of Elia's hair and neck.

"Is that yours or mine?" Kamryn mumbled, still refusing to open her eyes. She didn't want to know that it was morning, or that it was time to get up yet. She wanted to stay snuggled against Elia's back, curled around and spooning her for as long as humanly possible that day.

"Mine," Elia answered, though she didn't seem very happy about it either.

"Where is it? Turn it off," Kamryn whined again, pulling Elia tighter against her front. She *would* stay there as long as she could. Alarms be damned.

"Probably the living room." Elia seemed more awake now than Kamryn was ready for. Couldn't they stay here even longer? "I should get up and shut it off."

"But it's so warm here," Kamryn answered.

"And comfortable," Elia replied, and this time Kamryn could hear the smile in her voice. Elia wiggled around, turning awkwardly in the bed so that she faced Kamryn and trailed fingers across Kamryn's cheeks and then her arm before she pressed their mouths together. "We do have to get up and go to work, though."

Kamryn groaned again. She really didn't want to do that. She wanted to stay in this warm bed, she wanted to stay pressed up against Elia, she wanted to repeat exactly what they'd done last night. Elia kissed her again.

"You have a school to run, and I have classes to teach." Elia pressed her lips in a line down Kamryn's neck, her tongue dipping out to tease at the hollow of Kamryn's collar bone.

This was what she wanted.

Kamryn shook her head and burrowed in deeper. "Not yet."

Elia chuckled lightly, wrapping a hand around Kamryn's back and then against her ass. "Work is a necessary evil."

"We can call in sick."

"I think that would be suspicious." Elia massaged Kamryn's ass, and Kamryn could already feel her body waking up well before her brain. She wanted more of what they'd shared.

"Next time we do this, we do it on a weekend when neither of us has to work in the morning." Kamryn pouted but smiled when Elia swooped in to kiss her again.

"We're doing this again?" Elia asked.

"If you want to, yes. I would very much like to not let this be the only time." Kamryn found Elia's nipple under the covers and gave her a quick pinch.

Elia squeaked in response and shifted instantly. "Ugh, that alarm is annoying me."

"Me too, but I'm doing a decent job at ignoring it."

"I'm not." Elia pulled Kamryn in for a deep kiss, their lips melding together, their tongues tangling. Kamryn melted into it. Screw morning breath, screw the sleep-addled brain, and screw needing to get up for the morning. This was exactly what she needed and wanted this morning. Elia in her arms, tousled, warm, and so willing to touch. Elia broke the kiss and pulled away. "Time to get up."

Kamryn groaned again. "What time is it, even?"

"Five."

"Jesus, you're a masochist."

Elia laughed lightly as she slid out of the bed. "Now you know why I don't like staying awake until three in the morning doing whisk time."

Kamryn watched with rapt attention as Elia found a towel and wrapped it around her middle, covering up her glorious body.

"I'm going to shut that off and start coffee. We'll both need some."

"Buckets full," Kamryn commented, rubbing her hands over her face. "Do I at least get to shower with you before you make me leave?"

Elia paused, her movements jerky and stiff. "Make you leave?"

Kamryn nodded, squinting to see Elia in the doorway as she was just about to walk out. "Yeah, because... well, I don't really know why. I'm not very good at one-night stands."

"This is a one-night stand?" Elia was far too awake for this conversation while Kamryn was far too asleep for it. She couldn't keep up with what Elia was implying. "I think most one-night stands involve strangers."

"Friends with benefits?" Kamryn tried again, but that one also didn't sit right with her.

"Right, you figure out what we are to each other while I go turn off that alarm and start the coffee." Elia walked away without another word.

Kamryn winced. Had she messed this up already?

She stayed in the bed, trying to convince herself that she wasn't a complete idiot for everything that had happened, that she hadn't ruined a good thing. The conversation from the night before kept replaying in her mind, not just her and Elia screaming at each other, but the intensity of the ethics meeting that had blown her out of the water and made her show up here to begin with.

She really needed to figure out a better way to explain that to

Elia, so Elia didn't think she was ready to fly off the handle at the smallest upset.

"Are you coming?" Elia's voice reached her ears from the doorway.

Kamryn finally looked up. Elia was naked as the day she was born, and she was giving Kamryn a very pointed look.

"We both could probably clean up after last night," Elia added.

"Uh... yeah." Kamryn scrambled to get out of the bed, her muscles lagging and stiff. She definitely wasn't as spry as she used to be. She hadn't worked out in ages, and she was paying the consequences for that now.

Kamryn met Elia at the door, and they walked across the hall to an upstairs bathroom. This one looked far more lived in than the one downstairs. Elia's things were all over the countertop and in the shower. This was what had been missing before, and Kamryn hadn't even put two and two together until now.

Elia turned on the water and stepped under the spray instantly. Kamryn bit her lip. She really needed that cup of coffee to wake her brain up. Finally giving in, she followed Elia into the shower and stood awkwardly in the part with no spray. Her nipples instantly hardened in the cold as Elia dipped her head under the water.

But she wouldn't give this up for anything.

Elia was so relaxed. For the first time since they'd met, and Kamryn could see that now, Elia wasn't hiding anything from her. On impulse, Kamryn stepped in, wrapping a hand around Elia's back and pulling her in close. Their lips touched. The hot spray mingled with the warmth of their skin, their tongues sliding together as Kamryn and Elia both deepened the kiss.

Pulling away slightly, Kamryn pressed her forehead to Elia's shoulder. "I'm so sorry about last night."

Elia ran her hands up and down Kamryn's back. "What happened yesterday?"

"I should ask you that same thing." Kamryn couldn't stop

the smile from reaching her lips. The Elia from last night was the opposite of the Elia the other week in the hotel room, when she'd said no to a kiss. Last night had been...wild. Kamryn dragged in a slow, deep breath, steadying herself for what she knew needed to come. She had to explain, but she still wasn't sure how much to say. She didn't want to hurt Elia in the process.

Stepping away, Kamryn gathered herself. They really needed to talk and not be naked in the shower together for this. But time was short before they'd both have to go into the office, and Kamryn still had to go back to her apartment and change for the day. She ground her molars lightly.

"I'm still in the process of forming a new ethics team. It's one of the tasks that the board gave me when they hired me. Apparently, Miller was never interested in having an ethics team."

Elia visibly stiffened. Her eyes widened and were set on Kamryn's face, her lips slightly parted for a brief second before she snagged her shampoo and turned her back to Kamryn. She was upset by something that Kamryn had said, which was exactly what Kamryn had wanted to avoid.

"Miller was very good at parent-student relations. He wasn't very good at some of the finer points of administration and dealing with the board."

Kamryn hummed, the cold settling into her body now more than before. Her skin raised up with goosebumps, but she couldn't drag her gaze away from Elia's back.

"An ethics team is a good thing to have," Elia added.

"I wish you would be on it," Kamryn mumbled. "Then at least I'd have one ally in this fight."

Elia looked over her shoulder and shook her head. "You know I won't do that."

"I know," Kamryn answered sadly. "Doesn't mean I don't wish it was possible."

"And after last night, I think that's one more reason why you should think it'd be a very bad idea for me to be on the team, especially with you in charge of it." Elia ran her fingers through her hair, massaging the shampoo into the long strands.

Kamryn watched with rapt attention. Elia hadn't meant anything by that comment, had she? She hadn't just jumped Kamryn's bones to avoid being on that particular team? No, that would be too calculated and manipulative. Kamryn couldn't believe that Elia had that in her.

She refused to believe it.

"Yeah, anyway, the only people on this team right now are me, Susy, and Heather from the board. No one else has agreed to be on it. But instead of working to round out the team as a whole with differing opinions, Susy and Heather have kind of just taken on the work and are pushing it through." Kamryn paused, pressing her lips together hard. "At least what they think the work should be."

"You don't think they're doing the right thing?" Elia asked before dipping her head under the water to rinse out the shampoo. The suds traveled over her shoulders, down her breasts, and continued to move across her skin and down her body until it reached the shower floor and disappeared into the drain.

It was damn hard not to step forward and start touching. Kamryn wanted nothing more than to wrap herself back up in Elia's arms like she had the night before. It would be so much easier than this conversation.

"Why don't they like you?"

"I'm not very likable," Elia answered as she snagged the conditioner bottle.

Kamryn pursed her lips again and shook her head. She was freezing in the corner, but she wasn't going to ask to step under the water. Not until she had this out in the open between them. "This is more than a simple dislike, Elia. They're out to get you fired."

Elia wrinkled her nose and nodded. "They both have been for years now. The problem is that they can't find anything I've done wrong that is worth a termination."

"Why do they want you out of here so bad?" Kamryn wanted to reach out and touch Elia's hand, hold her again, have that physical connection so they could have more of an emotional one at the same time.

Elia shook her head, gave Kamryn a warning look, and then stepped back under the spray to rinse out the conditioner. This was definitely something that Elia still didn't want to talk about, but something must have happened that she hadn't disclosed yet for Susy and Heather to be harping on her specifically so much.

"I can't protect you from what I don't know." Kamryn was pretty sure she'd said that the night before in the heat of everything, but she couldn't quite remember. Either way, she wanted it to be said again, out loud and when she meant it the most.

"What'd you say?" Elia asked, coming back out from the water.

Kamryn could have face-palmed herself right then. Of course Elia hadn't heard her. "I can't protect you from what I don't know."

Elia softened immediately, and they were back to that same look that Elia had given her the night before. "I know you can't. And even then, you can't protect me from everything anyway. It's not in your best interest to do that."

"How is it not? I'm the Head of School. It's in my interest to protect all members of the staff and faculty."

"Not always," Elia replied, taking Kamryn by the shoulders and shifting them awkwardly around each other so that Kamryn was now under the water. "Sometimes hard decisions have to be made."

"I know that." Kamryn wrinkled her nose. "But you're not someone who is doing anything inappropriate with anyone."

"And what would you call last night?" Elia's tone was still light, teasing almost, but there was an undercurrent of sincerity that Kamryn didn't like.

"Consensual," Kamryn replied. "Besides, it'll fall more on me than you."

"You were my student. You think that there won't be questions about impropriety then?"

Is that what all of this was about? Kamryn dipped her head fully under the water to get it wet and then stepped out to look Elia dead in the eye. "Nothing happened twenty years ago."

"I know that, and you know that. But rumors can and will ruin lives." Elia said nothing else as she stepped out of the shower and snagged a towel and wrapped it around her middle. "I'll start some coffee and breakfast while you finish up."

Before she knew it, Kamryn was alone in the shower. The cold hadn't left her body, despite the hot water covering her skin. Something in the way Elia seemed to have just given up didn't settle right with her.

Finishing her shower quickly, Kamryn wrapped herself in a towel and followed the sounds of Elia's movements back into her bedroom. "I was upset last night because I couldn't stop them from trying to take you down."

"You won't be able to." Elia looked up as she pulled a white oxford shirt on and started doing the buttons. "And it's not your responsibility to, either. But I do appreciate the sentiment."

"Is that..." How was Kamryn going to ask this without sounding pathetic? She'd just have to come right out and say it. "Is that what last night was about?"

Elia paused, her movements stilling. "Kam..."

"I need to know if this was just a thank you, or a whim or...I don't know, something." Kamryn's nerves were at the edge, and she just needed someone to tell her that everything was going to be all right. "Because you told me no the other week, and then last night... that was definitely not a no."

"It was a yes," Elia agreed, walking right up to Kamryn and cupping her cheeks. "Last night was a yes, absolutely." Elia pressed their mouths together quickly. "And if you were to ask again today, it would also be a yes."

Kamryn sighed, relief flooding through her. She hadn't realized just how much she'd needed to hear those words, to have confirmation that what happened wasn't just a fluke but was something so much more—to both of them.

Elia kissed her again, this time lingering in the contact. "Last night showed me that I can trust you."

Kamryn melted, and all the tensions that had risen since she'd woken up vanished. "Elia."

"I *will* trust you," Elia whispered. This time when their lips touched, Elia became Kamryn's entire world. Her scent, her touch, her taste, the intake of her breaths and the exhalations on sweet, satisfied sighs. "I promise I'll trust you."

eighteen

"You look..." Abagail studied Elia carefully, her cup just at her lips, but she didn't take a sip of the steaming coffee. "...I'm not even sure how to describe it."

Elia's cheeks burned. She hadn't thought that breakfast with Abagail would turn into this. She'd intended to come and talk about Abagail's trip, but not much else. She hadn't thought that she would end up as the subject matter, and certainly not so close to the beginning of their meal. "I had a good week, that's all."

"Hmm... you lie, but I'll let it slide for right now."

Elia winced. "How was Italy?"

"Wonderful. Excellent."

"And your traveling companion?" Elia hated asking that question. It felt so odd in some ways, but she did always want to make sure that Abagail got what she needed out of the trips she took, including on the emotional and sexual front. Details she definitely didn't need, and thankfully, Abagail didn't typically share those, but she would usually talk about whoever went with her.

"Katelyn was stunning, as always." Abagail finally took a sip of the coffee she'd been holding and smiled in Elia's direction. "You really should try it some time. The no strings attached. You might actually end up liking it—and maybe yourself—better."

Elia's cheeks burned. Abagail certainly couldn't know, could she?

The pause was filled with tension, and surely Abagail would pick up on that.

Elia had to say something to distract them, to change the topic, to move it back to Abagail's exploits rather than her own. "Would you go back? With Katelyn?"

"No." Abagail set her mug down and started to dive into her eggs benedict. "Katelyn was fun for a few weeks, but I don't think I'll invite her on another trip. Don't think that your distraction went unnoticed. What was that look all about?"

Cursing under her breath, Elia picked up her fork and stabbed some of the home fries on her plate. "I've gotten closer with Kamryn while you were gone."

"While I was gone?" Abagail raised an eyebrow in Elia's direction. "I was only gone two weeks."

"Well, before then...and after." Elia tried her best not to mumble the last few words, but she definitely failed on that front. She wasn't going to get out of talking about this, so she might as well just embrace the fact that Abagail was her best friend and she'd find out eventually. There was no reason to keep anything a secret from her. Besides, Abagail could provide good advice. "We...had a night."

"Elia! You dog! Are you serious?" The interest in Abagail's face was intoxicating.

Elia was so used to trying to hide every part of her relationships from the world that it was a struggle to be more open about it. "Yes, it's been amazing, honestly. Something about Kam is so different from anyone else I've been with."

"Do you perhaps trust her?" Abagail raised an eyebrow at Elia.

"Maybe." Elia still wasn't sure how deep that trust ran, but they were working on building it up, weren't they? "Trust isn't built in one night."

"Neither was Rome." Abagail winked. "But I think this is a good thing for you. Even if she is your boss."

Elia's stomach twisted at that thought. "Yeah, that's a complication that I hadn't thought through."

"You need to." Abagail shoved the fork between her lips, a small dash of the hollandaise sauce lingering on her lip before she licked it up. "It could be disastrous for both of you, and because of what happened—"

"We don't need to talk about that," Elia interrupted. It was the last thing she wanted to talk about, especially when she was feeling so good lately. She didn't want to think about it either, even if it was a huge part of the reason why she'd finally made the move with Kamryn. The silence at the table was stilted, and Elia knew she'd hit some sort of sore point with Abagail.

Abagail cocked her head and pursed her lips, holding her fork and knife like she was going to attack Elia next instead of her food. "We have to talk about it."

"No, we don't." Elia dove into her own breakfast, needing the physical distraction now since the verbal one wasn't going to work.

"Fine, we don't have to talk specifics, but what you went through last time was in part because you didn't disclose who you were with. And you don't want to be running headlong into that same mistake twice, do you?"

"It wasn't like Kam and I were planning on being in a relationship."

"Are you?" Abagail gave her a very pointed look, but it wasn't filled with the excitement and joy that Elia had hoped her best friend would have for her. Surely Abagail should be excited for her to actually be in a relationship with someone instead of pining away over something she thought she'd never have again. "Are you in a relationship, Elia?"

"I… I don't know. We haven't really discussed…"

"Elia." Abagail set her silverware down and put her full attention on Elia. "You and Kam need to have a serious discussion about what it is you're wanting from each other. And you really need to tell the board what's going on. You can't keep this hidden like last time, especially because Kam is your immediate supervisor."

"It's not like that. She wouldn't..."

"She might not," Abigail interrupted. "But it wasn't Yara either, remember?"

The scolding had the desired effect. The elation that Elia had felt from the start of her relationship with Kamryn dissipated quickly.

"Kam was your former student, right?"

"Yes," Elia whispered, already knowing exactly where this conversation was going, and she really, really didn't want it to go there. She'd made that clear as day already, and yet she knew without a doubt that Abagail was going to take it that direction. "But nothing happened back then."

"I trust your word on that, but I also know you." Abagail picked her knife and fork back up and cut rather harshly into her food. She wasn't saying it. Elia knew that. But it did need to be said. More than that, Elia needed to take to heart the accusations that were likely to fly.

"But you think someone else will accuse me of that."

"Would you? If you weren't at the center of this situation, wouldn't you have questions?"

Abagail was right. Elia hated it, but she was. And once it came out that she and Kamryn were in some sort of relationship, even if it just remained sexual and just one night, it was going to be brought up that she was sleeping with a student of hers—even if it was twenty years later. There would be questions. There would be accusations. There would be pain and heartache, and fuck, she really didn't want to think about or talk about this.

She just wanted to live into the happiness for a little longer, maybe even get her feet under her if this was going to develop into something more. Because if Elia allowed herself to dream and have hope, which she had the last few days, she could actually see a future for them.

Or at least she wanted to see if that was a possibility.

Something about Kamryn grabbed hold of her and held on tightly. Something that Elia loved feeling again.

"What do you suggest?" Elia asked, taking another bite of her home fries, but not tasting them this time. "Since HR is your area of expertise."

That had been invaluable the first time Elia had gone through some of this drama. She'd leaned so heavily on Abagail during that time, and she'd never forget what her friend had done for her, the advice she'd ignored then that had landed her in the situation that she'd found herself in. Although Elia wasn't convinced that informing the board of her relationship with a student's parent really would have prevented the repercussions of their break up.

Nothing could have prepared her for that.

"I'm so glad you asked." Abagail seemed delighted again, and as much as Elia wanted to share in that enjoyment, she just couldn't bring herself to. "Because of what happened the last time..." Abagail wasn't actually saying the details out loud, and Elia was so grateful for it. "...you and Kam need to sit down and have a discussion about what you want from each other, and then you need to inform the board about the conflict of interest that you've now created."

Elia clenched her jaw tightly, the muscles in her cheeks hurting from how hard she did it. She hadn't done that in a long time, now that she thought about it, and the muscles weren't used to the pressure. So much for kicking that bad habit.

"And what do I do when *other* questions arise?" Elia again skittered around the topic. She wasn't ready to open that can of worms, to experience that hurt and pain again. It would be too hard, and she wasn't ready for it. She wasn't sure she'd ever be ready for it.

"You phone a friend and have a lawyer on retainer."

Elia dropped her fork with a loud clatter. "You think it'll be that bad?"

"I always plan and prepare for the worst, Elia, you know that. And I won't lie to you, this could get ugly, and it could easily cost you both of your jobs. And if you don't tell Kam what happened eighteen years ago, she's going to be blindsided by everything. You *have* to warn her."

Elia shook her head sharply. She definitely wasn't ready for that. "It'll change everything if I tell her that."

"It's part of who you are, and it's part of your job at this point. She needs to know." Abagail continued eating, but she kept her eyes on Elia the entire time. The silent message was clear.

This was non-optional.

This was do or die.

This would be her greatest downfall.

"There's no other option?" Elia asked, needing to be entirely sure that she was going to be stuck in this. That there was no way out without the entire school finding out about what had happened eighteen years ago. Not again. She'd barely survived it the first time. She wouldn't survive a second round of it.

"Quit. Retire. Leave Windermere. And end your relationship with Kam immediately. That's the only other option, and even then, I can't guarantee that it won't get out and come back to bite you in your pretty little ass."

None of that settled well with Elia. She'd been impulsive with Kamryn, that was for certain. And now they might very well be in over their heads. "And if I don't want to do any of that?"

"You really like this girl, don't you?" Abagail took another large bite of her food.

"I do," Elia admitted quietly. Why did that feel so dangerous to suggest? "We haven't talked much since... since that night, but I have a date with her in a few days, and we can talk then." Elia finally settled into that knowledge. She hated admitting things before she was ready, and Abagail was really good at making her do that. "I mean, we will talk then. We need to."

"That sounds more like the Elia I know."

"Really?" Elia frowned at her plate. None of this sounded like her at all.

"No!" Abagail laughed. "You in a relationship? One that you're this excited about? Doesn't sound like you. You've dated since Yara, yes, but no one has seemed to turn your head like this Kam. I'll have to meet her soon."

"Maybe." Elia wasn't sure she was ready for that, or that Kamryn was. Putting the two of them in a room would likely end in some sort of pissing match. Elia had never told Abagail this, but when she and Yara broke up, it had been mutual, but a lot of it had been because of Abagail. She and Elia were *too intimate with each other* according to Yara, and it had continued to put a wedge between them. And Elia hadn't been willing to give up the strongest friendship she had.

And she'd left Abagail out of that entirely.

Although she had put more distance between them after, wanting to be able to find love again at some point. Though over the years, she'd given up on that hope. Or at least, she thought she had. Still, whatever was between her and Kamryn felt good, and she wanted to continue exploring it.

"Yeah, let's do it when I come down for Thanksgiving."

"Hmm." Elia hadn't thought about that. She'd already forgotten to call her mother and let her know that Abagail would be coming that year. In fact, it had been way too long since she'd talked to her mother. She'd have to add that to her list of things to do for the week. "I'll have to talk to Kam and see what she has planned. We haven't exactly shared our schedules with each other yet."

"No, just swapping spit."

Elia rolled her eyes. Abagail could be so crass sometimes. Settled into the fact that a conversation desperately needed to happen—and sooner rather than later—Elia finished her meal in peace, still with the small fluttering of hope inside her chest.

Maybe this was a good thing after all.

nineteen

"Greer!" Kamryn flopped onto the couch in her living room after another insanely long day. She had the phone pressed to her ear and she sighed in absolute relief when she heard Greer pick up. "I miss you."

"I miss you, too!" Greer said on a laugh. "It's been way too long."

"Way too long," Kamryn agreed. They were so used to seeing each other frequently, but with the added distance between them, it was far too difficult to meet up regularly anymore. "What's new in your world?"

"Oh you know, same old, same old. Poopy diapers, screaming kids, lots of laughs and joy."

That was what Kamryn had been missing from her life—Greer's insane sunshine, bubbly joy that she never seemed to be without. Even when she was being laid off, Greer was happy about everything. Kamryn sank into that feeling, needing it more and more in her life now than before. The world of the school was bogging her down and dragging her under, and she wasn't going to be able to survive it without Greer in her life.

"You're my best friend, you know that?"

"Uh-oh," Greer answered, concern edging its way in. "Why are *you* getting all sappy now? You never do that unless..." Greer stopped. "Did Lauren call you? Are you two—"

"God no! Why would she call me?" Kamryn frowned, her nose wrinkling. She hadn't even thought of Lauren in the last two weeks. Since when had that happened?

Elia.

Her name swam through Kamryn's memory, the soft touches, easy kisses—fiery kisses more like. Kamryn smiled at that. They hadn't started off slowly, had they?

"Earth to Kamryn!"

"W-what?" Kamryn winced. "Sorry, what did you ask?"

"Lau-ren. Did she call you?" Greer sounded even more concerned now. Kamryn was going to have to rectify that. She didn't need Greer worrying about her when she had her own problems to deal with.

"No. Was she supposed to?"

"I thought she might."

There was definitely more in that statement than Greer was letting on. And Kamryn now wanted to know everything. She glanced at the clock on the wall. She had the time to dig for this. "Did she say she was going to?"

"She mentioned she might."

"About the wedding?" So it was twenty questions. Got it. Kamryn could play this game and win.

"No, it wasn't about the wedding." Greer's voice dropped.

She definitely was trying to not talk about this.

"Rosie? Did she break up with Rosie?"

"Uh. You know, she didn't say."

"Greer." Kamryn narrowed her gaze, annoyance peeking its way into her. She had to get whatever answer she needed now. She was tiring of this game quickly. "Lauren called you?"

"Yeah? I mean, yeah, she did. We still have regular calls, and she's trying to get me a job."

"A job?" A deep line formed in the center of Kamryn's forehead. "Are you that worried about work that you're asking her for help?"

"She said she might know someone," Greer said sheepishly. "And my layoff date is coming up faster than I expected it to."

"What do you mean?"

Greer let out a loud sigh. "They moved it up to the middle of November."

"Oh, Greer." Kamryn's heart broke. She hated this for her. It was part of the job, she understood that, but it still sucked. Greer deserved so much better than that.

"They said that the long goodbye was making it worse on the boys, and so they didn't want to let it linger."

"Jesus." Kamryn ran her fingers through her hair, shaking her head. "What a douche move."

"Yeah, it is a bit." Greer gave a light chuckle for that one. "But that means I don't have a lot of time to find a new family."

"No, you don't." Kamryn's heart broke a little more. "What will you do if you can't find anyone?"

"I don't know. I've always wanted to be a nanny, you know that. And if I can't find another job, or if most families think I'm getting too old for this—I don't know, Kam. Maybe I'll have to go back to school for my Master's or something."

"In what?"

"Something so I can teach?" Greer sounded so lost. Kamryn wished she could be there with her. "But enough about me, what about you?"

"You mean what about Lauren." Kamryn pushed. She still wanted that answer. "Why did she say she was going to call me?"

"She was... jealous. There."

"Jealous?" Kamryn's stomach flopped. "Of what?"

"Your *new* girlfriend. Have I mentioned I don't like lying to her? Or anyone for that matter."

"I..." Kamryn stopped. "She's really that jealous?"

"She is. Because you're happy, and she's clearly not happy with Rosie despite the fact that she won't admit it. I'm pretty sure she's stepping out on that one, and I don't blame her. I don't like Rosie one bit."

"No one does," Kamryn said offhandedly. "And she thinks I'm happy?"

"That's what she said. That at the bridal shower you and Elia were all lovey-dovey and holding hands, and you must really be happy. She said she couldn't remember the last time she'd seen you so happy."

"Huh." Kamryn mulled that one over. She'd never felt happier—at least from what she could remember. It had been a very long time since she'd felt relaxed and content. And despite the fact that work was a bitch and she hated being stuck working there for so long, she was happy with her life right now. Satisfied, even. "I guess I am."

"Really?" That seemed to surprise Greer, and Kamryn could imagine why. The only time they talked lately was when Kamryn needed someone to complain to and Greer was the best listening ear that she had. And she was damn good at it. And it was telling that she was the only one doing the talking because Greer hadn't told her about the moving up of her lay-off date.

"I've been a shitty friend." Guilt ate away at her stomach. "I should have done better."

"Kam, you've been busy."

"Yeah, but you needed me, and I wasn't there, and then I used you to whine too when I should have been listening to you."

"Kam..." Greer laughed lightly. "If I needed to complain to you, then I would have called you to complain. But I didn't need it. I'm sad, yes, but I'm not angry or upset about it."

"All right." That satisfied Kamryn slightly. At least it made her feel a little better. Still, she was going to do better in the future. She had to—for their friendship. "Then to answer your question, I am happy. And to answer your non-asked question, you might not really be lying when you tell Lauren that I'm dating Elia."

"What?!" Greer squeaked. "Are you serious?"

"I don't know." Kamryn grinned widely, a bubble of elation building in her chest. "But yes. We had... well, we've had several moments, and I don't know, we had one really big moment."

"You had sex."

"...Yes..." Kamryn dropped her head into the couch cushion. "Yes, we did that, once, and it was amazing, and the next morning was even better in some ways."

"How so?"

"Because it wasn't just sex, and it wasn't until the next morning that I think I really realized that. I thought... well, Elia's not exactly the easiest person to read, and she's very closed off and secretive about some things in her past, which is fine, she doesn't have to spill her guts to me in one session of lovemaking—"

"Lovemaking?" Greer devolved into a fit of giggles. "You didn't just call it that!"

"Well, *fucking* didn't sound right either in my head. I don't know what to call it. Getting sideways in the sheets? Except it didn't start in the bed. Hmm..."

"TMI!" Greer was still laughing, her voice trilling through the phone in a wonderful chorus. Oh, how Kamryn missed that sound. She definitely needed to make more time for her life and for her friends.

"Right, so I don't expect her to open up immediately, but the next morning, she really did do just that. Not with answers to the millions of questions that I have, but with the emotional side of things. I'm not even sure if I'm making sense right now. I feel all tangled up."

"You're making sense. I promise." Greer's tone softened. "You're smitten."

"Now who's using weird-ass words."

"I couldn't think of another one to describe it," Greer echoed Kamryn's thoughts. "And that's exactly what you sound like. Currently wrapped up in a new potential relationship and totally lost to the outside world. That's how it's supposed to happen, isn't it?"

"I suppose it is..." Kamryn trailed off. She'd been that way with Lauren once, many, many years ago, when they were so very young. And it hadn't ever come back, not even when they'd started dating again after a breakup. There was always that distance between them.

"You don't know?" Greer laughed a little again, that sunshine personality coming through. "But you and Lauren—"

"Weren't happy together for a very long time. I don't know if that's how it's supposed to be." Why did that hit her hard? She and Lauren had been in love, hadn't they? They'd spent so many years trying to make their relationship work, and yet it had still failed. Had they just not put in the effort or had the love been missing all along? "I'm sorry Lauren is feeling jealous because she thinks I'm happy. Was she going to call to wish me well or try to win me back?"

Greer's silence spoke volumes.

"Right." Kamryn nodded to no one but herself. "She wanted to try and get back in my good graces, see if maybe there was a chance now that I'm doing well."

"Something like that," Greer mumbled. "So I'm glad she didn't call you."

"Yeah. Will she be at the bachelorette party?"

"She will," Greer responded, her voice rising and lowering in just those two words. "And Rosie will."

"Great." Kamryn frowned. "Andra better appreciate me spending so much time with my ex for her."

Greer clicked her tongue. "She understands how hard this is for you."

"Good." Kamryn caught sight of the clock and nearly gasped. "Shit. I've got to get ready."

"Ready? Ready for what? It's like eight o'clock."

"Yeah. I've got a hot date." Kamryn stood up and rushed into her bedroom. She should have figured out what she was going to wear well before now, because now she was in an all-out panic over it. "What should I wear?"

"Where are you going?"

"No clue. Elia picked the place." Kamryn opened her closet and stared at her options. Everything was school-centered and not date-centered. She'd left so much of her stuff packed away in boxes because she knew she wasn't going to be here long, and now she seriously regretted that decision. She needed hot-date clothes, not prim-and-proper Head of School clothes.

"Is it a fancy place? Laid back?"

"I should have asked that, right?"

"Probably." Greer was laughing again, definitely at Kamryn's own expense this time. "When's your date?"

"We're leaving in twenty minutes."

"Oh, big date time. Does this mean you two are officially a thing?"

"I don't know," Kamryn added a whine to her tone. "I was hoping to talk about that tonight. And maybe... do other things."

"Like *make love?*"

"I knew that would come back to bite me in the ass, but yes, I'd like to get laid again." Kamryn laughed as she pulled out an outfit that she'd saved for special board meetings and interviews. This should do, shouldn't it? It was semi-revealing but still fairly conservative. She could get away with this at a super fancy restaurant or a more laid-back one. Probably not the fast-food joint down the road, though. Then again—they never really had too much judgment, did they?

"Kam!"

"Shit, sorry. What'd I miss again?"

"Wow are you distracted lately."

"I know. It's bad. I've got it bad."

"Yeah, you do." Kamryn could hear the smile in Greer's voice. "You get dressed. Call me tomorrow with all the details and tell me if I can stop lying to all our friends or not."

"Will do. Love you!"

"Love you, too. Go get 'em, tiger!"

Kamryn laughed as she hung up, really needing to pull herself together quickly. Luckily, she was fairly low-maintenance, unlike Elia, so she was changed and out the door in fifteen minutes and walking toward Elia's house.

Knocking on the door was so reminiscent of the other night, when she was filled with anger and frustration, when they'd definitely fucked on the kitchen counter. Kamryn's lips curled up at that memory. She wasn't ever going to tell anyone that. That was for her and Elia only. When Elia opened the door, Kamryn's breath caught.

She was stunning.

Her jacket was loose around her shoulders still, not buttoned up all the way, and it revealed a beautiful red dress underneath, smooth fabric that Kamryn could definitely imagine running her fingers up and over time and time again, if just to get in one more touch.

"Come inside a second," Elia said, her voice husky and deep.

Kamryn wasn't even sure what controlled her, but she walked inside and shut the door behind her.

"Much better," Elia said, grinning. "Can I?"

"Can you what?" Kamryn frowned in confusion.

"Kiss you," Elia answered, the most beautiful smile gracing her lips. She was chock full of confidence, with an added dose of sassy. "I didn't want to do it without asking."

"Fuck yes." Kamryn stepped in closer, immediately wrapping her hand around the back of Elia's neck and pressing their mouths together. Elia melted into her. She closed her eyes, doing everything by feel, overwhelming herself with the scents and touches and warmth of the moment.

Moaning, Kamryn nipped at Elia's lower lip before diving back in for more. All the tension from the day vanished into thin air, and she relaxed instantly in Elia's arms. She craved this, more than she'd known. Someone who could just hold her and manage to relax her. Someone who was there when she needed her to be.

"Kam," Elia whispered against her lips. "If we don't leave now, we're going to be late for our reservation."

"All right," Kamryn murmured back. "Just one more for the road."

twenty

"Kam," Elia tried again. "As much as I'd love to go upstairs with you, I really do think that we need to talk before we do that again."

"You're right." Kamryn kissed again quickly. "Dinner."

Kamryn took a purposeful step away, and Elia was so grateful for that. Her entire body was heated and raring to go, and not to dinner. She wanted to drag Kamryn upstairs and stay up there for the rest of the night. It was taking all her willpower to stay right where she was.

Buttoning her jacket purposely, Elia set her shoulders and straightened her back. They *really* needed to talk. Especially after her conversation with Abagail earlier that week. She couldn't avoid this one any longer. None of them could.

Kamryn held her arm out, expecting Elia to slide her arm into the nook of her elbow and walk together. Elia flicked her gaze down to Kamryn's arm and then back up to her face. She shook her head slowly. "As much as I would like to, I think it's probably a better decision not to at this point in time."

"Oh." Kamryn frowned, a dark cloud coming over her in an instant.

"It's part of what I want to talk to you about. I hope you understand."

"I do."

But Elia wasn't sure that Kamryn did. She hadn't been through the experiences that Elia had, and she wouldn't be as cautious. She should be, but she was far more innocent in this part of their relationship—if they even had one at the end of the night. God, Elia hoped they would.

"Come on," Elia said, snagging her purse and slinging it over her arm. "Let's go."

"Okay." Kamryn still had that cloud over her, and Elia really wished she didn't.

Elia had her hand on the doorknob and was about ready to turn it when she stopped. Making Kamryn wait for this was just going to torture them both. There was no reason they couldn't have the conversation now, and here, and then it'd probably be safer anyway. No one might potentially overhear them.

"If we're going to be in a relationship together, then we need to tell the board," Elia blurted out.

Kamryn stood frozen on the spot, her eyes wide, her face drawn. "Relationship?"

"Yes. Well, I think we should probably tell them what happened the other night too, kind of. Because it's a conflict of interest, and I don't want either of us to end up in trouble because of it." Elia dropped her hand off the doorknob. "So if we just tell them, then everything is out in the open, and we don't have to worry about it."

"Wait." Kamryn waved her hands in front of her. "Slow down. We're not even dating, Elia. Why would we tell—"

"Because it's the ethical thing to do."

"Now you want to talk about ethics?" Kamryn's eyebrows raised so high up that they very nearly disappeared into her hairline. "But you're not the ethical one, right?"

"I..." Elia stopped talking. She was walking into a trap, that was for sure.

Kamryn blew out a breath and stepped away again, shucking her jacket and tossing it over the back of the couch. "Let's talk about this, Elia, because that was my goal for tonight too. I'm glad we're on the same page with that. I want more from this."

"From what?" Elia's stomach twisted hard into knots.

"From whatever is between you and me, and yes, that will involve talking to the school board about our relationship, but I want a little bit more definition before I walk into that firing squad."

Elia cringed at that metaphor. If only Kamryn knew just how bad it could be. She wouldn't want to come near Elia any time soon. "We could both lose our jobs if they want us to."

"We could, but considering they're already short-staffed, considering Miller—well Maria—finally told the board this week that he won't be returning, and considering that you're my former teacher, the power dynamics and authority issues aren't as complicated as they might be."

But they were.

And Kamryn was so wrong to think that they weren't going to be an issue. "They'll wonder about us, you know."

"About us?" Kamryn furrowed her brow, leaning over the back of the couch, her fingers clenching tightly.

Elia needed to explain better, and she knew she was doing a bad job at it. She hadn't thought they'd talk here. She hadn't figured out a way that this conversation was going to go, and it was throwing her for a loop. She dropped her purse onto the floor next to the door and took off her own jacket. If they were really going to sit down and do this, then they needed the time to do it.

"About whether or not we were in a relationship when you were a student here."

"Why would they wonder about that?" Kamryn pulled a face —one that was akin to disgust and also horror. "Nothing happened then."

"No, nothing happened then. But they will question it."

"Then I'll tell them nothing happened then."

"It's not that simple, Kam." Elia sat down on the couch and crossed one leg over the other. "It's the board's job to protect the interests of Windermere, and if neither one of us is seen as doing that, the repercussions are going to be strong."

"Elia..." Kamryn slid onto the couch next to her, taking Elia's hands in her own. "It'll be fine. We just need to disclose to them because I'm your boss, and I can't be doing certain things while in this position. But when I'm gone—and remember, this job is just temporary—it'll be fine."

Elia wanted to believe that. She really, really did. But her gut told her that it wouldn't be, that everything she feared was going to come up would blow up, in a massive way, and the only ones that were going to be hurt were her and now Kamryn.

Could they hide everything until the end of the semester?

"But if Miller's officially not returning, won't the board ask you to stay on?" Elia wanted to hope that the answer was yes as much as she wanted to hope it was no. To spend more time with Kamryn, to continue to work with her in the capacity that they had been would be amazing. She enjoyed so much of their time together. But if Kamryn left, then they could be together without the hindrance of creating ethical issues at the same time.

"I don't know," Kamryn replied, shrugging a little. "And I'm not sure I'd tell them yes at this point either."

"You wouldn't?" Elia leaned into the hope that flared up. "Why not? I thought you enjoyed being here again."

"I am," Kamryn answered, staring down at her hands in her lap. "I really am enjoying my job and being back at Windermere. But I'm also really struggling with the board right now. I don't know if they would ask me to stay on or if I've even ruined my chances at potentially having another position here."

"Kam..." Elia touched Kamryn's knee. "Boards can be brutal and unrelenting sometimes."

"I have a feeling you're someone who would deeply understand that."

"I am," Elia admitted. She bit her lip, her mind working

quickly on what to say and do next. "Let's tell the board. Maybe not today, but soon."

"When?"

"When we think the time is right, and when we know exactly what we're going to tell them." Elia squeezed Kamryn's knee and then went to pull away, but Kamryn snagged her hands and pulled her back quickly, lacing their fingers. "Kam..."

"And what about us in the meantime?"

"Meantime?" Elia asked.

"I like you, Elia." Kamryn smiled then, and it lit up her entire face. Elia loved seeing it, the honesty behind it all. Kamryn lifted Elia's fingers to her mouth, kissing the backs of her knuckles lightly. "I really like you."

"Kam." But Elia didn't know what else to say. She was at a complete loss for words. She watched with rapt attention as Kamryn turned her hand and kissed the inside of her wrist. Shivers ran straight up Elia's arm and into her chest. "I wouldn't have suggested talking to the board if I wanted to end this."

"Wouldn't you have?" Kamryn kissed a little higher. "Because I do believe you said that we should tell them about the other night regardless of where we went from here."

She had said that, hadn't she? Elia's mind was blurring with the touches, and it was becoming harder and harder to focus as Kamryn worked her way up Elia's arm to her neck.

"What do you want? And be honest with me." Kamryn stopped. She pulled away, leaving a rush of cold over Elia's skin from her missing warmth. "Because I want to know."

Here she was again, at yet another crossroads. She had to say something, and she wasn't willing to mess this up. Elia raised her gaze, meeting Kamryn's brown eyes, the steadiness of her look, the confidence in it.

Fuck.

Hiking up the edge of her dress, Elia took the biggest risk she'd taken in years. She moved swiftly, straddling Kamryn as she sat on the couch, her back now pressed into the cushion behind her. Elia stared down at her, dropping her dress and curling her hair behind her ear. Saying nothing, Elia bent down and touched her lips to Kamryn's.

It wasn't enough.

She lowered her hips down, feeling Kamryn's hands against her waist, holding onto her. She pushed in, parting her lips and kissing Kamryn again. And again. And again. Elia slid her tongue out, tracing the edge of Kamryn's mouth and delighting in the moment when Kamryn echoed her movement.

Sucking in sharply, Elia pushed her body against Kamryn's—breast to breast, center to thighs. She had her fingers deep in Kamryn's hair, tugging and pulling tight as she lost herself in this one moment. She shut out the world around them, the naysayers, the worries, the anxiety that all of this would be taken the wrong way, and she focused solely on how she was feeling in this moment.

Nipping at Kamryn's lip, Elia pulled back and eyed her confidently.

"I want you."

"Fuck," Kamryn murmured, her heart thumping hard under Elia's fingertips on her chest, her thighs taut with tension. "Fuck," Kamryn repeated. "Yes."

"I want more than one night," Elia said, making sure that Kamryn understood exactly what she was saying.

"Me too."

"And I want more than just sex." Elia traced her finger along Kamryn's damp lips. "I want a relationship—or at least to explore one with you."

"Elia..." Kamryn eyes lit up, a smile blossoming on those kissable lips. "That's exactly what I want."

"Good." Elia slid back in, kissing Kamryn again. "But I don't think we're going out to dinner tonight."

"Next time," Kamryn muttered as she took Elia by the hips and flipped her onto the couch.

Elia settled, the weight of Kamryn's body resting between her legs as they kissed—deep and hard. She threaded her fingers into Kamryn's hair and tugged, scraping her nails along Kamryn's scalp. The resounding moan she received in response was music to her ears.

"Keep doing that and we're not going to make it to the bed again."

"Screw the bed," Elia answered, lifting her hips up in a little buck. She wanted this now, and she wasn't going to be apologetic about it, either. "Now. Here. I'm done waiting for good things in my life."

"I'm a good thing?" Kamryn said, the smile obvious in her tone as she moved to trail kisses down Elia's neck and over the top of her chest.

"Y-yes," Elia said, stuttering as Kamryn reached the tops of her breasts. "I didn't think so at first, but I was wrong."

"Not often Dr. Elia Sharpe admits she was wrong," Kamryn said into her skin, pulling the sleeve of Elia's dress down and revealing even more skin.

"Not often," Elia agreed. She wanted to touch and taste just as much as Kamryn was, but she couldn't find a way to do that in this position. The most she could do was touch Kamryn's head, tug on her hair, push Kamryn's mouth to exactly where she wanted—oh that was a good idea. Elia reached between them, sliding her dress higher up on her legs until she could reach the edge of her underwear.

She wasn't going to wait for this ever again. She'd waited so long for something amazing and wonderful to happen, something so unexpected like Kamryn Ogden walking in as the new Head of School. Elia slid her fingers against her body, finding her folds wet and swollen. She briefly touched her clit, biting back a groan at just how sensitive she was tonight.

"That's so hot," Kamryn whispered into Elia's ear, and then moved directly back down to her breasts.

Elia closed her eyes, feeling Kamryn's hair drag across her skin, the roughness of her clothes between Elia's thighs, the gentleness of her kisses. "I want you inside me."

"Fingers?"

"Yes," Elia said on a moan. "Fingers."

Elia parted her legs wider as Kamryn slid her hand up the inside of her thigh. She pulled Kamryn back up, kissing her again and again and again. Their lips melded in a sloppy wet kiss. Elia gasped when Kamryn finally slid two fingers inside her, when Kamryn's thumb gently coasted over her clit.

"Ahhh, yessssss," Elia hissed, her eyes fluttering shut and her back arching. "Just like that."

Kamryn hummed a response, starting a slow pattern, one that was no doubt going to torture Elia with a slow buildup of pleasure. But she wanted more, and she wanted it now. There was time for slow later, just like they'd done before.

"Don't tease," Elia said on a breath. She couldn't stop herself from wiggling and moving, needing more of every kind of touch that she could coax from Kamryn's fingers, all the pleasure she could possibly find in every simple touch and slide and glide. "Just...don't draw this out."

"What if I want to?" Kamryn's lips moved against Elia's neck as she spoke.

"Next time," Elia repeated Kamryn's words from earlier. "I've been wanting this all week."

"Have you?" Kamryn laughed lightly, sucking on Elia's skin and scraping her teeth. The subtle roughness was exactly what Elia had needed. She whined in the back of her throat, careening higher and higher toward her orgasm. "What exactly did you think about?"

Elia struggled to organize her thoughts. They went from *hard*, to *slower*, to *faster*, to *now*, to *shut up Kamryn*, to *keep laughing*, the sounds intoxicating. Then suddenly Kamryn stopped. Her fingers halted, her thumb moved away, and Elia's eyes widened as she glared at Kamryn.

"Why'd you stop?"

"Answer the question."

"What question?" Elia couldn't drag her gaze away from Kamryn, from the way the buttons shifted on her shirt to reveal creamy, smooth skin, the rise and fall of her breasts only adding to the tantalizing momentum they'd already found.

"What *exactly* did you think about this week?"

Elia whimpered. Did she really want to admit every fantasy she'd come up with? Absolutely not. Because she wasn't sure she could remember them all. "Next time we're in the hotel room, I'm going to kiss you."

Grabbing the back of Kamryn's head, Elia kissed her hard. Kamryn responded immediately. The heel of her palm pressed hard into Elia's clit, the pressure intensifying her pleasure immediately. Elia gasped, pushing her head back into the couch cushion.

"And then you're not leaving."

Kamryn laughed again. Elia was quickly becoming addicted to it. "I'm due for more walks of shame, that's for sure."

"We can always meet at your place."

Kamryn shook her head. "No, much more privacy here."

"Yesssss..." Elia hissed out the word as soon as Kamryn hit a particularly sensitive spot. Elia bit her lip and arched up again. She wanted so much more touch. She wanted every single moment the two of them could have together tonight. "Hold there."

Kamryn did as she was told.

Elia clenched down around her fingers, her entire body jerking sharply as she slid into the orgasm she'd been longing days for. She held Kamryn as close to her as possible, wrapping her arms around Kamryn's back and holding on tightly. Kamryn cradled her, pressing soft kisses into Elia's skin and hair.

"Elia..." Kamryn whispered.

"Hmm?"

"Not to be a pain, but do you think we can still make the reservation?" Kamryn kissed Elia's cheek and then along her jawline. "I promise that we'll come back tonight and do more of this, but I'm really hungry."

As if on cue, Kamryn's stomach growled. Elia's lips twitched upward into a smile. "We can call and see, but I'm going to need a few minutes to freshen up."

"Perfect," Kamryn bent down and kissed her again. "And I promise we'll pick up right where we left off when we get back."

"Don't make promises you can't keep."

"Never," Kamryn winked. She backed away from Elia and then helped her to sit up a bit.

Elia took a few extra breaths with her feet solidly on the ground before she managed to remember what she was supposed to be doing. Right, calling the restaurant. She stood up and rummaged through her purse to find her phone. When she turned back around, Kamryn was staring at her with a hungry look in her eyes—and it definitely wasn't for food this time.

"What?" Elia asked.

"You look damn good and fucked." Kamryn's smile turned bright and brilliant, gracing her entire face.

Elia couldn't stop the laugh that bubbled up inside of her as she headed toward the bathroom. She'd deal with Kamryn in a minute.

twenty-one

Kamryn pushed back in the chair, her toe digging into the floor of the conference room. The all-staff meeting was just about done, and she'd had to work damn hard at not staring at Elia throughout the entire meeting.

Unfortunately, Elia had chosen not to sit next to her but almost directly across from her. Giving Kamryn the perfect view of the prim and proper English teacher that she most definitely had a massive crush on right now. Kamryn couldn't stop the smile sliding over her lips from that thought.

Their dinner had been amazing.

And their night afterward had kept them both up into the wee hours of the morning before they'd crashed and crawled out of bed the next morning. The walk of shame had definitely been worth it. Kamryn couldn't have asked for a better night, or a better first date. It'd been a while since she'd been on a date, since the last time she and Lauren had broken up. But this one had definitely been worth it.

Elia thought so too.

At least, she'd shared as much during the morning shower, which was perhaps becoming a bit of a routine for them. Kamryn could live with that. It felt good to take the down time where they could be close but not sexually primed for whatever was coming next. It was simple and intimate.

"I think we'll have a really good send-off for the winter break if we keep this up," Kamryn added. They'd gone through just about everything that was coming up between now and then, and hell if she didn't admit that time was passing quickly. "I did want to officially let you know that Dr. Waddy will not be returning to Windermere. He won't be healthy enough to come back for at least a year while he's in recovery, and he and Maria decided that it was time for him to retire."

There was an audible gasp in the room. The faculty couldn't have honestly thought that he'd be returning, right? Kamryn had hoped that he would be when she'd started, but after seeing how long it took for him to leave the ICU and then for him to be discharged from the hospital to a rehabilitation facility—which had only just happened last week—surely they couldn't expect him to make a full recovery before then?

"I'm sure that Maria will be grateful for any help when she decides they'll be moving. I'll get more information about that when I can. But she's going to need all of the support that we can give her during this time. We're her family here, and we won't let Miller or Maria forget that."

"Will we have a sending-off party of sorts?" someone in the back of the room asked. Kamryn wasn't quite sure who it was, but she would figure that out later.

"We'll check with Maria and see what would be most useful for them. I don't want to overburden them at this critical time. But I also know that the closure for us would be helpful." Faculty nodded along in the room, agreeing with what Kamryn had said. "Right, so if that's everything, I'll see you all together in the same room in a couple of weeks for our next meeting."

Kamryn started to pack up her satchel just like everyone else in the room as they started to file out to get back to their regular routines. She glanced up to try and catch Elia before she walked out, but she didn't manage to make it in time. Frowning, Kamryn finished packing up her stuff, talked with a few of the other faculty members who had stayed for some more personal conversation and then headed back to her office.

What was she supposed to do now? Because she did actually need to talk to Elia about some things with the Speech team, including who was going to replace her as Elia's co-lead when Kamryn was no longer working at Windermere.

Kamryn quickly checked Elia's class schedule, noting that she didn't have any classes going on at the moment. That was pure dumb luck. Stepping toward her door, she glanced at Mrs. Caldera and nodded. "I'll be out for an hour."

"I'll hold your calls," Mrs. Caldera responded. "You really should think about putting together some sort of going-away gift for Maria and Miller. The faculty would appreciate it."

"Right." Kamryn slid her hands along her hips. "I'll figure something out."

Except she didn't really know Miller Waddy that well, and what she did know of him didn't exactly tell her what she should be getting him as gift. He was disorganized, could definitely use a calendar or three, and he really needed a new office chair. But that was the extent of her knowledge. He hadn't been at the school when she was a student, and she hadn't actually met him in person yet.

She'd have to ask Elia. Surely, she'd have more of an idea what that *something* could be.

And as it just so happened, Kamryn was headed in that direction.

Walking outside was a breath of cold crisp air. Kamryn had forgotten just how much the wind wasn't blocked out here by the trees. Not on this part of campus anyway. She really should have grabbed her winter jacket before leaving, but she'd completely forgotten about it. Clenching her jaw and hunkering down against the wind, Kamryn walked briskly toward the humanities building.

She was just entering inside when she stopped short.

Was that...snow in the air?

Turning around and facing the way she'd come, Kamryn gazed in awe at the small flakes of snow that were carried on the wind and continued to fall around her. She stayed there, watching them, forgetting that the wind was cold and the air was biting. The longer she stayed, the more flakes fell. It was going to be white all around her by the time she headed out of the office that night.

"Perfect," Kamryn whispered, a smile on her lips before she finally turned back around and headed inside.

The building was warm, especially compared to outside, and it gave it a stuffy feel that she couldn't get rid of. Kamryn's fingers were freezing as she made her way up to the third floor where Elia's office was. She was just about to step inside when she heard voices.

Frowning, Kamryn walked slowly and quietly to see who was talking. One voice was definitely Elia's. Kamryn would recognize her voice anywhere. And the other sounded like a student. They lacked the confidence that came with age. Kamryn pressed her lips into a thin line and checked her watch. She really did have an hour in her schedule that was free, but that was supposed to be her lunch hour.

Elia, however, didn't have that hour. Which meant she was going to be heading back into the classroom sooner than Kamryn wanted her too.

"Thanks, Dr. Sharpe!"

"You're welcome," Elia answered. "Come see me again if you're still having issues with it."

"Will do."

Kamryn waited stoically as Bristol walked out of Elia's small office, a backpack slung over her shoulder and her jacket hanging over her arm. She stopped short, eyeing Kamryn up and down before she plastered on a smile.

"Hi, Dr. Ogden."

"Bristol," Kamryn replied, nodding her head slightly. "It's

getting cold outside. If you're headed out, you'll want that jacket."

"Right." Bristol looked over her shoulder to find Elia standing at the entry to her door. "I didn't realize you two had a meeting. We could have finished up earlier."

Kamryn shook her head. "No, we didn't have anything scheduled." Kamryn flicked her gaze up to meet Elia's and frowned slightly. That didn't seem like a very happy look that she was receiving. Had she said something wrong? "I'll see you at practice tomorrow, Bristol."

"See you!" Bristol skipped a little as she walked down the hall.

When Kamryn faced Elia again, Elia nodded her head toward the inside of her office and then stepped in, leaving Kamryn alone in the hallway. This was a good thing, right? She did have actual business to discuss with Elia. This wasn't just a personal call. Surely Elia would know that and be fine with the small interruption.

"Hey, I wanted to talk to you about the next meet," Kamryn started as soon as she stepped inside and shut the door behind her.

Elia looked like she was going to object for a moment, her gaze lingering on the door that Kamryn had just shut before looking directly into Kamryn's eyes. "You shouldn't shut the door."

"Why not?" Kamryn frowned and glanced at it before stepping away.

"So that everyone can see or hear what's happening in here, so that there aren't any questions." Elia crossed her arms over her chest, leaned on the edge of her desk, and gave Kamryn a very pointed look.

"We're two adults, Elia. I don't think anyone is worried about what's going on in here."

"You might be surprised." Elia still wasn't giving up on this.

Kamryn pointed at the door. "Do you want me to open it?"

Elia waved her hand and shook her head. "What about the meet?"

"I'm not sure that Ethan should skip Info for Congress. He's really good."

"I know he is." Elia didn't move. "But he doesn't like Info."

"But he's amazing at it."

"But he doesn't like it," Elia countered. "And with the weather coming up, there's a strong chance that we're going to have to cancel the event entirely. I don't want to risk the safety of the students simply to be at a Speech meet."

"Oh, I hear you on that. I've been thinking that too, but I also just don't want to admit that's a possibility. I'm loving being involved in Speech again. I think wherever I end up next that I'll have to make sure I'm involved in something like it."

Elia hummed and nodded. "You haven't lost your touch in twenty years, have you?"

Kamryn smiled, her cheeks heating from the compliment. "I did also want to say thank you for the other night."

"You've already done that." Elia lowered her voice to just above a whisper, and again, she was glancing toward the door like someone was going to walk in on them. Was she that worried about it? Kamryn wanted to respect that if she was. They hadn't talked about what they were going to tell people aside from talking to the board—which they hadn't really put specifics on yet.

And if things kept going the way they were now...well, Kamryn was going to want to talk to the board as soon as possible.

"I know I did," Kamryn agreed, staying put when she would have much rather moved in closer. "But I just wanted to make sure that you heard me. I also wanted to ask if you were going to apply for the Head of School position, now that it's official that Miller won't be returning."

"Ah." Elia sighed heavily. "I don't know."

"Have you thought about it?" Kamryn was so curious. She was still debating herself whether or not to apply for the permanent position. Everything had seemed to calm down slightly now, and so she might still have a chance at actually being hired for it. Still, there was a worry in the back of her mind that because of her relationship with Elia, she was going to lose out on that. Or that she shouldn't even try. If for once she should put her personal life before the professional.

Hadn't Lauren always accused her of not doing that?

"I have thought about it." Elia crossed her legs, putting the weight of her entire body onto one heel as she rocked back slightly. "But I'm not sure that I've decided yet."

"Will you let me know when you do?" Kamryn bit the inside of her cheek. That would be telling, wouldn't it? That Elia actually trusted her.

"Will you let me know?" Elia raised an eyebrow at her. "Even if I do apply, I know they won't hire me."

"They might."

"Kam..." Elia shook her head. "They won't."

"Will you ever tell me why you believe that?"

"Maybe someday," Elia answered, standing up. "Until then, you'll just have to keep guessing." Elia smiled briefly before she stepped in close, taking Kamryn's hands in hers and pressing their mouths together.

The unexpected change from before when Elia had seemed so worried about someone seeing them was stark. Kamryn melted into the embrace, curling her hand around the back of Elia's neck and pulling her closer as their tongues teased each other. Kamryn eventually pulled away, instantly regretting the loss of touch and contact.

"You did really well at the meeting today, by the way," Elia whispered, sliding her hands around Kamryn's back and pecking her lips again. "They should hire you for the full-time position."

"Are you ready for me to continue being your boss?"

Again, there was that entertained and satisfied hum that Elia managed to do. It said so much and so little at the same time. Kamryn kissed her again, cupping her cheek and holding Elia close. Couldn't every day be like this? It was so warm here, so comfortable, and just damn easy. It would be a sad day when Kamryn couldn't just pop by and meet up with Elia for sweet moments like this or tender conversations together.

"I think I'd be fairly satisfied if you were my boss," Elia said, sliding her hands down Kamryn's arms and taking a step back. "And everyone knows that it's always good to satisfy the Chair of English. She's a cranky one."

Kamryn snorted. "Some might say she's a bit icy."

"Oh, definitely that." Elia slid into the chair at her desk, turning it toward her computer. "Keep the door open on your way out. I have office hours for the next ten minutes before class."

"Right." Kamryn smiled to herself as she put her hand on the doorknob. "We should take a walk in the snow later."

"Snow?"

"Yeah." Kamryn winked. "Looks like it'll be gorgeous when the sun goes down."

"And freezing," Elia responded.

"Perfect time to snuggle up with someone you like a lot." Kamryn laughed as she stepped out into the hallway. The look of shock on Elia's face had been exactly what she was going for. For some reason, it was never going to disappoint Kamryn to surprise her. She could do it for the rest of her life.

twenty-two

"Yara."

Elia nearly screeched to a halt on her way to Kamryn's office. She'd thought they could snag a late lunch together, but now her entire stomach was in knots just staring at her ex-girlfriend in the middle of the hallway of the administration building.

"Elia." Yara winced visibly, but then she plastered on the cool, confident mask that Elia had become so familiar with after their breakup.

Elia's heart was in her throat. What was Yara Cole doing here? Her kids had all graduated years ago, and Elia had never been more thankful to be able to close that phase of her life and truly move on from their breakup.

"It's been a while," Elia said, trying to open the conversation for something—anything—that might give her a hint as to why Yara was here. Because there had to be a reason. And it couldn't be because she'd applied for the Head of School position because it hadn't even been opened yet, and she hadn't even decided if she would or not.

"It has." Yara's lips twitched upward into a half smile before it faded. "I just had a meeting with our new temporary Head of School."

"Oh." Elia wasn't sure if that was a comment or a question. But she was definitely going to ask Kamryn about it as soon as they had a moment alone and away from the school.

"She's doing well, don't you think?"

"Yeah." Elia tightened her grip around her notebooks. The panic that she'd faced all those years ago was settling into her chest, and it was trying to overtake her, but she wasn't going to let it. Not again. And definitely not today. "She was well chosen for the position."

Yara nodded, still staying put and not moving. So this conversation—if it could even be called that—wasn't over yet. At one point, Elia had convinced herself that they were in love. But now she was fairly certain it had just been a strong dose of infatuation, one they'd both experienced. Elia was probably the only one willing to admit to that now, though.

"What are you doing here?" Elia asked, ending up being the direct one and breaking the stalemate between them.

"I was asked to join the ethics committee." Yara's look was pure satisfaction, crazed and elated satisfaction.

Elia's stomach dropped. She closed her eyes and sighed heavily. Of all people to ask to be on the team, Yara would be the last one that Elia would want. Even over herself. But they'd allow Yara on, wouldn't they? She was the innocent one in everything, and she'd made damn sure that the world had known that.

"I hope that doesn't bother you," Yara added.

Of course it damn well did, and of course Yara would be pleased to know that Elia was one of the first to find out, to know that Elia was going to go back to her home and struggle with this. Elia needed to catch her breath, and she needed to find a way to give as good as she was getting right now.

"Why would it bother me?" Elia raised her chin up high, steeling herself for whatever was going to happen next, because damn would it be major. "You're clearly the perfect person for the role, with your extensive experience in the area of politics and ethical violations. I'm sure the team will benefit from all your *experience.*"

Yes, she'd thrown that last bit in there to tick Yara off, even though it probably wouldn't work in the long run. It'd come back to bite her in the ass so hard, and she would regret it every second of the way.

"Yes, I do have quite a bit of experience in these things, don't I?" Yara fired back, but her shoulders tightened, and her jaw line was so sharp that Elia knew she'd at least gotten under her skin. No one else might be able to tell, but two years of dating didn't erase that. Elia could read her from anywhere.

"You sure do." Elia nodded sharply. "Too bad your efforts couldn't have been aimed in a more fruitful direction instead of at an innocent party."

"Innocent?" Yara choked on the word. "I hardly think *you're* innocent."

"No, you wouldn't think that, because you never even took a moment to listen to what I had to say, did you?" Elia spat out the words, all the anger rushing up and out of her. "It was only every listening to one side of it, and you know what? I'm glad you weren't on the ethics committee then, or the board. You wouldn't have provided an objective voice."

"Then justice might have *actually* happened."

"Really? After eighteen years, you're still going to hold this grudge?" Elia waved her off. "Give it up, Yara. Eighteen years is too long to hold onto something so negative in your life. Move on already."

"No." Yara took a step forward. Elia very nearly took a step back in response, but she held her ground. They were in the middle of the administration building, and there were cameras everywhere. If anything happened, then someone else would see it and know about it. This wasn't twenty-years ago when there was nothing to prove her right, to back up her claims of innocence.

"Excuse me." Kamryn's voice startled Elia. "What's going on?"

"Nothing," Elia said, stepping back immediately. "I was coming to discuss the Speech meet this weekend. I see you're busy. We can reschedule."

Without another word, Elia turned on her toes and walked away. Kamryn didn't say her name. She didn't follow her. She didn't even try to stop her. Elia could understand why. Yara had to be Kamryn's priority in this situation. Dealing with Yara had to be the reason why Kamryn was staying behind. Not because it was anything else.

And if Elia let her mind wander, she could come up with any number of reasons as to why she might be staying that were far beyond Yara. Elia rushed out into the cold air and held back her tears. Running face first into her ex-girlfriend at a time like this.

And to have Yara be on the ethics team?

Elia couldn't tell them now. They couldn't tell the board what she and Kamryn had been doing. That they'd been dating? It would ruin any chance of Kamryn getting the job, and it would instantly set Elia up for a termination. Yara would make sure of it.

Snagging her phone from her pocket, Elia called Abagail before she even made it back to her office. She wasn't going to stay there long, just enough to grab her stuff and walk straight home.

"We have bigger problems with the board."

"Uh-oh." Abagail clicked her tongue. "This isn't going to be a short conversation, is it?"

"No."

"I'll call you back in five." Abagail hung up.

It gave Elia enough time to grab her laptop and shove it inside her bag. She needed to get out of here. It'd be better if she lived off campus, because she really needed to distance herself from the school, but she couldn't—not today. She still had Speech practice that night, and she couldn't escape. Not yet.

She was just inside her front door when her phone buzzed. Staring down at it, she saw the missed messages from Kamryn. Elia immediately ignored them. She needed to talk to Abagail, someone who understood the situation. Someone she could fully trust.

Not that she couldn't trust Kamryn, but she had no idea what Yara had told her. She may have told her absolutely everything already, and Kamryn would certainly see that as a betrayal. Wouldn't she?

Elia answered and fell into her couch at the same time. She just wanted to cry.

"All right, tell me what happened."

"I was going to talk to Kam, and walked into the admin building, and right into Yara."

"Shit."

That was the exact response that Elia had been looking for. She didn't need to explain anything. She was so close to tears. The stress and anguish of the past years coming right back into her chest in a way that she wasn't able to get rid of. "Someone—and I strongly suspect I know who—invited her onto the ethics team."

"Elia..." Abagail trailed off. "Not Kam I hope."

"No, I don't think so. She barely even remembered Yara from when she was a student. I'm betting it was Heather."

"Heather-Heather."

"Yeah. *That* Heather." Elia closed her eyes. She hadn't told Kamryn that part of everything, not who Heather was to Elia and exactly why she knew she'd never be allowed on the ethics team, not while Heather was there. "She joined the board about a year ago but hadn't really caused any issues until Kamryn was hired."

"And you think she'll cause more?" Abagail asked.

"I know she will." Elia pinched the bridge of her nose, feeling the dampness from her unshed tears. She wasn't ready for this. She wasn't sure she'd ever be ready for it. "I can't tell the board about Kam and me now. It'll spell disaster for both of us. They won't listen to a thing we have to say. It'll ruin her career."

"And yours," Abagail added. "Or don't you care about it anymore?"

"I do." Elia frowned. Teaching was her life. She'd made it her life and she didn't want it any other way. She wanted her world to remain exactly as it was now. Where she could teach, live here, and have some fun on the side with someone she found really, really interesting. And she definitely found Kamryn interesting—and exciting. "I do care about it. I'm not ready to quit or retire. I *need* to teach."

"Then you're going to have to fight whatever they throw at you."

Elia had been afraid Abagail was going to say that. She wasn't sure she had any fight left in her. They'd taken it all those years ago, and she'd done her best just to fly under the radar until now. And now it wasn't even her fault. It wasn't like she and Kamryn had talked to the board yet.

"There's going to be so many questions," Elia whispered. "Not just about back then or now, but about Kam and me."

"There will be," Abagail confirmed. "And they'll be invasive. And they should be. Those questions are there for a reason."

"They are, but..." Elia sighed heavily. "Will it be worth it?"

"Only you can answer that question, E." Abagail shook her head. "But you need to come up with a game plan going forward, and you need to make sure that you have every possible outlier and base covered. You can't be alone with a student—ever. And you need to make damn sure that you're always in the view of someone."

"I didn't do anything wrong."

"No, you didn't. And unfortunately, when it comes to situations like these, it's never innocent until proven guilty."

Abagail was right. Elia had experienced that firsthand.

"So what do I need to do next?" Elia asked, already knowing the answer and already hating the fact that she knew what was coming.

"You need to talk to a lawyer, and you cannot tell anyone anything. And you need to talk to Kamryn, not about eighteen years ago, but you need to talk to her about your current relationship." Abagail sounded so sure of herself.

"And tell her what?"

"That you're done. End it now, before it blows up in your face."

Elia curled in on herself. "And Yara?"

"Yara is going to be your worst enemy if you let her. Don't. She doesn't need to get under your skin any more than she already has. She was always a brute, and she'll continue to do exactly what she thinks she needs to do."

"It feels like the whole world is out to get me."

"Not the whole world, babe." Abagail's tone turned tender. "But most of the people at Windermere, that's for sure. At least the ones in power right now. I don't know about Kam, yet. She might still be on your side."

"I'm afraid she won't be when she finds out." Elia sounded so small, so scared. And she was. She cared what other people thought about her—at least about this—and she especially cared about what Kamryn thought about her. It mattered. She mattered.

"There's only one way to know that," Abagail answered. "But now isn't the time to find out. You're going to have to live in the ambiguity a little longer."

"I hate that."

"I know you do."

Elia frowned. She checked the time on the wall and knew she was going to have to head back for the Speech practice soon. At least she'd gotten a small escape. Maybe she could take a few more minutes to put her head on straight and be able to hide the fact that she wasn't okay. The last thing she needed was Kamryn to start prying.

"I'll call you tomorrow," Elia said. "You should get back to work."

"Okay. I'm going to hold you to that, and if you don't call me, I'm going to sic the hounds on you."

That made Elia smile slightly. She could always trust Abagail to have her back. "Thanks."

"Anytime."

Hanging up, Elia went to the kitchen to pour herself a cold glass of water. She stared at her phone, knowing that she needed to read the texts from Kamryn. And then she needed to follow Abagail's advice. She needed to pull away and protect Kamryn as much as she could. Because this was turning out to be a disaster.

Sliding her phone open, she was relieved to see the first text was Kamryn saying she wouldn't be able to make it to the Speech practice that night, that she was going to be stuck in a meeting for a few hours. And then her stomach twisted hard at the next ones.

Are you okay?

Can we talk soon? I have time later tonight.

You're worrying me.

She was already in too far over her head, wasn't she? She'd thought briefly that this might work, but now, she wasn't so sure. Her mistakes from decades ago were going to come back and take her down again. And she wouldn't let Kamryn bear the brunt of her past.

twenty-three

"Hey." Kamryn slid into the seat next to Elia on the bus.

The day had been filled by the speech competition, so much so that Kamryn hadn't even had a moment to take a breath, let alone talk to Elia at all. And since they weren't staying anywhere overnight this time, she was stuck trying to talk to Elia on the bus with students chattering away behind them and passing around the whisk that Kamryn had brought.

"Hey," Elia answered, but she scooted away slightly, putting space between them.

For the last few days, Elia had been so quiet. The stark change from the weeks before was unnerving, and Kamryn had searched her brain and every interaction they'd had to try and figure out what had happened and what she'd done to set Elia off, but she honestly couldn't think of anything.

Except that interaction in the hallway with Yara Cole.

That was when all of this had started, and Elia had shut down on her. But Kamryn was determined. They'd had something good going, and Kamryn cared. That was her downfall every time, but she cared about Elia, and she wanted to make sure that there wasn't something she could do to help out with whatever the situation was.

"That was a good meet, don't you think?" Kamryn was going to start easy. They needed to slowly work into this conversation because she knew that Elia was going to be uncomfortable having it on the bus. And they weren't going to be able to find much time afterward since Kamryn was on call that weekend at the dormitories and she was damn sure that Elia was going to use that as an excuse not to come over and have an actual conversation.

"It was good," Elia agreed, but her heart wasn't in the conversation. Kamryn could tell that from a mile away.

"Yeah. I think the whisk thing is still going over well." Kamryn looked over her shoulder as the kids were sharing. It was the only chance they'd had to do it at this meet, and even though the bus wasn't ideal, the kids were committed to sharing their highs from the day. "Think you'll keep it up when I'm gone?"

Elia frowned before pursing her lips and looking out the window at the dark sky and the snow that was falling around them. In just about any other circumstance, it would have been stunningly beautiful. And Kamryn still wanted that walk in the snow that she'd never gotten with Elia.

Taking a chance, Kamryn slid her hand over and rested it lightly on Elia's forearm. She was met with an intensity that she hadn't expected. Elia glanced down at the touch and then straight up into Kamryn's eyes.

"Please don't."

"Sure." Kamryn moved her hand away immediately, an awkwardness settling into her chest that she hadn't felt since that night in the hotel room when she'd asked Elia for a kiss and been rejected. It had everything to do with her and not Elia, she knew that, but she wasn't quite sure where to go from here. "I'm sorry I didn't ask first."

"You're forgiven," Elia commented before going back to looking out the window.

"Do you mind talking to me?"

Elia shook her head. "Not at all. I think Bristol needs to work on her informational, don't you? She needs to dig deeper in order to round out her argument even more."

Kamryn frowned. That hadn't been what she meant. She didn't want to talk about the Speech meet. She wanted to talk about them. "Yeah, it's probably not a bad idea for her to do that."

They sat in silence again. Kamryn picked up on laughter behind her, but it all sounded innocent enough that she didn't feel she needed to turn around and observe. She followed Elia's gaze back out the bus window and cringed. What were they doing here?

"Can we find some time to talk this weekend? I can find coverage for the dorm—"

"I'm not sure that's necessary," Elia interrupted. "We don't really have that much to talk about."

"I think we do." Kamryn resisted the temptation to reach out and touch again. She knew Elia wouldn't accept it, that she didn't want it, even though it would help her to find some sort of connection between them again. "Everything's been off these last few days."

"It's just been me, not you," Elia answered, giving Kamryn a patronizing smile. "Don't worry about it, really. It's nothing you've done."

"Well, it's good to have confirmation on that front, but I wasn't thinking that it was anything I'd done." Kamryn rubbed her lips together as a thought occurred to her that hadn't managed to work its way into her brain before. "Was it something that I didn't do?"

Elia twitched at that, her entire body jerking with a start. "What?"

"Are you upset that I didn't do something you wanted—or maybe needed—me to do?" Kamryn held her breath, wanting this to be the answer that she'd been searching days for.

Elia blinked at her, as if trying to process that information before she shook her head. "No. Well, yes, a little, but it's not your fault. You wouldn't know any better."

"O...kay." Kamryn was more lost now than she was before. "Care to fill me in?"

"No," Elia answered simply, her voice ringing out in the bus seats like there was no one else there but them.

Was Elia not even going to try anymore? Or was she trying to push Kamryn out more now than she had before? Kamryn chose her words carefully. "I respect that it's your decision whether or not to tell me. It's just really hard for me to know where to go from here without some sort of direction."

"You're going to have to trust me on this, Kam. I don't want... We do need to talk, you're right. But now isn't the time or the place. And I need more time before I can have that conversation." Elia's face didn't betray anything of what was going on behind her eyes.

Kamryn wished it did. Because she really needed some sort of hint to figure out what wasn't being said. "All right."

Kamryn leaned back into the seat, giving in to the fact that she wasn't going to get any more information than what she'd already gotten. Elia was closed off for a reason, and until she decided to let Kamryn in, then Kamryn was going to be left on the cold outside like she'd never mattered. But she had mattered. Kamryn had seen that in Elia's eyes, in the touches they'd shared, and she wasn't ever going to doubt that.

"Just... one thing," Kamryn said, sitting up straight again. "Lauren always shut down like this, and it scares me that you're doing it, too. I don't want a repeat of my past mistakes, and so I don't want to push you if you're not ready, but I also don't want to leave you alone if that's the last thing you need. What I need is some guidance from you about what you need or want me to do."

Elia's lips parted before her jaw clenched hard. The muscles bulged at her cheeks, and then her face fell. "I don't want to repeat past mistakes either."

And then there was nothing.

Frustration ate away at Kamryn. She'd tried so many times and she wasn't getting anywhere.

"I can't let you suffer because of them," Elia murmured, her voice so quiet that Kamryn wasn't quite sure if she'd heard her correctly. She was about to ask Elia to repeat that when a loud scream echoed down the bus.

Kamryn leaned up on the seat and eyed the students in the back. "Volume down, please!" she reminded them all. She was going to have to say that a million more times, that was for certain. But that was why she was here, wasn't it? To teach and be with the kids.

Sliding back into her seat, she didn't have the heart to ask Elia to open up again. Kamryn threw her head back into the seat and closed her eyes for a moment, attempting to gather herself again. Opening her phone, she checked her work email. Frowning at a recent email that had come in, she hovered her thumb over it before opening it.

From: Yara Cole
Subject: Agenda to Follow

I thought it'd be pertinent to get this information out to you as soon as possible. I don't want to waste time. We'll have a meeting Tuesday evening at six, and we'll formulate a plan to make sure that our students' safety is our number one concern.

Thank you,
Yara

Kamryn's stomach dropped. She read the email three times over before she closed out of it and reached behind her neck to rub the tension out of the muscles. Except it wasn't working. She dug her thumb into the line of muscle from the back of her skull down her neck, and that seemed to help but only momentarily.

Yara wasn't an opposing voice to Susy and Heather, and instead of adding diversity to the team, Kamryn had unwittingly added nothing to it except more pressure against what her goals were. She really needed to start this over or she needed to get someone else in there quickly.

She ran through the list of names in her head, but she couldn't come up with anyone. Finally, she gave in and asked, because at the very least Elia could help her with this. "Hey, do you know anyone who might be good for the ethics team?"

"What?" Elia's voice wavered with surprise and worry.

"The ethics team." Kamryn furrowed her brow. "I told you that one of my jobs is to rebuild it. Since you won't be on the team, I need to find someone else, and someone who..." Kamryn paused. Could she say this without offending Elia? Probably. "... someone who has a differing point of view. And someone who can stand up for themselves and speak out when necessary."

"I'm really not the person to ask for this."

"Why not? You've been around the school long enough to know who might be interested and good at that."

Elia shook her head. "No. I've been at the school, yes, but I haven't been involved in the way you think I have. I'm not someone who fully understands the inner workings and who does what. I do my job and that's about it."

Kamryn frowned at that. She'd never thought Elia had been someone who was distant from other faculty or staff or even the board. Then again, now that she thought about it, Elia often ate lunch and dinner at her house or in her office—she didn't come down to the dining hall. And if she did, she usually sat quietly at a table with others instead of engaging them in conversation.

How had Kamryn not noticed that before?

"So you don't have any names I might approach?" Kamryn asked again, hoping not only for an answer to resolve her issue, but to pry more information out of Elia if she could, just something that might tell her more about who this woman was.

"No, I don't."

"Okay." Kamryn opened Yara's email again. "I won't be at practice on Tuesday."

"You missed practice on Thursday." Elia glanced over, her gaze dropping to Kamryn's phone. "Ethics meeting?"

Kamryn glanced up at her. "Unfortunately, and they didn't ask when I was available—just told me when we were meeting."

"Typical Yara Cole."

"Do you know Yara?" Kamryn asked, looking at her directly. "I mean, I guess you would because her kids went to Windermere."

"I do know her," Elia responded, but she tightened even more, pushing herself into the window as if to get away from Kamryn.

"I don't know her that well."

Elia didn't respond. She was shutting down even more than before, and it was obvious. Kamryn wished she could take it all back, that she could try to have this conversation at any other time, that they were standing up and yelling at each other, that they were doing exactly what they needed to get through to each other.

It might just be one hiccup, and that's what Kamryn was going to count it as. They were both busy and exhausted after a long day, and they really needed to take time to rest before they tried to talk about anything serious.

The school chant reverberated through the bus before a loud cheer went up. Kamryn smiled, facing Elia and shrugging slightly. "Seems *whisk time* is done for the evening."

"Seems to be that way." Elia glanced over the seat toward the kids. "We'll be back in the next ten minutes."

"Good timing then," Kamryn answered.

"Seems that way." Elia faced the window again.

Kamryn held her phone tightly in her hand and relaxed as

much as she could for the next ten minutes. As soon as they were back on Windermere property, she was going to have to dive straight back into work. And she'd have to find time to talk with Elia later.

She wished they had their own *whisk time* that night—just the two of them. Maybe then they could each figure out what the other needed.

twenty-four

"You got a minute?" Elia asked as she knocked on Kamryn's door. Mrs. Caldera hadn't been in when she'd shown up—not that Elia had intentionally waited until the lunch hour before coming to see Kamryn, knowing full well that she wouldn't be joining the rest of the school for lunch.

"For you?" Kamryn asked, looking up from her computer and grinning broadly. "Always."

That warmed Elia even though the last few days had been tenuous at best. Ever since they'd returned from the Speech meet, Elia had kept her distance. She'd purposely not met up with Kamryn alone, finding only time when they could be seen by others to talk. It was one way of avoiding, that was for certain, but it was also a way of protecting.

But now they needed to talk. Seriously. About everything that Elia had avoided the last few days while she got her head on straight and figured out what her next steps were going to be. And she'd taken advantage of as much time as she thought she could manage.

Elia left the door open, still wanting to be able to be seen if any questions were asked. She stood in front of Kamryn's desk, arms crossed, and she once again debated where to even start. She should have prepared better for this.

"I wanted to apologize, for my recent behavior," Elia said, her voice clear and strong. It probably came off as aggressive. Surely someone would accuse her of that.

"What exactly are you apologizing for?"

"Being distant," Elia said on a sigh. She couldn't go into this like an attack. It wouldn't end well for anyone if she did. Sliding into one of the chairs facing Kamryn's desk, Elia crossed her legs, then uncrossed them, then leaned forward and rested her elbows on her knees. "I haven't been myself lately."

"I'll say..." Kamryn answered, glancing toward the open door. "Do you want me to shut that?"

"No." Elia straightened up. "We need the space."

"We do?" Kamryn furrowed her brow, and Elia knew she was being confusing. But she wasn't doing it on purpose. At least, she didn't mean to be.

"I need it," Elia corrected. "There are a lot of things I'm working through right now. Well, one thing I'm working through, but it can have ripple effects that I don't want to have too much of an impact."

"You're talking in riddles, Elia." Kamryn sighed heavily. "What is this even about? Us? The school? Speech team?"

"All of it." Elia ran her fingers through her hair. "It's about all of it and none of it. I can't promise that it'll make sense at any point. But I really think that we might need to put a pause on us."

"A pause," Kamryn repeated, no doubt trying to process exactly what Elia was saying. And Elia should give her the time to do that. She'd been thinking about this nonstop for days now, ever since she'd run into Yara, and she needed to give Kamryn that same time to draw her own conclusions.

"Is that really what you want?" Kamryn asked, so sincere in her question.

Elia nearly broke then. It would be so easy to open up and tell Kamryn everything, but Abagail had advised against it. Not because they shouldn't share but because it was safer this way—for everyone involved. But with all of that, Elia knew exactly how to answer Kamryn's question.

"No."

"Lucky finding you two here," Yara said from the doorway.

Elia instantly tensed. Her spine went ramrod straight. She clenched her jaw, the ache already starting, and she couldn't force herself to look toward Kamryn. She couldn't see Kamryn's reaction to what she knew was coming.

"Yara," Kamryn said, straightening up before she stood. She walked forward and extended her hand toward Yara in a greeting.

Elia envied her ability to put on that mask, but with all the history between her and Yara, it was going to be impossible for her. And it would come off as so fake that Yara would smell it miles away. But she was regretting leaving the door open now. How much had Yara heard before she'd announced her arrival?

Had she heard and understood Elia's confession?

"I know I'm early for tonight, but I wanted to get a head start on going through some of the files." Yara clutched something to her chest. "Do you mind if I use the conference room?"

"I don't think anything's scheduled in there until our meeting tonight." Kamryn stepped back and glanced at Elia, catching her gaze. The concern in her eyes was there an instant before it vanished, and she turned back to Yara. "Were there any files you needed that I can get for you?"

"All files concerning current faculty and staff," Yara said while looking directly at Elia. "We want to protect our current students, don't we?"

Elia stood up, folding her hands together in front of her. She hardened immediately. This was the battle that she was going to be up against, and she was going to have to rely on the fact that the investigation eighteen years ago had been conducted well and that she was innocent. Once again, she was going to have to trust others to protect her, people who had no interest in her welfare.

"I think I'll leave you two to it," Elia said as she picked up the jacket she'd set on the chair when she'd come in.

"No, stay. I don't want to disrupt your meeting...again." Yara was looking directly at her. When had her eyes become so cold? "You two do seem to have a lot of meetings."

Kamryn jerked her head to the side then, pinning Yara with a sharp look. "I have one-on-one meetings with all the faculty on a regular basis, but considering that Dr. Sharpe and I both run the Speech team—yes, we have a few more meetings than the others."

Was Kamryn aware of just how dangerous defending Elia could be for her own future?

Probably not.

Elia swallowed the lump in her throat.

"I didn't hear a conversation about the Speech team," Yara crooned.

That answered Elia's earlier question. And she wasn't ready for it to come out into the open. Running was so much better than this. Sliding her arms into her jacket, Elia put it on. She was determined to get out of here. Quick and fast—that was the only way.

"What you heard was a personal conversation, and it wasn't meant for your ears." Kamryn squared her stance, spreading her feet out and glaring at Yara with everything that she had.

Elia had no doubt that even without hearing the words they were saying, Yara would be aware of the tension in the room, the tension between them. Elia could still feel it, she could still hear her resounding answer to Kamryn's intuitive question.

"I'm here to protect the students, Kamryn. That's why I was asked to be on the ethics team, and that's exactly what I'll do."

Elia shivered. The use of Kamryn's first name? That was a dressing down if she knew it. Since when had Yara become so hardened? It was amazing what eighteen years could do to someone, that was for certain. Elia just had to look at her own life for a prime example of that. She'd slowly shut down over the years, pushing people further away from her—until Kamryn. Until someone who seemed so interested in what was underneath the surface that Elia couldn't resist coming up from her hidey-hole to see what she'd been missing all these years.

"No one would ever ask you to do anything else," Kamryn answered. "And that's not what I'm asking you to do now."

Elia really wanted to leave. She didn't need to be here for this, did she?

"Having her here is a risk."

Shame filled Elia. This was how it was all going to come out, wasn't it? This was how her world as she knew it was going to end, and the second wave of bullshit was going to take over her life. And she still wasn't certain she could survive it a second time. Had she even survived the first time?

"Dr. Sharpe?" Kamryn furrowed her brow and looked from Yara to Elia and back again. "Elia has no open complaints about her. In fact, she hasn't had any in years."

Had Kamryn looked her up? Had she read Elia's personnel file? Because all that information would be in there. Violation ripped through her. She was exposed here, not just in a professional sense but in a personal one. Kamryn could so easily know so much about her if she just looked. And it sounded like she had.

"But she has had some." The sharp lines of Yara's face were so prominent when she was angry. "You shouldn't defend something that you know nothing about."

Kamryn closed her mouth then.

So she hadn't read that far into it.

Elia wasn't sure if she was happy with that or not. But it did mean that Kamryn trusted her—even if it wasn't warranted.

"I haven't met a teacher who doesn't have at least one complaint against them. I have complaints against me, not only as a teacher but also as an admin."

"We're not talking about minor complaints, Kamryn." There it was again, that tone that Yara used when she thought she had all the power in the room. "We're talking about career-ending accusations."

"I really shouldn't be here for this." Elia stepped away from the chair and tried to head straight for the door, but Yara stepped between it and her. Elia wasn't sure what to do next. She'd never been physically blocked from leaving a room before. "This is between you and the ethics team and Dr. Ogden, Yara. This isn't between you and me."

"It's always been between us," Yara said quietly, a threat in her tone. "And it always *will* be."

Elia gulped. It was career-ending this time. She had no doubts of it. If Yara was going to remain on the board in any capacity, then Elia wasn't going to have a position at Windermere. But she would hang on for as long as she could, because her kids mattered, and she wanted them to have the best they could for as long as she could.

And she would make damn sure that Yara never did this to anyone else.

"For Dr. Ogden's knowledge," Elia started, facing Kamryn with an apologetic look on her face, "Yara and I dated for nearly two years."

Kamryn paled. "When?"

"We broke up eighteen years ago." Elia lifted her chin in defiance. She clenched her jaw again. "It was a mutual break up—at first. But grudges have been held since."

"It'll all come out anyway." Yara sneered. "It's just a matter of time."

"It will come out." Elia wasn't going to back down. She'd done that once before, but she wasn't the same person she had been then. This was her life Yara was screwing with. Elia let the anger surge forward, filling her chest and the top of her head. "All of it will come out. Are you prepared for that?"

"Absolutely," Yara answered with a sickening grin.

"Good." Elia faced Kamryn. "We'll talk later."

"Yeah," Kamryn breathed the word out.

Elia had no doubt that she was completely lost to what was happening, to the war that she'd just walked into. All Elia could do was hope that Kamryn finally went and searched what she'd so obviously hadn't. It would tell her everything. But for now, it was out of her hands.

Shoving her hands into her pockets, Elia balled her fingers into tight fists. She stared Yara down and waited in silence. She would do that until Yara moved. She would hold her ground with everything that she had.

"Why don't I get you settled into the conference room?" Kamryn stepped forward, putting her hand out in front of her. She ushered Yara away, leaving Elia in the office.

Who had Elia been kidding?

This office would never be hers. She should have given up that dream decades ago when this had first happened. She should have never thought that she'd be allowed to be in that role and position. Relaxing slightly, Elia stared around the room some more. She slowly said goodbye to that dream and that hope.

No one had ever wanted her in that position. It had been a pipe dream at best, and it was time. Time to give it all up and to settle for what she knew she could have. And to fight to keep that. Because she was going to be lucky to keep it now.

"I'm so sorry about that," Kamryn rushed as she came back in.

How long had Elia been standing there? She shook her head, breaking her reverie. "It's not your fault."

"If I'd known you and her—"

"It wouldn't have mattered. I've made plenty of mistakes in my life, Kam. Dating a student's mother isn't the worst of it. Putting myself in a position that could ever seem unethical was. And I need to keep my promise to myself." Elia tightened every muscle in her body, because she didn't like what she had to do next. "I won't put myself in another compromising position."

"You mean us." Kamryn closed the door behind her this time, pushing on it to make sure that it was shut.

"I mean me." Elia pursed her lips, already deciding exactly what she needed to do next. And it wasn't going to be pleasant for either one of them. “You should look in my personnel file, Kam. Stop avoiding it. Better yet, get online and search my name. And you should do it now, before you walk into that ethics meeting.”

“Elia...” Kamryn stepped in close to her, immediately reaching for her arm, but Elia jerked back.

She had to protect herself from this. “Don’t touch me, Kam. I can’t...” Her voice broke on the word. “I won’t take you down with me.”

Without another word, Elia walked out.

She was doing this for both of them.

“Elia!” Kamryn followed her into the main office.

Elia halted by the outer door. This felt final. But it wasn’t. And yet, something about it seemed like an end. There was a chasm between them, and Elia needed to keep it there. It was Kamryn’s protection as much as her own.

“What do you want me to think?”

Shaking her head, Elia very nearly came to tears. She just wanted Kamryn to believe her. But she couldn’t ask that. It was too much. Biting her lip to prevent the tears from falling, Elia bolstered herself for what she knew she had to say.

“I want you to believe the victim.”

twenty-five

Time.

That was all Kamryn wanted.

And it was everything she couldn't have right now.

She'd ripped apart Elia's personnel file, and there was nothing in it. Literally nothing. At least nothing that Elia could have been referring to when she'd told Kamryn to look into it. Scratching the back of her head, Kamryn was just about to open up her computer and do an online search like Elia had suggested, but the knock on her door stopped her.

"You ready?" Heather asked, her lips curled upward.

One way or another, Kamryn was going to find out exactly what everyone was hiding. Tonight. She was tired of waiting for answers.

"Yes." Kamryn closed out her computer and took Elia's personnel file, shoving it into the top drawer of her desk and locking it. She grabbed her satchel with her laptop and her notebook, and she followed Heather out. There wasn't a chance that she was going to leave Heather alone in her office. Not now.

Kamryn walked into the conference room, surprised to find Susy already there. She shouldn't be though. These three were never late to anything. In fact, they were always way earlier than they should be. Pursing her lips, Kamryn sat down and pulled out her things. She was ready for whatever they were going to throw at her.

She had to be.

"Let's get started," Yara said, eyeing Kamryn thoroughly. "I wanted to specifically talk about Elia Sharpe today. She's gone unsupervised for too long, and in order to protect our students, we need to implement the protocols that were in place before."

Before?

Kamryn was so out of the loop, and nothing in the personnel file had said that Elia was on restrictions. Or that she'd ever been suspended or put on leave. Absolutely nothing. It reeked of someone wiping it completely.

"What were the restrictions before?" Heather asked, leaning forward on the table, all her attention on Yara.

That had been what Kamryn wanted to ask—at least one of the millions of questions that had gone through her head. The first question that kept ringing through her brain was *what the hell happened eighteen years ago?*

"She wasn't permitted to teach any extra curriculars. All interactions with students had to be supervised, and she had to pay for the assistant to supervise her. And someone must be present while she was teaching and on campus. And she wasn't permitted to live on campus." Yara put out a finger for each thing she listed off.

Those were insane restrictions.

How could anyone have survived those? It would have been better to have been fired. Or perhaps Elia would have done better to just quit. But those restrictions must have been dropped a long time ago because Elia had continued to teach Speech as far as Kamryn knew. Maybe those were just temporary restrictions during an investigation?

That would make far more sense.

Kamryn needed information. She picked up her pen and

poised it over her paper. "You're going to need to fill me in on what the charges were against Dr. Sharpe."

"Charges?" Yara looked confused by that word choice, but she shouldn't be. With restrictions as firm as the ones she was listing off, surely there would have been formal charges filed against Elia. And why she would have been allowed to stay at the school was lost on Kamryn.

Unless she'd been proven innocent of whatever it was.

"It's in her personnel file," Yara responded, wiggling her shoulders in discomfort.

"Actually, it's not. Which is probably the more egregious error that we should be discussing at this point. But there are no reports or complaints in Dr. Sharpe's file." Kamryn pressed her lips together hard.

"What?" Heather's eyes widened.

"That's impossible," Susy responded.

"It's not if someone took them out, and I, for one, would like to know who might have done that. Because, again, even if a complaint was found baseless, there still needs to be a record of what happened and why it was filed." Kamryn kept her pen on the paper, still waiting for some kind of answer to her earlier question. "So since I don't have access to whatever information you three are discussing, you need to fill me in."

Susy shook her head slowly in disbelief. "There was a complaint filed against Elia Sharpe, eighteen years ago, for sexual harassment against a student."

"A *female* student," Heather added with a snarl.

"Well, you can't fire someone for being queer," Kamryn commented, but her heart sank. To have someone make that accusation formally meant there was likely some sort of proof that it had happened. The lack of reporting was so stark, that if only one person had formally reported there were certainly others it had happened to who had kept their mouth shut over the years. And Kamryn would be responsible for digging up all that information.

"Eighteen years ago they could have," Yara added, dropping her gaze to the table in front of her.

Had that been why Elia had kept that relationship so under wraps? It would be a very good guess, especially at an all-girls boarding school. At least it had been all girls then. Kamryn eyed Yara carefully. "Yes, eighteen years ago, we could have fired her for that. But you can't now. And if you're looking to fire Elia Sharpe for something, you're going to have to come up with a far more egregious error on her part."

"Perhaps a personal relationship with the Head of School."

Ah, so that was going to come back and bite her in the ass. Kamryn dropped her pen onto the notepad. "I have a personal relationship with all of the faculty. It's impossible not to when you work closely with them and when you live on the same campus as most. And it's unlikely that I wouldn't have a personal relationship with Dr. Sharpe, or any of the other four faculty members who were teaching here when I was a student. I've known them for more than half my life at this rate. You can't require complete objectivity. It's impossible."

The lines around Yara's mouth were prominent when she frowned. She didn't like Kamryn's response, but she also didn't fight her on it. Probably because she didn't hear enough of the conversation in Kamryn's office to really know anything.

"What happened eighteen years ago?" Kamryn brought them back around.

"Do you remember Rylann Fowler?" Heather asked, looking solemn for the first time since she and Kamryn had been reintroduced. "Her older sister is Lucia."

"Okay, vaguely. She's a few years younger than me, right?"

"Four. She was in eighth grade when you graduated." Heather seemed so forlorn now. She absolutely believed what she was about to say. Kamryn had no doubts about it. "When she was a sophomore, she filed a complaint against Elia Sharpe for sexual harassment. She was on the Speech team, and she said that Elia harassed her not only in the classroom but also on the overnight trips that they took."

"Only harassment?" Kamryn asked, writing *sexual harassment* onto her yellow pad. She was finally getting somewhere with answers.

"Yes."

"No," Yara interjected. "Rylann also accused Elia of sexual advances and coercion, but she dropped that part of her complaint after the pressure from the school became too much."

Kamryn wrote that down as well. She was going to need to dig deep into the school archives for as much information as she could possibly find about the details. Surely, they had to be somewhere. At the very least, Mrs. Caldera should remember everything. She always did.

"Was Rylann the only student who complained?"

"She was," Susy jumped into the conversation. "At least about anything sexual. Elia had other complaints about being too hard on the students, expecting too much."

That would be Elia. Kamryn had those same complaints when she'd been a student, but Elia had never expected more than what her students could handle. She just held them to high standards, and now, twenty years later, Kamryn was glad Elia had done that. It helped her to raise the bar on herself several times over the years.

"So in the following eighteen years, disregarding this one situation, there were no other complaints filed against Elia about sexual harassment, sexual coercion, sexual assault, rape, or anything of that nature?" Kamryn was ready to hear it all, even if it devastated her in the end. She needed to know who she was dealing with—who she was falling head over heels in love with.

"Not as far as I know," Yara answered.

Both Heather and Susy shook their heads.

"But if the personnel file has been wiped of any incriminating reports, then we have no way of knowing tonight if there were other complaints filed against her," Kamryn added.

"We don't," Susy responded.

"And you couldn't tell me all of this before? When I suggested Elia for this team? When you hired me and told me that this team was top priority for the board?" Kamryn dropped her pen onto her notepad. "Because this is relevant information to how I run this school and protect the children we house and teach here. Without all the information, I can't do that. In my view, you're as liable as Elia right now, and as liable as whoever cleaned out her files."

Heather looked an odd shade of gray. Susy looked as though she'd just been scolded. Yara, however, seemed pleased as punch. Kamryn couldn't figure the three of them out. But at least they seemed to take what she'd said to heart.

"Let's do this..." Kamryn started with a sigh. "Let's meet again, soon. And in the meantime, Yara and I will begin to work through the files in the school and see if we can find the missing records. All of them, even if Elia's weren't the only ones. We need to make sure that they were or weren't. And then we're going to figure out who did it."

"Sounds good," Yara answered.

Of course she would be happy with this answer. She was basically getting what she wanted for now. And the *for now* part was what Kamryn had to remember.

"Heather, Susy—I want you to report back to the board about the missing records. Without disclosing the details of whose records are missing unless Yara and I find more information out before the next board meeting." Kamryn wrote each of these action items down, so that everyone was on the same page when they got back together. "In the meantime, we'll implement *some* of Yara's restrictions on Elia, but not all of them."

"What?" Yara's eyes widened in shock.

Kamryn shook her head, holding her ground on this one. "Those restrictions went away for a reason, and what you're asking for is over and above what would be required unless a new complaint was filed. And there hasn't been. I'll speak with Elia about supervision during classes and office hours and ask that she restrict her time in the main part of campus. Since I'm co-leading the Speech team, she'll be supervised by me on those trips and during practices."

"And you don't see that as a conflict?" Yara pushed.

"No, I don't. The board hired me for a reason. Let me do my job." Kamryn stared across the table at Yara, giving her a pointed look. "If you see my position as a conflict of interest, then you should recuse yourself right now.'

"Why would Yara need to leave?" Heather asked.

Kamryn held her hand out for Yara to explain. She didn't want to be the one to explain it. She was airing dirty laundry for sure. Elia had said the breakup was mutual, but that didn't mean that Yara felt that way. When Yara didn't answer, Kamryn jumped right back in.

"During the time of the accusation, actually, Yara and Elia were in a committed relationship."

"Not at the time of the accusation," Yara corrected. "Elia and I broke up before that happened."

"Lucky for you," Kamryn murmured. She couldn't imagine being in a relationship with someone who had been accused of that, having children at home, and then having to decide whether or not to support a partner.

"Yes, lucky for me," Yara agreed. "Not so lucky for Rylann. It ruined her."

Kamryn would look into that one too. She needed as much information as she could possibly find. "Yara, are you available to come in tomorrow?"

"Thursday, I can."

"Good." Kamryn put it into her calendar. "We'll start our investigation then. We'll meet together next week to discuss what we've found—or not found." Kamryn was ready for this to be done. She needed time to collect herself again.

They finished the meeting, and Kamryn made sure that the others left before heading back to her office. She fired off a text to

Greer, but she kept it simple. She couldn't exactly tell her everything. It was all confidential at this point. But she needed someone to vent to and to tell her worries to, and Greer was the best option for that. At least at this point.

"Hey," Kamryn said as she answered Greer's call. "I've had a hell of a day."

"Oh no, what happened?"

Shaking her head, Kamryn stared at her desk drawer where she'd shoved Elia's file. "I can't talk specifics."

"Okay." Greer knew the drill.

"People can be so cruel, but right now I'm not sure who to believe." Kamryn closed her eyes and let that sink in. Without all of the facts, she was left in a constant spinning loop of what-ifs.

"Who do you want to believe?" Greer asked.

"All of them." That was Kamryn's issue. She wanted to always believe the one who was coming forth and making the accusation, first and foremost. So she couldn't just let that go. "I want to believe all of them."

"Oh, Kam, that's so hard."

"Because it's impossible." Kamryn groaned and put her head on her desk. "What do I do?"

"You go straight to the closest source you can find."

Kamryn had known that was the answer, but despite having Greer tell her that to her face, she still didn't want to do it. This was going to hurt. Not just Elia, not just Kamryn, but it was going to hurt whatever was between them.

Wasn't it?

"Yeah. You're right. Thanks. I'll talk to you soon. Love you."

"Love you!"

Kamryn hung up, and without waiting to start doubting herself, she grabbed her jacket, locked up her office, and left the building. It didn't take her long to reach the humanities building and find Elia's office door wide open and the light still on. Speech practice would have ended only ten minutes before, and Kamryn was certain that Elia would be cleaning up to head home.

When she reached the door, Elia looked up at her, devastation clearly written all across her face. Elia was waiting for Kamryn to bring her bad news. But Kamryn wasn't ready to do that, not just yet.

"What did you decide?" Elia asked.

Kamryn pursed her lips and shook her head. "Not here. Take a walk with me, Elia."

twenty-six

They walked in silence from Elia's office toward her house. Everything in Elia's head told her to stop this right here and right now, but she couldn't. Abagail had been right. This was so hard, and she just wanted someone to believe her.

When they reached her house, Elia unlocked the door and let them in, dropping her things by the door before she nervously walked toward the kitchen. Tea would help, wouldn't it? Anything to keep her hands busy.

She risked a glance up at Kamryn, who was so still and quiet, as she took off her jacket and tossed it onto the arm of the couch. Kamryn knew everything at this point. Elia had seen it in the haunted look in her eyes when she'd shown up at her office.

"I don't know how you've kept this a secret for so long." Kamryn's voice was confident as she spoke, but it wasn't loud or an accusation.

Elia clicked on the electric kettle and crossed her arms over her chest in a move of protection. She didn't want to talk about this. She never wanted to talk about it. "It's not a secret."

Kamryn snorted, her lips twitching upward slightly. "Could have fooled me."

She walked closer to Elia, staying at the edge of the open

kitchen and not coming any closer. Was she afraid that Elia was going to try something? Was Kamryn afraid that it was all true?

"It's not a secret, Kam. You weren't here when it happened, but the entire school knew about it. The board knew about it. The local authorities knew about it. My name was in the news so many times that I lost count." Elia leaned against the kitchen counter, still keeping her arms crossed. It took everything in her to look up into Kamryn's eyes. "If you'd been here, you would have known just like everyone else."

"And in eighteen years the school's just, what...forgotten?"

Elia shrugged slightly. "It's in my personnel file. It's not forgotten. I'm required to have a co-leader for the Speech team. I can't take on any new responsibilities without it being double checked by my direct supervisor. And I can't move up into administration. No matter how many times I've applied for a new job, it comes up. I'm stuck here, Kam. I've never been able to escape it."

"It's not in your personnel file."

"What?" Elia's eyes widened. She stood up straight and put her hand out to her side. "What do you mean it's not there?"

"Your personnel file is wiped clean. Not one single complaint since you started working at Windermere twenty-four years ago." Kamryn crossed her arms now, the accusation in her words and her actions.

The cold rush of fear ran through Elia in an instant. Was she being accused of tampering with it?

"I walked into that ethics meeting knowing nothing, Elia. And you could have told me what I was walking into so many times over. Why wouldn't you just tell me what happened?"

There were so many reasons. Elia took a deep breath, calming her racing heart. She needed to explain this clearly, and she needed to tell Kamryn everything. She couldn't hold back any longer, even if Abagail wanted her to.

"Who erased my file?"

"Hell if I know, Elia. But I plan to find out, even if it was you.

And let me make it clear, if it was, I'm not going to hold back." Kamryn's lips drew into a thin line.

"I would expect nothing less." Elia snagged two mugs and set them on the counter. "What did they tell you?"

"Not a whole lot, honestly. I researched what I could after the meeting, and I have to say, Elia, these are dangerous waters you were swimming in."

"I know." Elia put the tea bags into the mugs and poured the boiling water over it to let the tea bags steep. "But you had to have also seen that it was ultimately decided the accusations were false."

"They were," Kamryn agreed. "But I want your side of the story. It's the only one that's missing for me right now."

Elia ran her finger in a circle around the top of the mug. She was going to hate this. Taking the cup of tea she'd made for Kamryn, Elia walked over and handed it to her. Their fingers touched as Kamryn took it, and Elia stared down at where Kamryn's fingers had slid against hers.

"Don't hate me after this, please." Elia didn't look at her as she walked around the peninsula of the kitchen and walked directly to the couch. Kamryn was going to end this tonight, Elia knew that. Kamryn was going to hear her side of the story, and she was going to walk out and not look back. Everyone always did.

Kamryn settled next to her on the couch. But there was quite a bit of distance between them. Elia felt it in her heart. It was why she'd never managed to hold onto a relationship since then. How did she even begin to explain that she'd been accused of sexually harassing a minor when she was that minor's teacher and that she wasn't some monster.

Because everyone thought she was.

"Yara and I broke up. It was mutual, just the end to a slow petering out of a relationship." Elia wrapped her hands around the mug, warming her skin from the cold walk home. "Everything was fine for a month. Heartbroken, but fine."

She couldn't believe she was even explaining this. It had been so long since she'd sat down with someone and run through exactly what happened. She curled her legs under her body and leaned into the corner of the couch.

"A month later, I was called into an emergency meeting with the ethics team, with the Head of School at the time—Jessup Watters—and no one else. They explained to me that there had been a formal complaint filed against me for sexual harassment by a student. They wouldn't tell me who. Not then, anyway. I was on an immediately paid suspension while they investigated. I was forced to leave my apartment in the dormitories for the safety of the students, and then I just had to wait." Elia sighed heavily.

"Where did you go?" Kamryn asked, her voice meeker than Elia expected it to be.

"I stayed with my friend, Abagail. She works human resources in Boston." Elia took a sip of her tea, burning her lips, the roof of her mouth, and her tongue in the process. She stared down at the liquid, unable to truly look at Kamryn. She didn't want to know the answers to the questions she refused to ask.

"I bet she was helpful during this situation."

"In more ways than one," Elia responded. "She also told me that I shouldn't tell you what happened." Elia frowned but glanced up at Kamryn then. "Because it'll cause more of a conflict of interest for you."

"And you're not taking her advice?" Kamryn raised an eyebrow in Elia's direction.

"No, I'm not. And I'm sure that I'll regret this decision later." She sighed and set her mug onto the coffee table. "When all was said and done, what was discovered was that Rylann made a false report. All charges were dropped, and I was allowed back onto the campus for the following semester. It took about six months for everything to be resolved."

"What did she say you did?" Kamryn asked.

Elia's cheeks heated. "She said that I made comments about how she was dressed, about how I liked the way she was dressed..." Elia slowed down, hating to say this out loud, but knowing that it was exactly what Kamryn was asking for. "...She said that I said sexual things to her, not asking her for sexual favors, but that I would say comments about other girl's bodies and her own, comments about what they should do together while in the dorms." Elia gulped. "She implied that there were emails exchanged between us, but those were never recovered or found."

"Because they were deleted or because they don't exist?" Kamryn asked.

"They don't exist," Elia confirmed. "Rylann was best friends with Heather and Felicity... Yara's oldest daughter. What Rylann finally admitted was that when Yara and I broke up, Felicity was the one who was hurt the most, and she wanted me to pay for what she thought I'd done, which was hurt Felicity and hurt Yara."

"So you were blamed for the breakup."

"Yes. And I didn't mind that Yara did that, especially with Felicity. I mean, if I needed to be blamed to make it easier for her, then by all means, blame me."

"But you didn't ask to be accused of sexual harassment over it."

"No, that I didn't." Elia brushed her fingers through her hair. "I tried to find another job after that, but anytime I would get an interview, I wouldn't be up for the job. No one wanted to hire me, not with my track record."

"And that's why you never applied to be Head of School when Jessup left."

Elia nodded. "Yeah, exactly."

"And now?"

"I thought it'd been long enough that maybe it wouldn't matter." Elia wrung her hands together. "I was wrong. The stigma, the accusations, all of it has followed me for the last eighteen years, and I've had enough, Kam. I'm not sure I want to fight it this time, and there will be even more questions now than there were before, because *now* they have a trend they can prove."

"A trend?" Kamryn squinted.

"You." Elia wasn't sure she could say the words out loud, but she had to. "You were my former student, and now... Yara isn't stupid, Kam. She knows there's more going on between us. We dated for two years, she's not oblivious. It's why I held back on telling the board, and with all of this coming back up now, I don't think it's a good idea."

"I agree," Kamryn responded. "Not only for your sake but for mine. I'm already tangled up in this enough without adding in that complication to the conversation."

Elia frowned. She hated that she was the cause of all of this. It would have been so much better if she'd just stayed in her lane, if she hadn't given in to wanting to know if there was more between them. "I'm so sorry, Kam."

"For what, exactly?"

"For so much." Elia stood up, that nervous energy shooting through her body in a way that she couldn't avoid even if she wanted to. "For not telling you sooner, for even thinking that maybe enough time had passed and I might have a chance at a relationship with you, for tangling you up in a mess that I've never been able to divorce myself from."

She roughly grabbed her tea and started back toward the kitchen, but Kamryn shot out a hand and stopped her. Elia froze. Her eyes locked on their fingers—touching—the tender grasp that Kamryn had on her. She shook her head when she looked directly into Kamryn's eyes.

"I wish you wouldn't," Elia whispered.

"Wouldn't what?"

"Kam..." Elia couldn't finish her thought.

Kamryn stood up, taking the mug from Elia's fingers and setting it back down on the coffee table. She slid her arms around Elia's shoulder and pulled her in.

A hug.

As simple as that. Elia stayed, lax, arms at her sides, in the safe embrace of Kamryn's arms. She buried her face in Kamryn's shoulder and sucked in a slow breath, becoming overwhelmed with Kamryn's scent, with her strength, everything that Elia wanted and couldn't have.

"Why are you still here?" Elia asked into Kamryn's shoulder, unable to turn away. "Why haven't you left yet?"

"I believe you," Kamryn whispered, tightening her grasp. "Normally I wouldn't be inclined to listen to your explanation, but everything you shared tonight lines up with what I found, aside from the lack of information in your personnel file. That's an issue I'm going to deal with." Kamryn pulled away slightly, her hand resting at the back of Elia's neck and tilting her head up so they could look into each other eyes. "You asked me to believe the victim."

"I didn't ask you to believe me." Elia couldn't tear her gaze away. She needed to hear those words.

Kamryn moved her hand up and brushed her fingers across Elia's cheeks, wiping the silent tears from her skin.

"You shouldn't believe me."

"Why not?"

Elia shivered. "Because anyone who has been assaulted should be believed the moment they step forward to say something."

"You're right. They should. They deserve that." Kamryn nodded, wiping even more tears from Elia's cheeks. "And you deserve to be believed, too. You did nothing wrong, and yet all those years later, you're still bearing the brunt of someone else's lie."

"She was a hurting kid, Kam. Rylann's home life wasn't great, and school was a sanctuary for her. She didn't know better than to lie."

"Not every bad behavior needs to be excused." Kamryn held Elia firmly. "Do you understand that?"

"Yes," Elia whispered.

"You deserved better from everyone. And I'm going to make sure that the witch hunt against you ends here." Kamryn gave her a sweet smile. "Whether or not our relationship continues, Elia, you deserve to walk into work every day with your head held high and to teach without feeling like you're going to be thrown under the bus every two seconds."

Elia let out a shuddering breath. She couldn't tear her gaze away from Kamryn, from the warmth in her eyes, the sincerity in everything she was saying. Taking a small step forward, Elia reached up and did the only thing she could think of.

She pressed their mouths together.

twenty-seven

"Elia." Kamryn broke the kiss. "I'm not sure this is the right time."

"The timing is never right," Elia answered. "But I wasn't lying in your office earlier. I don't want this to end."

Kamryn bent her head, pressing their foreheads together. Her mind was spinning with all the possibilities, and her body was telling her only one thing. Comfort would feel so nice right now. Comfort from someone she trusted and who trusted her. They'd shared something tonight, something far deeper than anything else that had come before.

This was their breakthrough.

Kamryn closed her eyes, trying to process each thought individually and make sense of it all.

Elia was under fire right now from the school board.

Kamryn was caught in the middle of it all.

Someone else was hiding what had happened all those years ago, and for what purpose?

Kamryn couldn't look at this situation objectively. She hadn't lied about that, but she was so much more tangled up in it than she'd wanted to admit to Yara.

And she trusted Elia's story.

It made sense.

It lined up with all those news reports that she'd found.

And it lined up with everything the ethics team had conveniently left out of the conversation.

But Kamryn was Elia's former student. And that alone could tear apart anything they did to build Elia's career back up.

"Kam..." Elia whispered, sliding out of her grasp slightly. "We don't have to. It's fine." She snagged the mug of tea off the table and started for the kitchen, leaving Kamryn still stunned and standing in the middle of the living room.

This shouldn't be so damn hard.

Why was love always so complicated?

Kamryn watched as Elia cleaned her cup and set it into the dishwasher, saying nothing as she worked. The sounds were so normalized, so mundane, and yet the entire conversation today had been about something so extreme. What if a little normalcy was all they needed to feel like they could make it through this?

Not on a whim, Kamryn rounded the couch and walked directly up to Elia. She said nothing as she took Elia by the hand and led her directly toward the stairs. Elia followed without resisting. As soon as they reached Elia's bedroom, Kamryn turned around and set her eyes on Elia.

"We'll figure it out tomorrow—at least start to," Kamryn said. "If this is what you want."

"Yes." Elia nodded, but she also didn't move to initiate. "Yes, this is what I want."

Kamryn reached upward, sliding her fingers along the edge of Elia's blouse, the V-neck not that low, but revealing small freckles and sunspots along Elia's chest. Kamryn touched them lightly before dropping her hand to Elia's hip and pushing her slightly so that she was between the bed and Kamryn.

"Are you sure?" Kamryn asked. With everything that had gone on, she needed to know that they were both okay with doing this, that they were both aware of the potential consequences—

perhaps for the first time fully aware of them. "Because I don't want to do this if you're not okay with it."

"Kam..." Elia brushed her fingers across Kamryn's lips. "You're the only one I want to be with."

A buzz filled Kamryn's body, one that was full of something she wasn't quite ready to name yet. She had to hope that her feelings for Elia weren't clouding what she was doing. That she truly was hearing and seeing what had happened all those years ago with a clear and level head. Reaching for the edge of Elia's shirt, Kamryn slid it over her head and dropped it to the floor.

"You're so beautiful," Kamryn murmured, tracing the curve of Elia's body from her ribs to her waist to her hip with just the faintest of touches from her fingertips. "So strong. I never in a million years thought that this would happen when I took the job here."

"Me either," Elia answered.

Reaching behind Elia, Kamryn pinched the clasp of her bra and let it drop to the ground along with her shirt. Elia's small nipples were already puckered and hard. Kamryn brushed them with the backs of her knuckles before leaving them alone. Everything she did, she did slowly, with reverence. She was going to hold every moment they had together tonight carefully.

"I didn't want to let you leave this afternoon." Kamryn pressed her cheek against Elia's, speaking quietly into her ear before dropping kisses along her jawline. Elia's skin was so warm and soft, beckoning Kamryn's every touch and taste. "I wanted to keep you there, talk everything out with you. But you have a damn bad habit of walking away instead of sticking around sometimes."

"Yeah, I do." Elia's voice was so breathy.

Kamryn scraped her teeth along the thick cord of muscle down Elia's neck. She didn't bite or make it hurt. With her tongue, she followed the line of Elia's collarbone to her shoulder, placing a gentle nip there. Elia gasped, and she plunged her fingers into Kamryn's hair, tugging on the strands and scraping her nails along Kamryn's scalp.

"I wish you wouldn't do that with me." Kamryn pressed a kiss to the center of Elia's chest. "I want you to stay and talk to me, not be afraid of my reaction."

Elia let out a small noise in the back of her throat. She tilted her head back as she guided Kamryn's mouth down her chest to her breast.

"I don't want to half the time," Elia admitted. "But old habits are hard to change, no matter how hard I try." Pulling Kamryn upward, Elia melded their mouths together, taking control of the kiss.

Kamryn melted into her, holding on tightly to Elia's back as she kept their bodies locked together. She skimmed her fingers down Elia's back, across her hips, onto her ass, and she tugged Elia into her harder, increasing the energy of the moment into something they were far more used to.

"Don't shut me out," Kamryn begged, finding the zipper on the back of Elia's skirt and pulling it down. "I don't want you to shut me out."

Elia pulled Kamryn back in, their tongues tangling as Elia took control of the kiss. Kamryn continued to slowly undress Elia, making all her clothes disappear to somewhere she didn't care about. Kamryn was just about to push Elia back onto the bed when Elia's fingers tugged at the fabric of her dress.

"Take it off," Kamryn said. "I want to feel you against me."

Elia pulled her hands upward, taking more and more fabric with her until she reached the edge. She didn't wait as she pushed the dress up and over Kamryn's head. Kamryn's breath caught when she saw Elia's gaze cascade down her body, from her lips to her chest to her hips and to right between her legs.

She'd always been a little self-conscious of her body, especially in the last ten years when she'd gained more weight than she thought she would during one of her breakups with Lauren. They'd never gotten back to sex like it had been before, and something in the back of Kamryn's mind always told her it was because of that.

But something about the way Elia looked at her—hungrily—had made those thoughts vanish in an instant every time, and tonight was no different. Elia reached up, palming Kamryn's breast and massaging before she followed the fabric of her bra to her back and pulled the material away from Kamryn's body.

"Against me," Elia murmured, as if in a trance.

That's what Kamryn felt like anyway. Completely focused on Elia, her body, pleasure that they would create for each other, and nothing else. All the worries and fears vanished into the ether where they couldn't be seen or heard anymore. And that was exactly where Kamryn wanted them to stay for now.

Kamryn stepped in closer, sliding one knee between Elia's legs and pulling her in closer. She pressed their mouths together before stepping back. This wasn't how she wanted this. Not yet anyway.

"Get on the bed." Kamryn stepped away and bent down, using the edge of the mattress to hold herself up as she slid her finger into her heels and tugged them off. Unlike Elia, she hadn't taken her shoes off as soon as she'd entered the house. While Elia sat on the bed and then moved into the center of it, Kamryn pulled off her underwear and then put her hands on her hips, looking Elia over.

This was how she wanted it. Face to face—intimate—raw. Climbing onto the bed, Kamryn knelt over Elia on all fours. She bent down, connecting their lips in yet another kiss before she dropped her weight down into the cradle of Elia's body.

"Touch me," Kamryn said. "Same way I'm touching you."

Moving just enough to get her hand between them, Kamryn slid her fingers firmly across Elia's chest again. Her nipples were still hard, and she palmed Elia's breast tightly. Elia gasped, but she finally lifted her hand to touch Kamryn in the exact same way, mirroring Kamryn's touches.

Kamryn held herself up with one hand as she fluttered her

fingers down Elia's side to her hip, across the front of her abdomen and then back again. Elia's hand wasn't much behind hers as they moved. Kamryn smiled down at Elia, settling into the pacing and the touching.

"I'm here for you, you know that, right?" Kamryn kissed Elia's cheek, closing her eyes and listening to the change in Elia's breathing. "Don't shut me out."

Elia put her hand behind Kamryn's head and pulled her down, kissing her feverishly. She said nothing in response, but Kamryn hoped that with that kind of reaction, Elia had at least heard and felt the sentiment that Kamryn was trying to give her.

"Are you ready?" Kamryn asked.

Elia nodded.

Moving her hand farther down, Kamryn pressed her fingers between Elia's legs. Elia did the same to her. Together they touched each other, first running two fingers across their swollen lips, then inside. Kamryn dipped her fingers into Elia's juices, always amazed that Elia would have this reaction to her. That someone this amazing would be interested in her.

"Don't stop touching me," Kamryn whispered into Elia's ear. "No matter what."

Elia nodded, biting her lip as she mimicked Kamryn's touches. Kamryn's fingers slid up to Elia's clit. Elia's cheeks tightened for a brief moment before they relaxed.

"Sensitive tonight?" Kamryn asked.

"Yesssss," Elia hissed back. That was probably a good thing. Kamryn was going to use it to her advantage at least. Especially because she wasn't as obviously sensitive as Elia was. "Yes," Elia said again, this time the word floating off into the air between them.

"Elia..." Kamryn breathed her name, wanting it to become the only thing she said tonight. Her name felt so good rolling off her tongue, the natural tone to it, the rhythm of the word as her tongue rolled on the 'l'. "Elia," she said again.

"Kam," Elia responded.

Kamryn couldn't stop the grin that lit up her face. They were absolutely lost in one another. Sliding two fingers inside Elia, Kamryn held her close. Seconds later, Elia mimicked Kamryn's touch. This was going to go perfectly—it had to. Kamryn bent her fingers, pulsing gently against Elia.

The groan Kamryn received in response was exactly what she'd been looking for. And when Elia got her brain together enough to do it on Kamryn, she didn't disappoint. Dropping her head onto Elia's shoulder, Kamryn used what was left of her concentration to keep herself somewhat upright and in the right position for this to happen.

She pumped her fingers—once, twice, three times. Kamryn pressed a kiss into Elia's shoulder before parting her lips and sucking at the skin at the base of Elia's neck, swirling her tongue in response. Elia lifted her hips up, straining to keep her body still.

"Let go if you're ready," Kamryn said against Elia's skin before she went back to sucking and teasing.

"So close, Kam."

"Then hold on a little longer." Kamryn wasn't anywhere near ready, but having Elia's hand between her legs still felt amazing. She focused her energy on what she was doing, on the way that Elia was struggling to follow the rhythm now, on the fact that Elia's body was twitching and jerking and moving out of her control.

"Kam!"

"I've got you," Kamryn said, holding tightly to Elia. She kept the movement going, even as Elia pulsed around her, as her breathing increased and then slowed, as her body tightened and then relaxed. Kamryn stayed right where she was, making sure that they were together through every part of this from beginning to end.

"Turn over," Elia said, her senses coming back to her.

Kamryn did as she was told, moving to lie on her back with her knees spread. Elia slid down her body, kissing her way in an aimless direction from Kamryn's mouth, across her breasts, and over her stomach. Her hair tickled as it followed the path of Elia's kisses. Smiling to herself, Kamryn brushed Elia's hair to the side so she could see her face and the intense look that Elia gave her in response.

"What are you going to do next?" Kamryn asked, a tease in her tone that she hadn't known she was capable of that night, but she was glad to hear it. She was far more at ease now than she had been earlier. This had been exactly what they both needed. Time where it was just the two of them and no one else to ruin it for them.

"Wouldn't you like to know?" Elia moved to the side, scraping her teeth along the top of Kamryn's hip and toward her belly button.

Kamryn cried out, her hips jerking instantly from the touch. She hadn't expected that move, not at all. She curled her fingers into the sheets, gripping onto them to hold herself right where she needed to be so that Elia could do anything she wanted.

"Did you like that?" Elia asked, looking directly up into Kamryn's gaze.

"Yes. A lot."

Elia just smiled in response before she did it again on the other side. "Can't go without equal treatment, can we?"

"No." Kamryn wasn't sure what she'd signed herself up for yet, but she was pretty sure it was going to involve a slow rise toward an orgasm that she wasn't going to be prepared to be hit by.

Elia licked a circle around Kamryn's belly button before moving her way back up Kamryn's body. She took Kamryn's left nipple into her mouth, sucking and using the flat of her tongue to pulse against her. Kamryn tightened her grip on the sheets, arching her back up. She really hadn't prepared herself properly for this. She should have, but she hadn't. Everything with Elia always seemed to happen so unexpectedly fast and slow at the same time.

Kamryn grunted when Elia flicked her nipple with the tip of

her tongue. Elia moved one hand back down between Kamryn's legs and put her fingers right back where they were before. Kamryn's knees parted a little more to give Elia better access.

She raised a hand over her head, gripping onto the edge of the pillow that her head rested on. She was going to hold still. She was going to let Elia do whatever she wanted tonight. And she was going to absolutely enjoy every single moment of it.

Elia pulsed her fingers against Kamryn. Then she flipped from Kamryn's left breast to her right, giving it exactly the same treatment as the other one. Kamryn should have guessed that would happen based on Elia's earlier comment, but she hadn't figured it out soon enough. It caught her off guard and she cried out as pleasure hit her quickly.

"Fuck, Elia."

Elia hummed against her, but if she was trying to say something, it was lost on Kamryn. She felt a surge of wetness between her legs, and the prickles of her orgasm begin to work their way throughout her body. Kamryn focused on Elia's fingers. She listened to her body tell her everything about the way Elia touched her.

"Keep going," Kamryn moaned around the words. "I'm getting there."

Elia moved back down Kamryn's body, pressing kisses against her stomach, against the top of her mound, and then against her clit. Kamryn's hips reared upward as she hissed. Elia flicked her tongue out just like she'd done to Kamryn's nipples. Then she covered Kamryn's clit with her mouth and sucked in that same way.

Kamryn did everything in her power to keep herself still and in place. She wanted to feel everything and more. She was so lost in the sensations that she wasn't sure if she was speaking, moaning, or just writhing under Elia's touch.

Taking one last breath, Kamryn held it tightly as she crashed through her orgasm. Her body rocked. Her heart raced, threatening to pound its way out of her chest. Her cheeks and chest were so hot that she worried she'd succumb to heatstroke if she didn't catch a breath of cold, fresh air. Elia stayed right between her legs, easing her through the orgasm, one lick at a time.

Finally, Kamryn pushed Elia away from her and shook her head. "Enough for now."

Elia said nothing as she moved back up Kamryn's body with sweet kisses that weren't meant to incite. Kamryn waited until Elia was close enough and then captured her in a kiss and a hug, the cool damp on Elia's lips and cheeks a reminder of what they'd just done. Kamryn sank into it.

This was pure. This was just for them.

She pulled Elia into her embrace, spooning her from behind and using her feet to pull the blanket up and over their bodies as they cooled. Kamryn had no idea what to say now, so she just held Elia close to her. She soothed the goose bumped skin when it became too cool for them, and she kissed the back of Elia's neck and shoulder as Elia fell into a slumber.

Kamryn stayed where she was, awake long after Elia had finally fallen asleep. Her mind already spinning with what tomorrow was going to bring.

If only their little oasis could last a little longer.

Then maybe they wouldn't have to hurt each other.

twenty-eight

Elia rapped her knuckles against Kamryn's hotel room door and waited. They'd spent hours talking since the last ethics team meeting, but that still left them in an awkward spot in terms of how they were going to handle everything. And Elia couldn't get it out of her head.

She'd been so hyperfocused on the kids all day to keep herself distracted, but now that they were tucked away in their rooms preparing to sleep, Elia was lost. She couldn't stop thinking about everything she'd confessed to Kamryn, about the ethics team, about all the upheaval that was playing out around her.

Kamryn opened the door, squinting at her behind a pair of reading glasses, which were absolutely adorable on her. Elia immediately felt her lips turn upward and her body relax a bit. "Hey, since when do you wear reading glasses?"

"Since I hit thirty-five and my body started to think I was an old crone." Kamryn winked. "Was there something you needed?"

Elia's lips parted in surprise because she wasn't being immediately invited in. She'd thought—well, hell, she'd thought that the intimacy they'd created between them so far wouldn't end this quickly.

"Just to talk." It was the simplest way for Elia to say that she needed to be in Kamryn's presence, and that she needed to feel and hear her voice, no matter what they were talking about. "About the ethics team."

"Right." Kamryn dropped her voice and glanced up and down the hallway. "Everyone is in their rooms?"

"Yes, and Bailey is going to check on them in an hour to make sure they're all asleep."

"Good." Kamryn stepped to the side and opened the door wider, allowing Elia to finally walk in.

The air was frigid. Kamryn must have the air conditioner turned on. Elia wrapped her arms around her chest and walked inside. The desk was littered with papers and Kamryn's laptop. There were even papers strewn about on the end of the bed. Kamryn immediately started to clean those up, sliding them back into the folders they must have come from.

"I got a bit lost in work, sorry." Kamryn shoved the folders onto the desk and closed her laptop, dropping her reading glasses on top of the lid. "In all honesty, I got the glasses because I've been staring at the computer way too much lately."

Elia stared hard at Kamryn. "Maybe you shouldn't work so much."

Kamryn snorted and shook her head. "Impossible right now."

Guilt slammed Elia hard. She had no doubt that this was because of her and because of Yara and Susy and Heather bringing up her whole sordid past in one go. And Elia hated it. She just wanted to make it all go away so that maybe she could go back to living in peace again. Not that she'd done too much of that before.

"Did you want to talk about the bachelorette party tomorrow?" Elia asked, sliding onto the edge of the mattress while Kamryn continued to stare at her.

It wasn't the reason she'd come in there, but it would at least be a distraction. Then again, hadn't she wanted to avoid distracting herself any longer?

"No." Kamryn sighed heavily. "What I want, right now, is to

go back a few more weeks and live like I didn't know any of this." Kamryn waved her hand over the papers. "These are the personnel records, kind of. They're the complaints that I've found, and I'm trying to piece them all back together."

"How many personnel files were wiped?" Elia wasn't sure if she should even be asking that question, or if Kamryn could even answer it.

Kamryn sighed again and ran her fingers through her hair, closing her eyes. "More than just yours, so that's a bright spot in your favor."

"Unless they think I erased everyone else's files to make me look innocent," Elia mumbled and stared at the odd design on the carpet under her feet. She shivered, the cold air hitting her skin in a way she didn't expect it to.

"I think it was Miller." Kamryn frowned.

"Really?" Elia looked directly at her. She could imagine Miller doing something like that. In the last few years, he'd definitely taken liberties in other things and thrown his weight around with the board, but there was no reason he'd go into her personnel file and erase that. He'd been fully aware of what had happened, just like he should have been.

"I don't know who else would have access to do it other than Jessup, but from what I can tell, there were files erased after Jessup left." Kamryn sat next to her, their shoulders brushing. "I don't know yet. I just started looking through everything tonight. I need to meet with the team on Tuesday—so I'm going to miss the next practice again—to go through even more of this."

"Kam, the kids need you at practice." Elia hated that she felt like she was trying to guilt Kamryn into everything. But if the kids were going to trust Kamryn to actually teach them, then she needed to be present.

"I know they do, but right now, I think you need me in those meetings more."

Elia needed her there? That thought warmed her from the

center of her chest. Kamryn did actually care about her, she just had to remind herself of that.

"Are you my knight in shining armor?" Elia meant it to sound like a light tease, but it didn't. It sounded pathetic, like she couldn't even manage to stand up for herself anymore and needed someone else to do it. That thrill of hyper-independence reared its ugly head, and Elia wanted to latch onto it.

But it had also been her downfall more times than she could count.

"Hardly," Kamryn answered. "If anything, I'm the bodyguard you never wanted."

"What?"

Kamryn frowned and then ran her hands over her face. "What I didn't tell you was one of the conditions that I agreed to in order to allow you more freedom."

"What are you talking about?"

"Yara wanted to bring down the hammer on you, put you on restriction after restriction, and I refused to do it." The stress lines in Kamryn's face were so tense. This was weighing so heavily on her, and she was right back to that guilt. "I agreed to one, and that was it."

"Which one?" Elia wasn't sure that she wanted to be asking that question. What would it mean for her ultimately? Could she even continue teaching? Had she already broken the rule that she didn't even know was in place.

"I get to supervise you, closely, while you're with students." Kamryn grimaced. "You already do everything else on their list aside from having a paid person to observe all your interactions with students."

Elia shuddered. She really was being thrown back eighteen years ago, wasn't she? "I had to do that for a while during the initial investigation."

"I know," Kamryn answered. "Yara was quite forthcoming with that information. And that you were required to pay for that person's time."

"I was," Elia whispered. It had been a strain on her finances, but Abagail had managed to give her a loan at the time, along with a place to live. "I was under a microscope, as I would expect with anyone accused of something like that."

"Yet they still allowed you to teach afterward."

"Because Rylann confessed that she'd made it all up."

"But where is that confession? Because I haven't found it yet." Kamryn pointed to all the papers on the desk. "And that's what I need, to prove that you were innocent eighteen years ago."

"I don't know." Elia worried her lower lip. "I wasn't ever given a copy of that because it was considered confidential on the school's side."

Kamryn wrinkled her nose. "I thought, originally, that the investigation into the complaints had been well done, and it might very well have been, but with no evidence to support that, I don't even know what to think any more."

"I hate what this is doing to you," Elia said, unexpectedly not just to herself but to Kamryn. The look on Kamryn's face was confirmation enough of that. "It's not worth it."

"Of course you're worth it," Kamryn retorted.

That hadn't exactly been what Elia said. She wasn't struggling with her self-worth. She was struggling with the drama that seemed to come from her, from the chaos that she seemed to bring with her into every relationship and every conversation lately. It would be so nice to just go back to how it was before.

"This isn't worth it," Elia reiterated. "Fighting them."

"Of course it is." A deep line formed in the middle of Kamryn's forehead. "First, I need to know what's going on at the school and what else was hidden. Your situation is just one of many that could be hiding away and causing issues that I don't know about. But second, I won't stand for injustice, Elia. You have to know that about me."

Elia did know that, but she also wasn't convinced that this was an injustice at this point. The accusations had been made years ago, she was found innocent of them, but it wasn't like that was happening anew this time. And she had to keep reminding herself of that. This wasn't a new threat. It was the same one that she had faced before and beaten.

"I do know that," Elia answered. "But also know this about me… I've been down this road before, and I'm not sure it's worth it to go down there again."

"Even if you have support this time?"

"I had support last time." Elia wouldn't discount Abagail, and she certainly wouldn't discount the fact that there were others who showed as much support as they could during that time. It was difficult, and eighteen years ago, she was convinced the entire world was out to get her. But looking back on it, that hadn't been the case. "Rylann is the one who needed support, not me. She was crying out for attention, and she got it, but it wasn't the kind that she needed."

Kamryn pulled away slightly.

"You've been teaching for years, Kam. You have to have known students like that."

"I do," Kamryn answered.

"I blamed her for years, you know. I blamed Rylann, I blamed Yara, and I blamed myself. I put myself in a position to be easily accessible to my students, to be seen more as friend than teacher, and that put me at risk. I refused to do that again since."

"Is that why you're so closed off now?" Kamryn touched the top of Elia's hand, curling her fingers around and squeezing lightly. "Because you're so different now."

"I am." Elia's shoulders stiffened. "And it's for good reason."

"In some ways, I'm glad you changed," Kamryn said, a glint in her eye that Elia wasn't quite sure where to place.

"Why's that?"

"I find the mystery behind an icy heart absolutely attractive." Kamryn chuckled nervously, as if she knew this wasn't the time and the place but she was stretching to lighten the mood.

"Are you saying that you wouldn't have found me attractive twenty years ago? If you were who you are now, I mean."

"Absolutely not." Kamryn winked. "Why do you think I liked Lauren so much?"

"Lauren." That was something that Elia hadn't really thought about or wanted to think about. Lauren had been one of those troubled students that Elia had tried to keep her eye on from a distance. She always seemed to have a dark cloud around her. And that was still the case all these years later. If Kamryn was attracted to the women who needed fixing, then it would make sense why she and Lauren had been together forever, and why she struggled to break it off entirely. "I want you to think about something."

"Sure."

Elia knew this could be the end of what they'd started, but she wanted to make it clear. "I don't need you or want you to fix me."

"Elia—"

"I'm serious, Kam. I don't want it. I can deal with my own problems and my own neurotic habits. I don't need you swooping in and thinking that I'm suddenly going to be someone different than I am today." That cold air wasn't the only thing bothering Elia, clearly. But she'd said her word, and she wasn't going to let it go this time.

"I don't want you to change," Kamryn said slowly. "I don't know why you think I do want that, but I don't. You have changed in the last two decades, just like anyone does, but I don't want to change you."

"It doesn't sound like that to me." Elia covered Kamryn's hand on hers briefly before removing it. "Let me know what you need from me for tomorrow."

"You're still planning on coming?"

Elia stood up and started toward the door. She hadn't really thought there was another option in that sense. She'd agreed to go with Kamryn, and she enjoyed spending time together. What harm would it do at this point, honestly?

"Sure. Besides, then you'll be absolutely certain that I'm not doing anything inappropriate with a student." *Ah…so that's where this is coming from.* Elia bit the inside of her cheek. "That was—"

"Anger," Kamryn finished for her. "Resentment, perhaps."

"Yeah," Elia agreed. "And I took it out on you." She really was going to need to find a way to navigate this, and the intricacies that they'd created and put into place that were causing so many complications and unintended hurts.

"That's fair," Kamryn responded. "I didn't exactly tell you before now what we'd decided on at the last meeting."

Elia pressed her lips together tightly, clenching her molars together. "You didn't. So, for tonight, I'll relieve you of your duties for a bit."

"Don't leave like this, Elia." Kamryn stood up and followed her. "Don't leave hurting."

"There's no way to resolve this hurt tonight." Elia touched Kamryn's cheek lightly, but she didn't pull her in for a kiss, the war inside her too strong for that to be a possibility right now. "Good night, Kam."

twenty-nine

"Andra!" Kamryn ran into the bar and wrapped her arms around one of her best friends. She'd needed this, probably more than Andra did. With the wedding tomorrow, and with all of the drama at the school picking up, Kamryn just needed a night where she didn't have to think about it.

"Hey there," Andra answered, squeezing her tightly. "And good to see you again." Andra moved away from Kamryn and extended her hand to Elia.

Except that.

With Elia here, Kamryn wasn't going to be able to avoid everything. And their conversation the night before had set her on edge far more than she'd anticipated it would. Stepping back, Kamryn slid her hand into Elia's, but she didn't squeeze.

"And you," Elia said, shaking Andra's hand. "It's good to see everyone again and relax a bit, don't you think?" Elia rocked her shoulder into Kamryn's slightly, which caused Kamryn to frown.

What was Elia playing at? She seemed so much more relaxed now than she did at the school. But was it only that? A change in environment? Surely not. Elia wasn't *that* good an actor.

"I see you have survived the relationship so far."

Kamryn tensed at Rosie's voice. Why did she let this woman

bother her so much? She really needed to figure that out already. Elia's hand tightened in hers before she swung her arm around Kamryn's back and pulled her in tightly to her side.

"We are." Elia said nothing else as she turned Kamryn away from Rosie and Lauren and moved toward another small group of friends nearby.

Kamryn wasn't even sure that she could get it together enough to say thank you for that maneuver. Elia stayed right next to her as a waitress came by to take their drink orders. Kamryn debated whether or not to get something strong, but when Elia leaned into her side and whispered, "Get whatever you want. I'll drive home." Kamryn didn't hesitate and ordered herself a double shot of whiskey.

"Thanks," Kamryn murmured, lowering her voice so no one but Elia could hear her. This shouldn't feel awkward, should it? They hadn't spent much time together, alone, since Kamryn had finally been brought in on what was going on, and she was placing a whole lot of trust in Elia, that she was the one telling the truth.

"Any time." Elia ran her hand up and down Kamryn's back. "Do you mind if we...ignore all the other drama in our lives tonight?"

Kamryn frowned, staring down into Elia's blue eyes, which seemed almost black in the dim light of the bar. "You want to ignore what exactly?"

"The inquisition." Elia stepped in closer, pressing her lips to Kamryn's ear. "Tonight I just want to be free. I don't want to be weighed down by past mistakes or hurts or questions about what my future is going to look like."

"I won't let them fire you."

"*You* can't control them. Just like I can't." Elia nibbled on the lobe of Kamryn's ear. "I don't want to think about it tonight. I just want to be me."

"And who are you?" Kamryn asked, that question resonating deeply in her chest and soul. Because up until this moment, she'd thought she'd gotten the true Elia Sharpe, the woman who was tightly wound with secrets but had such a caring heart that it caused her even more strife.

"Elia," she replied, kissing the corner of Kamryn's mouth. "Yours."

Kamryn moved in, pressing their lips together. She closed her eyes, feeling everything that she could and ignoring the people surrounding them. Elia was warm, comforting. Her scent was an embrace that Kamryn longed for every moment that she woke up in her own bed. Elia was brilliant, careful, concentrated. She was passionate in a way that Kamryn hadn't ever expected to experience after so many years teaching.

Their tongues touched.

The clearing throat startled Kamryn, and she pulled away quickly. The waitress stood next to them, Kamryn's drink in her hand and a soft drink in the other for Elia.

"Uh...thanks," Kamryn said, taking the drinks. "Sorry."

"Don't apologize for love, honey."

Kamryn frowned as she walked away. This wasn't love. It was far too complicated to be love. It was too hard to be anything other than lustful passion and a simple liking for each other. Besides, she was still in love with Lauren—wasn't she? She'd never not have feelings for Lauren. Handing Elia her drink, Kamryn sipped hers slowly. The alcohol filled her mouth, stung her lips and then burned her throat as she swallowed.

"Kam." Lauren walked over to stand next to them, eyeing Kamryn before she moved to look at Elia. "I'm still surprised that you two of all people ended up together."

"No one's more surprised than us, I think," Kamryn responded, trying to keep her tone light. But hadn't she just been thinking that and trying to figure it all out? Why was she so unsure now when she'd been so confident before?

Because Elia wasn't wrong.

Kamryn liked to fix broken situations and broken people.

That's what irked her. That comment, and the accusation

that Elia had made with it. But had that really been what she was trying to do?

"I'm not sure about that." Lauren tossed back the rest of her drink. "I'm breaking up with Rosie."

"Oh?" Kamryn raised an eyebrow, her entire body tilting toward Lauren out of habit. Here it was, wasn't it? The breakup that would inevitably push them back together. At least it always had in the past.

"Not tonight, though." Lauren dropped her voice so Kamryn had to lean in to hear her. "Maybe after the wedding."

Elia's lips thinned to a line as she watched the move, and immediately, Kamryn moved back. What was wrong with her? She stared down into the amber liquid in her hand and tossed it back. She needed another one. Kamryn walked away from Elia and Lauren, needing space. Her head was clouded. Her feelings were so mixed together that it was getting harder and harder to think.

"What did she say?" Elia asked, anger lacing her tone.

Startled, Kamryn looked over her shoulder, finding Elia right behind her.

"She's breaking up with Rosie. Can I have a double shot of whiskey?" Kamryn directed the question to the bartender. She leaned back down off her toes and looked Elia over. "I suppose she wants me to jump back into a relationship with her."

"And will you?"

Normally Elia would have touched her. By now Kamryn knew that. She would have slid her fingers gently, she would have touched Kamryn's back, but she didn't this time. Kamryn was giving off mixed signals galore tonight, and she seriously needed to stop it.

"Why can't love be easy?" Kamryn winced as the question left her lips because she wasn't talking about Lauren. She was talking about Elia, but she knew that wasn't how Elia was going to take it. Elia was probably the least selfish person she'd met, and yet

Kamryn couldn't stop fucking things up when it came to her relationships.

"Love *is* easy," Elia answered. "Being in relationships with actual people who are broken and traumatized and come with history is hard. The practical side of love is hard. But actually loving someone? That's just emotion."

Kamryn froze. She once again lost herself in those beautiful, stunning blue eyes, in the hard lines of Elia's aging features. "You might be right."

"I know I'm right." Elia straightened her shoulders and nodded toward the bar top. "Your drink's ready."

"Oh." Kamryn stared at it, not sure if she wanted it now. What was going on with her? She was all over the map. Taking the glass between her fingers, she spun it in two full circles before she threw it back and swallowed it. "I can't go back to Lauren. Nothing's going to change unless I make it change."

"You mean your relationship with her?"

"What relationship?" Kamryn muttered. "It's been the same for so long, and I don't want to be that person anymore." *I want to be who I am when I'm with you.* But Kamryn didn't say the last part out loud. She probably should have, but the buzz from the shots hit her swiftly.

"Then don't go back to her." Elia reached up and touched Kamryn's arm, wrapping her fingers around her bicep and squeezing. "Don't go back to her just because you feel obligated."

What was Kamryn supposed to say to that? Why did she always seem to say the right things when Kamryn didn't want to hear them? "Then what should I do?"

"What do you want to do?" Elia dropped her hand and the connection between them.

I want to be with you. But Kamryn wasn't sure she could say that out loud either. What did she really want? She wanted love without complications. She wanted to find herself in someone else. She wanted that fairytale that she'd never had. She wanted the promises she'd been told as a kid, all those promises about what love and life would look like that she knew now would never come true.

Kamryn eyed Elia carefully, from the curled ends of her hair with just a dusting of gray in them that no one would notice unless they were looking, to the way the corners of her eyes crinkled when she smiled—which she so rarely did. The lines of her lips, which she outlined carefully each day with a pencil before slathering on lipstick. The small freckles that littered her upper chest, probably from too much sun when she was younger.

Elia's lips parted, the tip of her tongue dashing out against them before they closed, and she swallowed. Kamryn's gaze was locked on her mouth, and she suddenly had the most outrageous thought. At least it would have been if she'd had it first.

Smiling, Kamryn cupped Elia's cheek and brushed her thumb across those beautiful lips. "I want to be free. Not weighed down by the past or the future, but just be me in this moment."

Elia gasped.

"You're right," Kamryn continued. "Let's not make promises that we can't keep, that the world or other people expect us to make. Let's just make one promise."

"What's that?" Elia whispered.

"Let's promise that when we're together we'll be ourselves, no matter what. We'll be free to be exactly who we are in whatever moment we're in." Kamryn grinned and pressed their foreheads together, her eyes closing. The world around them vanished again, and she was here to focus only on the things that felt good, right here and right now. "Promise?"

"Yeah," Elia answered.

"Can I kiss you?"

Elia didn't answer. Instead, she moved, tilting her chin up and capturing Kamryn's mouth. They both sighed simultaneously, easing into the kiss together, into the hope that they were finding in this moment. Kamryn needed to commit herself to this moment fully, because if she didn't, she'd focus too much on the what-ifs, on the fact that they shouldn't be doing this, on the worries that wouldn't stop plaguing her.

Maybe one day, she'd be at her own bachelorette party or planning her own wedding and her friends would be there to celebrate her. It wasn't today. It sure as hell wasn't going to be tomorrow, but Kamryn wanted the possibility to still be there.

She pulled away, her body relaxing and lightening as she made eye contact with Elia. "You have good ideas sometimes."

"Just sometimes?"

"Yeah, just sometimes." Kamryn grinned.

Lauren showed back up, a new drink in her hand, and she seemed nonplussed by the fact that Kamryn had just been making out with Elia in the middle of the bar. "So what do you think?"

"I think I'm good for now," Kamryn answered, barely sparing a glance to Lauren. Even if she and Elia didn't end up together—which at this rate it didn't seem likely that they would—she didn't want to go back to Lauren. She needed to give up those dreams and start some new ones, or at least find people who were better for her.

And Elia was definitely better than Lauren. On so many levels.

Kamryn laced her fingers with Elia's and faced Lauren fully now. "Where's Rosie?"

"Talking wedding details with Andra." Lauren groaned. "She acts like we're next in line to get married. "

"You better dodge that bullet quickly." Kamryn let out a single chuckle. "Don't want to be giving your girlfriend the wrong impression, do you?"

"Maybe I do." Lauren's gaze dropped to Elia and Kamryn's joined hands. "Maybe that's exactly what I want her to think."

"You might just want to tell her that you're determined to never get married. Don't want to make the same mistake twice. Even if you do, the drama's written all over Rosie. Head to toe."

"Yeah, it is, isn't it?" Lauren snorted.

"I always find the truth is the best answer," Elia chimed in, squeezing Kamryn's hand in the process. "Not that it's always taken at face value, but at least I feel better about myself."

Lauren hummed but didn't answer. Kamryn leaned in and pressed a kiss to Elia's cheek. "I do still believe you." She just wanted to make sure that Elia didn't forget that. Even if Kamryn had her doubts, she didn't want Elia to feel them.

"And I appreciate you." Elia gave her a sweet smile back. "But remember, we're not focusing on that tonight."

"No, we're not." Kamryn kissed her cheek again. "So for tonight we're two broads at a bachelorette party. What do you suggest we do?"

"Get shit-faced drunk," Lauren replied.

Oh right. Lauren's still here. Kamryn really needed to ditch her ex-girlfriend. She wasn't interested in showing Elia off anymore. Right now she just wanted to spend some one-on-one time with Elia and forget that the world outside of this bar existed. And that was exactly what she was going to do.

"The wedding's tomorrow," Kamryn whispered into Elia's ear. "What do you say we practice our dance for the reception?"

"I'm a little scared to ask what you mean by that, but I'll try it." Elia hooked her arm in Kamryn's and started to walk away from Lauren. "See you, Lauren."

Kamryn spun Elia in a circle before she dragged her close and started to move to the beat of the music. All the tension from before lifted, and she focused solely on the woman in her arms.

"Remind me we should do this more often," Kamryn said.

"Let's do it tomorrow."

"Yes!"

thirty

"I needed last night. Thank you for that." Elia had pulled Kamryn to the side at the wedding as they waited for the day's festivities to begin. They were there early so that Kamryn could make sure Andra didn't need anything, but that didn't mean Elia was ready to wait around either.

"I needed it too." Kamryn wrapped her arm around Elia's back. They'd already checked on Andra. They'd gotten the last few things that she'd forgotten, and they'd run interference with the groom when he very nearly walked in on the bride and bridesmaids. "I've never been so happy to just be a friend and not in the wedding party."

"Not your style?" Elia could barely contain the smile and laugh. "I can totally see you in blush pink with your hair twirled up on top of your head."

Kamryn laughed wholeheartedly. "I'd need you to help me out with that."

"With your hair or getting dressed?"

"Probably both."

Elia could see that happening. She'd watched Kamryn get dressed enough times to want to be there right in the moment, touching her. The sexual energy between them wasn't lost on either one of them. That wasn't the issue they had to contend with. It was everything else.

"Elia?"

Elia jerked sharply. Her heart in her throat. She spun around, instantly putting space between her and Kamryn and wiping the smile off her face. She put that mask into place and pretended she was the most aloof person on the face of the planet. "Simone."

Kamryn spun around instantly, and Elia winced. Kamryn wouldn't be as good at holding her own on this one. Elia braced herself, trying to figure out what exactly Simone was doing here, at a wedding that had nothing to do with the school.

"What are you doing here?" Simone asked, frowning.

"I was going to ask you the same thing," Kamryn said. "Andra's my best friend."

"That... doesn't explain why Elia is here." Simone looked over Elia's shoulder to Kamryn.

"She came as my guest." Kamryn stepped in closer, lowering her voice. "My ex-girlfriend is an absolute bear, and I needed someone who was cool, calm, and collected and who could verbally beat the crap out of her if I needed it."

Simone's lips twitched upward at that. "Oh, I understand exes like that." She looked around, her gaze skimming the room before she leaned in and lowered her voice even more. "And some current spouses."

"Right," Elia said, trying to stay present in the moment, but her brain was spinning. How could Simone Parks be here? Another teacher at Windermere was somehow connected to this wedding? Kamryn had promised no one was connected.

"So who are you here for?" Kamryn butted in.

Elia's fingers itched to reach for Kamryn's, needing that touch to bring her brain back to this earth and her heart rate back into a normal range of beats, but with Simone standing right in front of them she couldn't do that.

"Andra's my soon to be daughter-in-law...well, step-daughter-in-law, but that's a mouthful." Simone gave them a sweet smile before she frowned. "I married Garrett's dad right after he graduated college, so I haven't been that involved in the wedding planning. It's a bit out of my responsibilities."

"You didn't mention anything," Elia said, finally coming back to herself.

"It's not that big a deal to me anyway. I'm sure it is to Garrett and Andra. All they've done lately is talk about the wedding." Simone smiled, but it didn't quite reach her eyes. She wasn't someone who ever talked about her personal life, but Elia remembered when she'd gotten married and then when she'd gotten the job at Windermere shortly after. And that was about the extent of what Elia knew about her.

Not that she'd tried to get to know her better. Elia pretty much kept to herself.

Panic seeped its way into Elia's body, eating its way up her legs and into her stomach before reaching her chest. She tried everything she knew to tamp it back down. But if she and Kamryn were caught out like this, and with all of Kamryn's friends thinking they were in a relationship, she was screwed.

They were screwed.

Elia had to put a stop to this, not just for her own self-preservation but also for Kamryn's.

At least one of them should walk out of this unscathed. Elia took another step, putting even more space between her and Kamryn. She didn't want anyone to have even an inkling that they were attending this together as dates. Nope, she had to snuff out any and all of those thoughts immediately.

"Ah, there's Garrett." Simone smiled, and Elia followed her line of sight. Garrett was young, and he looked everything the perfect groom should. His hair was coiffed, his suit was impeccable, and he had his horde of merry men surrounding him.

"I've never met him," Elia commented.

"He and Andra met a few years ago when we were trying axe throwing for the first time. Which the ax throwing was a disaster, but the result... not so much." Kamryn smiled sweetly, no doubt reliving the memory of it. "I haven't spent much time with him, but what little time I have, I've liked him. He's very sweet."

"He can be," Simone replied.

Something in her tone put Elia's back up. As if there was a lie in there somewhere, but Elia couldn't figure out exactly what it was.

"If you'll excuse me, I need to play the part."

Don't we all? Elia thought, but thank God she kept her mouth shut. The last thing she needed was that getting out. She turned to Kamryn, who looked a few shades paler than she normally did.

"I can't—" Elia started.

"I know," Kamryn finished. "This was an unexpected hiccup."

"Unexpected in the very least." Elia folded her hands in front of her, trying to make sure that she wasn't tempted to hold Kamryn's hand or touch her unexpectedly. She'd gotten too good at lowering her defenses and forgetting to watch herself when she wasn't at the school, and she was around Kamryn. It would be far too easy for her to accidentally do something that would send out signals that they were together.

"Do you need to leave?" The worried wobble in Kamryn's voice would be obvious to anyone in the vicinity. But the sound was only meant for Elia's ears.

"I'm not sure. If it's just Simone, I might be fine if we keep our distance. But I'm worried about what your friends will say."

Kamryn hummed her acknowledgement. "I guess it comes out today that all of this was fake."

Was it?

Elia didn't want to believe that. There'd been so much that was real between them, so much that she had come to rely on in the last few months. She wasn't ready to let all of that go, to shatter the dreams that they had built together, even if they were on a false premise.

"Kam..." She was about to say something when she stopped, her eyes locking on the back of Susy Butkis's head. "Susy's here."

"What?" Kamryn flung around, frantically searching for Susy. "No. No, no no no no. Just no." Kamryn rolled her eyes, tears filling them. "I'm so sorry. I promised—"

"You made a promise you couldn't keep." Elia frowned deeply. "I need to leave."

"I don't want you to." Kamryn looked like she was so close to crying.

"I need to." Elia hated doing this. She hated being the one to walk away, but it had to be her. She was the one causing all of this turmoil. Not just the pain from her past, but the trouble now, standing in the center of a wedding that should have been fun and easy. "I'd appreciate it if you'd tell your friends, so that maybe we can do some damage control."

"Yeah. I'll uh...figure it out."

Elia turned slightly, a woman who looked very similar to Kamryn walking up to them with a huge grin on her face. Her hair was pulled up and out of her face, loose strands hanging around her cheeks. Her smile faltered when her gaze settled on the two of them.

"I was going to say nice to meet you, but I feel like I should be saying goodbye."

Elia furrowed her brow in confusion. Who was this?

"Greer," Kamryn said, supplying the answer without saying anything else.

This was Kamryn's best friend. This was the one person in her entire friend group who could know that all of this had been a lie, and she was the one that Elia was going to have to trust to help Kamryn set this right.

Kamryn stepped forward and wrapped her arms around Greer's shoulders, tugging her in tightly. Elia wished she could be in that embrace. That she could be standing there with Kamryn instead of Greer. She wanted to be that support, that shoulder to cry on. Instead, she was the one causing the tears.

"You must be Elia." Greer stepped back and held out her hand.

"Yes. It *is* good to meet you." Elia glanced at Susy to see if she'd noticed them yet. "But I'm sorry, I have to leave."

"The wedding hasn't started yet." Greer frowned deeply.

"I know. Kam can explain." Elia really hated doing this. She took the risk and touched the back of Kamryn's arm, the smallest of touches that she'd allow herself. "Will you be okay?"

"Uh...yeah. Greer's here. I'll be fine." Kamryn's face pinched in pain.

It was a lie. They both knew it. But Elia was going to have to accept it for right now. She couldn't dig into this one. Straightening her shoulders, she took a slow deep breath. She didn't want to stop looking at Kamryn. She didn't want to leave Kamryn here to deal with all the problems that she had created.

"I'll see you around, then." That sounded like such a goodbye. Not an *I'll call you later* and not an *I'll see you tonight when you get home.* Elia couldn't say any of that. Not in a room full of people who might overhear.

Elia walked out of the wedding hall and directly to where she'd parked the car. She couldn't look back. She had to protect both of them, and she had to be the one to leave. Andra was Kamryn's friend. Elia had no connection to anyone there—at least not any connection that she wanted to have.

The drive back to Windermere was quiet.

Elia didn't even turn the radio on. She wanted the silence. She wanted the spinning of her mind with all of the disastrous possibilities. And she wanted to name them all and then let them go. But when she got back to her house, there was only one that was truly bothering her.

Kamryn.

Taking out her phone, Elia called Abagail and waited impatiently for her friend to answer. She already knew what Abagail was going to say, but she needed to hear it again. She needed to know that she was doing this for the right reasons.

"What trouble have you gotten yourself into this time?" Abagail's words weren't as comforting as they should have been.

"What makes you think I'm in trouble?"

"Aren't you supposed to be at a wedding against my better advice?"

Elia winced. She had said that, and Elia had flat out ignored her and gone anyway. She really should have listened to Abagail. "Simone Parks was there."

"Shit, El."

"And Susy Butkis."

Abagail groaned. "I take it you left...immediately."

"Yeah, I did. But that's probably not going to stop the rumors." Elia pinched the bridge of her nose. "I should have listened to you the first time."

"Yeah, you really should have." Abagail sighed heavily. "How bad is the damage?"

"I don't know. I left, remember?"

"And Kam? What's she doing?"

"Damage control, if she can." Elia finally let the tears that she wanted to spill before burn her eyes now. She needed to figure her life out. She needed to take a step back from everything and find the best way forward. "What do I do now?"

"Retire, resign, leave. I told you that before."

"I'm not ready to be done teaching." Elia wiped her fingers under her eyes. "I'm not set up to take an early retirement anyway, but I don't want to leave my students high and dry."

"Then find another job doing something else so you can at least live until you can pull from your pension. But you need to get out of there. It's the simplest solution to this problem that you seem to be making worse by the week." Abagail's voice rose in accusation.

Elia couldn't avoid the guilt that was eating away at her. "I'm so tired of putting up this front." Her tone changed from angry and avoidant to melancholy in a snap. "I'm so tired of being someone I'm not just because it's safer this way."

"That's the decision you made eighteen years ago."

"Yeah, it is." Elia brushed away the tear that slid down her cheek. "And I'm done."

"What does that mean?" Abagail asked, alarm in her voice.

"I don't know yet." Elia stared out the window across from her, watching the first snowfall of the year. "I honestly don't know."

"You're scaring me."

"I'm scaring myself." Elia pursed her lips. "I'll call you when I figure it out."

"Elia!"

"I promise. I'll call you." Elia hung up, and when Abagail tried to call back, she didn't answer. The quiet was everything she needed right now, and she was going to take every single second of it that she could get.

thirty-one

"Well, that was odd," Greer said, watching Elia leave.

"It really wasn't." Kamryn wanted to cry. She had Greer with her now, but she still felt so very alone. "You've missed so much."

"I know." Greer frowned and tugged Kamryn in for another tight hug. "How's the bride?"

"She's fine." Kamryn snorted. "Rosie's in there making a fuss and everyone just wants her out of the damn room."

"Should I go kick her out?" Greer was ready to play mama bear, and Kamryn loved when she did that. She wished Greer would do it for her right now.

"No. I think Andra can handle her. Don't you think?"

"Maybe." Greer tilted her head to the side. "So what's with Elia?"

"Simone Parks...a.k.a. Andra's new stepmother-in-law teaches chemistry at Windermere."

"No shit!"

Kamryn frowned and nodded. "I didn't know that she was Garrett's stepmother, and neither did Elia, apparently. And Susy Butkis is here. She's on the board. I'm not entirely sure how she's related yet."

"Windermere is a really small world, isn't it?" Greer put her hands on her hips and scowled at the room.

Kamryn could have laughed at that look. Greer always had a smile on her face. She never allowed the world to get her down, and so her scowl looked so out of place. "It is. But so is the world in general. Six degrees of separation, right?"

"Ugh. Don't remind me."

"Why?"

Greer wrinkled her brow. "I'm struggling to get another job. And it looks like I might have to move back in with my mom."

"No!"

"Yes," Greer answered. "I'm not sure either one of us will survive that if we do it."

"Damn it. I wish you could come move in with me. You were my backup plan when I'm done with Windermere." It wasn't really the truth, but Kamryn had to give her something. If she could live with Greer, she would in a heartbeat. Greer had occasionally stayed with her and Lauren on a long short-term when she'd been between jobs, but it had never been more than three months. She missed those days.

"Guess you'll have to figure something else out." Greer wrapped her arm around Kamryn's back. "Looks like the wedding is getting started. Come on."

They found seats as close to the front as they could possibly get. Kamryn was already worn out from the day and now knowing that she was also going to have to tell her friends about the fact that she and Elia had been fake girlfriends was weighing on her. Elia really had left her in a bind to clean up the entire mess, hadn't she?

"Here she comes!" Greer clapped her hands lightly as the music changed.

Everyone stood up, and Andra started down the aisle. She was stunning. Kamryn couldn't have wished for a better day for her. It was exactly like she wanted it. The ceremony went swiftly, and before she knew it, Kamryn found herself at the reception, her arm still wrapped in Greer's for safe keeping.

"Where did Elia end up?" Simone stopped Kamryn as she headed toward the open bar.

"Oh, something came up and she had to leave." Kamryn forced the lie through her teeth. She wasn't ready for this. But it was all about to unravel now, wasn't it?

"That's a pity. I could use a friend at this thing."

"Friend?" Kamryn looked at Simone. She was a quiet teacher, rarely said anything during the staff meetings, kept to herself.

Simone shrugged slightly. "I always considered her a friend."

"You should tell her that then. She could probably use one right about now." Kamryn swallowed a gulp of the beer she had in her hand. She really shouldn't have said that.

"I heard about the accusations stirring up again. Pity. Elia's one of the best teachers Windermere has." Simone ordered a glass of wine, and then took Kamryn by the arm to lead her away from the bar. "Susy has been going on about it."

"Are you serious?" Kamryn's jaw dropped. Of all the people who were going to slip up and talk about confidential information, Kamryn hadn't expected it to be Susy Butkis. Yara, yes, but not Susy. She was going to have to report it with the board itself, and that was going to be its own drama for her to contend with.

"Yeah. It's really quite tragic."

"What is?"

"What happened." Simone gave Kamryn a curious look. "Don't you know?"

"I know some of it." That was always Kamryn's go-to answer when she wanted more information and wanted to make it seem like she was ignorant.

"There was a student who accused her of sexual harassment. And then when that one was proven false there were three others."

Kamryn's stomach plummeted. "What?"

"They were all proven false. All of them were from the same friend group, and once Rylann's story was disproven it was easy to disprove the others. They weren't as bad as what Rylann was saying anyway. But it was all because they were friends with Felicity Cole, and when she dropped her accusation, that was the end of it. Nothing else since then because it was all a bunch of bullshit."

Kamryn shook her head. "There were four accusations." It wasn't a question.

"There were, but all of them false, all of them from the same clique. They were out to get Elia fired. That was their goal."

"Were you working at Windermere?"

Simone shook her head. "I wasn't. But I was working at John Adams, and we heard all about it over there. When Elia tried to get hired there, they wouldn't even give her an interview."

The shock ran through Kamryn. If Simone knew this much, how many other people at Windermere knew about what had happened and were just refusing to talk? How many people knew where the recantation was? Because that's what Kamryn really needed to find.

"I hated what happened. It's so easy for that to happen to any of us." Simone touched Kamryn's arm lightly. "I hope you can figure it out to keep Elia around. I'd hate for her to get fired over something she didn't do."

"Right." Kamryn was flabbergasted as Simone walked away to join the family again.

"What was that about?" Greer asked, stepping next to Kamryn.

"I'm not entirely sure..." Kamryn still couldn't take her eyes off Simone. "But it's at least somewhat comforting."

"O...kay?"

"It's about that thing I can't talk about but apparently everyone else on the face of the planet is." Kamryn frowned at that. She really was going to have to report Susy for that violation. It was a massive breach of confidentiality.

"That doesn't sound good."

"It's not. But it's also a problem for future Kamryn. Tonight, I want to get drunk. I want you to crash in my room with me. And I want to wake up so hung over in the morning that we can't pull ourselves out of bed for the stupid brunch that Andra insisted on having."

"Deal," Greer answered. "Because when else is a good time to get sloshed than with your best friend at a wedding!"

Kamryn chinked her beer bottle against Greer's. "Bottoms up."

Without hesitation, both of them tipped their bottles upward and started chugging their drinks. They might not get completely wasted, but they'd at least get a good buzz on before the end of the night. And Kamryn was no happier to do that than with her best friend. God, she'd missed Greer.

"I needed this," Kamryn said.

"Me too," Greer responded with a laugh. "We can do it more often now."

"Yes!" Kamryn went over to the bar and ordered them new drinks. Finding a quiet corner where they could talk was fairly easy. Kamryn leaned against the standing table with a candle on it. "I do need your advice though."

"Shoot. That's what I'm here for." Greer leaned in closer. "Are you finally going to let me in on all the secrets?"

"No." Kamryn laughed lightly. "Well, some of them. There's a group at the school who's trying to fire Elia. One of them is here tonight. That one." Kamryn pointed the top of her beer bottle toward Susy.

"Susy?" Greer narrowed her eyes in that direction. "That's Garrett's aunt, I think."

"Are you sure?" Kamryn asked.

"Pretty sure, but I could be wrong. If we're sober in the morning, we might be able to find out."

Kamryn hummed, her brain processing that information. "She's on the board."

"And the plot thickens."

"Not really."

"Here's what I don't get," Greer changed the subject. "What does any of this have to do with Elia and you?"

"With me and Elia?"

"Yeah." Greer nodded emphatically. "Because from the reports that I've been getting from the crew, you two have gotten mighty close in the last few months."

They had. But when it was in front of Kamryn's friends it had all been an act. Hadn't it? They'd agreed to that. It was part of their deal. The fake dating routine, the keeping things strictly off property. Well, they'd failed at that one spectacularly, hadn't they? And Kamryn wasn't even sorry about it. That was the worst part. She didn't regret one moment of the time that she'd spent with Elia. Not a single one.

"What's that look for?" Greer pushed.

"Nothing," Kamryn mumbled into her beer before she took a long chug from it.

"Oh, don't lie to me now. You've never lied to me before." Greer gave her a serious look, one that meant business, and she didn't let up.

Kamryn withered under that stare. But she had no idea what to say. She didn't understand what to do next or if she could even begin to find the right words to even explain it to Greer.

"Maybe you're not lying to me," Greer said, pressing her hand over the top of Kamryn's on the table. "Maybe you're lying to yourself."

"I'm not lying to myself," Kamryn muttered. She hated when Greer called her out like this. Her shoulders tightened, something like a string being pulled in the center of her back. She looked around the room again, wishing that Elia was there with her to experience this.

"You keep looking for her, don't you?"

Fuck you, Greer. How was she so damn good at this? Kamryn immediately pulled her gaze back to her drink, her cheeks flushed.

But she wasn't sure if it was from embarrassment or if it was from the alcohol.

"Lauren's breaking up with Rosie."

"I heard about that," Greer responded. "And I assume that she hit on you?"

"At the party last night." Kamryn nodded her agreement. "She implied she and I should get back together again."

"And will you?"

Kamryn pressed her lips together into a thin line as she thought. The longer she'd had to think about it, the more solidified she became in her answer. She wasn't going to do that to herself. When she'd said that the last time was the last time, she'd meant it. Even though she'd said that before, she actually meant it now.

"No."

"I think that's the most resolute I've seen you when it comes to this."

"It is." Kamryn breathed in deeply, sucking down the rest of her beer. "I can't keep going back to her, Greer. I can't keep living my life and expecting her to change or thinking that I can change her." Those words that Elia had said really were coming back to bite her in the ass.

"What changed this time?" Greer seemed so sincere when she asked that. And she would be. She'd genuinely want to know, and she would truly care about the answer that Kamryn gave.

Shrugging, Kamryn started to rip the label off the bottle, trying to get it off in one piece. "Elia."

"What about Elia caused the change?" Greer was fishing again, but Kamryn didn't mind it.

Kamryn wasn't ready to answer that question.

"Kam..." Greer pointed at her. "Quit avoiding."

"Elia is...someone special."

"Obviously."

Kamryn smiled at that. Her cheeks rushed with heat, and she shook her head. "Like I told you before, it wasn't all fake."

"But how much of it was real?"

"All of it," Kamryn whispered. "All of it and more."

Kamryn wanted another drink. But she stayed where she was, trying to make sure that she did exactly what Greer had asked her to—stop avoiding. Greer wasn't wrong. She really needed to figure this out.

"If the circumstances were different? Hell yes, I think we'd be in a relationship together." Kamryn circled her finger around the rim of the beer bottle. "But with everything else going on right now? I don't think it's possible."

"Love is the easy part, right?"

Kamryn snorted at that and then rolled her eyes. "Sure it is. If that's what this is."

"Are you going to argue with your best friend?" Greer put her hand over her heart and feigned hurt. "How dare you?"

"You're a jerk sometimes, but no, I'm not arguing with you."

Greer stilled. "Are you serious? You're *in love* with her?"

"I don't know." Kamryn wrung her hands together before straightening up. "And even if I am, I'm not sure it matters in the long run. She's not here, is she? I needed her tonight, I asked her to be here, she agreed, and then she left."

"Yeah, but it sounds like she didn't leave without good reason. She *was* here. She did show up." Greer looked stern. "Don't get angry over something that isn't worth it."

"But isn't it? I'm not going to be in a relationship with someone who runs out on me. Not again."

"Ah, so that's where this is coming from." Greer sighed. "Elia definitely isn't Lauren. You honestly couldn't have chosen someone more opposite of Lauren."

"I'm not sure they are all that different." Kamryn had been pondering that one for a while now. She was cleaning up both their messes. Lauren's she'd cleaned up for decades, and now she was cleaning up Elia's. They were both people who were followed everywhere by an inordinate amount of chaos. "I think I just need to focus on work right now. I need to figure out who's been messing with the records, and I need to get everything in order for when I leave."

"That's it?" Greer asked.

"That's it."

thirty-two

"I promised I'd call her." Elia handed Abagail a glass of wine as she slid down onto her couch.

"And have you?"

Elia frowned. She hadn't. She hadn't been sure what to say, and she figured that if Kamryn really wanted to know that she would have called her already. "No."

"Why not?" Abagail sipped her wine and crossed her legs. She was still in her outfit from work, the heels showing that she hadn't even taken the time to head back to her condo before driving all the way out here. She'd been so worried since Elia's last call with her, but Elia had needed time, and she couldn't fathom doing that with a sounding board. Not yet anyway.

And it wasn't actions that she had to figure out.

She needed to know what she was feeling.

"I love her," Elia said simply. She'd said those words out loud already, but she hadn't actually said them to anyone else. And she really shouldn't be talking to Abagail now.

Abagail's entire body tightened, frozen in place. "What?"

"I love her," Elia repeated. "And I can't be objective when I make decisions about what happens next and how to deal with this situation. I can't."

"Well, you're picking a hell of a time to figure that out." Abagail put her glass onto the coffee table, hard enough that Elia worried it might break. Abagail stood up sharply, and she paced in front of the large windows in Elia's living room. "Are you serious?"

"Am I ever not?" Elia asked. She'd never seen Abagail like this before. She'd never witnessed this type of agitation from her, especially not over something as benign as this. "I don't know what to do about it though."

"About love?" Abagail's voice cracked on the last word. "I'm sorry." She ran her fingers through her hair and then rubbed circles into her temples. "I'm not… I wasn't expecting this."

"Neither was I," Elia responded, setting her own wine glass onto the table. She couldn't drink. Not at a time like this.

"What do you want me to do with this?" Abagail whirled around, her hands flying out around her.

"I want you to help me figure out what I'm supposed to do." Elia couldn't understand why this was so difficult. She always called Abagail for advice, and this was no different. "Not about my relationship with Kamryn. About my job, and hers."

"You want me to save *her* job."

"Yes." Elia was pleading now. She needed Abagail to understand why this was so important. She needed Abagail to tell her exactly what to do because she couldn't figure it out. "I've spent days and weeks and months trying to answer this and find a way where I can have everything and Kamryn can too, and I just can't."

"Because there isn't a solution, El." Abagail gave her a hard look, her chin dimpling in anger. "There isn't a way where you both can come out of this the winner and be in a relationship and keep your jobs. It's impossible."

"Then what do I do?" Elia wasn't sure she could force herself to ask that question again. She knew that having everything was going to be next to impossible, but up until this point, she wasn't sure what the best solution would be for everyone, especially

Kamryn. "I can't take her down with me, and if I have to sacrifice myself for her, then I will."

"Sacrifice? God, Elia. Do you hear yourself?" Abagail fumed.

Elia was so taken aback. She stayed rooted to the spot, her toes pushing into the ground as she refused to budge. "Do you hear yourself?"

Abagail stilled. "Yes. Sorry." Abagail ran her fingers through her hair again, tugging on the strands before she seemed to settle right before Elia's eyes. "This was unexpected."

"Like I said, it was unexpected for me as well."

"I thought you two were just...having some fun."

"We were." Elia shrugged slightly. "We did." And then it had turned into something so much more along the way, but Elia wasn't really sure when that had happened. She'd been trying to pinpoint the moment, but she couldn't quite figure it out. Aside from that first time when Kamryn had come into her house so mad—raging on Elia's behalf.

"All right." Abagail sighed heavily before moving back to the chair and plopping down in it. "Fine."

"Fine?" Elia asked, sliding onto the couch next to her. "You'll help me?"

"I can't not help you. No matter how hard I try." Abagail groaned and covered her face again. "All right, there's only one way for her to keep her job if that's what you really want."

"I can find another job." Elia had no clue where, but she could find something that would support her financially until she could start drawing from her pension. That would give Kamryn the time she needed here to apply to be the permanent Head of School.

"Are you prepared for all that involves though? And I'm not just talking about applying for new jobs and interviews."

Elia pursed her lips. What was Abagail talking about?

"You need to end it with her, completely. And you need to stay as far away from her as possible. No more dates, no more fake dates, no more individual meetings in her office or yours. None of that, Elia. You need to be done."

The news rocked through Elia. She'd heard it all before, but this time it felt so much more real, and so much harder. With the confession of love still ringing through the air and still filling her soul, she hated that this was what she was going to have to do in order to save Kamryn from Elia's mistakes.

"And then what?"

"Then you quit." Abagail pointed at her. "And you move out of this house, and you go jobless for a while until you find something new."

Elia nodded slowly. "All right." She blew out a slow breath as it sunk in. "All right."

"So how are you going to do this?" Abagail asked, her voice softening back into the compassionate friend that Elia had longed to have with her tonight.

Elia did need to figure that one out. Sipping her wine, she crossed her legs and sank into the couch. It was going to be a long night. Even if she planned everything out, she wasn't going to be able to sleep. She was going to spend hours writing up her resignation and editing it and then staring at it while she pretended she wasn't going to hand it in hours from when she finished scribbling her name across it in black ink.

"Tomorrow," Elia said firmly. There was no other way. She couldn't wait. It had to be now or never. And if she left, them Kamryn could stay. She could still run the Speech team and keep the kids learning and debating exactly as they should. Elia picked at invisible lint on her slacks. "I'll do it tomorrow after the staff meeting."

"Effective immediately?" Abagail asked.

Elia knew that should be the answer that she should give even if it wasn't the one she wanted to hear. Nodding as her only answer, Elia kept her lips closed firmly.

"The end of the semester?"

"Effective immediately," Abagail repeated. "You said you

couldn't make any decisions about this, that you would listen to everything I said."

"I did." Elia finished her glass of wine and set it on her knee, spinning the stem between her two fingers. Abagail was right, and Elia had been right. She couldn't look at this objectively. Maybe if she got all of these negotiations and avoidant tactics out with Abagail then she wouldn't do them tomorrow with Kamryn.

"So, effective immediately. Your contract says you have what... sixty days to move out?"

"Thirty," Elia replied. She'd read it over that morning in preparation for this conversation. It still didn't help her. She was going to lose in any scenario that she'd come up with so far.

"All right, so let's start looking at apartments tomorrow."

Elia frowned. She hated thinking about this. It was devastating to leave her home after this long. It wasn't just the house, it was the people, it was Windermere. She didn't want to leave, and the more she and Abagail talked about it, the more that sentiment solidified in the center of her chest. This was going to be the hardest thing she had ever done.

"I'm not sure I'll be ready for that."

"You have thirty days, Elia. You can't hold off on this. You have to plan."

"I can take a day or two." Elia settled in, looking around her house at all of the things that she was going to have to pack up and put away. She'd been planning to help Maria and Miller move out next month, but now she'd be moving out first.

What a cruel twist of fate!

"What do I do if the board finds out about Kam and me?" Elia changed the topic. She needed the slight distraction.

"There's nothing you can do." Abagail shook her head. "That's why I told you not to do it."

Well, that hadn't worked very well. Love was fickle in that sense, and Elia had ridden the lust train for as long as she felt she could. She and Kamryn needed to talk, seriously. Except that would also go against Abagail's rules of never being alone in a room together again.

Maybe she could just drop off her resignation on Kamryn's desk, leave and not come back. That might be the easiest way, but Kamryn would probably come after her then—in anger, in accusation, in frustration. Kamryn wouldn't let Elia off easily. And that thought brought a smile to her lips.

"I can't believe you," Abagail said.

"I can't either," Elia agreed. "I never thought this would happen."

Elia relaxed into her couch. "I'll give her my resignation after the staff meeting tomorrow, and I promise you that I'll leave the door open when she confronts me about it. Because she will confront me."

Abagail clenched her jaw and shook her head. "You're going to screw this up somehow. I know you are."

"I won't. I promise." Elia gave her a wry smile. She took Abagail's glass of wine. "More?"

"We're going to need it, aren't we?"

"Probably." Elia made her way into the kitchen. "We should probably order some food to go with the wine. Especially if you're going to help me write this letter of resignation that I'm turning in tomorrow."

Abagail laughed. "Now I'm writing it for you?"

"Well, I imagine you've seen far more of them than I have." Elia grinned at her. "Besides, isn't that what best friends are for?"

"Best friends?" Abagail gave her a hard look. "Aren't best friends supposed to know when their friend is in love?"

Elia shrugged and headed back toward the couch. "I didn't admit it to myself until this morning, so it's not like I've withheld information from you."

"Admit it?" Abagail took the offered glass of wine and pointed it toward Elia. "You mean you truly didn't know before now?"

"I didn't." Elia sat back down. "I might have if I'd taken the time, but I didn't. I didn't want to."

"Because of everything that happened eighteen years ago?" Abagail sipped her wine, but she kept her gaze locked on Elia.

"Yes, because of that," Elia agreed. "But also because I wasn't ready to admit that perhaps love isn't as bad as I had become to believe it was. Maybe Kam was right."

"Right about what?"

"Loving someone is hard. Kam meant loving someone else, but I think loving ourselves is one of the hardest things we can possibly do." Elia settled into that thought, to the realization that for the last eighteen ears, she'd done anything but love herself. She'd tried to be someone she wasn't, and she'd tried to hide away from the world she had once thought would support her no matter what.

"Damn, that's deep." Abagail pointed her glass toward Elia. "You get deep when you drink wine."

Elia smiled sweetly. "Sometimes."

thirty-three

"You got a minute?" Elia stood in front of Kamryn, most of the faculty already leaving after the staff meeting that morning.

Kamryn's heart raced. She was still feeling some of the effects of her overdrinking at the wedding, and while her brain was moving slower than she wanted it to, her body clearly wasn't. She couldn't stop herself from looking at Elia, from noticing the small things about her that made her so damn attractive, and the way that Kamryn instantly relaxed in her presence. Even if she knew she wasn't going to like the conversation that was coming.

"Sure," Kamryn answered, staying seated.

Elia looked around the room and shook her head. "If we could go to your office..."

"Oh." So it was serious. Sure, it'd been a bit of a test, but Kamryn had gotten her answer relatively quickly and without any harm. She cleaned up her workspace and slid everything into her satchel. Elia carried her notebook with her as they walked slowly and silently out of the conference room and toward Kamryn's office.

Kamryn had no clue what to say. She wasn't even sure what this conversation was about, and it'd be unlike Elia to bring up the wedding and consequences now. That promised phone call had never happened, and Kamryn was pretty sure it would never happen at this rate.

Did it really matter in the long term?

Or was it just because Kamryn wanted an excuse to spend more time with Elia?

Then again, they were at an odd place in their relationship. Kamryn pushed open the door to her office, keeping it open until Elia stepped all the way inside. Kamryn immediately started to shut it, but Elia shook her head.

"Leave it open."

"Okay."

Elia had gotten more finicky about those types of things, and while this conversation might be serious it might not be confidential either, which meant the door could remain open. Kamryn kicked down the door stop so that it stayed in place before heading to her desk to drop her stuff on the top of it. She didn't sit down in her chair, but leaned against the edge of her desk, crossed her arms, and waited for Elia to begin whatever conversation she decided they needed to have today.

She looked so uncomfortable. Elia kept glancing between Kamryn and the door that she had requested stay open. Her face was drawn, and any of the joy that Kamryn had discovered there in the last few months was completely gone. Everything in her wanted to step forward and wrap Elia up in a hug, soothing whatever this upset was, but she was going to respect boundaries.

At least for right now.

Because they could both be professional, couldn't they? They'd had fun while the relationship lasted, but the wedding was over. Which meant so was the deal they'd made. It seemed so silly now, to even think that Elia would consider making that deal with her and that Kamryn would even agree to it. They'd both been so reckless, but they'd used that as a way to get their feelings for each other out into the open.

Kamryn didn't doubt their attraction to each other.

She doubted whether or not their relationship was sustainable.

"I wanted to give you this in person," Elia finally said, sliding her notebooks around and pulling out a white envelope.

Kamryn's stomach plummeted. Her heart sank. She didn't move to reach forward to take it. Elia held it out in front of her, still keeping quite a bit of distance between them. Kamryn gave her a hard stare, her fingers balling into tight fists as she continued to stare at Elia.

After everything they'd been through so far, this was how Elia was going to end things?

"Why?" Kamryn asked. She was trying to hold back her tears first and foremost. This was such a betrayal of everything she'd been trying to do behind the scenes, of everything she was trying to fix.

"It's the only way this is going to work."

"I don't believe you." Kamryn tightened her grip on her crossed arms and shook her head. "And it's unacceptable."

"You can't reject my resignation." Elia dropped her hand to her side, her eyes wide in surprise.

"I know I can't." Kamryn clenched her jaw, her brain spinning with all the possibilities of how she could get out of this. "That doesn't mean you resigning is the answer to a problem you didn't create."

"I did create part of it," Elia answered.

"Stop blaming yourself!" Kamryn's voice came out far louder than she expected it to, and that ticked her off even more. Standing up from the edge of the desk, she paced to Elia and then back again when she caught sight of her flinching.

Kamryn glanced out toward the main office where Mrs. Caldera sat at her desk, no doubt hearing absolutely everything that was going on in there. Because why wouldn't she? It was her job to run interference for Kamryn when she needed, and it was her job to know things so that she could help the school run more smoothly.

"This isn't your fault," Kamryn said, lowering her voice so that hopefully only Elia could hear her. "I told you that I was working on a solution, and that I was looking for the evidence that we're missing. There's no reason that eighteen years ago should come back to haunt you again."

"It's not eighteen years ago that's going to ruin my career now." Elia's lips thinned, and she barely moved.

How the hell did she manage that?

She was so calm while Kamryn could barely contain the fire that was raging inside her. "Then what is it?"

"You."

That one word took all the air out of Kamryn's lungs. She halted her pacing, staring at Elia with wide eyes and parted lips. Once again, Elia glanced toward the open door and shook her head slowly.

"Please accept my resignation."

"Elia..." Kamryn didn't want to do it. She didn't want to take that letter and read the words, she didn't want to file it away and start the paperwork. She wanted to fight for what was right. She wanted to stand up for the victim and stop the blaming that was never-ending. It wasn't right. This wasn't justice.

"Please, Kam." Elia sounded so pained, her voice breaking on the words. She held her hand out again, the letter loose between her fingers.

Kamryn stared at it. That piece of paper folded inside was the enemy that she had in no way been prepared to face. "I want you to be honest with me."

"I've always been honest."

"Then I don't want you to keep any more secrets." Kamryn took the envelope and tossed it onto her desk without opening it. She couldn't face that right now.

Elia swallowed, the line of her throat moving as the tension increased in her cheeks and neck and shoulders. Would anyone else even be able to notice how hard this was for her?

"What happened at the wedding?" Kamryn stood right in

front of Elia. She wanted the full story of everything that she hadn't gotten. She wanted that promised phone call with the explanation of a lifetime. Because it wasn't just about Simone or Susy being there. This was about something else, and Kamryn was once again left out of the loop.

"Nothing happened," Elia whispered.

"Stop keeping secrets. They're never good for anyone, and you've been carrying enough of them around for years to know that." Kamryn stared her down. "Trust me. That's all I've ever asked from you."

Elia let out a shuddering breath, tears welling up in her eyes and threatening to spill over the brim. In any other circumstance between them, Kamryn would have walked up to her and comforted her. But she was too hurt to even contemplate that. She was still reeling from that damn piece of paper with Elia's resignation.

"What happened at the wedding?"

A few of those tears spilled down her cheeks. "Please don't make me say it."

"I want to hear it." Kamryn's heart was breaking in two. "I want to hear *you* say it."

"It wasn't fake." The words slipped from Elia's lips. "It never was."

Kamryn sucked in a sharp breath, the truth flooding into her. That was exactly what she'd needed to hear, and it was exactly what she was feeling. "It wasn't," Kamryn agreed. "And I don't want it to end."

"It has to," Elia confirmed, and Kamryn watched as she steeled herself. Those little microcosms of change in her body language, the intensity in her gaze and determination filtering through to the rest of her. "This is the only way."

"For once, Elia, I don't believe you." Kamryn took a step forward and halted.

"Is she in?" Simone's voice rang through to Kamryn's inner office from the outer one.

"She's with someone at the moment," Mrs. Caldera answered. "I'm not sure how much longer it'll be."

"I should let you go," Elia murmured, taking a step away.

Kamryn reached out quickly, snapping her fingers around Elia's free wrist and stopping her forward momentum. "You don't get to resign and then just leave, Elia. We need to talk about this."

"No, we don't." Elia had that same hard look as before. "It's done. I'm done. I'm not fighting this."

"You're not fighting alone."

"I know I'm not." Elia dropped her gaze from Kamryn's eyes to her lips. "I never was." Elia broke Kamryn's grip and stepped back. "Thank you for all you've done."

"Elia."

"I'll start packing up my office first."

"Elia," Kamryn tried again, but it didn't work. Elia was already walking away. She was already disappearing into the outer office and nodding to Simone and Mrs. Caldera.

Kamryn didn't even have a second before Simone popped her head into the doorway. "I couldn't help but overhear some of that."

Great. That was the last thing that Kamryn needed.

"Which was what I wanted to talk to you about anyway." Simone stepped inside and shut the door with a resounding click. "The wedding."

Kamryn sighed heavily and plopped herself down into one of the two chairs facing her desk. She wasn't going to be ready for this talk either, was she?

"Is there more going on between you and Elia than merely friendship?" Simone carefully slid into the seat next to Kamryn. "Because if there is, you should know just how dangerous that can be."

Kamryn knew. She wasn't just risking her job and Elia's by pursuing a relationship there, but she was risking her future career. She could so easily end up with a black mark like Elia had. She'd never be hirable anywhere else.

"Just make sure that you're making decisions for the right reasons," Simone continued. "When I married Howie, I thought it was for the right reasons."

Kamryn flicked her gaze up to meet Simone's eyes. "I'm not in a relationship with Elia."

"I thought since you two came to the wedding..." Simone's eyes widened in surprise.

Shaking her head, Kamryn doubled down on the lie that she'd started because that was where the truth was now. "She came to support me because my ex-girlfriend is also still friends with Andra. And it was a contentious breakup. Hence why I'm living in the dormitories as a house parent." Kamryn put her hands out to her sides. "Elia was an outside person who could help me through that and who knows the players. Lauren was also a student here twenty years ago."

"Oh." Simone frowned. "I just thought with the way you two were acting..."

"Nothing more than friendship." Why did that hurt so much to say? Because that was the only lie she'd told so far. They'd had so much more than just mere friendship. And Kamryn still wanted more. She should have known better than to let herself get tangled up in this. "Was there something else you needed, Simone? I've got a lot of work to get done today."

Simone eyed her over carefully. "You seem upset."

"I am, but it's not by anything you said. I promise." Kamryn plastered on as much false bravado as she could muster. She clapped her hands onto arms of the chair and started to push herself to stand. "I'd appreciate it if you wouldn't spread this conversation around. Rumors can be fierce amongst teachers."

"They can be. That's why I came to talk to you and no one else." Simone furrowed her brow. "Because Susy Butkis was asking questions. I didn't tell her anything, because she's known for spreading gossip and I didn't want that to happen. I like you here, Kamryn. You're good for this school in ways that no other Head of School has been. You get stuff done."

Kamryn hummed as she sauntered back toward her desk and picked up the envelope that she'd thrown down on it earlier. She needed a way around this one. And she was going to have to force her hand on it. Elia wasn't going to be happy about it either, and it would push them further down the rabbit hole of separating their relationship, but it was the only way to keep Elia at the school until Kamryn could sort everything else out.

"Elia's not exactly the most popular teacher here at Windermere," Simone said. "The most recent board has been out to get her for a while, and I never truly understood why. She didn't do anything wrong."

"But she did," Kamryn said, using Elia's own words to justify her point. "She left enough questionable space to allow the possibility. And that's all that's needed, isn't it? The mere question of possibilities."

Simone paused, nodding slowly. "I suppose you're right."

Kamryn swallowed the lump in her throat. "I appreciate you coming to me. I'll speak with the board about some of the events that have happened recently. They really need to be informed about *everything* that's gone on." And by that Kamryn meant everything. She wasn't going to mince words or her own accusations. She was going to throw Susy under as many busses as she possibly could.

The school wasn't the problem.

Elia wasn't the problem.

The board was.

And Kamryn was going to do everything in her power to make things right. Even if it cost her the job of her dreams and the love of her life in the process.

thirty-four

"She hasn't said anything?" Abagail asked, sitting across from Elia at a high-top in their favorite coffee shop in town.

"Nothing," Elia answered, sipping the tea she'd ordered in the oversized and pretty mug. She'd needed to feel better about herself, so she'd willingly spent extra money just for the thrill of being frivolous for once.

"Nothing at all."

"No." Elia groaned. "She hasn't even officially accepted the resignation. I'm not even sure if I can tell the other teachers or start to prepare for my replacement when I leave."

"It's been days, Elia."

"I know." Elia had stayed as far away from the administration building as possible since she'd handed in her resignation. The devastation that she'd caused Kamryn wasn't lost on her. And yet there had been radio silence since.

"You might need to confront her."

Elia groaned and closed her eyes. That was the last thing that she wanted to do. She just wanted to pack up her life quietly and move on. She'd already started figuring out which things she was going to keep and which ones she was going to toss and collecting boxes to prepare for her move.

"I need an answer. I want to tell the students and prepare them as soon as I can. We have a meet this weekend, and I can't imagine holding that in and not trying to prepare them for this transition." Elia stared down into her tea, wishing the leaves would have more information than she did. But unfortunately, she wasn't a witch, and she wasn't going to be able to read the leaves at the bottom of the cup.

"She's really said nothing?"

"Nothing," Elia confirmed again. Abagail seemed more surprised than Elia was. It made sense to Elia why Kamryn would avoid it. She was probably still looking to see if there were any other viable solutions to this problem.

Elia knew there weren't.

Hell, they both knew that.

It was just a matter of actually admitting it, and then making plans to move forward from there. So why wouldn't Kamryn talk to her already? Because the silence was killing Elia slowly. She finally took a sip of her tea, bringing her gaze back up to Abagail.

"You've really got it bad," Abagail said. "You weren't even this tortured with Yara."

"Yara and I broke up mutually. The relationship wasn't going anywhere, and we stopped trying. Kam and I haven't even had a chance to start." Elia sighed. "We'll never get a chance." She had to keep trying to convince herself of that because she didn't believe it yet.

"And you and Kam..."

"Didn't break up," Elia answered confidently. They'd have to have an official relationship to break up, right? Wasn't that how these things worked? Whatever they were to each other had ended, though. Elia had made sure of that, and the silence from Kamryn was the confirmation she didn't want but needed. "I'll talk to her Thursday at practice, before we leave Friday morning for the Speech meet."

"You really want to do that before you're stuck on a bus with her?"

Elia shook her head. "I'd rather not wait until afterward." She needed the closure. And the more this tension lingered in the air, the more she felt that was true. "But enough about me. What's going on with you?"

Abagail groaned. "You won't believe what I'm doing."

"Tell me." Elia needed someone else to focus on, someone who wasn't herself. She was tired of the insular thinking that was dragging her down.

"I'm dealing with a new company that we were hired by." Abagail frowned. "And there's a lot of complications with this one. We weren't prepared for it." Abagail sipped her tea. "It's been a nightmare, actually."

"Really?"

"Yeah, I'm tempted to drop them, but Ivy really wants me to keep them."

"Ivy?" Elia had to work hard to remember exactly who they were talking about. She vaguely remembered the name, but the exact details weren't coming forward in her brain.

"Ivy Villegas. I hired her at the end of the summer to be my second." Abagail frowned at Elia. "Don't you remember?"

"Right, now I do. You haven't talked about her much."

Abagail sighed. "Because I've had some regrets in that hire."

"Oh really?" Elia was curious now. There were always certain regrets for Abagail, but she hadn't heard too much about Ivy.

"I hired her on the cusp of a divorce. I didn't know that, not that it would have necessarily affected my hiring of her, but I probably would have planned in more training time and transition time than I did. She's had to go in and out of court so many times in the last few months. Apparently, the custody battle is getting nasty." Abagail wrinkled her nose.

"That's always so hard, especially on the kids."

"And she's got a slew of them. Three, I think." Abagail frowned as if she was trying to remember exactly how many kids there were. "Yeah. Three. There's also a whole nanny situation that's driving me up a wall and I'm not even involved in it."

"Oh." Elia sipped her tea again. She had missed a lot it seemed. She really needed to not be so wrapped up in her own drama that she couldn't also be there for her friend. Her only friend that she really had anymore. She couldn't lose that relationship. "So Ivy wants to keep this new company?"

"It's her friend's company." Abagail pursed her lips. "Normally I'm opposed to those kinds of business relationships, especially when it involves HR issues, but when I hired Ivy, they came with her, and Ivy agreed that she wouldn't be the lead contact for them any longer."

"So who is?" Elia asked, her brow furrowing.

"I am." Abagail sighed heavily. "And let me tell you something, if I never hear the name Nathalie Coeur again, I'll be one happy woman."

"Is she your problem child?"

Abagail nodded. "And owner, who comes with its own complications."

"Wonderful," Elia muttered. The bell above the door to the coffee shop jingled as it opened.

"I have many regrets lately." Abagail's look faltered, and she didn't lift her gaze up to meet Elia's either.

Elia was just about to pry when out of the corner of her eye, she caught some movement as two women spun in a circle, trying to find a place to sit. A shiver ran down her spine. She knew one of those voices so well, and it'd been impossible to get it out of her head lately. So much for focusing on Abagail for a little bit, although she didn't think that Abagail minded in this scenario.

"Kam's here," Elia murmured.

"Oh, is she?" Abagail's eyes lit up, and she looked around the room. She found Kam and Greer immediately. A smile slid over her lips, and it scared Elia. Just what exactly was she thinking? "Maybe now's the perfect time to talk to her."

"Abagail!" Elia hissed as Abagail stood up. But she was too late. Abagail was already walking away from her with an extra sway to her hips that held so much sass.

Elia was ready to crawl in a hole and bury herself alive. This wasn't what she was ready for. She hadn't worked out what exactly she was going to say to Kamryn either. Abagail put her hands on the smalls of both Kamryn's and Greer's backs, ushering them toward the table that she and Elia were sharing, the one conveniently with two extra seats in this very busy coffee shop.

"Elia—Kam and Greer are going to join us."

Thanks so much for asking. Elia tried not to let that thought show on her face, because she had no doubt that it was going to worry Kamryn even more than this situation already was. Elia shifted in her seat slightly but said nothing as Greer immediately sat down.

"We didn't really get much time to talk the other day," Greer said, grinning from ear to ear.

And Elia had thought that Kamryn was all sunshine. She was nothing compared to Greer. Abagail sat next to Greer in the seat she'd occupied before, which left the one right next to Elia for Kamryn.

Fucking perfect.

Elia couldn't glare any harder at Abagail. But she also had to turn on her nice brain as she focused on Greer. Because Greer didn't deserve the wrath that Elia wanted to unleash on her best friend. Kamryn sat stiffly next to Elia, saying nothing.

"We didn't." Elia finally broke the silence and focused on Greer. "How was the wedding? Kam and I haven't had much of a chance to catch up since then."

That was an understatement, and Greer's hesitant look told Elia that she was as aware of the silence between her and Kamryn as Abagail was. And probably just how tense and awkward it was.

"It was good," Greer said. "Though the brunch thing the next morning was awkward."

Elia nodded. "It seems to be a new trend, however."

"It does." Greer sighed and folded her hands together in front of her. "I don't think I'll do that when I get married though."

"Is there someone in your life?" Abagail asked, wrapping her arm around the back of Greer's chair.

Elia eyed her. This was a clear sign that Abagail thought Greer was cute and queer, but that didn't necessarily mean the immediate attraction was reciprocated. Elia would make sure to watch that one. She really didn't want Greer to get caught up in any drama related to Elia. That was the very last thing she needed. Kamryn would no doubt hate her then.

"No." Greer grinned again. "But if there ever happens to be, I like to be prepared."

Abagail nodded slowly and leaned in a little more. Kamryn must have noticed because she tensed next to Elia. The waitress showed up just in time.

"What can I get for you?"

Greer flashed another brilliant smile and ordered swiftly. Kamryn was a bit slower to respond, and she kept flicking her gaze to Abagail like she was the enemy now. Which honestly, Elia should probably be happy with, right?

When the waitress left, Kamryn stayed poised at the ready, as if she was going to jump in and defend Greer with everything she had in her. Elia hoped it didn't come down to that. "Kam told me that you were laid off from your last job."

"Yeah." Greer's lips twitched upward. "It was time. The boys are in school now, and there's just not a whole lot for a nanny to do when the kids are gone most of the day." Her cheeks were a beautiful rosy red, but it didn't seem like embarrassment. "I stayed with Kam this week because of the wedding, but I'm going to be crashing with Lauren next week."

Kamryn tensed again, jerking sharply in her chair. "You are?"

"Yeah, sorry I didn't tell you before. I didn't think you'd mind."

"You can stay with me longer." Kamryn was rushing into things.

Greer couldn't stay at the school longer. The houseparent quarters weren't built for that. Elia would offer her spare room if she wasn't moving out. But perhaps Kamryn could move into her house and then there'd be room for Greer to move in with her until she found another job.

But this wasn't Elia's problem to try and solve either. And she really needed to stay out of everyone else's business. That's what had gotten her into trouble in the first place, hadn't it? Getting too close to Kamryn?

"It'll be fine," Greer responded. "I won't be there long."

"Did you say you're a nanny?"

"Uh...yeah." Greer nodded. "I've been a nanny for fifteen years now. I was thinking about going back to school for my MBA, but I'm not sure that's what I want to do."

"You have to have a plan to use your degree before you get one."

"Which is why I dropped out halfway through the program before." Greer winked. "I was more interested in nannying anyway. I adore kids."

Elia could understand the sentiment, though small children weren't exactly the age range she preferred to teach. She much preferred teaching high-school–aged kids. "Seems you're the odd one out, Abagail."

"Seems I am." Abagail leaned back in her chair, seemingly having given up on her interest in Greer. That was a good thing. Elia really didn't need one more complication to add to what was already going on.

"If you'll excuse me." Elia left her drink on the table and stood up. She needed a breather. And it didn't seem like Abagail was going to be ready to leave any time soon. But she really had to get her head on straight. Walking straight to the back of the small cafe, Elia stepped into the bathroom.

The air was much cooler in here. The scent of coffee wasn't overwhelming. She closed her eyes as she let the differences sink in. She wanted a break from the intensity, and she'd certainly got it. Now if only this break could last. Or better yet, the conversation she knew she had to have with Kamryn didn't go horribly in a direction neither of them wanted it to.

"Are you hiding from me?" Kamryn's voice reverberated through the small bathroom.

thirty-five

"I think it's probably the other way around." Elia's comeback was quick.

In truth, Kamryn had been avoiding her. She still wasn't sure how to take Elia's resignation, and the longer she could hold off on dealing with it, the longer Elia would remain at the school. She'd given until the end of the semester, but Kamryn was determined to at least push that to the end of the year. She just hadn't mentioned how much of a hard-ass she was going to be about it yet.

"Why won't you talk to me?" Kamryn frowned. She kept a reasonable distance between them, not wanting to invade Elia's space at all, but still wanting some kind of answers. "You've always talked to me, even when you wouldn't tell me things."

Elia's mask cracked. "I can't talk to you."

"Why? I don't understand." Kamryn had struggled to fill in that one particular blank for days now. And they were running out of time. The ethics meeting had been pushed back, which meant that Kamryn had far more time to think about Elia and her odd behavior lately.

"Kam..." Elia's lower lip quivered.

Was she going to break? Kamryn wasn't sure she could handle that, especially if she was the reason behind it all.

"You told me that this wasn't fake and then you walked out." The hurt in her voice was evident. Surely Elia would be able to hear it. "I'm sorry that I put you in this position. That I threatened your job even more than it already was."

"You should know more about whether or not my job was threatened than anyone else. You hold all the power in this, Kam."

"Do I?" Kamryn frowned. She wasn't sure about that. She'd never thought Elia felt as though she'd been forced into any kind of relationship with her. "Did you feel like you didn't have a choice to be with me?"

"No." Elia's hard mask immediately cracked. She reached out and took Kamryn's hand in hers. "No, I never felt like that."

"Then where's this coming from?" Kamryn broke the grasp Elia had on her. She wasn't sure she could touch Elia after an accusation like that. Yes, Kamryn was Elia's boss, but she'd never —if anything it was the opposite, wasn't it?

"Accept my resignation, Kam. Stop putting it off. Let me have a clean break and move on."

"Where will you go?" Kamryn dropped her gaze to her feet, unable to meet Elia's eyes.

"I don't know, but I need to put an end to this."

"End to what?" Kamryn already knew the answer though, and it did include whatever relationship the two of them had going forward. Elia might not have said as much but Kamryn was certain that's what Elia had meant.

"Everything." Elia looked at her directly in the eye. "I can't do this anymore. I can't be someone I'm not."

"I'm not asking you to be."

"No, you're not." Elia smiled sadly then. "But everyone else is."

Kamryn shuffled forward slightly. She wished they weren't in a bathroom in the middle of an insanely busy cafe. She wanted more time with Elia, more quiet intimate time with her than she was going to get here. Kamryn wrapped her fingers into Elia's, lacing them together and squeezing lightly. "I want to fix this."

"You can't fix everything," Elia whispered.

"But I *can* fix this." Kamryn nodded, more confident now than she was before. She'd been doing so much research on who had erased the files and wiped Elia's record. She'd eliminated Jessup as a possibility already, and Elia. "I promise you I can fix this."

"But at what cost?"

"At what cost is it if you don't let me try?" Kamryn cupped Elia's cheek. "Because I love you."

"Kam—"

"No, it's my turn to talk. You blindsided me with that, and it's my turn to say something." Kamryn stayed still, making sure that Elia understood the importance of this conversation. "I don't know if it'll work out in the end for us, but I wasn't lying when I said there was more, that it was never fake between us. It'd have been so much easier if it was, but it wasn't. It's not," Kamryn corrected herself. "And I'm not lying or holding back now."

Kamryn dropped her gaze to Elia's lips, to the way she continued to stay where she was, nearly pinned between the wall and Kamryn, as lost in this moment as Kamryn was.

"I love you," Kamryn repeated. "Please just trust me."

Elia turned her cheek into Kamryn's hand. The softness of her skin, the warmth, was everything in this moment. Kamryn smiled at it, at the way that Elia's eyes fluttered closed briefly.

"Let me love you," Kamryn whispered.

"I can't stop you from loving me," Elia said opening her eyes again. "I can't stop you from doing anything that you set your mind to. Just like you can't stop me."

"Are you that determined to leave Windermere?"

Elia was shaking her head before she said the word. "No. Windermere's my home."

"Then stay. Fight."

"I won't be chained anymore." Elia placed her free hand over

Kamryn's on her cheek, holding her tightly. "I won't let them take my freedom from me again."

"I won't either."

"It's not you that I don't trust, Kam. Don't you understand that? It's them. It's the school board, Susy and Heather, and Yara." Elia rested her shoulders fully against the wall now. "They won't stop until they've made me leave the school."

"But what if they do?" Kamryn asked, knowing far more about what was going on with that situation than Elia. She had to. Elia had to be kept out of it, because if she was in the middle, it'd make everything so much harder.

"Don't make promises that you can't keep. I'm so tired of those." Elia's tongue dashed across her lips, and she'd barely managed to drag her gaze away from Kamryn's mouth.

Was she thinking about something else? Or was she still talking about the school board? Kamryn leaned in closer, her breath fluttering across Elia's mouth. What she'd give to have all of these tensions relieved, not just the sexual ones, but the pain and heartache that the school was causing.

"I'm not letting you resign until your contract is up. I'll withhold your pension and fine you if I have to." Kamryn cringed. She hated herself for saying that. "I need you at Windermere. The kids need you."

Elia jerked sharply, pushing Kamryn away. "You can't do that."

"I can, and I will." Kamryn stepped away, a rigidity forming along her spine which she was struggling to not feel the pain from. The look of betrayal on Elia's face was all she needed to know that she'd perhaps gone too far. But this was the only card that Kamryn had left. "You signed a contract, Elia. And if you break it, the consequences in it are very clear."

Elia's jaw dropped.

Kamryn pressed her lips together, her chest tightening from the ache. She reached up and rubbed her fist right in the center of it. She just needed more time to sort everything out. She hated that this was taking so long, that she was the one who seemed to be holding things up, but she didn't want to walk into the next ethics meeting or the next board meeting without all of the information and all of the answers possible.

"I can't believe you'd do this," Elia accused. "I just want to leave."

"And you'll be able to. On July first, when your contract ends." Kamryn shoved her hands into her jeans pockets and rocked up on her toes. She shrugged, playing everything so nonchalant, but inside she was a twisting fury of anger, hurt, and devastation. She hated this so much.

"Kam—"

"It's just business, right?" Kamryn clenched her jaw, hardening her gaze. "I'm your boss, remember? I hold all of the power in this relationship."

She couldn't stand there any longer. She couldn't bring herself to hear Elia's reaction.

"I'll see you tomorrow, Elia." Without another word, Kamryn walked out of the bathroom. God, she hurt. Her muscles ached, but her heart was shattered. She nodded toward Greer when they made eye contact and then jerked her head toward the door.

Greer immediately said something to Abagail and then stood up. Kamryn didn't wait for her. She walked out of the cafe and straight onto the street. The air was cold, biting almost. The next snowfall was due that night, and they'd likely need to bump up their departure time for the next Speech meet in order to give them enough time to get where they were going.

Again, she didn't wait as she slid behind the wheel of her car. Greer jumped into the passenger seat, confusion written all over her. "What happened?"

Kamryn bit back her initial retort. She started the engine and then pulled out onto the street before she said anything. "We're going back to Windermere."

"Okay. But what happened, Kam? This is so unlike you."

Shaking her head, Kamryn focused on the road in front of her. "I told Elia exactly what she didn't want to hear."

"Which is...?" Greer was entirely focused on Kamryn, and it was so unnerving. Her gaze was scolding.

"That she can't break her contract without consequences. And that I love her."

"You—what?" Greer squeaked. "What did she say?"

"Nothing. Absolutely nothing." Kamryn took a hard turn, faster than she probably should have, but the energy from the conversation in the bathroom still sizzled through her veins. She hadn't managed to dissipate it.

"Wow."

"I need to figure out what I'm going to say at the next ethics meeting." Kamryn hit the main road toward Windermere and stepped on the gas. She was running out of time, and she couldn't let any of it go to waste now.

"What will you say?"

"First I need to figure out who erased the files." Kamryn pulled into Windermere and parked in her spot. She didn't hesitate as she got out of her car and walked swiftly up to her apartment, Greer hot on her heels.

"Do you have any idea who might have done it?"

Kamryn shook her head. "I know Elia didn't. But that doesn't..." Kamryn stopped. A corner of a folder stuck out from under the edge of her door. She frowned at it and bent down, sliding it back out before standing back up.

"What's that?" Greer asked, peering over Kamryn's shoulder.

"No clue." Kamryn flipped open the folder and bit her lip. It was Rylann's confession, everything hand-written in bubble letters about how she'd lied about everything. "Holy shit."

Kamryn slapped the folder shut and looked down the hallway both ways. Who'd slipped this under her door? There was no one there, and she'd been gone close to an hour. Anyone could have put it there in the meantime.

"Damn it," Kamryn muttered. She unlocked her door and

stepped inside, looking up and down the hallway one more time as if that would give her the answers she was looking for. But of course, it didn't. She moved to the couch and immediately laid the folder out on the coffee table, pulling out all of the papers.

It was Elia's personnel file. All of the missing parts of it. And it was the case file for the investigation that Kamryn hadn't been able to find yet. She skimmed through each of the papers inside of them before going straight back to the beginning and reading everything word for word.

This would relieve all of the newly resurfaced accusations against Elia. Everything Kamryn had been told so far was true. Elia had maintained her innocence from day one, Rylann had lied. The other accusations that had followed Rylann's disappeared with similar confessions of lies. And it all came down to Felicity.

This was exactly what Kamryn had needed.

But who the hell had it this whole time?

"I tore about the office and the storerooms looking for this." Kamryn flipped it closed and sank into the couch. She rubbed circles into her temples before glancing at Greer. "Seriously, the number of hours I've spent looking for these files is astronomical and then they suddenly appear at my apartment?"

Greer shrugged. "My guess is that whoever erased them or took them in the first place dumped them off for you."

"Yeah, that'd be my guess too." Kamryn sighed heavily, a weight lifting from her chest. She hadn't realized how awful it had felt for so long. She wanted to run to Elia and tell her everything, but after her threat at the cafe, Kamryn knew that'd be the worst idea ever. She'd basically thrown the biggest punch she could in Elia's direction.

Running her fingers through her hair, Kamryn couldn't tear her gaze away from the folder on the coffee table.

"What are you going to do now?"

"I'm going to figure out who left me this." Kamryn snagged her phone from her back pocket and dialed a number immediately. It was after hours and she knew she'd be lucky to get hold of security now, but at least she'd be able to do the one thing that she knew she could tonight.

Track down the mystery person.

She was going to walk into the next ethics meeting with her head held high and with all the information she could throw at them. This was going to end immediately. Enough with the witch hunt. Elia deserved to stay at Windermere, and she deserved be able to teach without looking over her shoulder for the next item that was going to come up.

"But what are you going to do about Elia?"

"What about Elia?"

"You told her that you loved her." Greer touched Kamryn's knee. "You've never said that to anyone other than Lauren."

"Yeah, I haven't." Kamryn frowned. "And right now, I'm pretty damn convinced that I'm not going to tell anyone that ever again. Screw love, Greer. It sucks."

"It can't be all bad."

"No. It's awful. Elia was wrong. Love is hard."

thirty-six

Elia's feet dragged as she walked back toward her house from the humanities building. The day had been exhausting, and it shouldn't have been. She was so used to long days at this point, but it seemed to be getting harder and harder to keep it together. Still, Elia couldn't figure out why she could barely pick her feet up to walk down the sidewalk toward home.

Kamryn.

The administration building was on her way to the row of houses dedicated for faculty, and Elia was going to have to pass it in order to reach home. Elia looked down, hearing the rustlings of the students as they walked by going from one place to the next, their muffled voices in the cold air a welcome reprieve. They hadn't talked since the coffee shop, and the weekend Speech meet had been tough to get through with that. But Elia had loads to say.

Her feet took her down the neighboring sidewalk and straight toward the administration building, but she wasn't entirely convinced it was of her own volition. Elia's breath came in short rasps, and she stood in front of Kamryn's office, debating whether or not to actually knock on the door. This wouldn't end well, would it?

Her knuckles hurt against the door.

Elia waited with bated breath for Kamryn to answer. When she did, she seemed surprised to see Elia standing there. "Did you need something?"

"To talk."

Kamryn's lips twitched forward. Was that an objection that she wanted to make? Did she want to hide away in this pain too? Or was she willing to put some of this away?

"I don't think it's a good idea for us to talk here."

"I seem to make very poor decisions when you're around." Elia put her hands out to the side. "I'm tired of not talking, Kam. Please indulge me."

Kamryn hesitated again, but she did open the door to let Elia inside. When the door clicked shut, Elia's heart was in her throat. This was a bad idea. The entire room smelled like Kamryn, and it was a strong, overpowering scent that sent her body into overdrive. Kamryn followed her inside, crossing her arms and staring at Elia.

"What do you want to talk about?"

"Please let me resign now. Don't make me wait this out." Elia's lips tingled, her tongue dry in her mouth as the words spilled out. She hadn't thought that she was going to talk about this. She'd wanted a more reasonable way to navigate the conversation with Kamryn, but she was tired of watching her step and her words.

"This isn't the time for this conversation," Kamryn responded. She relaxed and sat down at her desk, which was covered with papers again.

Stepping closer to Kamryn, Elia glanced down at the papers and squinted to read them. The paper looked old, but as soon as she saw Rylann's name, Elia panicked. "Did you find it?"

"Find what?" Kamryn muttered back.

"The confession." Elia reached down, touching the papers before picking up the handwritten confession from Rylann. "I've never read this before."

"Never?" Kamryn turned around to look up at her and furrowed her brow in Elia's direction.

Elia shook her head. She read through the confession, word for word, her heart hammering away loudly. It was hurting with how tight her chest was. Her hands shook. "Where did you find this?"

"I didn't," Kamryn replied, taking the paper and shoving it into a folder. "You shouldn't be seeing this."

Elia reached forward swiftly and took the other papers before Kamryn could stop her. "These are the other girls' confessions?"

"Yes. Everything that was in the original investigation folder. And the rest of your personnel file—though I left that back at my place." Kamryn leaned back in the chair and rolled her shoulders, seemingly relaxed. "You don't have any idea how it ended up in my possession?"

"No." Elia continued to read. Each word brought back all that pain from eighteen years ago, but also the vindication she'd had because she had been right, and she'd told the truth the entire time. She wouldn't have fought it otherwise. "Felicity made one?" Elia was so near to tears. "I didn't think...of all of them, I never expected her to do this."

"She was the one whose accusations were the most benign." Kamryn took the papers and settled them down. She took Elia's hands in hers, squeezed once and then let go.

"I never wanted kids of my own, but I could see myself playing stepmother to her." Elia frowned, struggling to tear her gaze away from the papers on the desk. "That hurts more than Rylann."

"You said you didn't care if Yara blamed you."

"I didn't." Elia's nose stung with tears. "I didn't, but I didn't think that Felicity would turn it into something like this."

"Well, she did. She got her friends to start a mob against you, and then she barely helped to make it stop when they were called out on it." Kamryn crossed her legs and stretched them out.

Elia stumbled back slightly, her chest tightening even more.

This school hadn't ever done anything for her. It'd only ever caused pain and suffering. "Please just let me leave, Kam. I can't keep doing this."

"No." Kamryn closed the top of her laptop and spun around in the chair, staring Elia down.

"No? Just no. You're not even going to negotiate this with me?" Elia's voice struck a nerve. She knew it would. "You're just going to ignore the fact that *this* is what I want?"

"I don't believe for a second that this is what you want." Kamryn sat up straighter and squared her shoulders, preparing for an argument.

"How would you know?" Elia raised her voice, her anger getting the better of her.

"Because you've told me as much." Kamryn crossed her arms looking so damn pleased with herself, as if she'd caught Elia in her own lie.

"I changed my mind." Elia gripped the edge of the desk as she leaned over it. "I want to leave now."

"I still don't believe you." Kamryn wrinkled her nose up. "Stop lying to yourself, Elia. The only person who can help you with that is yourself."

"Kam, I'm done with this school. I'm done with fighting fights I won't win. That's why I resigned. It's better for everyone."

"Again, I don't believe you." Kamryn stood up now, her hands in fists as she leaned over the desk. "And I think if you believed it then you would have been in here each and every day that I didn't respond to your resignation."

"You're full of shit, do you know that?" Elia straightened up and glared. "I turned in my resignation. I was going to give you until the end of the semester, but I changed my mind. I want to resign effective immediately."

"It doesn't matter what you want. I already told you my terms." Kamryn came around the desk. Elia had never seen her play hardball like this before. She wasn't even sure that Kamryn had it in her, but seeing this Kamryn now? It was no wonder she'd gotten the position over Elia.

"Those aren't my terms." Elia was going to stand her ground. She was tired of being pushed around by administration.

"Then leave, Elia. But you won't get what you want out of it." Kamryn crossed her arms.

Elia didn't want to leave. Yet again she was stuck in the middle of what she knew she should be doing and what she actually wanted to do. Abagail's advice had been so clear and precise, and still she struggled to follow it.

Here they were, alone in Kamryn's office. Anything could happen. Anyone could walk in on them and hear their argument. Anyone could so easily find out what was going on.

"We shouldn't be here," Elia said, pointing to the door. "You know they're talking about us, right?"

"Who?" Kamryn said obstinately.

"Teachers, students, staff—I've heard. They're commenting on how close we are, on how much privilege I have over other teachers." Elia was clawing for words now. She wasn't lying when she said she'd heard the rumors. Simone had come to talk to her after the wedding, to mention that it looked bad that Elia had been there, even if she left before Susy had seen—and thank God for that tidbit of information. "You know it's bad when the students hear the rumors."

"They don't know anything," Kamryn hissed. "Because there's nothing to tell, is there?"

Elia jerked sharply at that.

"It was all a lie, right?"

"No, it wasn't," Elia disagreed. She softened, wanting to make sure that Kamryn understood what she wasn't saying. What she couldn't say. Because it would tear both of them up.

Kamryn stomped right up to her. She ground the words out. "I told you I loved you and you walked away!"

"It was for your own good," Elia responded, the same pain as before hitting her full-on right in the center of her chest. Why did she keep ending up in situations like this? Why couldn't she just tell Kamryn? Right, because it was for Kamryn's own good. If she said those words, then Kamryn would cling on even stronger than she was now.

"And what about now, Elia? Is this also for my own good?"

"Yes."

"I'm not a child for you to make decisions for. I'm *your* boss." Kamryn's look of anger cracked, and Elia could see the discomfort underneath it.

She wanted desperately to reach out and caress her, to touch Kamryn and make all this better. But she held her ground. She had to. "Let me go."

"I will," Kamryn answered. "You're gone from my personal life. You told me that. But I won't let you go from this school—not yet anyway. You signed a contract, and I expect you to fulfill it."

"This is ridiculous. We're just going in circles."

"I agree." Kamryn started to step to the side, but Elia stopped her with a hand on her wrist.

She clenched her jaw, the muscles in her cheeks working overtime as her brain spun with what to do next. Finally, Elia looked up into Kamryn's brown eyes and said, "I don't need you—or want you—to protect me."

"I'm not protecting you. I'm protecting this school."

"Kam..." Elia trailed the words off.

"No. Stop being so self-centered, Elia. I can't find a replacement for you tomorrow. Hell, I'll be lucky to find someone for next semester. This isn't for you. It's for the school. Your students need you, and I'm not going to let them suffer because you're choosing the easy way out."

Elia nearly stumbled backward, but she didn't move. "It's not for you?"

Kamryn snorted. "It's never for me."

Was she really that self-centered? Had she been so stuck in the what-ifs where they concerned her that she hadn't been able to see the bigger picture? Perhaps. But Elia was still stuck there. Abagail had told her to stay there. And she'd promised that she would do what Abagail told her, where it concerned her job anyway.

"For the record, Kam—because I want you to understand before I walk away this time—I do love you." The words took the air from her lungs. Elia couldn't tear her gaze away from Kamryn's, from the way that Kamryn looked at her. Betrayal first, and then understanding, and then pure lust in its truest form. "Kam?"

"What?" Kamryn bit out the word, as if she was trying to control herself.

Elia nodded slowly in understanding. This was so hard for both of them. It was hurtful. "I need to leave now. It's just how this has to be. I hope you know that."

"Know that you're choosing this path? Or know that we haven't explored every alternative."

"Know that this is the decision that I'm making, for the both of us, because it's the right choice." Elia stepped away from her. She reached the door to Kamryn's office and opened it slowly, startling when she found Mrs. Caldera standing on the other side of her. She had a file in her hands, but she looked worried.

"I didn't want to interrupt," Mrs. Caldera said. "So I just waited."

Did she have a meeting scheduled with Kamryn? Elia tossed a look over her shoulder toward Kamryn in a question, but she didn't receive an answer. Elia swallowed, wetting her mouth at the same time. How much of the argument had she heard? If it was everything, then the rumors would definitely get worse. Then again, Mrs. Caldera was probably one of the few people on the campus who could keep a secret.

How did Elia ask if she was going to be discreet or not?

Mrs. Caldera put her hands up. "I haven't said a word since I first suspected."

Well, that answered at least one question. Elia's cheeks burned. She couldn't even force herself to turn around and look at Kamryn, because Mrs. Caldera had literally just proven the point that she'd made earlier. People at Windermere knew. And it was only a matter of time before the board found out and they were both screwed.

"Perfect," Elia muttered under her breath. She pushed past Mrs. Caldera and made her way toward the door. She needed to get outside, into the cold air. She needed to find a way to work out the rest of her contract and not feel this way every time she was in the same room as Kamryn.

And for that only time would help.

Time they so obviously didn't have.

thirty-seven

Kamryn was left reeling in Elia's wake. But she'd called Mrs. Caldera there for a reason, and from the look on her face, she knew exactly what this was about. This had better work out for the benefit of everyone—at least as much as it could.

"Sit down," Kamryn said, shutting the door behind Mrs. Caldera.

She never wanted to have a conversation like this with anyone. But it was impossible to avoid this time. Kamryn wasn't ready for this. Then again, she was fairly certain she never would be.

"This weekend you slid a folder underneath my apartment door." Kamryn tensed, eyeing Mrs. Caldera to study what her reaction was going to be. She wanted to know everything that she possibly could. "I know it was you, despite you not leaving a note or telling me."

"H-how?" Mrs. Caldera stuttered.

"There's cameras all over the school, including the hallways to the dormitories and the entryway. I had security pull the footage." Kamryn flicked the pencil between her fingers back and forth, waiting for some kind of useful information that she could write down. "Where did you get the file?"

"I've had it in my desk." She sounded so small, and she was so pale.

Kamryn hated this for her. "Why?"

"I kept it there for safety. No one ever looks in my desk."

That was true. Kamryn had torn apart the entire office except for that one place. And the worst part was that Mrs. Caldera knew exactly what Kamryn had been looking for. And she'd flat out ignored it, lied about the fact that she didn't know where the paperwork was.

"I took it a while ago." Mrs. Caldera wrung her hands tightly in her lap. "Before you started working here, when Miller told me that Heather was put onto the board."

"I'm not sure I understand." Kamryn tapped the end of the pencil against the paper, just waiting for information. This was something she could do well, and she was going to.

"Heather and Rylann became best friends after high school."

Kamryn jerked her head up at that. "What? How do you know that?"

"Windermere's a small school, Kam. And because I run into a lot of the admissions and records questions, I'm aware of where most students end up post-school. It took a few years, but they're best friends now." Mrs. Caldera was shaking, her entire body trembling. "I suspected when Heather was elected to the board that Elia's past might come up. It was horrible the first time. She doesn't deserve to relive that again."

"So you altered her personnel file?" Kamryn bit the inside of her cheek. She wanted Mrs. Caldera to give a full confession of what she'd done, but at the same time it was better to live in ignorance some days. At least ignorant, she wouldn't have to fire Windermere's longest standing employee.

"And a few others to not put the blame on her."

Premeditated. It was the word that came straight to Kamryn's mind and bounced around like a pebble stuck in a shoe.

"Do you have those records as well?"

Mrs. Caldera nodded. "In my desk."

Kamryn pressed her lips together hard. "Just...why? Because not having these has proven to be a bigger issue than if we'd just had them."

"I gave them back."

"But why?"

"Because you and Elia..." Mrs. Caldera stopped speaking. "You two deserve to be together. I think you're a good match, and Elia has never truly been happy since she and Yara broke up. You can see it in her face how happy she is with you."

Kamryn would disagree. Especially with the way their last conversation had gone.

"I know it doesn't seem that way now, but she'll come around."

Kamryn sighed heavily. Even if Elia decided to be in a relationship with her, that didn't mean the board would approve or that it would end up with a happily ever after. They still had a lot of problems to work out in the meantime.

"I appreciate you giving me these files," Kamryn started, pointing to the paperwork on her desk. "Especially since I'm about to walk into a board meeting. But this goes beyond what a reprimand can do."

"I know," Mrs. Caldera answered. Her lip quirked up, the same bright red lipstick that she'd worn twenty years ago. She laid her hands flat on the table. "I know you have to fire me. And I still believe it was well worth the intervention."

Kamryn was speechless. No words formed on her tongue. She'd fired people before, and she'd never had an experience like this. What was she supposed to even say to that? She shook her head as Mrs. Caldera stood up.

"I wrote out a letter, explaining what I did, so you can have it for the board meeting tonight. I'll print a copy for you, and I'll start cleaning out my desk. I've also written up notes and procedure books for my replacement."

"Is this how you wanted to leave?" Kamryn frowned. "Have you been planning this?"

"Planning for the possibility." Mrs. Caldera nodded. "It's time for me to retire, Kam. And it's time for you to step up to the plate. This school needs you. Don't let the board tell you otherwise."

And she walked out.

Kamryn watched in utter bewilderment as she started to pull things out of her desk. What the hell had just happened?

Mrs. Caldera was gone with one small box of personal items before Kamryn had to walk into the board meeting. She held the folder that contained everything she needed to prove that Elia was innocent, and this was all a witch hunt against her. Because some people just couldn't move on from the past.

Sitting down at the table, Kamryn waited for the ethics team to be called up to give their report. Yara started, explaining everything they'd done so far and the restrictions they'd put onto Elia. She was just about to start down the road of adding more when Kamryn jumped in.

"I'm going to stop you there."

Yara seemed surprised, along with Susy and Heather. Kamryn slid the copies she'd made to each person sitting in the room. "This is Elia Sharpe's personnel file, along with the records from the investigation that happened eighteen years ago. I'll get to where I found these in a minute, because that's an issue that's been dealt with but needs to be on the record."

Kamryn sat back down. Her heart was racing and in her throat, making it so hard to talk. She was nervous and breathy, and she fucking hated it.

"As you can see, all the accusations against Elia were recanted and then disproven. I want it on the record that there have been many conflicts of interest in this case." Kamryn looked around the room. "Yara Cole and Elia Sharpe dated for two years prior to the accusations. Heather is best friends with Rylann, the initial complainant about Elia's behavior."

"And you..." Susy added, giving Kamryn a pointed a look.

"Yes, and me." Kamryn tensed. "We can also talk about that in a minute." Kamryn needed to make sure that everyone in this room understood what had happened. "It seems that when Heather was elected to the board late last school year, she came in with an agenda, which was to continue the plot against Elia Sharpe that began eighteen years ago when she and Yara had a mutual breakup."

She hated that she was airing this all out in the open again, but most of it was knowledge they'd all have access to anyway.

"You can see the recantations in these files and read them for yourselves. All charges were dropped against Elia, and she was reinstated. It's why she has remained a trusted member of the faculty at Windermere for the last eighteen years. I believe it's unconscionable to have brought these accusations back up in the way they were."

"She wanted more power," Susy jumped in.

Kamryn shook her head and pointed at Susy. "What she wanted was respect. And the board here never gave her that. You refused her an interview for the Head of School position—one she's most definitely qualified for—and not only did you refuse it, you ignored her entirely. You didn't have the decency to even tell her that she wasn't being considered. And then you forced an ethics team that would look into her because you wanted her gone from this school."

Susy paled. Which was exactly what Kamryn wanted. She needed Susy to be on the defensive.

"I want to add in to the fact that you breached confidentiality, repeatedly, where it concerns Elia Sharpe's personal records and the business of this school." Kamryn was about to go in for the kill. "I've had repeated reports of information that came directly from you about the conversations we were having in the ethics team meetings, and about Elia's past records—which, as I've proven with this, have been expunged."

"I haven't—"

"Kamryn isn't the only one who's received these reports."

Kamryn whipped her head around, eyeing Simone. She

hadn't expected that. Simone was usually so reserved, but she was glaring at Susy with everything she had.

"And I have to say, I find it appalling," Simone added. "I'd move for a vote of no confidence if I thought that the board would accept a motion."

Shock rocked through Kamryn again that evening. She couldn't have asked for something better to have happened. She looked around the room, hoping against all hope that someone else would speak up. She didn't have a vote, she only had a voice, but that didn't mean the others there wouldn't listen.

"I've never seen these before," Yara murmured as she flipped through the photocopied papers that Kamryn had passed over. "I always thought..." She stopped speaking. "Felicity made a report?"

How had Yara not known about that? Policy was to contact the parents, especially in a situation like this. So how had they avoided that eighteen years ago? Kamryn was about to ask when Yara shoved the papers away from her.

"I don't know what to say right now." Yara pressed her lips together and stared at Kamryn. "You were right."

"And you wouldn't listen to reason."

Yara nodded. "I wouldn't." She faced Susy. "I'm resigning from the ethics team. I'm not the person you need." She rolled her shoulders and touched the edges of the papers again. "And I need to talk to Felicity."

Kamryn was about to speak when Yara stood up and nodded toward her.

"Thank you."

The room settled quietly after Yara left it. Kamryn stared at Susy. "And are you going to defend yourself?"

"No." Susy frowned. "I did make the mistake of breaking confidentiality."

"Then I move that you step down as president." Simone wasn't going to back down from this one, was she? "I can't get behind a board president who isn't going to keep the school integrity first and foremost in her mind. Do you know how bad this could have gotten if Elia decided to sue? You're damn lucky she didn't."

Did Simone know that Elia had contacted a lawyer? Kamryn wasn't sure what the outcome of the meeting had been, but Elia had mentioned it, and it would have been the wisest thing for her to do regardless of the outcome.

"Are you stepping down, Susy? Or are we forcing you to step down?"

Kamryn watched with awe as one after the other, board members stood up to Susy, and forced her hand to resign effective immediately. As soon as she walked out, that left Heather. Kamryn held her breath, the tension tight in her chest to see what Heather would do next without Yara and Susy there to back her up.

"Heather?" Kamryn asked. "I think it would be appropriate for you to resign as well."

Heather's jaw dropped. "I...I thought we were coming here tonight to fire Elia."

"No, we're not." Kamryn stayed right where she was, feeling so much more confident with the support of the board behind her. "We're proving that she was right all along, and that Elia is the true victim in what I would call a witch hunt against her."

"So you just want me to leave?" Heather screeched.

"I think it'd be a wise decision if you did."

"You'll regret this." Heather stood up. "All of you will regret it."

"I don't think we will," Kamryn responded coolly. Because she knew for a fact she wouldn't. Heather raced off in a huff. Kamryn looked around the room and excused herself. She'd had security on call in case something like this might happen, especially when it came to Mrs. Caldera. She gave them a heads-up and then had them escort Heather and Susy off the property. She'd deal with the rest later.

When she got back to the room, the conversation was alive

and energetic. They'd already solved the problem of a temporary board president. Kamryn waved them down to try and calm the conversation. She needed to get this under control because she had more that she needed to tell them, and more she needed to confess.

"You all should know that I fired Mrs. Caldera tonight." That got everyone's attention. Kamryn wasn't quite ready for the next point of conversation, but it needed to be said. Secrets needed to come out, and promises needed to be kept. "And there's one more point of discussion that I need to add into the many conversations we're going to have tonight. Please expect this meeting to last later than you originally thought it would." Kamryn's stomach twisted hard. This was it. This was what she'd been working toward all night.

"You should be aware that Dr. Elia Sharpe and I have been involved in an intimate and personal relationship for the past few months now. And it's a conflict of interest for me to remain as Head of School."

thirty-eight

"You figured out why I didn't get the interview."

Elia stared at Kamryn as she cracked open the door to her apartment. Her heart raced, and her body was filled with unrestrained energy that told her she had to do something, anything, to make it dissipate. But there was no direction to it at all. So she'd ended up here. Just before midnight, standing in front of Kamryn's apartment, and begging to be let inside.

"I did." Kamryn stood up straight, her eyes still alight with the energy from the day. But she looked exhausted. She looked worn out and torn down. "Come on in."

She opened the door wider, stepping to the side. Elia brushed her fingers across the top of Kamryn's hand as she walked by, her heart skipping a beat or two briefly before she was fully ensconced in Kamryn's world.

"What the hell happened tonight?" Elia asked, still standing in the center of Kamryn's living room with her jacket wrapped tightly around her.

"Want a whiskey? I think I deserve a drink after this, and it's much better to drink with someone than alone." Kamryn strolled toward the kitchen, not answering Elia's question. "Take your jacket off, this is going to be a while."

Elia was stunned speechless. Kamryn seemed to have none of the energy that Elia did. She was all sorts of calm, and just that fact irked Elia. She was once again left in the dark, not knowing exactly what happened. The call from the apparent new board chair hadn't relieved all of her concerns, and it didn't answer all of her questions. She almost hadn't even answered the phone since it was so late, but both Kamryn and Simone had texted and told her to answer it.

Elia pulled at the buttons on her jacket and dropped it onto the back of the dining room chair. She curled her fingers around the top of it and leaned. Kamryn was taking her sweet time finding glasses in her cabinets and then pouring them each a good dose of whatever whiskey she had in her hand. Elia couldn't make the label out from there, not that it mattered.

She just wanted answers.

"Kam..."

"I promise you, I'll answer everything you want to throw at me. Just give me a second. It's been a hell of a week." Kamryn capped the bottle and snagged the drinks, her hips swaying but more from exhaustion than intention as she walked back around and handed Elia a glass. "Can we at least cheers to the fact that this is mostly over for now?"

"But...how?" Elia held her glass dumbfounded, unmoving when Kamryn held hers out.

Shrugging, Kamryn sipped her drink and then moved toward the couch. She sat down heavily, sighing as she toed off her shoes and made herself comfortable.

"Kam..."

"Elia," Kamryn answered, a tease in her tone. "I figured for someone as smart as you that you would have asked as many questions as possible during that phone call."

"I was a bit stunned and blindsided." Elia moved around and sat next to Kamryn on the couch, their knees bumping. "I didn't exactly have the wherewithal to come up with any questions."

Kamryn frowned and took another sip. "Mrs. Caldera is the

one who altered your personnel file."

"She... but why?"

"To protect you." Kamryn took another sip, raising her eyebrows in Elia's direction as if she was making a point, but Elia didn't follow her line of thought. "You have more friends here than you may have realized."

"She didn't want anyone to read it?"

"She thought it was time that the past faded into the past, and she was worried with Susy as president of the board that it would come back up. She wasn't wrong, but her methods leave a lot to be desired. I had to terminate her."

"Oh, Kam." Elia reached out and touched Kamryn's arm, her fingers curling around Kamryn's wrist. Heat seared into her skin from just the touch. Elia didn't want to let go either, so she lingered there as long as she felt safe before retreating back into the bubble that she had created.

"Susy, Heather, and Yara are no longer on the board."

"Jensen told me that. Did they step down?"

"Mostly. Heather threw the biggest fit. I found out at the wedding that Susy has been spreading rumors about you, some true, most untrue. Simone helped me to uncover even more and to trace them back. Susy has had a vendetta against you, and the creation of the ethics team with Heather and Yara was fully with the intention of getting you out of Windermere. We were able to prove that tonight. In case you're wondering, Simone has taken over chairing that team, and I'm working with her to rebuild it from scratch, again."

"Simone will be good for that." Elia lifted the crystal glass to her lips and finally took a sip of the amber liquid. It burned going down but not as much as everything else lately had.

"For now, Jensen has taken over supervising your position at the school."

Elia jerked her head up at, locking her eyes on Kamryn's in confusion. Kamryn was staring at her intently, as if trying to read between the lines for what Elia was thinking and feeling.

"It's only temporary until Marshall Dean returns from parental leave in a few weeks," Kamryn added.

"I'll be supervised by the Assistant Head of School? Not by you?" Elia tightened her grip on the glass, but she wasn't understanding something. Kamryn wasn't telling her something intentionally, and she was completely lost as to why the change was happening.

"I told them about our relationship."

"Kam." Elia's heart sank, and that same fear from before came rushing back. "They fired you?"

"No, they didn't fire me." Kamryn's lips twitched upward, a small smile taking over what had been exhaustion for such a brief moment. "They extended my contract to the end of the year."

"What?"

"And in order to avoid a conflict of interest and favoritism, they're placing you under different supervision. Marshall will be back in a few weeks, and I'll update him about the changes going forward."

"I don't even know what to say." Elia set her drink onto the coffee table. "I don't know whether to be pissed off that you did all of this without talking to me first or to thank you."

"Both is probably a good place to start." Kamryn knocked back the rest of her drink and added her glass to Elia's. "I couldn't tell you about a good portion of that."

"I understand, but it still involved me." Elia stared down at her hands. "And to tell them about our relationship? We're not even—"

"I want to be," Kamryn interrupted. "And I want to make that very clear. If you want to be with me, Elia, then be with me. But even if you're not because of our history, the board deserved to know. I need to be as open with them as I possibly can, and our relationship causes a conflict of interest when it comes to certain things, even if we don't continue to be in a relationship together."

Elia steadied. Kamryn still wanted to be with her? She wasn't sure she'd be as gracious as that, not with the way Elia had treated her lately. She'd ignored all sides of a personal relationship between them—or at least she'd tried to.

"You don't have to answer me about that tonight if you don't want to. I know this is a lot to take in at once." Kamryn stretched out her legs and pointed her toes. "And you haven't had a lot of the information that I've had."

"You asked me to trust you, and I didn't."

Kamryn turned sharply to her at that.

"I didn't trust you," Elia repeated, making sure that her point was clear. "I pushed and nearly bullied you into accepting my resignation, and you just stood there and took it."

"In all fairness, Elia, I pushed and nearly bullied you just as hard. I just needed you to stay long enough for me to get things in order and make things happen. I needed you to stay until after this meeting, so you could choose to leave on your own terms. And if you want me to accept your resignation, then I will. I won't hold you here any longer. I'll curse you when I have to teach your damn classes until I can find a long-term substitute, but that's the extent of it."

Elia's lips parted in surprise. She was free to leave. And it was the first time that she'd truly felt that. She had all the power now, to leave or to stay, to make the decisions about whether or not their relationship continued. Kamryn had laid it all out so beautifully for her, giving her all the options and more, and the absolute freedom to make these choices.

"I don't want to leave," Elia whispered. That much she knew to be true right in this moment. She'd never wanted to leave Windermere. It'd been her home for so long and she was comfortable here.

"I'm glad to hear that." Kamryn snagged her glass and started toward the kitchen.

Elia stayed on the couch, sitting in silence as she processed through everything she'd just been told. It was so hard to not be the one doing anything, to not be defending herself, to not be trying to keep up with all the accusations and politics that came with teaching and especially with teaching in a private school.

"So can I burn your resignation? Because I've been dying to do that, in all honesty." Kamryn sat back down heavily, but she hadn't returned with a refilled glass.

"Sure." Elia smiled at the comfort and ease that they'd found again. "The board didn't have questions about when you were my student?"

"They did." Kamryn ran her fingers through her hair. "But they didn't seem to question my answers when I gave them."

"Because they're the truth."

"Yeah." Kamryn grinned and rubbed her hands over her face. "I know it's not all done and solved, and now I have to hire a new administrative assistant and get a temp in this week, but I feel like I can honestly say that the drama is done."

Is that what this odd feeling was? Completeness? The end to what Elia had never truly believed would end? Had Kamryn finally succeeded in doing that? Elia blinked, looking Kamryn over in a new light. She hadn't truly seen her as admin before this week, but with the way Kamryn had held herself during their confrontations and with the ethics team and the board?

"You deserved this job, Kam. Far more than I did."

Kamryn's brows drew together, a definite sign of her confusion as she threw a look in Elia's direction. "You would have been just as good if not better as Head of School."

"No. I wouldn't have." Elia had never been more confident in that. The jealousy that she'd allowed to take over her when Kamryn had first started was completely gone. "You're really good at this job."

"Well... thank you." Kamryn smiled again, her cheeks tinging pink from the compliment. "That's high praise coming from you."

Elia smiled in response, her heart fluttering lightly. "You deserve it."

"So do you. Still one of the best damn teachers that I know."

The last bit of tension disappeared from Kamryn's face.

Elia wanted to bring it up, and she'd half expected Kamryn to. Then again, that wasn't exactly Kamryn's style, was it? Elia snagged the glass off the coffee table and tilted her head back, swallowing the rest of the liquid in one long gulp.

She stood up, copying Kamryn's moves from before to put the glass away. She needed just a few more seconds to center herself. When Kamryn had said they could be together, her heart had leapt right before fear had taken over its place. She was so used to living in fear, wasn't she? It was almost like she hadn't been living at all for the last few years. She'd simply been existing within the world in a way that she would make as little impact as possible.

But Kamryn had paved the way for her to do something different, to live more truly to herself than she had been. And she couldn't ever be more grateful to Kamryn for that. The silence was loud, and the call to fill it with something was strong.

But what exactly did she want to say?

What did she want to do?

She still had all these decisions to make and things to do, but there was only one thing that called through that loud echo of silence.

Kamryn loved her.

Love.

She hadn't let that sink in until now, but Kamryn had told her in the coffee shop bathroom that she loved her. And she'd been so unapologetic in it. She hadn't wanted anything out of it, she hadn't wanted anything from Elia, and here they were.

Elia set her glass in the sink and turned around, eyeing Kamryn over the back of the couch. Her hair was pulled back in a ponytail, and she'd already pulled off her suit jacket. Elia's lips tingled, the memory of their almost kiss in that bathroom coming back fully. What she would have given for Kamryn to give in and just push her against the wall, to take the decision from her so she didn't have to make it.

But Kamryn wouldn't ever do that.

That wasn't who she was.

The memory of their last kiss, the tenderness and hope and fear that had mingled all within it. The memory of their first kiss —or at least what Elia considered their first true kiss. Kamryn all hot and bothered by the board dealing with the very issue she'd now resolved. She'd kept all of those promises, hadn't she?

And that first kiss.

Wholly unexpected, awkward, and hot as hell. Elia hadn't been touched so reverently by someone before, hadn't been held so closely and carefully, and never in such a public setting. Each of those memories was one that Elia never wanted to forget. But more than that, she wanted to make more.

"Kam?"

"Hmm?" Kamryn replied from the couch, barely moving.

"Did you want another drink?"

"No." Kamryn yawned. "I think I'm done for the night. I could really use the rest instead of staying up later."

Right. Kamryn was exhausted. Elia had seen that the moment she'd laid eyes on her that evening. She couldn't imagine the number of hours and the tension that Kamryn had been holding in the last few weeks. Rinsing out her glass, Elia dried her hands on the towel on the counter before heading back to where Kamryn sat.

Elia walked around toward her jacket, intending to leave, but she stopped short when Kamryn's gaze reached hers. She didn't want to leave. She wanted to stay and take care of Kamryn and make sure that she got the rest that she needed.

"Did you have any more questions?"

Elia shook her head, biting her lip before she settled on what she wanted to do next. Instead of grabbing her jacket, she strode back toward the couch and slid onto the cushion next to Kamryn. She had one more chance to get this right, and that was exactly what she needed.

"Yes," Elia said, full confidence in the word.

thirty-nine

"Yes?" Kamryn asked, thoroughly confused. Hadn't Elia just said no? And now she was saying yes? But it didn't feel like she was answering the same question as before. "What questions?"

"No questions." Elia had a hint of a smile on her lips.

Kamryn's brain was struggling to keep up with everything. The relief as she walked out of that board meeting had been overwhelming, and she'd dragged her feet back to her apartment. She'd had every intention of curling up on the couch and probably falling asleep in her clothes because she couldn't be bothered going to the bedroom and changing.

"Elia, you're going to have to catch me up on what you're talking about." Kamryn was ready to sink into these couch cushions and sleep the night away, but at the same time it was such a struggle to keep her eyes closed and turn her mind off. She hadn't been able to stop thinking about the last few hours and all the conversations sprouting around the table, not to mention the last week, as everything had come to a head.

"Yes," Elia said again.

Okay, Kamryn was really missing out on something now. She was just about to ask for more clarification when Elia answered her.

"Yes, you can kiss me. Yes, I want to be with you."

Kamryn stilled. She hadn't realized they were even talking about that. She'd mentioned it earlier, but Elia hadn't seemed remotely interested. Then again, she might have just been overwhelmed by everything that had happened. Kamryn had more time to digest it all.

Sitting up a little straighter, Kamryn reached for Elia's hand and took it in her own. "You can think about it more if you want. I'm not in any rush."

"I am." Elia raised her chin up, her lips still curled upward in a true moment of happiness. One that was so fucking rare for Kamryn to see from her. "I'm in a rush."

"Why?"

"Because I'm tired of holding myself back." Elia lifted Kamryn's hand to her lips, kissing her knuckles gently. "I'm tired of living in fear and in the shadows. I'm ready to live."

Kamryn's heart raced. "Even if this doesn't work out?"

"Even if it doesn't work out." Elia turned Kamryn's hand over and kissed the inside of her wrist.

The touch of her lips sent shivers racing up Kamryn's arm and straight into her chest. She couldn't drag her gaze away from Elia's mouth, the closeness between them mocking her to do something, but she was stunned speechless.

"I want you to kiss me," Elia murmured, pressing another kiss, this one higher up and very near the inside of Kamryn's elbow. "And I want to kiss you."

"Yessss," Kamryn whispered, the word barely audible over the blood rushing to her head. "I love you, Elia."

Elia grinned fully then. She reached up, cupping Kamryn's cheek with her hand, the softness of her fingers so tender and loving in the caress. Kamryn closed her eyes and leaned into the touch, reveling in it, savoring it. She needed this. They both needed it.

"Fucking kiss me already," Kamryn demanded, keeping her eyes closed as she waited for what Elia would do next.

It didn't take long for their lips to brush, for the brush to become more intense, for Kamryn to part her lips and move into the embrace. She threaded her fingers behind Elia's head, holding her close and sighing into the kiss. God, she'd missed this. It hadn't been that long, but it felt like forever. All that tension that had been pushing them apart had completely dissipated. Kamryn was ready to reconnect.

She moaned when Elia pulled her lower lip into her mouth, sucking gently before diving back in and deepening the kiss. Kamryn gave her whole self over to this moment, to the touches and the kisses, to the hope that was rekindled between them. They were actually doing this. They were going to be together.

"Elia..." Kamryn murmured before being completely distracted by yet another kiss. She started to lift up, pushing Elia back slightly. Kamryn caressed her neck, her shoulder, dropped her hand down to Elia's and squeezed before breaking the kiss. "Elia, you're sure?"

"More sure than anything. I promise you I'm not going to hold back." Elia kissed Kamryn's cheek, then her other one. She kissed her forehead. "I want to be with you tonight, to stay here and take care of you. This hasn't been easy on you."

Kamryn snorted lightly, shaking her head in agreement. "It's been awful."

"Then let me take care of you." Elia kissed her lips again.

"Make love to me," Kamryn begged. She was already pulling at her shirt to get it loose and away from her skin. "Make me forget these last few weeks for a little bit."

"Are you sure? You don't want to rest?" Elia was already helping Kamryn pull the shirt off, lifting it over her head and dropping it to the side of the couch.

"I'm sure."

Kamryn stood up, taking Elia by the hand and leading her back toward her small bedroom. She didn't look over her shoulder, and Elia didn't tug or slow down either. As soon as they were inside, Kamryn cringed. Her room was a mess. It had definitely been a rough few weeks. The only advantage was that Greer had been around for a while, and she'd kept everything in the main area spotless while she tried to avoid her own problems.

"Just love me," Kamryn requested. She pulled Elia in for another kiss, delighting when Elia started running her fingers up and down her back, touching her skin anywhere and everywhere that she could. Elia flicked the clasp on Kamryn's bra and pulled it down, their tongues still tangled.

Immediately, Elia's hands were around her front, cupping and massaging and teasing Kamryn's breasts. Kamryn moaned and she reached for Elia's shirt. She struggled to find the edge of it, her hands fumbling, especially when Elia bent down slightly and pressed her entire mouth over Kamryn's left nipple and sucked.

Hissing, Kamryn had to stop everything she'd been trying to do just to concentrate. Being this exhausted and adding sex into the mix was making her entire body come alive. She didn't have to fight her brain to feel things. She didn't have to concentrate on anything because she literally couldn't think about anything else except what was happening right here.

"I can't think about anything but you," Kamryn said with a little laugh. "Fuck, this feels so good."

Elia hummed, but she didn't move away from Kamryn's body. She continued to tease until she moved to Kamryn's other breast, giving it exactly the same treatment. Kamryn stumbled backward and braced herself against the small full-sized bed that the apartment had come with. She fell back, pulling Elia with her.

"Sorry!" Kamryn said.

Shaking her head, Elia stood back up and dragged her blouse over her head, her hair settling around her shoulders and framing her body perfectly. Kamryn could never get enough of looking at this woman. She wanted more every single time.

Elia bent down and pulled down the zipper on her boots, taking them off and tossing them to the side. "I want to taste you."

For some reason, those words sent a ripple of anticipation and pleasure through Kamryn. Elia had never been lacking in confidence when it came to sex, but this version of her was something else entirely—confident, sexy, but completely in control. And Kamryn was more than ready to let Elia take the reins and guide their night.

Moving her hands to her waist, Kamryn pulled at the snap and zipper before she shuffled the fabric down her legs and onto the floor. She didn't even bother to watch where they landed, because her eyes were locked on Elia's face. She wanted to see only Elia in this moment, hear and feel exactly what Elia was hearing and feeling.

Elia stepped in between Kamryn's thighs, trailing her fingers up and down the tops of her thighs as she stared down between Kamryn's legs hungrily. That was a look Kamryn could get used to. She loved when Elia looked at her like that, as if she was the entire world, and as if Elia would do anything for her pleasure. And right now, Kamryn was pretty sure that was true.

"El..."

Elia's lips quirked up at the nickname, and she swiftly moved down and pressed their mouths together. Fire and heat led the kiss, their tongues tangling as the speed increased. Kamryn fell backward, dragging Elia with her as she went.

Cradling Elia between her legs, Kamryn held her there. She loved the skin to skin, the press of Elia's chest to hers, even if Elia's bra was still in the way. She'd deal with that later. Elia broke the kiss, breathing heavily. She stared down at Kamryn, a hand pushed into the bed above Kamryn's head as they looked at each other.

"I love you," Elia said. "I told you that, and I'm not going to take it back."

Kamryn's lips quirked up. "I never doubted your feelings for me."

Elia faltered at that. "You doubted me?"

"I doubted whether or not we could make this work. But I never doubted that you care for me."

Humming, Elia bent down and kissed her again. "You're right. I never doubted what I felt, just the possibilities of hope and what it would be to be loved and to love someone again."

"Loving someone is the easy part, right?" Kamryn tried to hide her satisfaction at throwing that one back at Elia.

"It's so easy to love you," Elia responded, standing back up and taking off her slacks. She nodded toward Kamryn, indicating she wanted Kamryn to move farther onto the bed. Following the direction, Kamryn pulled herself backward. "It's been much more difficult to love myself."

"You're so worthy of it, though. You're amazing."

"Kam," Elia said in a warning. "I know that here." Elia tapped the side of her head. "It's a bit harder to make myself remember it when it's easier to run the other direction."

"It's easier in the short term."

"Once again, the student is wiser than the teacher." Elia chuckled lightly as she climbed onto the bed, hovering over Kamryn on hands and knees. "It's a good thing I'm out of lessons for you."

"Oh, I don't know about that." Kamryn couldn't resist any longer. She traced the curve of Elia's breast as it pushed against the cup of her bra. "I've learned plenty from you in these last few months."

"Have you?"

"Yeah, like don't turn in my resignation if I'm not ready to fight for it."

Elia snorted loudly. "Fair."

"And don't think that I'm alone in a fight for my livelihood when I really do have allies all around me. If I'd only just ask for help." Kamryn held Elia by her hips, ready to flip them over so that she was on top.

"Ouch," Elia answered, but she was smiling just the same.

"You have a whole team of faculty that's behind you, who are willing to risk their own careers for you." Kamryn slid her fingers into the elastic of Elia's panties. "Don't you know how loved and revered you are?"

"By you? Or by the faculty and staff?"

"Us and more." Kamryn pulled Elia's panties down as much as she could, revealing the little bit of hair between her legs. Ideas worked their way into Kamryn's mind, how she was going to go about continuing what they'd started. "But I'm ready to worship your body, that's for certain."

Elia hummed that knowing hum before she took Kamryn's mouth with her own and moved her hips out of Kamryn's reach in one swift move. Kamryn grunted her disappointment until Elia parted Kamryn's knees with a sure hand. Kamryn let her, locking her gaze on Elia's face and grinning when Elia looked directly back up at her.

Where the hell had all this energy come from? Kamryn had needed it hours ago, not now. Although she'd take it now for sure. She threw her hands above her head, gripping onto her pillow as she waited for Elia's next move.

She started with kisses, soft gentle ones, against Kamryn's hips and then the inside of her thighs. Kamryn struggled to stay still and let Elia do whatever she wanted. Because she wanted Elia's mouth against her immediately. She didn't have the wherewithal to wait any longer, not after the desert they'd just come out of.

"What are you thinking?" Elia asked.

"What? Why?" Kamryn winced at her tone.

"Because the look that just crossed your face was...interesting. And I'm not sure what it meant." Elia put the flat of her tongue against Kamryn's skin, licking her inner thigh firmly.

Kamryn groaned, her eyes fluttering shut as she could just imagine what Elia was going to do with that tongue next. God, she'd never wanted to be touched this much before. She'd never truly understood just what it meant to beg to be touched, but she got it now.

"Kam," Elia said before licking her inner thigh again. "What were you thinking?"

"That this might be the best sex I've ever had, and we haven't even gotten to the main show yet." Where had those words come from? Kamryn chuckled nervously while Elia cocked her head to the side.

"Best sex?" Elia asked.

"Uh... yeah. I mean, if we get to that portion of the night." Now Kamryn felt awkward and useless. She'd ruined everything they'd been going for, hadn't she?

Elia grinned before she licked her lips and shook her head. "It's good because it means something, don't you think?"

"Uh huh," Kamryn readily agreed. "But are we going to... move on? I'm not sure how much energy I have left for staying awake."

"Message heard." Elia moved back down, once again pressing gentle kisses to Kamryn's skin.

She worked her way closer and closer to where Kamryn wanted her. As soon as Elia's lips covered her clit, Kamryn sighed. She closed her eyes, tilting her head up and focusing only on the sensation of Elia's mouth against her, the flick of her tongue, the licks, the sucks, the slow pattern that she finally started as soon as she stopped exploring.

Kamryn slowed her breathing, resting into the touches and feelings that were rolling through her body. Elia was so good at this, at finding exactly what Kamryn needed in these moments and delivering on them. Kamryn tightened her muscles, she prepared her body for the pleasure she knew was going to surge through her, and the inevitable rush of heat that would overtake her. But she knew without a doubt that Elia would be there with her through it all, that she would soothe and touch and taste and continue to care for Kamryn every second of the way.

And when she crashed through her orgasm, Elia did exactly that. She ran her fingers along Kamryn's thighs, she slowed the flicks of her tongue, she tasted Kamryn's juices, swallowing them and taking as much of her on her tongue as she possibly could. Kamryn beckoned Elia up with a wave of her hands.

Elia crawled up the bed, sliding against Kamryn's side so they could kiss. Her lips were still damp, and Kamryn loved the sensations of hot and cold that it brought. She deepened the embrace, moving her hand down Elia, to her hip and back up again to tangle her fingers in Elia's hair.

"I love you," Kamryn whispered again. "But take this fucking thing off already." She plucked at the strap of Elia's bra before palming her ass and pulling her in closer. As much as Kamryn wanted Elia naked and next to her, she wasn't sure she wanted to give Elia the space to do that.

Elia reached behind her and snapped the clasp of her bra. But she didn't move very swiftly to divest herself of the fabric. Was she feeling the same way? Kamryn started to push Elia's panties down with her hand, at least what she could manage in the positions they were in. She didn't want to stop kissing Elia. She didn't want to stop touching her. She wanted to stay right here and never go back to where they were that afternoon.

Elia finally sat up and pulled the rest of her clothes off. As soon as she was free from them, Kamryn pulled her back down and kissed her.

"I didn't think you'd want to talk to me again after this afternoon," Kamryn said, still worried about how everything had happened. She could have done such a better job of explaining and holding that tension.

"I didn't really want to talk to you again," Elia answered but kissed her anyway. "Not until I got some answers anyway."

"I'm really sorry about that."

"Seems it won't be too much of an issue any longer since you won't be my boss anymore. Hmm?"

"Yeah." That was one good thing to come out of this situation. Kamryn smiled at that thought. It did allow them to have moments like this.

"Just use your fingers, Kam, and then we'll go to sleep."

"Good." It was getting harder to keep her eyes open, the orgasm doing exactly what it was supposed to do and stealing the last vestiges of her energy. Kamryn moved her hand between Elia's legs, glad when Elia parted her knees and propped one leg up to give Kamryn easier access. "I can't wait to fall asleep in your arms."

"Me either," Elia replied. She clasped her arm around Kamryn's neck and kissed her hard, their lips pushing into each other. "Fuck me, Kam."

Not having to be told twice, Kamryn slid two fingers deep inside Elia. She was soaking, and her juices pooled onto Kamryn's palm, which was exactly what Kamryn needed. She pulled out slightly and wet Elia's clit before she started grinding the heel of her palm against Elia's clit and tapping the fingers inside her.

The pace Kamryn started was brutal. This wasn't meant for slow and sexy, for lingering in touches. This was meant as a relief of pent-up emotions and sexual tension and frustration. This was meant for comfort and release. And they were both going to get exactly what they wanted. Elia tightened her grip around Kamryn's shoulders, pulling her upper body into Kamryn as her own pleasure intensified.

Kamryn could see it, not just in the way she moved but in the intensity of her gaze, in the brilliance of her smile, in the way Elia breathed rapidly and the rush of red to her cheeks from the exertion. Kamryn moved in harder and faster. She watched with rapt attention as Elia got closer to the pinnacle, closer to where they both wanted her to be. It was beautiful to watch—in fact, Kamryn wasn't sure she'd ever seen something as wonderful as this before in her life.

Each time Elia pressed against her, each time Elia allowed her to touch and taste and bring pleasure, it amazed her. Kamryn was in complete awe, and she wanted so much more for each of them. She never wanted to stop this.

Elia let out a small groan, and Kamryn grinned in response. She pressed kisses against Elia's cheeks and neck, to her lips. Elia clasped tightly onto Kamryn's back, pulling her in and pressing their mouths together in a wild, passionate embrace.

"S-slow down," Elia whispered.

Kamryn eased up on the movements, finally able to feel Elia pulsing against her, the clenching of her body around Kamryn's fingers a sweet embrace that she'd been looking for. Kamryn hummed her own pleasure as she kissed Elia's parted lips quickly.

"Please say you're staying the night," Kamryn said.

"Yeah, I'm staying," Elia answered, her chest still rising and falling rapidly as she lay back on the bed. She smiled as she stared up at Kamryn. "That was good."

"Wait until you see what I can do next time." Kamryn winked. "But not tonight. Too tired tonight."

Elia nodded her understanding. Kamryn forced herself to half-sit up and she reached for the bottom of the bed for the blanket. She was about to curl around Elia when Elia opened her arms, inviting Kamryn to snuggle into her side.

Lying next to Elia, Kamryn closed her eyes and absorbed her scent, her warmth, her comfort. She rested and relaxed to the feel of Elia's fingers in her hair, combing through the long strands lovingly. Kamryn was going to stay here for as long as possible. She didn't want to get up and leave. She wanted this.

Simple love.

And promises of more.

forty

"This house is gorgeous!" Kamryn's jaw dropped as Elia opened the door to her mother's home.

She hadn't expected this kind of reaction, but it was so nice to see at the same time. Elia stepped outside into the lightly falling snow and wrapped her arms around Kamryn's shoulders before kissing her. "I'm glad you got here safe."

"Uh-huh. Seriously, Elia, this house is amazing."

It was a small cottage-style house in Western Massachusetts. Elia had grown up there, and her mom still lived there. Though she had thought about moving after Elia's dad passed away ten years ago.

"Come on." Elia took Kamryn's hand and led her into the house. She pulled Kamryn into the kitchen where her mother sat at the dining room table with Abagail. "Mom, this is Kam. Kam, this is my mom, Janet."

"It's good to meet you." Kamryn held her hand out and shook Janet's.

Elia kept her hand locked in Kamryn's. It'd only been two days since they'd seen each other, but it felt far longer. Elia had been spending most of her free time with Kamryn, and since they were still co-leading the Speech team and it was the height of the season, they were rarely apart aside from the eight hours in the middle of the day when they were at work.

"Nice to see you again," Kamryn said to Abagail, nodding at her.

Abagail flicked her gaze down from Elia's face to her joined hands with Kamryn and hardened. She'd been acting so odd lately, ever since the drama at the school had mostly resolved and since Elia hadn't followed her plan to a T. It was strange. Elia couldn't remember a time when they were at odds as much as they were lately.

Still, she was glad that Abagail had come for Thanksgiving. It was tradition after all, ever since Elia and Abagail had graduated college and Abagail had scorned most of her own family. She still had close contact with them, but she wasn't very familiar with them. Janet had become the second mom that Abagail always wanted. At least, that's what Abagail had said.

Elia pulled Kamryn a smidge closer. "I'm going to show Kamryn upstairs. I'll be back down to help in a minute."

It didn't take her long to get Kamryn settled into the room that they were going to share. And by the time they were done eating the festive Thanksgiving, Kamryn stayed in the kitchen to help clean up while Elia settled onto the sofa with a glass of wine, Abagail still giving her an odd look.

"I was hoping for a minute to talk to you alone," Abagail said, sliding onto the sofa next to Elia. "I didn't want to say this in front of Mom or Kam."

"Go for it." Elia sipped her wine and relaxed. She could tell that something was bothering Abagail all evening, so now it was finally time to have it out. This would be a good thing.

"I don't think you and Kam should be in a relationship together, and it's not because I think she's too young or not right for you or this is an HR nightmare. I've already told you all of that."

"You have," Elia agreed, trying to figure out where this was heading.

"It's not even because I don't like her. I do like her." Abagail twisted her wine glass between her fingers, not even looking up at Elia. "I just like you more."

Elia laughed lightly. "We've been friends for decades. Of course you like me more."

Abagail shook her head slowly, and Elia's breath caught. "No, not like you think I do."

Elia's stomach tightened. She looked out toward the kitchen, hearing Kamryn's laughter with her mom, and steadied herself. "What are you *not* saying?"

"I'm in love with you."

"Abagail..." Elia's body went cold. "We're best friends."

"I know we are. It's why I haven't said anything before now. You were never interested in me in that way, and I never thought that I'd say anything, but seeing you and Kam together? I can't help but wonder what if it was me?"

It had been Abagail. For years when Elia had been single, she'd used her friendship in that way, relying on Abagail for the support that she would normally rely on a partner to help with. That hadn't been right of her. But they were best friends.

"I'm not in love with you like that," Elia lowered her voice, again looking toward the kitchen. She couldn't have Kamryn walking in on this. It would blow up, it would be a disaster, and they had finally found even footing lately.

"I know you're not." Abagail lifted her chin up, sadness sweeping through her gaze. "It doesn't mean that I'm not in love with you. I always have been." Abagail reached out and rested her hand on Elia's knee. "And seeing you so happy with Kam is fucking hard, Elia."

"I can't imagine." She couldn't. She'd never been in a situation like that before. She'd always been the one on the outside looking in but never with the feelings and the emotions attached to it. Looking around her mother's house now came with an entirely different feel. Had she been giving off the wrong signals for years? Had Abagail found places where Elia had accidentally told her that she was interested in a more romantic partnership? Had she taken advantage of Abagail's feelings without even considering the cost to their friendship?

"Don't do that," Abagail whispered, squeezing Elia's knee before she moved her hand. "Second guessing the last three decades isn't going to win you any favors."

"How did you—?"

"I know you." Abagail frowned into her wine. "And I love you, so of course I pay attention to how you behave." Abagail shook her head. "I don't want you to be with her, not because she doesn't make you happy, but because I want to be with you."

Elia had no idea what to say. She'd never heard any of this from Abagail before.

"I think I'm going to go," Abagail said, standing up and putting her wine on the table. "Will you tell Mom I'll call her next week?"

"Uh... yeah." Elia stood up, following Abagail toward the front door to the house. She again was at a loss for words. Did she say she would call Abagail? See her soon? This put her in such an awkward spot, and they hadn't really resolved anything. Abagail had just dropped this bomb on her lap and now she was leaving.

At the front door, Abagail snagged her jacket and scarf, putting them on. All the while, she kept her gaze on Elia, and a sad smile on her lips. "I'll call you soon. I promise."

"I'll hold you to that," Elia said, glad to have at least that little bit of hope.

"I'm just going to take some time. Okay? I want you to be happy, and I see that with Kam in ways I never saw with anyone else." Abagail stopped, she stared down at Elia, and then she took a step forward. "I want something just like this."

Abagail moved swiftly. She cupped Elia's face and pulled her in, pressing their lips together in a swift kiss. Elia's stomach twisted sharply, and she pulled away, immediately moving her hand up to her mouth and wiping her lips.

"I'll call," Abagail said as she stepped out the front door. She looked at Elia and then over Elia's shoulder, nodding before she stepped away.

Elia knew without turning.

Kamryn was standing there. The voices in the kitchen had gone silent. The blood rushed into her ears, making her head spin, and she felt like she was about to collapse to the floor in a puddle of something she wasn't sure she could even name.

"I didn't..." Elia started.

"I saw," Kamryn answered. But she stayed so far away that Elia wasn't sure what to make of it.

Elia swallowed the lump in her throat, glued to the spot where she'd been when Abagail had kissed her. What fresh hell was this?

"Just give me a minute." Kamryn put her hand up as if to stop Elia from approaching. "Just a minute."

Elia stayed where she was, wanting to rush forward and tell Kamryn that she had no idea what had just happened. They continued to stare at each other in the silence until Kamryn nodded at her.

"All right."

Elia moved swiftly then, walking right up to Kamryn and shaking her head wildly. "I have no idea where that came from."

"If you couldn't tell that girl was in love with you for years, you're more blind than me!" Elia's mom piped up from behind Kamryn. "I could have told you that was going to happen when you brought Kam home." Janet snorted. "Serves her right though. If she's going to wait around for years and not do anything about it, then she's going to have to pay the consequences."

Kamryn gave Elia a pained expression. Elia reached for Kamryn's hand and laced their fingers together. "I'm so sorry."

"It's not your fault." Kamryn gave her a weak smile. "Not easy to see, but not your fault."

"Are you sure?" Elia asked.

"Yeah." Kamryn lifted Elia's hand and kissed her knuckles. "Want to talk?"

"Yes." Elia smiled. "Let's take a walk."

"I'll get dessert ready." Janet wandered back toward the kitchen.

Elia stepped into Kamryn's space, hugging her tightly. "I'm so sorry."

"Again, Elia, it's really not your fault." Kamryn rubbed her hands up and down Elia's back in a soothing motion. "Come on, let's walk and talk."

Once they were bundled up and outside of the house, Elia felt much better. Just being out of that space gave her a clearer head. "Are you sure you're not mad?"

"I saw and heard enough to know it wasn't your idea, and you weren't particularly interested in it." Kamryn chuckled. "Trust me, I know when you want to be kissed."

Elia's lips quirked up slightly at that and she tightened her grip in Kamryn's hand. "I didn't know she felt that way."

"You and Abagail have something in common. That much was obvious from the moment I met her." Kamryn walked across the street to the next. "You're both cold as ice until you decide to let someone in. And then you warm right up. You're just very picky about who those people might be."

"You," Elia answered. "I let you in."

"You did." Kamryn grinned brilliantly. "And Abagail hasn't yet. She might get there, and she might not. That's a decision for her to make."

They walked another half block before Elia found herself going right back to that moment when she turned around and Kamryn was there, and the look of satisfaction on Abagail's face. That was what bothered her the most, like Abagail had intentionally caused drama between them. But she wouldn't do that, would she?

"Are you sure you aren't upset?" Elia asked again.

"I'm sure." Kamryn laughed lightly this time. Not in a making-fun way, but a *this is ridiculous* way. She moved in and kissed Elia's cheek.

Elia instinctively turned and pressed their lips together. The cold air bit at her cheeks, but Kamryn was all warmth and comfort, a welcome reprieve from what Elia had been experiencing. She backed away slightly and smiled up at Kamryn.

"You know the first time you asked to kiss me, I was so taken aback by the question that I told you no."

"That's why you said no?"

Elia nodded, taking hold of both of Kamryn's hands and lacing their fingers. "No one has ever asked me that before. And I have to say, I prefer it."

"You prefer it?" Kamryn grinned brightly.

"Yes." Elia took a small step in closer. "I like when you ask me to kiss you or you ask to kiss me. It's consent, it's permission, it's a decision that we make together."

Humming, Kamryn bent down and put her lips a breath away from Elia's. "Do you want me to kiss you now?"

"Yes." Elia breathed the word.

When Kamryn's mouth touched hers, Elia melted. She stayed right where she was, giving Kamryn everything that she wanted and more. Elia closed her eyes, holding tightly onto this moment —one where they were understanding each other, where they were going together in hope for what might come next. Pulling away, Elia licked her lips and smiled.

"We do need to talk, though."

"Talk?" Kamryn raised an eyebrow. "What's there to talk about?"

"Whether or not I'm staying at Windermere."

Kamryn's step faltered. "What do you mean?"

"Don't you think it'd be better if I started applying at other schools? Especially if you apply for the permanent position?" Elia started walking back toward the house. She was getting chilled to the bone far more quickly than she anticipated. And she wanted to get warm.

"It's an option, but I thought the way things were going so far was fine. Marshall's back, and that takes our conflict of interest one step farther away."

"But it's still going to be there no matter what we do. There might be work-arounds, but it doesn't mean that students or other staff and faculty won't try to play that out when they shouldn't." Elia kept her hand locked in Kamryn's. She wasn't going to let go. "I just think that maybe I should. It'd be easier for me to find another job than you."

Kamryn frowned, and she stopped Elia just in front of her mother's house. She shook her head. "Stay."

"I'm not leaving you."

"I know that." Kamryn kissed Elia's cheek. "But I want you to stay at Windermere. I enjoy getting to see you so often, and I don't want to give up what little time we have together. Besides, if you go to another school, then we'll be opponents at Speech. And you'll know all of our tricks."

Elia laughed lightly. "As if there are tricks in Speech."

Kamryn shrugged. "Stay. Please. I want you to."

"I love you, Kam." Elia leaned up and kissed her quickly. "You're so understanding, even when you probably shouldn't be."

"When shouldn't I be?"

"I don't know." Elia relaxed. "I don't know if I would have been as calm if I'd found you and Lauren kissing."

"Lauren and I have a very different history than you and Abagail. You really can't compare the two. It'd be like Greer and me. And that has never happened, nor will it." Kamryn wrapped her arm around Elia's shoulder and pulled her in tightly against her side. "I have a very particular question for you."

"Okay?" Elia looked up into Kamryn's dark eyes, even darker when the sun was down. "What's the question?"

"Is sex off limits when we're at your mother's? I don't want you to feel uncomfortable."

"You want to have sex?" Elia wrinkled her brow. "Now?"

"No, not now!" Kamryn snorted. "But maybe tonight. I don't know. Maybe tomorrow. Maybe next time you drag me here."

"Drag you here? Are you coming for another holiday?"

Kamryn shrugged slightly. "I will if you invite me."

That was music to Elia's ears. She loved thinking that they were going to be spending more time together, and more holidays together. It meant that their relationship truly was one that might last. And with all the drama and fear she'd had in the beginning about that, she was glad to see that they were defeating the odds against them.

"Yes, we can have sex."

"Oh good. Now, just how deaf is your mom?"

"Kam!" Elia playfully hit Kamryn's arm. "Don't you dare."

"Dare what? Make you scream."

"Shhh." Elia stepped toward the front door and pulled Kamryn with her. "Come on, Mom's sweet potato pie is to die for. Some might say...orgasmic."

forty-one

"Ugh, I'm stuffed." Kamryn sat down heavily on the mattress, watching as Elia pulled the earrings from her ears and tossed them into the small plate on the dresser. How often had she done that growing up? Kamryn wasn't sure that she could imagine Elia as a teenager, or as a teenager in this house in particular. Would she have been a straight-A, goody-two-shoes teenager? Or would she have been a rebellious one?

Elia chuckled as she started pulling off her shoes and tossing them to the side. Kamryn was completely entranced with every single move that she made. She wasn't sure if she'd ever get over Elia. And sure, they still had problems they would need to work out, but at least they were working on them together.

"Are you trying to be a tease?" Kamryn asked. "Because if you are, you're succeeding at it."

"Maybe." Elia gave her a wicked grin. "I do have a gift for you, though."

"A gift?" Kamryn frowned. She hadn't realized they were exchanging gifts... at Thanksgiving... What tradition was this? She pulled herself to sit up on the bed and pulled off her own shoes. If Elia was getting comfortable, she was sure they were going to be staying in here the rest of the night.

Elia smiled over at Kamryn from the dresser that she was leaning against. This seemed almost like a trap, Kamryn wasn't sure. But there was such an ease from earlier in the night, and Kamryn was so happy. She'd been worried after Abagail left with her...parting gift...that they were going to struggle to get back into the swing of things, but she was glad to find that it was easy.

Standing up, Elia turned around and took a medium-sized wooden box from the dresser and started to walk toward Kamryn. That was her gift? It'd been in plain sight the entire time? Also, who gives gifts at Thanksgiving?

Kamryn was still stumped on that last one. She ran her fingers through her hair and eyed the box as Elia came closer, sliding it into Kamryn's fingers before she sat next to her on the bed. "I couldn't help myself when I saw it online."

"Online?" Now Kamryn was even more interested than before.

"And I couldn't wait until Christmas to give it to you either."

Were they planning for Christmas? Absolutely. And that thought alone made Kamryn so happy. She remembered all those times she'd planned for holidays with Lauren and then they'd break up before they got there, only to get together again last minute and Kamryn would have to scramble to get anything ready for the holiday.

Everything with Elia was so much calmer and easygoing. It really was easy to love her. At least now it was.

"Are you going to open it?" Elia asked, nearly as impatient as a toddler on Christmas morning.

Kamryn eyed her carefully. "I'm scared to open it."

"Why?"

"What could you possibly have come up with for a gift?" Kamryn ran her fingers along the smooth and polished edges of the wooden box. It was gorgeous. Even if the box itself was the whole gift, then Kamryn would love it. But she had a feeling there was something else inside. Elia didn't do things half-assed at all.

"You'll have to open it to find out."

Kamryn hesitated only a moment longer before she slid the lid of the box off and immediately burst into laughter. Inside, nestled in red fabric, was a whisk, and not just any whisk, but a golden whisk. She plucked the item out of the box, and grinned down at it, reading the engraved handle.

Promise Whisk.

"You got me a whisk?" Kamryn very nearly burst into tears. She'd never gotten such a heartfelt gift before. Not one that would mean so much to both of them. Kamryn ran her fingers along the metal and couldn't stop smiling.

"You gave your whisk to the kids. I figured you needed a new one."

"To cook with?" Kamryn snorted. She couldn't remember the last time she cooked in her apartment. She usually ate at Elia's. "You think I'm going to use a golden and engraved whisk to make my scrambled eggs in the morning?"

Elia laughed lightly and shook her head. "Well, no. Probably not. But the whisk is all about telling truths and highlights, and I wanted you to know what a highlight you've been to my life. I can't imagine how this semester would have gone without you in it, to walk right alongside me, to be with me, to *protect* me."

Kamryn took in a shuddering breath. "I couldn't have done it without you."

"I know I couldn't have done it without you." Elia moved in, kissing Kamryn's cheek. "But the whisk is just the added good-luck charm that I think we both needed."

"It's not a good-luck charm." Kamryn ran her fingers over the wires again, admiring the way the light shone off them. "It's a truth teller, it's a positivity master, it's what I want to keep in the forefront of my mind always. I don't want to live in the negative, and I think the world would be better off if we tried to be more positive."

"You've always believed that," Elia said, "even when you were a student at Windermere."

Kamryn nodded. She had always believed that. She'd also

forgotten it a time or two in the meantime. The whisk was the perfect reminder. "I'll treasure this." She settled the whisk back into the box and closed it up. "Thank you."

Leaning in, Kamryn pressed their mouths together.

"Thank you, really. I love the gift."

"Good." Elia swiftly moved in and kissed her again.

Kamryn sank into the embrace. She let go of the box and threaded her fingers into the hair behind Elia's head, pulling her in even closer. "Are we really doing this?" Kamryn asked.

"If you want to," Elia answered, kissing her again. "And for the record..." another kiss, "I want to." Elia was pressing their bodies together. "I want to remember why I love you so much."

Kamryn smiled at that. "And you need sex to do that?"

"No," Elia whispered, pressing their mouths together in a quick kiss. "Just time with you, and a promise that you won't ever let me forget."

Kamryn grinned at that. She moved to put the box on the nightstand next to the bed and immediately pulled Elia with her onto the mattress. She wanted to get lost in Elia's body tonight, to be completely taken over by what they could do together and more.

"I feel like I owe you a gift," Kamryn murmured against Elia's neck as she pressed kisses down on her collarbone. "You should have warned me that you were getting me something."

"Gifts given in surprise are better. Don't you think?" Elia moaned lightly, arching her back against Kamryn as they laid down together.

"I don't know," Kamryn said, pulling Elia's shirt upward. "Please tell me you have a lock on the door."

Elia frowned before she glanced over Kamryn's shoulder at the door. "Yes."

"Good." Kamryn jumped up from the bed.

She had the door locked in a snap. Instead of immediately going back to the bed, Kamryn started to strip off her clothes. Elia watched her carefully from the bed, one hand tossed over her head in a pose of relaxation. Kamryn knew it was exactly the opposite though. She unzipped her jeans and shimmied out of them. She loved that Elia wouldn't look away from her. She'd never felt more attractive than when Elia was watching her like this.

"Are you going to get undressed?" Kamryn asked, wishing that she could watch Elia just like Elia had watched her.

"Do you want me to?" Elia asked, dragging her gaze all over Kamryn's naked body.

"Hmm, yes." Kamryn's lips quirked up at her. "So much yes."

Elia moved to sit up, starting with her shirt. She slowly stripped herself while Kamryn stood watching. This could very well be her favorite part of their sex life so far. The slow pulling off of all the responsibilities and weights and masks that they wore throughout the day so that they were purely themselves and no one else. Kamryn had never thought of it like that before Elia. But she could see how this was the way that they came together authentically, them together and only them.

When Elia lay back on the bed, Kamryn winked. "I'd love your mouth."

"Then that's what you'll have." Elia started to move, but Kamryn knelt on the bed and pushed her back down, shaking her head.

She wanted this to happen a certain way, the idea coming to her far too late in the game, but she wanted to make sure that she and Elia could do this together—she absolutely loved it when they did that.

"Lie down," Kamryn said. "On your back. I'd like to be on top."

"Oh!" Elia's curiosity turned into a wicked joy. Kamryn wished she could bottle that and keep it. She adored Elia more and more each day that they spent together, the hopes and dreams that they were weaving around each other, individually and as a couple. It was like they were made for each other sometimes, and Kamryn leaned into those moments every chance that she got.

When Elia had a pillow under her head, Kamryn climbed onto the bed, walking on her knees until she was straddling Elia's waist. She wasn't going to wait or drag this out. The day had been long, and what she wanted most was to connect with Elia in a way only the two of them managed to do.

"I love you," Kamryn said, not sure if Elia was paying any attention to her words or not. Elia was running her hands up and down Kamryn's thighs, her gaze locked right between her legs, that hungry look back in her eyes again. Kamryn touched Elia's nose lightly with one finger to get her attention. "You ready for this?"

"Absolutely."

Kamryn lifted one knee over Elia's shoulder and then the other, planting herself firmly over Elia's face. She had longed for this for weeks now, but she hadn't been bold enough to ask for it. Not until tonight.

Elia grabbed Kamryn's ass, pushing her forward and right where both of them wanted her. Elia's lips curled upward quickly before she dove right in. Kamryn sighed in pleasure, the sensations rolling through her instantly. Elia was so damn good with her mouth. Kamryn adored it. And she never wanted to forget moments like these where she'd absolutely lose her mind just to be tongue-fucked by this powerful and no longer icy woman under her.

Kamryn took her time centering her balance so she knew she wouldn't accidentally topple over. Then she leaned back, sliding her hand along Elia's body, from her waist to her hip and down her leg and right back up it. Kamryn grinned to herself as she pressed her fingers between Elia's legs and waited for the hitch of a hiccup.

Instead, she was greeted with a widening of Elia's knees so that she could slip her fingers as deep inside Elia as they would go. Elia didn't falter in her pace. She licked and sucked just like she had been before. Now Kamryn was just damn determined to get Elia off track.

From this angle, it was super easy for Kamryn to slide her thumb along Elia's clit. She touched. She teased. She tried to stare down at Elia's face to see her reactions, but she couldn't see over her own body and still reach to touch Elia in the way she wanted. Elia shifted Kamryn, her hands against her back as she moved them closer together.

Kamryn moaned, biting the sound back as best as she could. She needed to make sure that she didn't let loose entirely in this house. She continued to touch Elia as best she could and wait for any kind of reaction other than the wetness against her fingers and the deepened breathing as Elia sucked in sharp breaths.

They stayed like that, concentrating on each other. Kamryn never wanted to give this up. She knew she'd been right to take the risk on Elia. Maybe not that first night, but definitely after that. There was something about this stunning woman that stole her breath every single day. They were so happy together.

Elia lifted her hips right when Kamryn was struggling to focus. Maybe Elia wasn't as far behind her as Kamryn originally had thought. But it was getting harder and harder to concentrate. She continued to move her hand, trying to keep her pussy right where it was, against Elia's mouth and face.

Elia pulled away sharply, dragging in a deep breath. She eyed Kamryn and closed her eyes. Kamryn continued to touch her, teasing her into the orgasm that she longed for. As soon as Elia could, she pressed her face against Kamryn's body again, picking up right where she left off. Kamryn moved her hand and pushed up on her knees, changing the angle entirely.

This sent a new wave of pleasure through her. She had to press her hands against the wall to keep herself upright. She bit the inside of her cheek to hold back her moan. She'd essentially promised Elia that she wouldn't scream or be too noisy, and she would be damn sure to keep that promise. She careened through her orgasm, pushing against the wall to hold herself up so she didn't collapse on top of Elia's face.

Kamryn laughed as she finally fell to the side, her legs still entangled with Elia's arms. She stayed right where she was as she caught her breath. Elia turned on her side and started to move around, and it took Kamryn a while to open her eyes and see what was going on.

"Elia..."

"What?" Elia asked, her tone sharper than she probably intended it, but they were in a much smaller bed than normal, and nothing was quite the same as being at Elia's house or Kamryn's apartment.

"You didn't scream."

Elia let out a grunt before she finally tapped Kamryn's hip. "Get up so we can pull the blanket down, would you?"

"Ready for bed already?" Kamryn said, yawning. All that turkey she'd eaten was catching up with her faster than she'd anticipated it would.

"I've been up cooking all day. How about you?"

"I drove here," Kamryn whined lightly and then wrinkled her nose. "Nope, I can't complain. And dinner was amazing." She finally got herself together enough to shift so they could move the blanket out from under them.

Turning to face Elia, Kamryn kissed her, softening the moment back to what it had been before. She slowed the embrace, not wanting to incite any more than she already had. "Turn over. Let me hold you."

"I'd love that," Elia murmured as she settled into a position.

They lay there, listening to the sounds of the house and each other's quiet breathing. Kamryn was so lost in the moment that she nearly missed Elia's words.

"Will you make me a promise?"

"Sure. Anything," Kamryn answered.

"Promise me that you won't leave Windermere. The school needs you."

Kamryn's heart stuttered. She'd thought about leaving more times than she could count. But it wasn't just the school drawing her back there now, it was the students she'd made a connection with, the staff and the board and the faculty. But more than anything, it was Elia.

Kissing the back of Elia's neck, Kamryn closed her eyes. "I promise that I'll think about it."

forty-two

"I've got wine!" Abagail cheered loudly as she stepped into Elia's front door.

It had taken two weeks after Thanksgiving for Abagail to call Elia, and it had taken another month before they'd agreed to get together. Elia's stomach was in knots, but they both needed this. Abagail's kiss, but more her confession of her feelings, couldn't ruin a friendship that had been so strong for decades. Elia wouldn't allow it to happen.

"Perfect," Elia said, leaning in, pressing a kiss to Abagail's cheek like she always would, and hugged her. But she hesitated, and she could tell that Abagail could tell. She sighed. They'd get better at this with time. At least that's what Kamryn kept telling her.

"Kamryn just went to get Greer, so they should be here shortly." Elia took the two wine bottles that Abagail had brought and headed toward the kitchen. She needed a drink to steady her hands already. She had really wanted Kamryn to be back before Abagail got there, but she was out of luck.

"How is everything going with Kam? You haven't talked about her much lately."

Elia had specifically avoided that while on the phone with Abagail, due to circumstances. But she couldn't avoid it forever, and she needed to work on getting over it so that she could work on her relationship with her best friend.

"It's going well. Marshall is back, so he's been my direct supervisor for the last month. It's been an adjustment, but it'll be better in the long run I think." Elia pulled out the sour cream from the fridge and started to scoop it into a bowl.

"You think that'll be enough to avoid some of the conflicts that come up?"

Elia shook her head. "No, but it's a start. This school hasn't had this kind of relationship conflict to navigate in a very long time, and no one was around the last time, it was in the fifties. Things were vastly different then. Kam and Jensen have spoken with a few other schools to get copies of their policies to try and create some for Windermere." Elia ripped the bag of dried french onion soup and dumped it into the sour cream.

"My HR brain still thinks this is an awful idea, and no one is going to come out the other end of it well."

Elia agreed. "I know, but I think it can work out." She had to believe that, because she'd rescinded her resignation and stopped looking for new jobs for the upcoming year. Kamryn still hadn't told her if she was planning on applying for the permanent Head of School position, but Elia suspected that she would. Windermere was in her blood, and she'd want to stay there since she'd spent so long trying to get back.

Abagail frowned. "My *new* hire, remember her? Ivy?"

"Yeah. Is something wrong again?"

"She can't keep a nanny to save her life." Abagail groaned. Maybe if they stuck to talking about work then they could ease back into their friendship. "Actually, I don't think it's her who's the problem. Remember when I said we were hired by her friend's company?"

"I do." Elia stirred the dry soup mix into the sour cream with a spoon and spared Abagail a glance.

"They share a nanny, and I think she's the problem. But would Ivy listen to me? Nope. Apparently since I don't have kids, I shouldn't have an opinion."

Elia pursed her lips. "As her boss, you do get some opinion."

"Right? That's what I said. I don't care who takes care of her kid, but if the nanny constantly doesn't show up so she can't come into work, then that's a boss opinion." Abagail threw her hands up before she grabbed one bottle of wine and rifled through the drawer for the corkscrew. "And trust me, if it was just once in a blue moon, I wouldn't care, but we're talking repeated issues every single month. It's affecting the office."

"That's gotta be hard on you." Elia finished the chip dip and started to pull out some more food that she'd gotten for the small get-together they were having. She should have started this sooner, but she had been so nervous about seeing Abagail again that she'd avoided it.

Abagail blew out a breath in an exaggerated fashion and rolled her eyes. "It's awful."

The front door opened, and Kamryn came in with Greer right behind her. She stopped briefly before plastering on a smile and taking off her jacket. Greer looked a lot worse for wear than the last time Elia had seen her at the wedding. Kamryn hadn't been lying when she said that she was worried about her best friend.

"Wine?" Abagail asked loudly from the kitchen. "I just opened the bottle."

"Yes. Please," Greer said, stepping forward and coming directly toward them.

Kamryn stayed behind a little as she continued to observe the situation. Elia had seen her do that several times throughout the years, and now was no different. Kamryn was trying to size up everything that was happening and everything she didn't know about without asking direct questions. It was adorable, honestly, along with the fact that she was still so protective of Elia even though Elia could definitely handle herself in this situation.

With everyone in the kitchen while Elia worked on the snacks she'd bought for the night, it was crowded. But it felt so good. For so long, Elia had believed that her life was going to remain lonely, that she wouldn't have friends or family to join her for special events like this or for holidays. But in the last four months that had completely turned upside down. Kamryn had encouraged her to reach out to other staff and faculty and continue to build on the relationships that were already there instead of holding them at arm's length.

It meant that Simone and Andra were coming over shortly. Andra with her new husband, though Simone said she wasn't going to bring hers. Elia hadn't thought twice about it until Kamryn had said she'd found that odd.

Kamryn set a wine glass in front of Elia and trailed her fingers down Elia's arm before settling her hand on the small of Elia's back. She leaned in, and Elia turned to press their lips together in a small and welcome kiss. She sighed into it and relaxed, silently letting Kamryn know that everything was okay.

"Andra said they're on their way," Kamryn said, her voice quiet. "I brought some card games to keep ourselves entertained if we need them."

"Good idea," Elia murmured back, lifting her chin up for a fuller kiss from Kamryn. When their lips parted, Elia really settled into the moment. These were the people that she was creating her family with. And it was amazing just to even have that opportunity now instead of before when she thought it would never happen.

Elia was happy, and it rested on her shoulders so well. She didn't want to give this up. It didn't take long for the four of them to finish plating up the food and setting it on the dining room table. Elia kept close to Kamryn, needing the physical support from her to stay present in the moment.

She was used to backsliding into the past, and with Abagail's latest drama added in, Elia was sure to stick with the one person she knew would be safe.

The knock on the door was excited. Kamryn touched Elia's arm lightly before she went to answer it.

Andra squealed as soon as she stepped inside, wrapping her arms around Kamryn's shoulders and squeezing her tight. Greer frowned slightly at the move. "Is that not normal?" Elia asked Greer.

"No, not really. She seems...forced. We'll see." Greer walked over to join in the fray, hugging her friend. Simone, however, stood a step back, gripping onto her purse strap tightly. This was the first time Elia had invited her over to her house, and it was going to be awkward at first. At least until they could start to figure out who they were outside of the work environment. But she had full confidence that they'd be able to do that.

Elia played hostess, getting everyone drinks and showing them the snacks. When they were settled onto the couches, she couldn't help but notice the odd behavior between Simone and Andra. Elia wasn't the only one who noticed it either.

Andra sat close to Greer, with Simone on the other side of her, leaving Garrett to fend for himself in one of the uncomfortable dining room table chairs that they'd dragged over to have the right number of seats. Elia felt bad for the poor guy, being the odd man out.

"Garrett and I moved in with his parents," Andra said, frowning slightly.

Elia couldn't tell if she meant for it to come out so sad or not.

"It's just temporary, for a few months—we hope. We don't want to impose."

"It's not an imposition," Simone chimed in. "You're welcome as long as you need."

Except that also seemed strained. Elia had known Simone for many years now, and she'd never seen that tight pull on her face, or the squinting look that she just gave. There was definitely more to the story there that she'd have to find out later. But she wasn't sure that a room full of other people was the place to really dive into it.

"I'm living with Kam for a while," Greer chimed in. "Life changes rapidly, and sometimes, we just need friends and family who can support us." Greer threw her arm around Andra's shoulders and nodded. "Isn't that right, Kam?"

"Yes, it is." Kamryn slid onto the arm of the chair that Elia was sitting in. She pressed her hand against Elia's shoulder and smiled down at her.

"If I could get another job, then I could move out any time." Greer scrunched her nose up. "I didn't think it would be this hard to find a long-term nannying position."

Abagail's eyes lit up. "I forgot you were a nanny."

Greer grinned. "Yes, I love it. I'm not sure I could do anything else with my life."

"I might have just the solution for you." Abagail raised an eyebrow at Greer.

That could work to the advantage of both of them. Kamryn leaned in and whispered to Elia, "Do you think that's a good idea?"

"Do you trust Greer to make her own decisions?"

"Most days. Except when there's gin involved."

Elia would have to ask about that later. "Let her figure it out then. She needs a job, and Abagail was just bemoaning her newest hire, Ivy, and her problem situation with the lack of a consistent and good nanny."

"Oh, well then, Greer might be the perfect solution. And it would get her off my couch. Though I do enjoy coming home to a clean apartment and fresh cooked meals every day." Kamryn chuckled lightly. "I'm not exactly a good housekeeper."

"Hmm, never would have guessed that one." Elia's lips twitched upward in a slight smile. The tease was there, although light, and Kamryn grinned in response, accepting it for what it was. "Let them talk. Will you help me with refilling drinks?"

"Absolutely." Kamryn stood up first, and then held out her hand for Elia. They walked hand-in-hand to the kitchen.

Elia wasn't quite ready to let go, so she pulled Kamryn in a bit. "I never thought I'd be the one with the full house for an early Christmas celebration."

"You just didn't realize how popular you actually are." Kamryn winked before leaning in for a kiss. "Or how popular you could be."

Elia smiled. "I think you have me mistaken for someone else. Five guests is hardly popular."

"But it's a start." Kamryn kissed her again. "I forgot to mention to you that I turned in my application on Friday."

"For Head of School?"

Kamryn nodded. "I needed to make a decision, finally, and what better time than right before the Christmas break?"

"Are you nervous?"

"Hell yes." Kamryn curled her hair behind her ear. "I don't know who else is applying, and I want to know, but at the same time, I don't want to know at all."

"Well, I'll spoil one thing for you." Elia squeezed Kamryn's hands. "I didn't apply this time."

Laughing, Kamryn shook her head. "Oh no! You were my greatest competition. Now I'll wipe the floor with the rest of them."

Elia grinned as she snagged the bottle of wine to start to head back to the living area with the rest of her guests. She didn't want to neglect them by focusing too much on Kamryn. But Kamryn pulled her back, putting her hand on the wine bottle and setting it onto the counter.

"Not so fast, Dr. Sharpe. I need to know why you didn't apply for the Head of School position." Kamryn slid her fingers from Elia's cheek to her neck to the top of her chest. "Is it perhaps because you want to avoid any more conflicts between you and a certain someone?"

"Maybe." Elia's breathing increased. She looked up into Kamryn's eyes. "Maybe it's because I know that I won't get hired."

"We're not back to that, are we?" Kamryn frowned, genuine

concern filtering through what had been fiery passion and flirtation.

"No. We're not," Elia confirmed. "I just realized that I'm happy where I am. I don't see the need to change a single thing."

"Not one thing?"

Elia shook her head. "Nothing."

"What if... and bear with me on this because it's not something that would happen right away, and I don't want you to panic your little heart out. But what if I did get the job, and what if I moved into the Head of School house." Kamryn dropped her gaze to Elia's lips, and Elia knew that she was debating whether or not to kiss her.

"So you move." Elia furrowed her brow, not quite following Kamryn's train of thought. "It'll be a whole lot nicer than the apartment in the dormitories."

"It will be," Kamryn agreed. "Far more...privacy than even your home here."

"Yes." They could use that to their advantage, though they'd never seemed to have issues with Elia's house either. "Kam, I'm not sure I'm following."

"If I get the job, move in with me." Kamryn flicked her gaze up to Elia's. "I'm serious."

"And if you don't get the job?" Elia asked.

"Then I'm going to be jobless and homeless and probably crashing on your couch." Kamryn's grin was full of cocky flirting.

Elia adored it. She pulled Kamryn in for a quick kiss. "Let's be honest here. You won't be sleeping on the couch."

"Good to know." Kamryn kissed her again. "And the other thing?"

"We'll figure that out when it becomes an actual possibility."

"Promise?"

"Yes, I promise." Elia kissed her again. "Now, my guests are without wine, and I know how cranky Abagail gets without it. Let's get back to them, shall we?"

"If you want to." Kamryn smiled, the move lighting up her entire face. She took Elia's hand in hers and they walked back to the living room together. It couldn't have been a more perfect night. It was exactly what Elia had been wanting for years.

forty-three

"You ready?" Simone asked.

Kamryn was ready and not ready at the same time. And there was nothing she could do about it now. "As ready as I can be," she muttered.

Simone opened the door to the conference room filled with board members. Kamryn swallowed the lump in her throat and begged the nerves that were taking over to dissipate sooner rather than later. She had advantages this time that she didn't have last time, ones that no one else had.

The problem?

She was still in a relationship with Elia. And that could cause a conflict that the board wouldn't want to continue to deal with.

Kamryn sat down at the head of the table and tried to plaster on a smile that meant she was calm and easy and ready for this interrogation—whoops, interview. Although it definitely felt like the former. The questions started easy, and Kamryn was readily able to lay out what her plans were for the future of the school.

Having been there the last six months helped drastically in how she made her plans. She was able to make them very specific, and she knew exactly where the majority of the problems were. Once Kamryn got into the flow of question and answer, she started to actually enjoy herself, and the outfit she'd worn that day didn't feel confining or like it was trying to strangle her.

"The board wanted to ask a few questions that are a bit personal in nature," Simone started, and she looked uncomfortable.

Kamryn had known these questions would come up. They had to, especially since she'd outed herself and Elia earlier in the school year so boisterously. If she was the permanent Head of School, then it was going to really come into question whether or not she and Elia could work together, especially if a breakup happened.

"That's all right," Kamryn answered. She and Elia had prepared for these questions and had planned answers ready. With some help from Abagail. It was a good thing that that relationship was going much better.

"We know that you're in a relationship with Dr. Elia Sharpe. Thank you for informing us of that." Simone sounded so professional. Kamryn had to hand it to her. The board she had met six months ago wouldn't have been prepared for this conversation in the least. They were letting Susy run everything and had no interest in participating in the conversations.

"I am." Kamryn smiled at just the memory of when she'd told them, and the fact that they'd all stayed three hours late to figure out some sort of temporary solution so they could both stay on for the rest of the year. Their support of her and Elia had been clear in that moment.

"The concern the board has is for reducing conflicts and conflicts of interest, and what ideas you had moving forward."

"Understandable. Right now, Dr. Marshall Dean is in charge of all supervision concerning Elia. And that's worked well for us. Though it's only been in place a few months at this point." Kamryn stilled, trying to ease herself into this conversation. "We would propose that the current processes in place continue, but also add in that Dr. Dean's reports will be shared with the board, and that he will be mediator should any conflicts arise about my influence in Elia's position."

"And should your relationship end?" Simone asked.

Kamryn nodded. "I don't anticipate that happening, but should it happen, both Elia and I have the experience and maturity to keep it away from the school. Marshall will continue to be her supervisor in that case. I wouldn't want there to be any question of ethics or confidence in my position where it concerns Elia. I do think that what we have in place is sufficient for now, but I also believe that we can do better with our policies. Marshall and I have been working with other schools in the area to improve our policies surrounding these potential conflicts as they come up and prior to them arising. The policies at Windermere are seriously outdated, and they all need to be updated and brought into the twenty-first century."

That was as much as Abagail had told them to give. Kamryn settled her hands into her lap, and Simone easily navigated the conversation back to more normal interview questions. Kamryn spent half of the day with the board, unlike the outside candidates who would spend the entire day with them.

As soon as Kamryn got back to her office, she sat down and stood right back up. Her nerves were on fire, and she just wished she had the answers now. Though it did feel like it had gone well. She wanted to call Elia, but she was in the middle of class. Which meant that she was stuck pacing her office with the lingering energy coursing through her veins.

Picking up her phone, Kamryn video-called Greer and held her breath that she'd be able to answer and not be busy.

"Hey!" Greer's smiling face filled the screen. "Just so you know, I'm with some of the kids right now, so it might get chaotic."

"Sure. Just hang up if you need to. I understand." Kamryn held the phone away from her face so she could see her best friend. "How is the new job going?"

Greer pulled a face before she rolled her eyes. "*Chaotic* is probably a very good word for it, honestly. I'm working on pulling together some kind of schedule that works for everyone, but it's just not happening. There's one particular holdout."

Kamryn knew who that was already. She and Greer had spent time on the phone brainstorming how Greer could handle Nathalie Coeur. With three families sharing a nanny, Greer was overwhelmed. But Nathalie? She was an ice-cold queen who didn't give an inch. She was Abagail's pain in the ass, as well, so they could at least complain together.

"I don't envy you on that one. I much prefer the school system. Structure is already built into my job." Kamryn laughed lightly and set her phone against her computer so she could talk to Greer hands-free.

"And...?" Greer asked, getting more excited than Kamryn had at the very end of her interview.

"And what?"

"How did it go?"

"I think it went well." Kamryn paused, glancing toward the main office where her new temporary office administrator was working. "I think it went really well, actually. I'm still concerned about the whole Elia-and-me thing, but overall, I feel really good about this."

"Eek!" Greer waved her hand in the air excitedly. "I mean, I do wish you'd move closer to Boston so that we could spend more time together, but if you get the job of your dreams, I guess I'll survive."

"I only wish you could have the job of yours," Kamryn countered, frowning slightly. She was worried with how much stress this was putting on Greer. The situation was way out of the ordinary for her, but the three families sharing one nanny did offer a safety net that Greer never had before. And it helped that all three of them were going to have to agree in order for her to be fired.

"Yeah. We'll see. You never know where this job might lead me."

"Yeah, you're right. You never know." Though Kamryn would

definitely take closer together as the best option. She was about to say something when there was a loud crash that echoed through the phone. "What was that?"

"Shit," Greer mumbled under her breath. She stood up, leaving the phone where she was and walked away.

Kamryn stayed on the phone, watching from a distance as Greer started to clean something up. She was just about to hang up to give Greer the time she needed when the phone suddenly moved. She was greeted with a curious face of a little blond boy who was missing his two front teeth.

"Hi," Kamryn said, trying in vain to remember his name or which kid he was and which parent he belonged to. But there were a lot of kids there, and since she hadn't met them yet, it was a struggle to remember. "Tell me your name again."

"Alaric!" He giggled wildly as he held the phone so Kamryn was basically looking up his nose. Then he must have started running because it was like watching an episode of the *Blair Witch Project* with a shaky cam that was liable to make Kamryn want to throw up if she watched for too long.

"Hey bud! Slow down!" Kamryn said, trying to get him to calm down a little. "Where are you running off to?"

"I'm hiding from the babies." He seemed to be crawling under something now, but Kamryn couldn't quite be sure.

"Are they loud?"

"They spilled their cereal."

"Ah." So that must have been what Greer had gone to clean up. "You don't want to help?"

"No! I'm not their brother."

So this must be Nathalie's kid. She was the only one who had one child while each of the other two families had two kids. "You know, even when my brother was little, I didn't want to be his sister sometimes. Especially when he was loud and trying to get me into trouble."

Alaric laughed wildly. "Leon tries to get me in trouble all the time."

"Oh, no. That's not good."

"Especially at school."

"Alaric?" Greer called, her voice quieter than it should have been.

Kamryn took the opportunity. "Alaric, let me finish talking to Greer, will you?"

"Sure." He climbed out from wherever he had climbed into and handed the phone over to a frazzled Greer. "He's a cutie."

"Most days." Greer sighed and pushed her hair away from her face. "There's no school today."

Kamryn glanced at her computer and all the emails that had come in. "So you have all five kids today?"

"I do, and it's been chaotic since the twins woke up. Then again, it's always chaotic."

That must be her new word of the week, but Kamryn wasn't going to mention anything about it. "I'll let you get back. Call me tonight if you want to. I'd like to talk to you without little ears that can hear everything."

"That sounds amazing. Maybe a video call date later?"

"Absolutely." Kamryn looked at the screen and smiled at Greer. "Let me see if Elia was planning anything tonight and then I'll let you know if I can."

"Planning something?"

Kamryn shrugged. "I'm not sure. We haven't had a second to compare schedules in a while."

"Sure." Greer laughed when there was another crash. "Crap."

"Catch you later, Greer!" Kamryn hung up without waiting for a response. Greer had bigger fish to fry.

Kamryn spent the rest of the day in her office working, trying to ignore the fact that her interview had only happened a few short hours ago.

The knock on her door wasn't the knock of her administrative assistant. When Kamryn looked up, she wasn't surprised to find Elia filling the doorway. "You didn't call or text."

Kamryn winced. “I didn’t want to bug you while you were teaching.”

Elia hummed and walked into the room, not bothering to shut the door. She immediately stepped close to Kamryn and kissed her. “How did it go?”

“Excellent.” Kamryn cupped Elia’s cheeks and pulled her in for another, deeper kiss. “I really do think it went well.”

“Good.” Elia sat on the edge of Kamryn’s desk. “This office won’t feel the same without you in it, you know.”

Kamryn canted her head to the side and squinted. “Are you saying that I won’t get the job?”

“No.” Elia crossed her arms. “I’m saying that you better get the job because this school won’t be the same without you.”

“You said this office.”

“You know what I meant.”

“Maybe.” Kamryn stood up and took Elia by the hand. “Do we have any plans for tonight? I was talking to Greer, and she could really use a drunk video call.”

Elia laughed lightly. “I had thought that I would take you out to dinner, but if you’d prefer to drink with Greer, that can be arranged.”

“Dinner? As in a date?” Kamryn walked over to the wall where she’d hung her jacket that morning.

“Yes, a date.”

Kamryn raised her eyebrows. They hadn’t been on a proper date in a long time. The busyness of the new year had swept both of them off their feet, especially with Kamryn’s interview and the time she needed to prepare for it.

“Hmm, a date with my girlfriend or drunk video calling my best friend. Such choices are these.” Kamryn slid her arms into her jacket and buttoned up the front of it.

“You can always do both if we call it an early night.”

“Oh, perfect.” Kamryn went back to her desk to pack up her laptop to bring it home to work on it later. She still had a ton to get done before the long holiday weekend.

As Kamryn was ready to leave, she took Elia by the hand and closed the door behind her. She never wanted to stop touching Elia like this if she could. She'd found so much comfort in the simple touches that they could have now that there was no need to hide their relationship, at least in front of faculty and staff. Students were another thing entirely. They tried to stay as professional as possible when they were around the students, especially their Speech kids.

Kamryn kept Elia's hand in hers until they stepped outside into the cold winter. Snow still covered the ground, and it looked like a warm blanket with tracks through it from the students running from one building to the next. Kamryn hiked her satchel up higher onto her shoulder as she started walking back with Elia toward her small house at the end of the row for faculty.

"So where are we going for dinner?" Kamryn asked. She hadn't realized just how hungry she was, but she hadn't managed to eat breakfast or lunch that day because her nerves had taken over her entire body.

"I was thinking Italian."

"Carbs. Perfect." Kamryn grinned at her. "We probably should talk about what we're doing if I don't get the job."

"What do you mean?" Elia frowned. "Of course you'll get it."

"I love your positive attitude, but let's be honest for a minute. I might not."

"Kam—"

"Just humor me, please." Kamryn clenched her fingers. "I've been looking at schools around here to see if they have any openings, but you know how hard it is to find jobs like these."

"Especially if you want to stay in administration."

Kamryn hummed her agreement. "So I also widened the search to the Boston area."

"You'd be closer to Greer."

"Yeah, I would be." *And farther from you.* Though Kamryn didn't say that. It was something that weighed heavily on her. "I could find another kind of job so that I can stay close by."

"Kam... wherever you end up, you and I will figure out what we're doing then. I'm not going to let you go now."

Relief flooded through her. She hadn't realized just how worried she was about that. That without the constant contact they currently had that their relationship would shift and change to the point that it would break them down. It still worried her, but at least having Elia thinking about it made her feel far less afraid of the reality she didn't want to experience.

"Like I said before, I'm not sure what this place would be without you." Elia let them into her house, but she didn't take her jacket off. "Now, let's celebrate your interview, and distract ourselves from the future what-ifs that we can't answer."

"Sounds like a good plan," Kamryn said as she dropped her bag onto the kitchen table. "Are you driving, or am I?"

"Me," Elia answered. "I've ridden with you before. Trust me, I'm driving."

"I'm not that bad!"

"Sure you're not. Maybe you should start teaching driver's ed so you can learn a thing or to."

"Elia!"

But Elia was laughing as she stepped back outside the house. Kamryn shoved her hands into her pockets as she followed. She'd let Elia drive—this time. It wasn't worth it to fight it.

forty-four

"Let's run some mirror drills today. I know you all have plenty of practice, but I've seen some bad habits forming lately. Break up into teams of three—" Elia stopped talking as the door to the Speech room opened loudly.

She'd been expecting Kamryn to show up late since she had a phone call that was taking longer than she expected and had texted as much, but she didn't anticipate the force with which Kamryn slammed open the classroom door.

All of the kids stopped to stare at Kamryn, and then looked at Elia. She set the dry erase marker onto the desk in front of the white board and focused all her attention onto Kamryn. She wasn't moving. Her hand was on the doorknob, and her chest was rising and falling in little breaths, but she didn't look worried or afraid. So it couldn't be anything bad.

Elia faced the kids again. "I told you to break up into teams of three—"

"Dr. Ogden, what's wrong?" Ethan asked, always the one who would bring something up and point out the obvious. That kid seriously had no fear.

"Nothing's wrong," Kamryn rushed out the words.

Elia paused again. What was she supposed to do with this?

Kamryn wasn't saying or doing anything, and all of the kids were waiting for some kind of explanation of this random behavior from their temporary Head of School.

"Why don't you all split into groups, and I'll talk to Dr. Ogden," Elia said, trying to get the attention of the classroom back on her, but the kids continued to ignore her.

"Is something on fire or something?" Bristol asked, grabbing for her bag.

"No, nothing's on fire. Nothing's wrong," Kamryn reiterated, but she still hadn't moved from the door. "You got a minute, Elia?"

Elia?

Kamryn was always so careful to use her salutation and last name in front of the students. This wasn't a work conversation. It was a personal one. There was a quiet hush around the room while the students murmured amongst themselves, trying to figure out what the hell was going on. Elia was going to have to come up with some sort of explanation when Kamryn finally told her what was happening.

Focusing on the kids, Elia was about to remind them again to start their practice, but she gave up. They wouldn't listen anyway, not with Kamryn acting so oddly. Elia dropped her hands to her sides and strode toward the door. She was just about to walk out of it when Kamryn caught her arm and stopped any forward movement.

"They offered me the job," Kamryn whispered.

Elia had to lean in to make sure that she'd heard correctly. "What?"

"They offered me the job—Head of School. Officially."

"What?" Elia's eyes widened, the excitement she now saw in Kamryn's face lighting her up. Elia's chest felt like it was going to explode. She grinned broadly as she pulled away to say something.

Before she could speak, Kamryn rushed forward and pressed their mouths together and wrapped her arms around Elia's neck.

Cheers went up from the rest of the classroom, and immediately Elia jerked back with a start. Kamryn winced and frowned.

"Crap," Kamryn said.

"Crap is right," Elia answered, putting even more space between them.

This wasn't how they wanted this to get out.

"Do you think they heard me?" Kamryn whispered.

Elia shook her head as the cheers continued. "I think they're cheering for other reasons."

"Really?" Kamryn popped her head around Elia's shoulder and glanced to the classroom behind her.

"Really." Elia straightened her back and snagged Kamryn's hand. She walked into the classroom and shut the door firmly, making sure that Kamryn stayed right next to her but still kept a good distance between them.

"We can't tell them yet," Kamryn mumbled. "They haven't officially announced—"

"Again, I don't think that's what they're cheering about. You might have saved yourself explaining the other one." Elia put her hand up to calm down the ruckus that was happening. But when she went to speak, she was struck dumb. No words would leave her lips.

"I just have one question!" Bristol raised her hand. "When did you two...hook up?"

"Oh Jesus," Kamryn muttered. "Poor choice of words, Bristol."

Elia's cheeks burned. Is that what all the students thought they were doing?

"And it's really not relevant to this conversation," Kamryn added.

"But it is!" Ethan called. "We need to know who won the bet!"

"Bet?" Elia's voice was a whole lot squeakier than it should have been.

"Oh yeah, we made a bet at the beginning of the year after the first meeting. We need to know who won," Ethan explained.

"What exactly is the prize?" Kamryn asked, keeping her hand locked in Elia's. "Maybe we'll get to pick the winners." She sent Elia a look, having way more fun messing with the kids than Elia was.

Elia was mortified—at least somewhat. The fact that the kids seemed so excited was more than what she'd been hoping for. And she wasn't clueless about the fact that she knew the kids were talking about her relationship with Kamryn. She just hadn't thought it had gone so far as a bet.

"The loser has to wear a clown costume to the next Speech meet," Bristol said.

"Oh, no. That's a no on that one," Elia jumped in. "It'll turn our next meet into a joke."

Bristol laughed. "We knew you'd say that, so we came up with an alternative. They don't wear it during the competition time, just before and after and all the other time we're there."

Elia pursed her lips. She didn't like it, but she couldn't argue with it. "And how do you determine the loser?"

"Whoever had the farthest date."

Kamryn glanced at Elia and nodded her head, as if asking if Elia wanted to tell them or not. "What's the prize for the winner?"

"A hundred bucks and a pair of AirPods."

"Not a bad prize," Kamryn commented. She turned to Elia, squeezing her fingers. "How much fun do you want to have with this?"

"I'm not sure what you mean." Elia's chest was still tight with tension. "I'm not sure *we* can have fun with this."

"Sure we can." Kamryn faced the class full of kids again, and she leaned forward toward the desk to grab the dry erase marker off the desk. "We'll start with January. How many of you picked dates in January?"

Kamryn walked up to the white board and wrote down the

month on it. Then she started to write names under it. She went backward from January all the way to August before she stopped.

"All right." Kamryn turned back around and glanced at Elia with a smart look in her eyes.

Elia wasn't sure she was ready for this. Not that she ever would be.

"For those of you who thought it was before August, I'm going to tell you right now that you're wrong." Kamryn put her hands on her hips and looked around the room, eyeing each one of the students. "And by the way, after we finish this, I expect you all to jump into groups of three so you can do mirrors. All right? No complaints."

Elia stepped closer to her and leaned in. "What date are we actually talking about? Because I can think of *several* that could be relevant."

"Crap, you're right." Kamryn wrinkled her nose. "That first ethics meeting."

Elia had to think about which date that was, because it wasn't their first time kissing or even the first time that Kamryn had asked her for a kiss. But it probably was the first time that she had given in to the fact that she wanted more with Kamryn, and when they'd made some sort of commitment to try a relationship.

"All right."

Turning back to the class, Kamryn pointed at January. "You all lose the bet."

The groans echoed through the room, although that month hadn't held the majority of the names on it. In fact, it was September, which would be the correct month. Had they been that obvious? Elia took the marker from Kamryn and walked up to the white board.

"Who had what date?"

Bristol read off the specific days, and the one student who had picked January thirtieth groaned loudly.

"Eddy, seems you're the loser."

"That sucks."

Elia shrugged at him and then handed the marker back to Kamryn. "Gotta keep you on their good side at least for now. Since they'll soon learn that being in the administration isn't about wanting to be liked."

Kamryn chuckled. "Fine." She walked up to the white board and immediately started crossing out names under each month other than September. The kids reacted each and every time she put a line through a name.

When they got down to the month of September, Kamryn asked again, "What date did everyone choose?"

Bristol, who apparently was the official record keeper, listed them off.

"All right." Kamryn stepped back and studied the white board. "I'm half tempted to just not tell them now."

"What? You have to tell us!" Ethan whined. His name was still on the board.

Elia eyed him over before shaking her head. "For the record, Ethan, it's not the thirteenth."

"Shucks!"

Elia walked up and crossed out Ethan's name. What had tipped off most of the students that they'd started a relationship in September? She would be curious to know, but she also wasn't going to ask them—ever. That was something that was going to remain a mystery. Along with many other things, because as entertaining as this was, Elia wasn't comfortable with their relationship being on display for the entire Speech team.

Kamryn took the marker from Elia's fingers and immediately crossed out two more names. "Just to make this fun, everyone who would pick September sixth over the thirtieth, raise your hand."

Only five students raised their hands. Kamryn then pointed at the thirtieth. "And this one?" Everyone else raised their hands.

With a smile on her lips, Kamryn moved the marker toward the thirtieth, but instead of crossing out the name, she circled it in bright red marker.

"Kayla, you're the winner of a brand-new pair of AirPods and a hundred dollars, apparently."

The cheers were so loud that Elia's ears were ringing. The kids were high-fiving each other and chattering loudly. Elia's cheeks were still on fire, but she managed to raise her voice loud enough to get their attention.

"Mirrors!"

The kids immediately parted into small groups of three. Elia touched the small of Kamryn's back and nodded toward the door. "Hallway. Now."

"Yes, ma'am." Kamryn walked in front of Elia until they stepped outside. "I think that was a good deflection from the real news, don't you?"

"Sure. We can *not* do something like that again."

"Deal." Kamryn held both of Elia's hands and leaned in to kiss her again. "I do have some not-so-good news when it comes to a condition of my hire."

"What's that?" Elia hummed, already knowing that she wasn't going to like this conversation.

"You need to find a new co-leader for the Speech team. They don't want us traveling together or staying together during the Speech meets. They'd like to not expose the students to anything that might have repercussions."

Elia frowned. "I'm not sure I understand their reasoning."

"Not all parents are comfortable with a lesbian couple leading the Speech team together."

"How many parents?" Elia asked.

"Enough that have loud voices. But it just means that you'll still run the team with a new co-lead, and I'll have less responsibility on my plate." Kamryn tried to smile, but it didn't reach her eyes.

"I don't like it."

"It's a small concession, Elia."

"I still don't like it."

"It was the only part of the negotiations that I was opposed to, but I'm here to stay." Kamryn relaxed instantly. "They want to keep me on."

"That's really great news. Truly." Elia smiled. "I'm glad they value you as much as they should."

"You too," Kamryn whispered. "They wouldn't have kept me here if they didn't want you to also stay. That came up in conversation, that if I left, you might also resign and move to another school—one that would allow us to be together."

"Interesting." Elia wrinkled her brow. "I think you're more adept at negotiating contracts than anyone I've seen before."

"Well, I had a leg up with all those Speech meets I won in high school."

"Must have had a good coach."

"The best." Kamryn moved in again and stole yet another kiss from her. "Everything's going to work out. I promise it will."

"I trust you," Elia answered. "When will they announce formally?"

"End of February. So we'll need to plan to tell the Speech kids that I won't be there next year."

"I think they can handle it."

"Probably." Kamryn started back toward the classroom. "You coming?"

"Yeah. Absolutely." Elia wouldn't miss the rest of this year for anything. Even if it was the last few months of them co-leading. Elia would savor what they had for now, and she'd look forward to what they could have in the future.

epilogue

Six months later...

Kamryn held onto Elia's hand tightly as they walked together into the reception hall. Cheers went up as the music played loudly. Kamryn couldn't stop smiling. She'd honestly tried at one point and then completely given up. She'd never been so happy before.

Once they got to the center of the dance floor, she spun Elia in a circle and then held onto her waist and started to rock side to side as the music changed into something with a slower tempo. She couldn't look away. Elia was stunning in her sleek white dress with her hair pinned up at the back of her head.

Kamryn had already tried to tangle her fingers in it, but Elia had scolded her. Leaning in, Kamryn pressed her cheek to Elia's. "I love you."

"I love you, too." Elia's response was exactly what Kamryn needed to hear.

This entire day had been about the two of them, and they were surrounded by friends and family. Even Miller and Maria Waddy had managed to make it there, which had been amazing to see. Kamryn kept the slow dance moving, not quite ready to sit down at the long table in the front of the room.

Kamryn didn't hesitate at all as she leaned in for another kiss. The cheers went up again around them. She could so get used to this. Kissing Elia without fear of any repercussions was perfect. Too bad they wouldn't get a long honeymoon, or really any honeymoon until the holiday vacation at the end of the year, but they hadn't managed to find any date other than the end of September.

She was pretty sure they'd manage to wait.

"Can you believe that we're finally married?" Kamryn whispered.

"Yes," Elia responded, always the practical one. "We've spent the last six months planning it and arguing over the details."

"I wouldn't call those arguments," Kamryn countered. Some of them could definitely be called that, but in the end, it had all worked out. They were here, they were married, the paperwork was all signed, and now they got to just enjoy their time together until they had to go back to work on Monday morning. "Just... next time let's get married when there isn't school in session."

Elia cringed. "Agreed, not that there's going to be a next time."

"Um, vow renewals are a thing for a reason."

Groaning, Elia shook her head. "I'd rather not think about planning another major event for the next few years."

"Deal." Kamryn slid her hand up higher on the small of Elia's back, reveling in the warmth of her skin underneath the thin fabric of her dress. "But speaking of major events, I do believe people are expecting us to sit down at some point so they can give their speeches."

"Hmm, do we have to?"

"I think we do, since we planned it and all." Kamryn kissed Elia's cheek before guiding her to the table. They sat down in between Greer and Abagail. Immediately people started chinking their silverware against their glasses. Elia's cheeks were pink when

Kamryn moved in to kiss her lightly. "Better get used to that, my people get riled up by it."

"No doubt," Elia replied.

"You two are ridiculous," Greer said with a laugh. "We just love seeing you so happy."

"I'm sure that's all it is," Kamryn said to her best friend. She'd never been so happy as to have Greer there with her. All her friends were there, Andra and Lauren included. It had taken some time for her and Lauren to start talking again in a friendly way, but they'd managed it, especially when Kamryn had made it abundantly clear that their last breakup had truly been their last.

"Of course it is!" Greer looked partially offended.

"Just wait until you get married, Greer. Payback's a bitch." Kamryn chuckled, but the sad look that crossed Greer's face took her off guard. "What's wrong?"

"I don't think I'm going to be getting married." Greer frowned. "At least not in the traditional sense."

"What?"

Suddenly, Abagail stood up and tapped on a microphone. Kamryn winced at the loudness of it.

"I'll tell you sometime soon. I promise. It's all good."

"You better." Kamryn focused on Abagail, listening to her retell stories about Elia and then stories about her and Kamryn together. Luckily everything was kept appropriate. Kamryn held Elia's hand under the table as they waited for Greer to start her speech.

By the time Greer finished, Kamryn took the microphone and stood up.

"I wanted to say something." Her heart pattered away. Janet, Elia's mother, nodded at her in affirmation of what was about to happen. "I don't want to embarrass Elia any more than she already is. As many of you know her, you understand that she is not someone who likes to be the center of attention."

There was a round of light laughter that filled the room.

"But sometimes she needs to be the center of attention."

Kamryn stared down into Elia's blue eyes and smiled again. "Because she is the center of my world, and trust me when I say that I never would have guessed that would happen. Not with the way we started out. I could have sworn she hated me at first."

"I did… a bit." Elia wrinkled her nose before she winked, so Kamryn knew she wasn't being entirely serious.

"Right, so when I got the job as Head of School instead of Elia, she was a bit jealous. Can you imagine? Elia Sharpe jealous? Crazy, right? And she let me have it. And then one night, while I was out with some friends, I had a little too much to drink and I was trying to make someone else jealous and I kissed her, and then I begged her to be my fake girlfriend while Andra was getting married. All so that I could protect myself from what I didn't want to deal with."

Kamryn ran her hand along Elia's shoulder before she brushed the backs of her fingers across Elia's cheek. "Well, the joke's on me, because she said yes. First to fake dating, and then to real dating, and then finally to marrying me. Elia," Kamryn turned to her wife—gosh, it was crazy she could say that now—and she smiled down at her. These words were just for Elia and no one else. "I love you, and I never would have imagined that all of those crazy decisions and insane start to our relationship would have turned out this way, but it did. And I'm so very glad that it did. I love you. And I promise to love you each and every day."

"Kam…" Elia whispered, her voice cracking.

"I love you." Bending down, Kamryn pressed their lips together in a long, sweet kiss. When she stood back up, she turned to the group with a grin.

But Elia stood up next to her and took the microphone. She trembled. Kamryn held her hand tightly, looking curiously into Elia's eyes. This was so out of the ordinary for her. Kamryn hadn't lied when she said that Elia wasn't someone who liked any attention.

"I just have one thing to say," Elia started, and she turned to look directly at Kamryn. "Who knew that fake dating my boss would end up like this?"

The raucous laughter filled the room. And Kamryn had no doubts in her mind. This was the woman she was meant to fall in love with. And she wouldn't have it any other way. Kamryn kissed Elia hard, tilting her backward slightly as she held onto the embrace for as long as she possibly could. Then she pulled back and whispered, "Thank God we didn't keep that promise."

"To keep this fake?" Elia asked.

"Yeah, that one."

thank you!

Thank you so much for taking the time to read this book. I wrote it after a particularly chaotic time in my life when I just couldn't find the time to sit down and type words.

But Elia and Kam were pushing me to write their story the entire time, so as soon as I was able to sit down and type, they blossomed on the page before my eyes.

Love is always so complicated, isn't it?

I really appreciate you taking the time to read this book and to explore a world with me, and maybe take a risk on a new author.

If you want to continue to support me, you can sign up for my newsletter on my website and get a free book!

I appreciate all of you, each and every reader who takes a chance on my creation.

Peace & Love,

AJ

about the author

Adrian J. Smith has been publishing since 2013 but has been writing nearly her entire life. With a focus on women loving women fiction, AJ jumps genres from action-packed police procedurals to the seedier life of vampires and witches to sweet romances with an age gap twist. She loves writing and reading about women in the midst of the ordinariness of life.

AJ currently lives in Cheyenne, WY, although she moves often and has lived all over the United States. She loves to travel to different countries and places. She currently plays the roles of author, wife, and mother to two rambunctious youngsters, occasional handy-woman. Check out her website for signed paperback editions!

adrianjsmithbooks.com

nanny in the middle

Stuck in the middle of three head-strong women, will Greer come out unscathed?

Greer Lockheart is a nanny to her core. When she takes on a new job of working for three families at once, she's not sure she can see her way through the chaos. As the days tick by and she falls more in love with each kid in her care, she can't help but also fall more in lust with their mothers. But these women are complicated. And Greer keeps running face first into their pasts, especially Ivy's ex. Who seems bent on taking the family down, beginning with the weakest link, Greer.

Nathalie Coeur, Lachlan Norris, and Ivy Villegas have been friends for a long time. Working together is second nature to them, but that doesn't mean their life is without problems. With Ivy's soon-to-be ex-wife making threats and breathing down their necks, they close ranks to fight for justice, just hoping they'll come out unscathed on the other side.

They protect their kids first and each other second. But what happens when their rank breaks because they can't keep their hands off the nanny?

Will their family falter?

Or will they have one, or two, more to add to their numbers?

Paving the way in a polyamorous relationship isn't easy, but with these four, they might have found the key to lasting love and support.

my boss's stalker: spoiler it's not me

An unrequited crush. A stalker on the loose. Will she be able to save her boss?

Zoe's boss is a force to be reckoned with. And Zoe has had a crush on Gwen Fudala for the last three years. In a twist of events, Zoe drunkenly ends up on the phone with Gwen while in a compromising position. But it sparks a wildfire that neither can put out.

Still, something isn't right.

Gwen is being stalked. Vowing to let nothing happen to her boss, Zoe winds up tangled in the stalker's game. Unable to see which way is out and loyal to a fault, Zoe sticks by Gwen's side through thick and thin.

Can they navigate a relationship under the watchful eye of a perpetrator?

Or does the stalker have a new target?

My Boss's Stalker is a steamy age gap sapphic romantic suspense. Follow these two as they navigate complicated relationships, fear, and unexpected serenity.

Printed in Dunstable, United Kingdom